GIFTS FOR THE ONE
WHO COMES AFTER

"Helen Marshall is a writer who creates real people in real situations, then uses the fantastic to pry her way inside her readers' ribcages and break us wide open."

—Neil Gaiman, international bestselling author
of _The Ocean at the End of the Lane_

"Helen Marshall whispers in your ear when she fits the noose around your neck, filling you with wonder and dread, urging you into a startling, beautiful darkness. These stories—which sometimes feel more like spells—are the very best kind of unsettling."

—Benjamin Percy, author of _Red Moon_, _The Wilding_, _Refresh_,
Refresh and _The Language of Elk_

"Helen Marshall is one of my favorite living writers. Her elegant, grotesque stories are best encountered like this, gathered together in a book and in conversation with each other; only then can you appreciate the staggering variety of her imagination. What unifies them, and what elevates them from being merely great fantasy to being literature, is the ache of human experience that informs them all: the yearning; the heartbreak; the desperate, misinformed love. This is life, in all its beauty and sorrow."

—Nathan Ballingrud, award-winning author
of _North American Lake Monsters_

"Helen Marshall's _Gifts for the One Who Comes After_ is in turns chilling, heart-wrenching and uplifting. Marshall has a way with words that makes even the most peculiar seem possible, and the stories here are each so layered with character and meaning, they are like perfect, condensed novels."

—Kaaron Warren, award-winning author
of _Through Splintered Walls_

Sno-Isle Libraries

WITHDRAWN
Sno-Isle Libraries

PRAISE FOR

HAIR SIDE, FLESH SIDE

"Sometimes a book comes along that is so original, so vibrantly alive, so beautifully imagined and so much a law unto itself that the only comment or advice a reviewer can offer is to say: go read it."

—Nina Allan, *Strange Horizons*

"Stories subtle and unsettling: Helen Marshall clothes the uncanny in new flesh and then makes it bleed."

—Kelly Link, author of *Pretty Monsters* and *Stranger Things Happen*

"Sometimes you hear people talking about the new face of horror. Well huddle closer, children . . . *Hair Side, Flesh Side* is it. . . . Marshall's stories are frightening, touching, quirky, sexy and deeply lyrical."

— "Best F/SF Books of 2012," *January Magazine*

"*Hair Side, Flesh Side* is a strong first collection of speculative fiction borne out of faded manuscripts, old libraries and the memories of the past. However, it's how Marshall sees us reconcile these ghosts with the world of the living that give her stories the weight of immediacy. She is a talent to be discovered."

—*The National Post*

"Helen Marshall's debut collection reads like a fanciful walk through her dark imagination. . . . Strangely touching, disturbing and weird as hell, Marshall proves herself a potent new talent."

—*Rue Morgue Magazine*

"A tour de force of imagination, this remarkable debut collection uses the conventions of dark fantasy and horror as the framework for some of speculative fiction's most unusual stories. VERDICT Fans of experimental fiction and exceptional writing should find a wealth of enjoyment here.

—*Library Journal*, starred review

GIFTS FOR THE ONE WHO COMES AFTER

BY HELEN MARSHALL

INTRODUCTION BY ANN VANDERMEER

ILLUSTRATIONS BY CHRIS ROBERTS

ChiZine Publications

FIRST EDITION

Gifts for the One Who Comes After © 2014 by Helen Marshall
Cover artwork © 2014 by Erik Mohr
Illustrations © 2014 by Chris Roberts
Interior design © 2014 by Clare C. Marshall

All Rights Reserved.

This book is a work of fiction. Names, characters, places, and incidents are either a product of the author's imagination or are used fictitiously. Any resemblance to actual events, locales, or persons, living or dead, is entirely coincidental.

Distributed in Canada by
HarperCollins Canada Ltd.
1995 Markham Road
Scarborough, ON M1B 5M8
Toll Free: 1-800-387-0117
e-mail: hcorder@harpercollins.com

Distributed in the U.S. by
Diamond Comic Distributors, Inc.
10150 York Road, Suite 300
Hunt Valley, MD 21030
Phone: (443) 318-8500
e-mail: books@diamondbookdistributors.com

Library and Archives Canada Cataloguing in Publication

Marshall, Helen, 1983-, author

Gifts for the one who comes after / Helen Marshall. -- First edition.

Short stories.

Issued in print and electronic formats.

ISBN 978-1-77148-302-5 (pbk.).-- ISBN 978-1-77148-303-2 (pdf)

I. Title.

PS8626.A7668G54 2014   C813'.6   C2014-904065-2
                                               C2014-904066-0

CHIZINE PUBLICATIONS
Toronto, Canada
www.chizinepub.com
info@chizinepub.com

Edited and copyedited by Sandra Kasturi
Proofread by Michael Matheson

Canada Council   Conseil des arts
for the Arts   du Canada

We acknowledge the support of the Canada Council for the Arts which last year invested $20.1 million in writing and publishing throughout Canada.

ONTARIO ARTS COUNCIL
CONSEIL DES ARTS DE L'ONTARIO
50 YEARS OF ONTARIO GOVERNMENT SUPPORT OF THE ARTS
50 ANS DE SOUTIEN DU GOUVERNEMENT DE L'ONTARIO AUX ARTS

Published with the generous assistance of the Ontario Arts Council.

Printed in Canada

To Laura:
My gift to you.
I owe you much more.
(But you already knew that.)

We shed as we pick up, like travellers who must carry everything in their arms, and what we let fall will be picked up by those behind. The procession is very long and life is very short. We die on the march.

— Sir Tom Stoppard, *Arcadia*

TABLE OF CONTENTS

Sno-Isle Libraries

Introduction:
Stories that Hurt So Good

BY ANN VANDERMEER

Helen Marshall has an uncanny way of getting under the readers' skin with her stories. We are itching and uncomfortable and yet . . . we are attracted to the scratch. *Gifts for the One Who Comes After* is Helen Marshall's second short story collection. Her first, *Hair Side, Flesh Side*, was embraced by readers all over and met with critical success. It dealt mostly with themes concerning the individual. Those stories were focused on the internal conversations we have with ourselves as we try to make sense of the world around us. Some of those stories explored how we fit into the universe.

In contrast, this collection deals with the connections we strive to make with others—those close to us and those that are merely in our way. Within these stories we have to deal with the legacies of the past—the histories of our ancestors, families and neighbourhoods. How do we maintain those traditions and yet still move confidently into the future? Will maintaining those traditions hold us back? And if we do abandon them will we lose something ultimately priceless in the process?

The collection opens with "The Hanging Game," which centres on what looks like a harmless children's game. Yet this game is deeply ingrained in the history of this small town community. So it's much more than just a children's game; it's the town's heritage as well.

If we are not deeply connected to others, if we push them away when they come close, what are we left with . . . an empty life? Perhaps as empty as Leah in "In the Year of Omens," who is waiting for the right signal. She wills it to come as it came to all the others. "There had always been signs in the world." But Leah is still looking for hers. She does not want to be left behind.

There are things better left unsaid—left undone—things that will cut you down in your prime if you give voice to them. Things that hang there on the periphery of your vision—you want to look but as soon as you turn your head, they disappear. As Melanie says in "Supply Limited, Act Now," "Why ya always gotta go doing that? Why ya always gotta go making things small just so that you can grow up? It doesn't have to be like that, you know? Why do ya wanna go on being the kids that just wreck everything because ya don't know better?"

The characters in Marshall's stories would do well to heed the advice of those that went before. They should think twice before leaving their long-held beliefs and traditions behind, because if they do discard these precious values, what will they be left with? In "Crossroads and Gateways" we hear from Dajan, "If only it were so easy to change the past." He struggles to make sense of what is expected of him. Yet he takes the next step. It is the only thing he can do.

So, let's talk about the legacy of the family. "Ship House" is full of family obligations and expectations, however, "It was home, it was home, but it didn't feel like home any longer." Eileen reluctantly returns to Ship House only to be surprised at the affection she feels, instead of feeling repelled. "Now Ship House felt strange on the inside to Eileen: too small and too large at the same time." But still, she can't turn away.

These tales demonstrate how families are the most complicated of relationships. Marshall's characters go through so many stages of connection to reach out to each other. In "The Gallery of the Eliminated" we are introduced to a different kind of natural history exhibit that makes you question your place in the wider world. You think about the inheritance you will leave once you are gone, "It's bewildering, you know. To realize that you are next. Link by link, generation by generation, the chain of your people are yanked into death. And you are *next*—the link before you? Gone. Your last protection. But losing a child is different. It's like seeing the end of the chain. Watching it dangle over the abyss." And yet in "The Zhanell Adler Brass Spyglass" we meet Danny who is only trying to figure out what went wrong in his parents' past so he can fix it and make everything right again. So, you see . . . it goes in both directions.

Then there are the stories where the familiar is strange and the strange becomes familiar, the memories are locked inside finding their way out when visuals stimulate the memory. Whether you are dating Death or trying to know and understand who your parents were before you were born; whether you are finally giving away the secrets of who you are or disappearing through someone else's magic, it's all about the connections with others. Families, neighbours, friends, lovers and exes.

You can't imagine your life without them even as they seem to want to change you or to destroy who you really are. Or maybe they know you better than you do and you've only been fooling yourself. Even when you try to escape your destiny, it comes back with a vengeance and claims you. That's what these stories will do. They will claim you . . . and you will *want* them to do this. They will itch inside and out, but oh the feeling! Just as the song says, it will hurt so good when you can finally scratch that itch.

"I give you to Hangjaw, the Spearman, the Gallows' Burden.
I give you to the Father of Bears."

THE HANGING GAME

There was a game we used to play when we were kids—the hanging game, we called it. I don't know where it started, but I talked to a girl down in Lawford once, and she remembered playing it with jump ropes when she was about eleven, so I guess we weren't the only ones. Maybe Travers learned it from Dad, and from father to father, forever on up. I don't know. We couldn't use jump ropes, though, not those of us whose fathers worked the logging camps, climbing hundred-foot cedar spars and hooking in with the high-rigging rope just so to see that bright flash of urine as they pissed on the men below.

For us the hanging game was a sacred thing, the most sacred thing we knew save for one other, which I'll have to tell you about too, and that was the bears.

What you need to know was that north of Lawford where we lived—Travers and I, Momma, Dad sometimes, when he wasn't at the camps—that was a country of blue mountains and spruce and cedar so tall they seemed to hold up the sky, what the old men called Hangjaw's country. They said the bears were his, and the hanging game was his. We all had to play, cheating death, cheating Hangjaw but paying him off at the same time in whatever way we could. Living that close to death made you kind of crazy. Take Dad, for instance. Dad's kind of crazy was the bears.

I remember one summer he killed nine of them, which was still two short of old Sullivan, the skidder man, but enough of a show of guts, of tweaking Hangjaw's beard, to keep him drinking through the winter following. He'd caught the first one the traditional way, see, but he didn't clean it how he was supposed to. He just left it out on the hill and when the next one came he shot it clean through the eye with his Remington Model Seven. He took another seven throughout the week, just sitting there on the porch with a case of beer, just waiting for when the next one came sniffing along, then down it went until the whole place smelled thick with blood and bear piss, and Dad decided it was enough.

But we were kids and we couldn't shoot bears, so for us it was the hanging game. That was the kind of crazy we got into. Bears and hanging.

The first time I played it I was just a skinny kid of twelve with her summer freckles coming in. I remember I was worried about having my first period. Momma had started dropping hints, trying to lay out some of the biology of how it all worked, but the words were so mysterious I couldn't tell what she was saying was going to happen to me. It scared the bejesus out of me, truth to tell.

That was when Travers took me to play the hanging game.

He was fifteen, copper-headed like me, just getting his proper grown-up legs under him. He brought a spool of high-rigging rope he'd scavenged from the shed, and we went down to the hollow, my hand in his, a stretch of rope with thirteen coils hanging like a live thing in his other hand. It had to be high-rigging rope, he told me, not jump rope like I guess they used in Lawford. High-rigging rope for the logger kids for whom the strength of rope was the difference between life and death.

Travers stood me up on the three-legged stool that was kept for that very purpose. I remember the wind tugging around at the edges of my skirt, me worried he might see something I didn't want him to see, so I kept my fist tight around the hemline, tugging it down. But Travers, he was my brother and he wasn't looking. He tossed the end of the rope over the lowest hanging branch, easy, and then he fitted the cord around my neck.

"Close your eyes, Skye," he said. "That's a good girl."

There were rules for the hanging game. This is what they were. It had to be high-rigging rope, like I said, and you had to steal it. Also it had to be an ash tree. Also you had to do it willingly. No one could force you to play the hanging game. It couldn't be a dare or a bluff or a tease, or else it wouldn't work.

I remember the rope rubbing rough against my neck. It was a sort of chafing feeling, odd, like wearing a badly knit scarf, but it didn't hurt, not at first. I let go of my dress, but by then the breeze had stilled anyway. My eyes were closed tight, because that was how you played the hanging game, we all knew that. We all knew the rules. No one had to teach them to us.

"Take my hand now, okay, Skye?"

Then Travers's hand was in mine, and it was as rough and callused as the rope was. It felt good to hold his hand, but different than on the way over. Then he had been my brother. Now he was Priest.

"I've got you, Skye, I've got you. Now you know what to do, right?"

I nodded, tried to, but the rope pulled taut against my throat. Suddenly I was frightened, I didn't want to be there. I tried to speak, but the words got stuck. I remember trying to cough, not being able to, the desperation of trying to do something as basic as coughing and failing.

"Shh," murmured Travers. "It's okay, it's okay. Don't be afraid. You can't be afraid now, understand? Be a brave girl with me, Skye, a brave girl."

I squeezed my eyes shut. Calmed myself. Let a breath go whistling out through my lips.

"Good girl," he said. "Now lean to me."

This was the tricky part.

The stool tilted and moved under my feet. It was an old thing, and I could tell the joints were loose just by the feel of it. That movement was sickening to me, but I did like Travers said, I leaned toward him, his fingers warm against palms going cold with fear. I leaned until the rope was tight against my throat, drawing a straight line, no slack, to where it hung around the tree branch, my body taut at an angle, my toes pointed to the ground. The edge of the stool pressed into the soft space on my foot between the ball and the heel.

"Good girl," Travers told me. "Good."

God, it hurt. The rope cut into my throat, and I knew there would be bruises there tomorrow I'd have to cover up. But this was how we played.

I knew the words that were coming next but even so, they sounded like someone else was saying them, not Travers. "Skye Thornton," he said, "I give you to Hangjaw, the Spearman, the Gallows' Burden. I give you to the Father of Bears." And he touched my left side with the hazel wand he had brought for that purpose. "Now tell me what you see."

And so I did.

I don't remember what I told Travers.

None of us ever knew what it was we saw, and no one was ever allowed to talk about it after the fact. Those were the rules. I remember some of the stories though.

When Signy played the hanging game she told us about how her husband in ten years' time would die high-climbing a tall spruce spar while he was throwing the rope and getting the steel spurs in. Ninety feet from the earth it'd get hit by lightning, crazy, just like that, and he'd be fried, still strapped to the top of the thing. But the problem was she never said who that husband was gonna be, and so no one would ever go with her, no one ever took her out to the Lawford Drive-In Theatre where the rest of us went when the time came, in case she wound up pregnant by accident and the poor boy sonuva had to hitch himself to that bit of unluckiness.

That first time I wasn't afraid so much of playing the hanging game, I was afraid of what I was going to see in Travers's eyes after. I was afraid of what he might know about me that I didn't know about myself.

When he took the noose off after and he had massaged the skin on my neck, made sure I was breathing right, I remember opening my eyes, thinking I was going to see it then. But Travers looked the same as ever, same Travers, same smile, same brother of mine. And I thought, well, I guess it's not so bad, then, whatever piece of luck it is that's coming my way.

It was stupid, of course, but we were all taken by surprise that day things went wrong. There were four of us who had gone to play the hanging game, Travers and me, Ingrid Sullivan, the daughter of the skidder man who had killed two more bears than Dad that summer, and Barth Gibbons. Ingrid was there for Travers. She'd told me so before we set out, a secret whispered behind a cupped hand when Travers was getting the rope from the shed. But it was Barth I was there for. Barth was a year or two older, a pretty impossible age gap at that time to cross, but that didn't matter much to me. All I knew was Barth had the nicest straight-as-straw black hair I'd ever seen and wouldn't it be a fine thing if he slipped that coil around his neck and whispered something about his future wife, some red-haired, slim-hipped woman, when I was the only red-haired girl north of Lawford. That's what I remember thinking, anyway.

It was Travers who played Priest. Ingrid and I were there, really, just as Witnesses, because sometimes it was better if you had one or two along, just in case you were too busy handling the rope and you missed something. Old Hangjaw didn't like that.

But as it was when Barth went up and played the hanging game he didn't say anything about a red-haired, slim-hipped woman after all. He said something about a she-bear he was going to cut into one day at the start of a late spring, holed up asleep in one of those hollowed-out, rotten redwood trunks. And when he tried to open the wood up with a chainsaw, how the woodchips and blood were just going to come spewing forth, take him by surprise. There was kind of a sick sense of disappointment in me at that, but we marked down the blood price of the she-bear anyway so that we'd be sure to let Barth know how much it was and how he could pay it when the time came.

Then up went Ingrid, and Travers, who was still Priest, which was what Ingrid wanted, held out his hand for her. She giggled and took it. She didn't seem the least bit afraid, her corn-yellow hair tied behind her, smiling at my brother, leaning toward him when he told her to.

Like I said, I don't know why we had never thought of it. I mean, of course, I'd thought of it that first time I was up there, that the stool was a rickety old thing. I'd felt it moving beneath me but then that was how it was supposed to feel, I thought, that was part of it.

But then while Ingrid was leaning in, we heard this noise, all of us, this low growling noise so deep you could feel it in the pit of your stomach. Then there was the rank smell of bear piss, which is a smell we all knew, living out in bear country.

Ingrid screamed, although that was the stupidest thing to do, and she twisted on the stool. Snap. Just as quick as that it had rolled beneath her and her feet were free, tap-dancing in the air.

It was quick as all get out.

Barth had turned and was staring into the woods, looking for that damned mother of a she-bear we had all heard, and so he hadn't seen Ingrid fall.

But I had.

She was choking bad, and her tongue had snuck out of her mouth like a thick, purple worm. Her eyes were screwed up into white gibbous moons, that yellow hair of hers twisting in the wind.

Travers had long arms even then, the biggest arms you'd ever seen, like a bear himself, and he tried to grab her, but Ingrid was still choking anyhow. I was scared of the bear, but I was more scared for Ingrid so I took the Sharpfinger knife that Travers kept on his belt for skinning, and I made to right the stool and cut her down.

Travers, I think, was shaking his head, but I couldn't see him from behind Ingrid, whose limbs were now flailing, not like she was hanging, but like she was being electrocuted. It was Barth who stopped me. He was thinking clearer than I was.

"The wand," he said, "do it first, Skye. You have to."

And so I took the hazel wand, which Travers had dropped when he grabbed hold of Ingrid, and I smacked her in the side so hard that she almost swung out of Travers' arms. I tried to remember what Travers had said for me, but all I could come up with was Hangjaw's name. Then Travers had her good, and I was able to get on the stool and saw the blade through the high-rigging rope just above the knot. She tumbled like a scarecrow and hit the ground badly, her and Travers going down together in a heap.

I looked over at Barth, absurdly still wanting him to see how good I'd been, to get her with the wand and then cut her down, but Barth, because he was still thinking of the she-bear, wasn't paying a whit's worth of attention to me.

So I looked at Ingrid instead. Her face kind of bright red with the eyes still rolled back into her skull, body shaking and dancing even though she was on the ground. Travers had gotten out from under her, and now he was putting his ear next to her. At first I thought he was trying to tell if she was still breathing, but of course, he wasn't, he was listening. He was listening to make sure he caught every word she said.

It could have only been a few seconds, that whispery grating voice I couldn't quite catch. But still it scared me even worse than seeing that stool run out underneath her feet, the sound of Ingrid's truth saying. I don't know what she said, but Travers's face went white, and when she was done her body stopped its shakes.

"Travers," I said. Even though I was scared, I wanted to be Witness still, it was my job, and so I wanted him to tell me. "Just whisper it," I told him then. "Go on."

"No use," Travers answered, and I couldn't tell quite what he was talking about but then it became clear to me. Travers let go of her head. I realized how he'd been holding it steady so he could hear, but then the neck lolled at a strange, unnatural angle, and I knew it had snapped like a wet branch during the fall.

"Old Hangjaw wanted her to pay her daddy's blood price," he said.

That frightened me something fierce. Not just that Ingrid had died—well, I'd seen death before—but the way I had seen her mouth moving even though her neck had been snapped clean through. We never played the hanging game after that. Some of the men from the camp brought down that ash tree and burned all the wood away from town where no one would breathe the smoke of it.

And so we all grew up. Those of us that could, that is.

A couple of years down the line Travers won a scholarship and followed it south past Lawford and out of bear country. I was lonely, but I never could blame him. Dad did, though, and they never spoke much after that. And me, well, I married Barth Gibbons, even though he never whispered about a red-haired, slim-hipped woman. I guess we can all make our own luck. That's what I did that day when I was seventeen, and I went with Barth out to the Lawford Drive-In Theatre. I didn't know at the time how easy it was for something to take root in you, but several months later after I'd been retching for a week, convinced I had a helluva stomach flu, Momma told me she reckoned I must be pregnant.

She was right, of course. Dad was pissed for a while but after Barth proposed and we got properly married then he was okay. The baby, though, didn't come the way we expected it to. She came two months too early, in a slick of blood that sure as hell smelled to me like bear piss though no one else would say so. I lost the next one that way too, and the next, just so many until I wouldn't let Barth touch me because I didn't want to see all those tiny, broken bodies laid out in the blood pooling at my legs.

Then one day, after the spring Barth bit into that she-bear and I had to knock him in the side with the hazel wand until he bled just to keep old Hangjaw happy, Travers called me up. I'd just lost another, a little boy who I had already starting trying out names for even though the doctor told me that was a godawful bad idea to do so. And Travers said to me, "Okay, Skye, I know we can't talk about it, I know we're not supposed to, but I'm going to say anyway. You just keep going, okay, Skye? You're almost paid up."

I didn't have the heart to tell him that I couldn't do it anymore, I'd seen all of the little bodies that I could and all I could smell was bear piss. But I loved Travers, I always had, and I remembered what it was like to hold his hand out there by the tree. I remembered the hanging game.

And so that night, though he was tired of it too and his eyes were bright and shiny and he said he couldn't face another stillbirth either, still, I kissed Barth on the mouth. Nine months later out came little Astrid, as clean and sweet smelling as any a little baby was.

So now I'm cradling that body of hers close to mine, her little thatch of black hair fluffed up like a goose and the rest of her so tightly swaddled there's nothing but a squalling face. I'm looking at her and I love this child of mine so much, more than I can rightly say. "Shh," I'm saying to her. "It's okay, it's okay. Don't be afraid now, girl."

But I can't stop thinking about that hill Dad left covered in bear bones that one summer way back when. Can't stop thinking about the nine little bodies I had to bury in the dirt before this little child of mine came along. As I'm holding her in my arms, feeling the warmth of her tucked tight against me, that thing which feels like the best thing in the world, I'm also wondering if she'll ever go out one fine afternoon to play the hanging game, and I'm wondering about the things our parents leave us, the good and the bad, and whether a thing is ever truly over.

"Magic can only give you a thing you want that badly, that desperately. No one can work magic over you. You can only work magic over yourself."

SECONDHAND MAGIC

A bad thing is going to happen at the end of this story. This is a story about bad things happening, but I won't tell you what the bad thing is until you get there. Don't flip ahead to the end of the story. Stories like this only work if you don't know what the bad thing is until you get there. Wait for it to happen, don't try to look ahead, don't try to stop it from happening. Because you know how magic works? When you try to cheat it, it just gets worse and worse and worse. That's the way of it. So, please. Just wait for it. I'll ask nothing else from you. Cross my heart.

Sayer Sandifer had very few of the ingredients necessary to be a true magician. His patter? Weak and forced on account of a childhood stutter he got when he turned four. His fingers? Short, stumpy things that couldn't make a silver dollar disappear no matter how long he practised. His sense of timing? Awful. And worse yet—crime of all crimes!—he had no assistant. The fact of the matter is that lacking any of these things might not have been enough to sink him, but all of them? What chance did the poor boy have? And at twelve years old he was just learning the first and only real lesson of being grown-up: that wanting a thing so bad it hurt didn't mean getting a thing, not by a long shot.

The only thing Sayer *did* have going for him was the prettiest set of baby blues you ever saw. That wasn't nothing. Not for a magician. And those eyes were only useful for one thing: getting an audience. When Sayer put on his star-spattered cloak and the chimney-pot hat he had swiped from Missus Felder's snowman the winter before; when with utter seriousness and intent he knocked on your door at eight in the morning while the coffee brewed and the scent of fresh-mown grass drifted through the Hollow; when you had just kicked up your heels to browse the paper in search of discount hanger steak and sausages, then Sayer would be there.

"Missus S-S-Sabatelli," he would stutter. Or if he was having a particularly bad day then he might not get that far, you might see him swallowing the word like a stone and searching out a new one. The first name instead, "Marianne," he might say and bless him for being so formal. "I require your attendance this afternoon at the house of my mother and father. Please bring gingersnaps."

And maybe you'd fall in love with him just a little bit right then, the way you could tell just by looking that he knew he didn't have the right stuff in him yet for magic, but he wanted it, oh, he wanted it. He'd chase it even if it meant looking a fool in front of all his mother's friends. He'd stand there, trembling, waiting for you to deliberate. Waiting for you to make some sort of pronouncement upon him. And you'd know how badly you could hurt him, that was the thing, you'd know you could crush him right there if you were of a mind to do so.

"Whatever for?" you might ask, hoping to surprise him, hoping to give him a moment to deliver a staggering statement of pomp and circumstance of the kind you knew he ought to have rattling around inside his head, because, *God*, you just wanted this kid to have it in him. Have that special something, even if it was just a flair for the dramatic. But, no, Sayer didn't know the turns of phrase yet, he didn't know that a magician was supposed to do something besides magic. You couldn't expect him to, not at twelve years old, not even if he had studied the masters like Maskelyne, Thurston, Houdini and Carter. Which he hadn't. All he had was a "Magic for Beginners" tin set an uncle had gotten him for Christmas—the same Christmas Missus Felder's snowman had lost its chimney-pot hat and knitted scarf.

What Sayer didn't know was that magic was never at the heart of being a magician. There was supposed to be something else. Something kinder.

But, as I said, what Sayer did have—what made you say "yes, sir, gingersnaps it is!"—were those wide baby blues of his. Eyes a kind of blue I never saw before, blue like a buried vein. His father's eyes.

Joe Sandifer had all the things that Sayer lacked: clean and polished patter; his fingers long and grateful like he'd filched them off a piano man; a near perfect sense of when to come and when to go; and you can bet your bottom dollar that he was never without a partner. Us girls, married though we were, still resented Lillian Sandifer a little for managing to grab hold of good old Joe. Handsome Joe. Joe who could lie like it was easy and beautiful.

Sayer might have had the beginnings of what Joe had, and would surely have discovered more as he passed the five-foot mark, but for now he was too much of a kiddie. A little lamb. All he had was his dignity, which he tugged as tight about him as that star-spattered cloak. And that dignity was the one thing that we in the Hollow were scared to death to take away from him.

Thus, we dreaded that Tuesday morning knock.

Thus, we dreaded that chimney-pot hat.

We dreaded the hungry eyes of Sayer the Magnificent.

Maybe it seems cruel to you that I'm talking like this about a poor runt of a kid with his heart stitched onto the red-and-black satin handkerchief he tugged out of his sleeve—courtesy, again, of that "Magic for Beginners" tin box. I swear I'm not trying to be cruel. It's the world that's wild and woolly. The world that cursed a stutterer—who couldn't holler "sunshine" or "salamander"—with a name like Sayer Sandifer.

You want to know I'm not cruel? Shall I prove it to you? Let's make him a Milo. Milo's a good name for a kid his age. Milo Sandifer. Easier with that "M." At least for a little while. Until he grows out of it. We can do that much for the little guy, can't we? The poor duckling?

When the time came, and we all knew it without really having to look, we went over as late as we possibly could. We being the women of the Hollow, me with my plate of gingersnaps. Just as the boy asked.

Lillian had set up the backyard with lawn chairs. An old red-striped beach umbrella in the northeast corner, just past the rhododendrons. Card tables covered with plastic cups and lemonade for the parents. Nothing is quite so apologetic as homemade lemonade in these circumstances.

"Thanks for coming, Minnie," Lillian whispered as I laid down a plateful of gingersnaps like the boy asked.

"It's nothing worth mentioning," I told her. "I need me some magic today, you hear? Must be he's got a sense for these kind of things after all." I let her smile at that. "It's a good day for it too."

"Some kind of good day," Cheryl Felder muttered. She scowled at the top of her chimney-pot hat poking out from behind the stage and curtains that Joe constructed special. Poor Milo. He never quite figured out that of all the women in the Hollow, Cheryl was the one you didn't want to mess with. Most kids know this sort of thing; they can sense a real witch with a bee in her bonnet if you catch my drift. Or maybe he was just bolder than we gave him credit for.

The other women were coming in then. They laid out licorice strands and tuna fish sandwiches with trimmed corners, whatever the boy asked for. Lillian didn't meet our eyes at first, but then she all of a moment did and, you know what?—give her credit, her eyes were just blazing with pride for little Milo. That buttered us up some. You could see it changing people. Missus Felder's face, well, her face was the kind of face you might associate with sucking lemons, but even it got a little bit of sugar into it.

And the rest of us? Well, I'd always liked the boy. He had a proper kind of respect and reverence, and if there's two things a magician ought to fluff his hat with, it's respect and reverence, magic being no easy business, magic being a thing that ought to be done carefully. Not that I ever suspected poor Milo could mend a cut rope or pull the secret card, but there you have it. He would try, and we, the ladies of the Hollow, we kept company mostly by Hoovers and the Watchtower babble and crap society; we would smile those husband-stealing smiles of ours come Hell or high water.

And so the show began.

"And now for the Lost Suh-suh-suh . . ."

Milo's face screwed up with concentration so hard you could see a flush of red on his neck. Lillian was saying the word alongside him in the audience, but he wouldn't look at her. Missus Felder shifted in her chair.

"And now for the . . ."

His hands palsied and twitched as he shuffled the oversized Bicycle deck, patterned blue flashing in front of our eyes. But no one was watching the cards. We were all watching his mouth. We were all clenching the edges of the Sandifers' lawn chairs.

"For the Lost Suh-s-s . . ."

He paused again. That moment stretched on and on like putty. Just when we thought it was about to snap. Just when we thought *he* was about to snap—you could see Missus Felder leaning forward now, *she* might've said something, none of us would've dared, we knew you didn't speak for a stutterer, not ever, but she would've, she had the word on her lips and she was going to give it to him—that was when Milo swallowed, pushed up the brim of the chimney-pot hat with his wrist.

"Beg pardon, ladies," he murmured ruefully, but it was out and the words were solid. "And now for the Lost . . . Sisters."

The applause was bigger than it had been for any of the other tricks. Milo took it as his due.

"For this I need a volunteer. Anyone?"

No one budged. We couldn't, not yet. We weren't ready for it.

"Anyone? Ladies, please. Ah, good. You there. The . . . missus is the blue dress."

It was Ellie Hawley from across the street in the blue cotton frock with the raglan sleeves her husband brought back from Boston. We were all a bit thankful. She was a good sort. The type who knew to bring licorice strands to a boy's magic show.

"I'm hard of hearing, boy," Missus Felder said. "Which was that?"

God, we were thinking together, do not make him say it again.

It was no good though. She was smiling. Her words were sweetness and light, and she was smiling like she was some sort of old biddy about to offer him tea and biscuits. You couldn't trust a smile like that. Oh, boy, not ever.

"I, uh, suh-suh-s-sorry, folks." The hat tilted forward again. Milo pushed it up, and licked his lips. "I meant . . ." He paused. Why was he pausing? Don't pause here, boy, we were thinking. Stick with Ellie Hawley. She's already getting up. She's halfway to the stage now, boy. Stick with her.

But we could see the look coming over his face. It was a proud look . . . and something else, something I couldn't quite tell yet. A look older than he was. He knew that Ellie was the easy choice. He knew it the same way we knew it. He knew this was a trap, but there was something in him that wouldn't let it go. We were watching. We were waiting. Milo was fighting with this thing, and we let him do it.

" . . . you there, in the front. Missus Felder. Puh-puh-please. Come on up here. Ma'am."

No, we were thinking together, do not ask for her. Do not do it, boy. Do not call on her, boy. Can't you see the Devil has come to your garden party? Can't you see the Devil has gotten into Missus Felder, and there ain't no way to cheat the Devil if you let her up on stage with you?

Missus Felder, she just smiled.

She took her time getting there, walked almost like an old woman even though she didn't look forty yet. Passed Ellie Hawley along the way, just swished past her blue dress with the raglan sleeves.

"Well, boy," said Missus Felder.

"Thank you, Missus Felder." Milo said like he meant it. He shuffled the cards again, each of those big, blue Bicycles. Missus Felder watched primly, patiently, hips swaying slightly as she shifted her weight from side to side. As he was shuffling, you could see Milo starting to look for the words, starting to line them up in his mind like bowling pins so they'd fall down easily once he got going.

Just as he opened his mouth to start the patter, Missus Felder piped up:

"Aren't you going to ask me my name?"

Milo paused at this, chewed back those words he had all lined up for the show. "Nuh-no, Missus Felder. They all nuh-know it already."

She nodded at this, like it was what she had been expecting all along. We all breathed a sigh of relief, but half of us were saying something pretty foul with that breath, let me tell you. Milo smiled a little wobbly smile and got with the shuffling again until he was all good and ready.

This time he got three words into the patter—three perfect words, three flawless, ordinary, magical words.

Then: "Aren't you going to ask me where I'm from?"

Milo shook his head, and his Adam's apple bobbed up and down. His hands missed the cards and three of them went flying out: an eight of spades, a red jack, and the two of diamonds. Milo tried snatching them out of the air, but he missed with those little hands of his and they fluttered like white doves to the grass.

He placed the deck down steadily on the card table, and all the while Missus Felder was watching him with a look as wide and innocent as his own. There was a hush. We all knew something was coming. The kid knew something was coming. The kid was the kind of kid born with enough sense to know when something was coming but not enough to figure how to get out of the way. We could see the poor kid's hands were trembling. He stooped to grab the cards, and as he was stooping, off slid that the black magician's hat.

Missus Felder was faster than a rattler. Like lightning striking or tragedy.

The hat was in her hand then. She was holding it up to the audience. She was squinting at the inside of the brim of it.

"My boy," she said, squinting away, "my boy, it seems as if you've dropped this."

Milo straightened up right away with only the red jack in his hands. He was staring at the hat. He was staring at Missus Felder.

"Aww, c'mon," someone whispered in the audience; we didn't know who, but we loved that person.

"Come now, Milo, we can't have the magician without his hat, can we?"

Milo didn't move. No one moved. No one dared to. Only the breeze tickling at the edges of his star-spattered cape.

"Come here, boy. Now." Her voice cracked like a whip. Milo couldn't ignore it. None of us could ignore it, our feet itched to stand. Ellie Hawley went so far as taking that first step forward before she caught hold of herself and paused.

Milo, though, he was too young to know better. He had been trained to obey voices like Missus Felder's. He was stepping forward, he was stepping forward, and there—he was forward, he was just in front of her, and she was putting down the hat, she was resting it gently on his head, and she was tugging just so at the brim to set it straight.

And she was tugging at it.

And she was tugging at it.

And down came the hat an inch farther.

And down came the hat another inch.

She was still tugging at it, still smiling like she was doing a favour for Milo, but none of us could see his face anymore. The hat was past his nose. The hat was past his mouth. The hat was past his chin, but Missus Felder just kept tugging it down and down and down. Now his shoulders were gone, and it was taking the boy up into it, Milo, he was just disappearing into the hat, disappearing to his knees and his shin and his ankles until the hat was resting on the ground.

Missus Felder blinked as if she was confused. She blinked as if she didn't understand what had happened. Then she picked up the hat. Quizzical. She held it out to the audience, showed us all the inside and it was empty. Perfectly empty.

"Well," she said, almost apologetically. "I guess that's that, then."

And she stepped off the stage.

The thing about magic is it only works when you let it. It only works when you believe in it entirely, when you give yourself over to it entirely. Magic can only give you a thing you want that badly, that desperately. No one can work magic over you. You can only work magic over yourself.

Cheryl Felder knew something about magic.

There were stories about Cheryl Felder, stories that poor Sandifer kid ought to have known the way that all kids know whose trees not to filch apples from and which backyards shouldn't be ventured for Frisbees and baseballs. Some might say that these sorts of stories were nonsense and spoke only to the curmudgeonly tendencies of the grumbles who reside in any town block.

But those people would be dead wrong.

After Sayer disappeared not a single soul spoke, not a bird twittered, not a skirt fluttered in the breeze. You could see those faces, each of them white as snow, white as a snow-woman caught in a melt.

Lillian trembled, but she said nothing.

She watched Missus Felder pluck a crustless tuna fish sandwich off the platter and vanish it with three remorseless bites.

"Could use some cayenne," she said with a sprung smile, "but all around, fine work, Lillian. Thanks for the show."

Cheryl Felder knew something about magic, and the biggest trick she knew was that people don't like messing with it. Messing with magic was like sticking your hand down a blind hole, you never knew if there might be treasure at the bottom or if it might be some rattler's hole. And all those women, they had something to lose, they had sons of their own, they had husbands, they had pretty hair or blue cotton frocks—something they didn't want vanished. So after a while each of them stood up and collected leftover plates still piled high with uneaten licorice strands or oatmeal-raisin cookies and then each of them filed silently past Lillian Sandifer with neither a glance nor a touch nor a whisper of comfort.

Don't be too hard on them.

They had loved that boy. We had all loved that boy.

They tried to make up for it over the next couple of months, knowing as we all did what a bad time Lillian would be having with that empty room at the top of the stairs, the room filled with arithmetic workbooks and bottle rockets and adventure paperbacks. They dropped off casseroles. Their sons took over the raking of the lawn and the watering of the flowerbeds. Ellie Hawley brought over a fresh-baked apple pie every Sunday. But it was never spoken of, why this neighbourly hospitality was due.

And Missus Felder, she did the same as she had always done. She shopped at the grocery store, squeezing peaches and plums to be sure they were ripe. She got her hair done once a week at the salon at the corner of Broad and Vine.

The missuses of the neighbourhood never spoke to her of it. None could manage it. I wanted to. I did. That little boy had a way of being loved that seemed a brand of magic all his own, but if there was one thing

I knew it was that I couldn't meddle in this.

Once I saw Lillian try, but only once.

This was about three weeks after it had happened. Poor Lillian was looking wasted and fat at the same time, her cheekbones sharp as fishhooks but her chin sagging like a net. Joe had gone on one of his business trips out of town, leaving her by her lonesome for the big old holiday weekend. All the ladies of the Hollow were bringing out bowls of punch and wobbling gelatin towers filled with fruit and marshmallows, while the children lit up Burning Schoolhouses and Big Bertha firecrackers. There was a fizzy feeling to the air on those kinds of days, as it exploded with pops and whistles and sparks and the smell of hamburger sizzling on the grill.

Missus Felder, she came out too for the block party and she brought with her a bowl of plump, red strawberries. She set them up at the end of her driveway on a little wooden table with a lace cloth thrown over, and she handed them out to kiddies as they whizzed by.

Now she was trimming the hats off them, one by one. *Snip!* A little stalk and a flourish of leaves went skidding onto the sidewalk. *Snip!*

And there was Lillian standing in front of her, trembling, thin-boned, in a yellow print dress that made her skin seem old as last year's newspaper.

"Please," Lillian said. Just that. Just that word.

"Careful," said Missus Felder, never looking up, her fingers dusted white to the knuckle as she pinched strawberries out and laid on the confectionary sugar. "You'll spoil your makeup if you keep up with that. You've too pretty a face for tears and if I'm not wrong there's others around here that'd be willing to hook that husband of yours. A nice man, Joe. A handsome man. He deserves a pretty wife."

Lillian didn't say anything. Her lips trembled. They were chapped and unrouged, and maybe she was wondering why she hadn't put a touch of red on them. Missus Felder plucked up another strawberry and she looked at it carefully.

"You're a beautiful woman, Lillian, and children wear you out. They trample the roses of youth, leave a woman like some tattered thing hanging out on the clothesline. Let the boy go. He was ungrateful, selfish. Have another one if it's in your heart to do so, but let that one go."

"But he's my son, Cheryl. Please."

"Son or no son." Now Missus Felder sighed a worn-out, old sigh as if the weather had gotten into her bones and really, she was just an old woman, why was she being troubled with this? "Do as you like, Lillian. But I'll tell you for nothing that some children are best let go."

And that was that.

The last flickers of September's heat burned out in the flood of a ravenous, wet November that shuttered the windows and played havoc with the shingles; by the time December whispered in, we were all thankful for it. All of us except for Lillian Sandifer.

There were some women who could take a loss and find their own way through, but Lillian, bless her, had had an easy life. Joe was everything you ought to have in a husband. He treated her gently. He brought her back fine cotton sheets from Boston, dresses and trinkets, a music box, a tiny wind-up carousel. Lillian loved all beautiful things. She had come as close to a life without loss as one can. But when December blew in—an easy December, full of light snows and bright silver days—it was like she took all the harshness, the cold, the cutting, fractured freeze into herself, and she let it break her.

And then we all saw the snowman in Missus Felder's yard.

The snows had been light, as I said, barely enough for a footprint, really, but there it was: round as a turnip at the bottom; a thin, tapering carrot for a nose; two silver dollars for eyes; and a fresh knitted scarf in green and gold hung beneath its hawkish, polar jowls. It was a king snowman, the kind of snowman that children dream about making before their arms give out from pushing the ball around the yard, the kind of snowman that wouldn't melt until halfway through May.

And on its head was a black chimney-pot hat, creased somewhat at the brim with a red silk ribbon drawn around it to set off its colouring.

A beauty, that hat; gorgeous to the eyes of a child and pure pain to his mother.

I could never do a big thing with magic, and that has always been both a blessing and a curse to me. Oh, there are ways and there are ways, and I know this is true, but the ways have never worked for me. It's an easy thing to change a boy's name. It's a little thing, particularly if it is a thing done kindly, if it is a thing that might be wanted. Then the change comes easily. But I cannot get blood from a stone, nor flesh from bread, nor make healthy a woman who wishes she were sick.

That is the province of my sister. And if it is none of mine to meddle with that greater magic, then it is at least something of mine to meddle with her.

It was a month into the hard end of winter I finally broke my silence.

"You must let the boy go," I told Cheryl, stepping in out of the cold, stamping my boots off to shed them of the slush that had begun to freeze around the edges. Winter always followed the two of us, winter and spring, summer and autumn, they had their own way about us whether we willed it or no.

"I will not, Minnie. . . ." She paused like the name was bitter to her. "Minnie, they call you. Ha. They have a way with names, don't they? Marianne. No, Marianne, I cannot." She closed the door quickly. She hated the cold, kept a thin blanket wrapped around her in the winter. I could see her curved fingers clutching at the edges. Winter turned her into an old woman as surely as summer made her a young one.

I gave her a look. It was not the dark and hooked scowl that came so easily to *her* face, no, it was a look entirely my own.

"It's time. It is long past time."

"Too skinny, and what has that husband of yours got you doing with your hair? I could never abide him, you know." Her mouth twisted as she looked me up and down

"I know. You could never abide any of them."

"I abided my own well enough," she said. "The poor duckling. The little lamb. Let me fetch you some cake." She did. Tea, as well, the heat of it warming through the bone china cup. Her movements were quick and sharp as a bird's.

She settled us at the kitchen table. I remembered this house, I knew the ins and outs of it. The gold December light filtered softly through the window, touching a lace cloth, a badly polished silver candle holder. She never had an eye for the details, no, and this was what came of it.

"Where is the boy, Cheryl?"

She touched her tongue to her lip, scowled something fierce. "You know as well as I do."

"Let him out."

"No."

"They will come to hate us." I knew she knew this. I could see it in her eyes, in the way she twisted at the lace cloth, but she could be a stubborn old biddy sometimes. "He was a good boy, and it was a small thing," I said.

"It was not a small thing!" she cried so harshly it took me by surprise, that her voice could go so ugly. So sad. I looked at my sister, and I saw then the thing that they all saw. That missus of nightmares and twisted stories, the hooked woman, the crone; she who devoured baseballs and Frisbees and footballs; she who stole the bright heart of summer and cursed the strawberries to wither on the vine; the son-stealer, the child-killer.

"It was," I said gently. "You know as well as I do that it was, and it is only spite and pride that keeps you from letting him go."

"You are a meddler too, Marianne, so mind your tongue," she muttered but the words stung nonetheless. "No," Cheryl whispered, chin curved down, and she was retreating, drawing in upon herself. "I know it as well. It was a mistake, all of it, nothing more than that." She cupped the bone china in her hand and blew on the tea to cool it. "I did not mean for it to happen, you know I did not, I would not do such a thing to a child. To his mother." She paused, took a sip, eyes hooded, lips twisting. "I know that the woman is dying. I know she will not live through the winter, but I cannot touch her, don't you see that? Don't you see, sister? I cannot heal the mother, I cannot summon the child. I cannot force a thing that is not wanted, and the boy will not *come out*!"

I could see the truth of it written on her face.

She was not a monster, she had never been a monster, and how I wished I could take her in my arms, her frail bones sharp and splintering as a porcupine; how I wished I could whisper the words of comfort to her. But she did not wish to be comforted. Her spine was made of sprung steel. She would not break herself upon this, for she knew what loss was and what mistakes were and the hardness of carrying on anyway. My sister knew this. She had buried a husband she loved. She had cried tears for her own lost boy, and knitted a scarf for him in green and gold, and hung it upon the cold reminder of his body in the yard.

Her fingers twitched, knuckling the bone china cup. I wanted to take her hand, but I knew something of her pride, the pride and the grief and the love of all of us missuses of the Hollow.

"Let us do something," I say. "Even if it is a small thing."

It is an easy thing to take a handful of snow and fashion it into a boy, easier than most anyone would believe. Snow longs to be something else. Bread does not wish to be flesh, water does not wish to be wine, stones do not wish to bleed—but snow, snow wishes always to be the thing that is not, a thing that might survive the spring thaw and live out its days whole and untouched. And a boy, a boy who is loved, well, what finer shape is there?

And so we two fashioned it into a shape, and we set the silver dollars for its eyes and we wrote its name upon its forehead. Then, of course, it was not a thing of snow any longer but a thing of flesh: a thing with Milo

Sandifer's bright blue eyes, barely nudging five-feet, and still as tongue-tied as any boy ever was.

"Missus Suh-s-sabatelli," he whispered, trying out that fresh new mouth of his.

"Yes, boy," I allowed with a sigh. "That I am. Now get you home to your mother, she's been calling after you, and don't you bother her with what you've been getting up to. Just give her a kiss, you hear?"

"Right," the boy said, "Yes, of course. I'll do that. Thank you, ma'am."

Already his tongue was working better than poor Milo's ever did. But it wouldn't matter none, I reckoned. Missus Felder unwound the scarf from around the king snowman's neck. The hole in its chest where we had dug out the boy yawned like a chasm. Like Adam's unknit ribcage.

"Here," she said, and she wrapped the scarf around Milo. "You ought to keep warm now. Little boys catch cold so easily."

He blinked at her as if trying to remember something, but then he shrugged the way that little boys do. Then he was off, scampering across lawns and driveways, home to his mother. I looked on after him, staring at the places where his feet had touched the ground, barely making a dent in the dusting of white over the grass.

"What do you reckon?" I asked Cheryl. She'd gone to patting away at her snowman and sealing him up again, eyeless, blinded, a naked thing without that scarf, only the hat on him now, only that gorgeous silk thing to make him a man and not just a lump.

"He'll last as long as he lasts," she said with a sniff. "Snow is snow. Even if it wants to be a boy."

"And Lillian?"

She didn't speak for a time, and I had to rub at my arms for warmth. For me it had already gone February and the little snowflakes that landed upon my cheeks were crueller things than the ones the other missuses would be feeling as they took their sons and daughters to church.

"Maybe it's a kindness you've done here, and maybe it isn't." She wasn't looking at me. Cheryl couldn't ever look at you when she was speaking truths. She smoothed the freeze over the place where she drew out the boy, and her fingers were like twigs, black and brittle, against the white of it. "You can't ever know the thing a person truly wants, but you keep on trying, don't you? I hope your husband is a happy man, I hope you give him children of your own one day."

"Well," I said, but I didn't know what more to add to that.

She was right, of course, she always was about such things: maybe it was a blessing and maybe it wasn't, but the boy came home to find his mother curled up in his bed surrounded by arithmetic workbooks and bottle rockets and adventure paperbacks. And he kissed her gently on the forehead, and she looked at him and smiled, her heart giving out, just like that, at the joy of seeing him once again. But the boy had been made good and sweet, and so he wrapped himself in her arms, and he lay next to her until the heat of her had faded away entirely.

That heat.

Poor thing didn't know any better. But snow is snow, even when it is flesh. A thing always remembers what it was first. When Joe Sandifer came home it was to find his wife had passed on, and from the dampness of the sheets he knew she must have been crying an ocean.

Joe was a good man and a strong man; his fingers were long and graceful. He pulled up the sheet around his wife, and he kissed her gently, and he buried her the following Tuesday. Perhaps it was hard for him for a time; it must have been, for he had loved his wife dearly, and he had lived only to see her smile, but the spring came and went, and then a year, and then another year, and he was not the kind of man who needed wait long for a partner. It was Ellie Hawley in the end, childlike and sweet, whose husband had brought her the blue dress with the raglan sleeves, whose husband had left her behind when he found a Boston widow with a dress that didn't make it past the knees and legs that went all the way to the floor. Ellie was the one who managed to bring a smile to Joe's face and to teach him that there were still beautiful things left in the world for a man who had lost both wife and son.

And so it goes.

And it goes and it goes and it goes.

Until one day Milo came back.

"Missus Sabatelli," he said when I opened the door to him, that bright June Tuesday with the scent of fresh-mown grass drifting through the neighbourhood, nine in the morning, just like he used to.

He was a grown man then, the height of his father, with his father's good looks and easy smile. A handsome man. The kind of man you'd fall in love with, easy, but the kind of man you'd never know if he loved you back.

"Milo," I said, and I had to hold on to the doorframe. I was half expecting him to be wearing that star-spattered cloak of his, to chew on his words as if they were gristle in his mouth. But he didn't.

"Thank you for that kindness," he said, "but I'm not Milo any longer. I've learned a thing or two since then." I saw then that he was right. Whoever he was, he wasn't little Milo Sandifer.

"You've come back," I said. I shivered. For him it was June, but for me the wind was already blowing crisp and cool, carrying the smoky scent of September with it. Time was running faster and faster ahead of me.

"Yes," Sayer said, lingering on that "s" with a lazy smile as if to show me he could do it now and easily at that. "I've come home again. Would you mind if I stepped inside, Marianne? I'm not one to gab on porches, and if it's not too impertinent I could use a cup of coffee something fierce."

"Of course, boy."

He chuckled, and the sound was rich and deep and expansive. I stepped aside, and he took off his hat as he came in. Not *the* hat, of course. The one he wore was an expensive, grey Trilby that matched his expensive, grey suit and his expensive, leather shoes. He followed me into the kitchen: I regretted that I hadn't had time to clear up properly that morning, but he didn't seem to mind so much. He said nice, polite things about the colour of the curtains and about the state of things in general, and when he sat it seemed as if he were too big for the chair, as if that chair wanted to hold a small boy in it but had now discovered a man instead. The coffee's aroma was thick in the air, and I found I could use a cup myself so I poured for both of us, and served it plain. He seemed the sort to take his coffee black.

I was nervous. It had been some time since there had been a man in my house.

"You found your way then?" I asked him.

"I did, ma'am. I surely did."

"And you know about your mother?"

He smiled, but this time there was something else to the smile. "I do," he said. "Missus Felder told me of all that, and I'm sorry for it, I suppose. She whispered it to me while I was gone. She cajoled, she begged, and she pleaded. She has a tongue on her could scald boiling water, Missus Felder does, could strip paint off a fence."

His eyes were bright blue, and surprisingly clear. I wondered if he was lying to me. I could see he had learned how to lie. Like lying was easy and beautiful.

"You didn't come back for her," I said.

"I did not." He paused, and breathed in deep, like he never smelled coffee before and found it the finest thing in the world. "I could say that I was unable." He glanced at me underneath a fan of handsome eyelashes, quick as a bird. "But you know that's not true, you know that's not how magic works, don't you? I wanted to stay. I wanted to stay, and it didn't matter. What Missus Felder did—your sister, yes, I know about that— what she did was cruel in its own way, sure, but not in the way you'd think—"

"No, boy," I cut him off. He looked surprised at that, like he was not used to people cutting him off. I wondered who this new boy was, this boy that Cheryl and I had made. "We figured it out, of course, though it was too late for anything to be done. You were always a boy who was looking for magic, even then, even then you were, and we knew it, Cheryl and I both knew it, but we had hoped it might be a different sort of magic. A kinder sort."

"But it wasn't," he said.

"No, it wasn't. You found something in there, didn't you?"

"I did."

"And you stayed for it."

"I did."

"And now?"

"Now I have taken what I need from it," he said, and he flexed his fingers, long and graceful. They were not the fingers he had when he was a boy, those poor stubby things that couldn't palm a quarter or pull off a faro shuffle. These were magician's fingers.

"So I see you have, my boy. Has it done ill for you or aught?"

At this he paused. I could see he wanted to get into his patter now, and it was not the same kind of pause as when he was young, when he knew the word but still it tripped him up; this was a different beast.

"I don't know," he said at last. "I want you to tell me. That's why I'm here, I suppose, Marianne."

"No one can tell you that, Sayer."

He took to studying his fingernails. Maybe he learned that trick from Cheryl, not looking at a person. "I think you can. I think you are afraid to tell me."

A shiver ran down my spine like ice melting. I tried to shake the feeling though.

"No, boy." He looked up at that word. "Your sense of timing was always characteristically awful. You never learned how to wait for a thing. Don't you know that? When you try to cheat magic, it just gets worse and worse and worse. What you found in that hat—some sort of secondhand magic I'm reckoning, that piece of truth you were looking for all that time—it's yours now. It ain't your daddy's magic. It ain't Lillian's either. Poor, sweet Lillian. You've suffered for it, and you've caused suffering for it, so it's yours to own, yours to do with as you will."

"There is a bad thing coming at the end of this," Sayer told me. He reached out that long-fingered hand of his, and he touched me on the wrist.

"I know, boy," I said. "We always know these things. Time's always racing on for us; even if most other folk can't see it properly, you can. But, God, the thing we never learned right, Cheryl and I, is that magic is about waiting, it's about letting the bad things happen. It's about letting the children pass on into adults, and the mothers grieve, and the fathers lose their way, or find it, and the sons come home again when they are ready to come home. That is the thing you will not have learned in that place you went to, because that is only a thing you can learn out here. What are you going to be, Sayer Sandifer? Why, whatever it is you choose to be. You saw what was coming that day when you invited her up on the stage with you. Boy, there were twenty people out in the audience who loved you, who would have waited with you, who would have helped you get there on your own, but you wanted what she had and so you took it."

The words were hard stones in my own mouth, but I had chewed them over so long that I had made them round and smooth and true.

"Where is my sister?" I asked him.

"She's gone now," Sayer told me, and this time I could tell that he wasn't lying. I didn't know what kind of a thing he was, this man drinking his coffee in front of me, this man who had taken power into himself but not knowledge, not wisdom, not the patience of a boy who learns to speak for himself.

"Well," I said, and the word hung between us.

I felt old. I felt the weight of every summer and winter hanging upon me.

I knew it would only happen if I let it. I knew it would only happen if I wanted it to happen. I knew this just as my sister knew it.

Then Sayer laid down his grey Trilby on the table, and, lo and behold, it was the thing I'd been looking for after all. The hat, the chimney-pot hat. That little piece of secondhand magic. He turned it over so that I could see that yawning chasm inside—the pure blackness of it, deep and terrifying. The place he disappeared to. The place he found his way out of.

"You could marry me," he said. "You always loved me, and I can see there's no man about now. Living like that can be awful lonely."

The words pulled at something inside me. He was right. I was lonely. This life of mine felt old, misshapen, stretched out by the years. But I did not want him. I did not want that stranger. "No," I said.

He sighed and shook his head like it was my tragedy. My funeral.

"I'm not cruel," he said to me in that handsome, grown-up voice of his.

And he looked at me with eyes wide as two silver dollars, but flat-edged and dull as if the shine had been worn off them by residence in too many dirty pockets. "I swear I'm not trying to be cruel. It's the world that's wild and woolly."

And I knew that magic only worked if you let it. I knew that magic only worked on a thing that wanted it. But I was tired, and I was tired, and I had lost my husband, and I had lost my sister, and I had lost that little boy I loved.

Sayer pushed the hat toward me.

I took it up carefully, studied the dilapidated brim, fingered the soft black silk of it.

And Sayer smiled. Just once.

And then the bad thing happened.

"Honey, I don't know what now is. A way station maybe. A pit stop on the Road to Somewhere Else."

I'm the Lady of Good Times, She Said

It's barely past midnight on the crumpled asphalt ribbon of Route 66, west of Ash Fork, just past the bridge at the Crookton Road exit on Interstate 40.

We're in an old, beat-up Studebaker Champ, and disaster is playing like a love song on the radio.

Carl rides shotgun.

You wouldn't like Carl much. Not many apart from Juney do, but Juney's got a blind spot for hard luck cases and Carl's the most hard luck case of all, not counting myself. I know Carl. I bailed him out the time he beat up that girl for short-changing him at the 7-Eleven. The cops told me they had to haul him away, screaming, "For a two-buck tip you better show me your cock-chafing titties, you little whore!"

I never told Juney about that. We aren't much the kind to keep secrets, but he's her brother, and I spent enough nights on the couch in the early years to know when to let a thing go.

The Lady of the Ill Wind Blowing, indeed.

So Carl's riding shotgun and I'm in the driver's seat, because I sure as Hell wouldn't let him touch the fucking steering wheel. Even now.

Carl's angry. You can tell by the way he's grinding his teeth—been doing that since he's a kid, I imagine, so's now they're small and smooth like pebbles, rubbed down to raw little nubblins that hurt him to chew, but he does it anyway.

The other way you can tell Carl's angry is the Colt. He's got it trained on me. He's draped an old U of A football jersey (rah rah, Wild Cats, huh?) over the barrel. Only we two know there's a gun under it.

It's my pappy's Colt. Same one he used to renovate the back of his skull when I was seventeen. I don't like guns. Must be the only fella in Mojave Country who don't, but once you've seen what a Colt does, what it's made for—which is turning a living, breathing human bean into ground chuck—well, the shine goes off fast.

Juney and Carl were raised different. Carl's been shooting beer cans out in the desert since he was five. I seen him at his place with an old air rifle he musta got as a kid. He could pump it just right to knock flies outta the air, leave 'em stunned but whole. Kept 'em in canning jars until they suffocated, bumbling like drunks up against the glass.

Carl knew guns. He knew where I kept the Colt, and I only kept it for Juney. So she'd feel safe. That's a laugh now.

Carl's shifting the gun. I can't see under the shirt but I can feel instinctively—hair on the back of my neck prickling with sweat—that he's got his finger on the trigger. He's stroking it. My skin crawls because he could be masturbating for all I can see, that wet gleam in his eyes and his tongue darting out like a lizard's between his cracked lips.

He'd be crazy to pull the trigger now. I've got my hands on the wheel and we're clocking over sixty, it'd kill us both. But that look in his eyes? He don't give a damn. That's what scares me.

So we drive.

I can feel the barrel trained on me. I can see the twitch of his finger. Clutch and release. Clutch and release.

It's past midnight. Nothing but grassland and the odd thicket shape of juniper bushes jumping in the glow of the headlights. The blue gloom of buttes in the distance. Faded neon signs. We pass the ruins of Hyde Park ("Park Your Hide Tonight at Hyde Park!!") and I wonder if that's what Carl has in mind, if he wants to park my hide somewhere out in the desert.

I try not to think about that, just feel the road underneath me, the scream of the engine. I'm almost relaxed. I can feel my body unspooling the way the road does.

It's a mistake.

Carl senses it, his body goes rigid and he grins a mad-dog grin. He's been baking in the sun for too long.

"Enough," he says. "Pull over."

"Hey, man," I try but my lips have gone dry. My throat is raw. "Hey."

"Don't shit with me, Smiley. Just pull over the fucking car."

"I can explain," I start. The line sounds funny in my own head.

"Sure," he says. "Sure." But he's got that grin and I don't think he gives two shits about what I'm going to say. He wants this. I'm used to reading people. You can't sell a man what he don't want in his heart, whether it's God, a Cadillac, or pills for the perfect boner. A man wants what he wants.

I'm releasing the gas and the car starts to shake as we pull off the asphalt. There's nothing out here but sage and sky and the road and us—him with the Colt and me with one shot at selling him something it's clear he don't want to buy.

Otherwise . . .

Otherwise . . .

I'll be ground chuck when that damned Arizona sun turns the road into the world's hottest grill.

"I'm the Lady of Good Times," she told me. "I'm the Lady of Turn Up the Heat, Boys."

Here goes.

I didn't mean to cheat.

I know that's what every cheater since Eve met the snake claims, but it's no less true. I didn't mean to cheat on Juney. The only defence I got is I'm human, I'm human, and what executioner ever gave a damn for that old song and dance?

Let me try again.

I only saw a ghost once before this all got started. That was the night Pappy died. Don't even know if it was real. When you've seen a man's grey matter splashed over the concrete you're bound to dream any number of things in the small hours.

I was lucky. What I saw was kinder that I had any right to expect. Which is to say I woke up to find Pappy standing at the foot of my bed. Some younger version it must have been. He still had the head of hair my mammy fell in love with. Whatever bad news came to him later in life—pulling the skin around his eyes with the fishhooks of too much worry—it still hadn't found him yet.

There he was. Some shadow of him slivered by the wedge of light from the hall come sliding into the room.

"G'night, Smiley," he said. Just that. He grinned a sweet old grin at me like he had, I imagine, when I was a babe rolling around in the crib.

"G'night, Smiley," he said and then he was gone.

And so I'm thinking about death and ghosts and the trouble men get into but somewhere else I'm stumbling through sand and cholla. The night smell of creosote is heavy. I don't know where Carl is leading me.

Carl's everything that I've ever been afraid of in the world. Ugly and brutal. A man who comes into the world with his fists balled and plans on going out the same way.

Maybe it's the same for him though. Maybe I'm everything he is afraid of. A man who smiles. A man who's had the shit kicked out of him but still knows how to whistle a tune. A man who could make his sister happy— Looney Juney, he called her. God.

A man who could make her cry too. I admit it. I broke her heart more than once. Poor Juney. She was the only person in the world who'd found a way to care for him, and a sumbitch like me has the thread of her love cat's-cradling between my fingers. God, he must've had that hard-on of hate for a long time.

And right now I'm thinking that maybe I deserve this. That's the thing. Right now I'm thinking maybe he has a right to put a bullet in me.

I never saw another ghost but Pappy until three months ago.

It started off with a sound like crying. Wailing, really. I thought maybe it was a bobcat in heat—some critter, maybe, with tire treads crushing half of him. Nothing left to do but cry his grief to the night.

Juney and I had never had kids. We talked about it, well, years ago, but it never got much past talk. One of the ways I broke her heart, I guess, though I still think maybe I did her a favour. My parents got unlucky with me—they couldn't afford a kid, but Mammy had grown up in the light of Jesus, so once I had taken hold in her belly there wasn't much for it. But one was enough. Whatever they got wrong that night they never got wrong again.

So I wasn't much used to the sound of babies crying, which is why I'd been thinking about some dying thing.

Juney didn't hear it. She worked the night shift at Dunkin' Donuts, and I didn't ever see her 'til the sun started in.

I didn't think much on it, but then it happened again. This time it weren't crying. It was singing. A drunk's tune. A little of this, a little of that. But sad.

I went into the kitchen. I had the Colt in my hand because wasn't that what my little Junebug made me keep it for? In these parts a man who wanders into another man's house is liable to end up six feet under. Half the folk think they were born from a misplaced squirt from Billy the Kid's cock.

Not me. Sins I have in plenty but I never thought it in me to kill a man. Not without asking his name first.

Still, I kept my finger on the trigger. I ain't stupid neither.

But the man. Well. When I saw him standing like nobody's business in my kitchen with that sad song on his lips, I knew I recognised him. Not enough to wave to, but enough to know I'd seen him before. It took me a moment but I'm good with faces. I'd given him a dollar or two when I had one to spare. Bought him a Coke outside the drugstore once. Sure enough, I looked down and there were the two bald knuckles of his left hand rapping lightly against my kitchen table. His sign had said he was a war vet. He had that half-vacant look in his eyes. True or not, I believed it.

He catches me looking and his lips twitch. He flips me a slow, three-fingered salute, and I swear, just like Pappy, the moonlight takes him. It seemed clear enough whatever I meant to do with the Colt, worse had already happened.

He wasn't back the next night, but three nights later he was. I woke with that itch between my shoulder blades that someone was in the house. I didn't say nothing to him, but he looked so sad. And something else too. A sharpish, black-eyed look. I sat with him a while. And the next night too. And the next.

Until he didn't come back no more.

✻

This is how I discovered girls.

If you know this, maybe the rest will be clearer. Maybe.

I was sitting with Pappy at the bus station getting ready for my first real haircut. Maybe six years old? Haircuts were a big deal in my family. We were dead broke, but it was my birthday and Pappy was clear about one thing—the cut makes a man. I was nervous. I knew this was a grown-up thing and Mammy and Pappy had fought about it. A big ole screaming match. I knew this was Big Boy stuff.

Pappy knew I was nervous. He starts horsing around, trying to let me know that it's no big deal. But I'm this sullen cinderblock. I don't move a muscle. I don't smile.

So he gets down on his knees in front of me, dusting up his best pair of trousers in the dirt. He's pulling faces. At first I won't crack a grin, but the faces get bigger and bigger. And there's Pappy down on that dirty floor with all the other folk staring and he's yanking at his lips and tugging at his nostrils. Now some of them are laughing, and now I'm laughing too, these giant *yuk yuk* laughs that are half hiccups. My chest is sore from laughing. Now I'm on my knees, half running, half crawling through the rows of chipped orange chairs because this big ole monster of a pappy is grunting and chasing after me.

I duck and juke, then I skid to the end of the last row.

I hardly notice someone's *there*.

A woman.

Ten seconds ago I was twisting on skinned knees but suddenly I'm transfixed, staring straight up the skirt of this young college girl with legs smooth as stripped timber and black stockings running up her perfect thighs.

I have never again seen such an elaborate set of machinery as the garter belts that kept those stockings in place. Erector sets had nothing on whatever those were. Nothing.

I'm telling you this because there is still nothing sweeter than those fancy snaps and laces that make a lady a lady. To this day I swear it was seeing the buckle of Juney's garter slipping out from under the hem of her church dress that stopped my breath. That sly sweet smile when she caught me looking.

I was in love. Same feeling at six as it was at twenty-six.

I never meant to hurt Juney. I swear. But women have always been my weakness.

The second woman I loved was Kelsi Koehler. She was a regular feature at the Glendale 9 Drive-In. A scream queen of the highest calibre. The leading lady of every wet dream I had between the ages of twelve and sixteen.

Miss Koehler had this thick, glossy hair and the most adorable way of shrugging her shoulders and quirking her eyebrows so they almost kissed at the centre of her forehead. The best part was you could find her every other night for the cost of admission. It was Boomtown for the Weissman family during those years—no more fights over haircuts, not then!

It wasn't the hair toss or that perfect little smirk that got me though. It was her voice. The super-sultry huskiness of it. "I'm the Lady of Good Times," I remember her saying. "I'm the Lady of Good Things Coming." When she said that it was like she was speaking directly to me. Her voice low and sexy, cutting the cuteness the way whisky cuts coke.

After that I dedicated every pencil erection my teenage self got to her. She was my queen. My goddess. My Lady of Good Things Coming. I worshipped her with paper route money and discount ticket stubs every Friday night.

And three days after the dead vet flashed me his final three-fingered salute, there she was.

The glorious track of red hair. The girlish set to her shoulders. The B-Movie smoulder.

My Lady of Good Times. My Lady of Love at First Sight.

And then she winked.

Here's the thing you got to know about my pappy. Billy Weissman was a Bible salesman. It always struck him as funny that a Heeb like him could get work slinging the gospel. He had a big Jew nose just like I got, but people took him for a cheech. Or a wop. An Apache, even.

He was gone most of the time when I was growing up, but when he was in town it was always a party. Mammy and I'd get in the car and we'd drive out to God knows where and Pappy would take out a bottle of whatever was rolling around in the back. We'd watch the stars. Sing old Hank Williams songs. Pappy would drink the road dust out of his throat and get a bit friendly until Mammy gave him that look all men know.

I loved those nights. All three of us together.

What I didn't know was that wasn't his first bottle. It might not even have been his second. Maybe Mammy was happy. I don't know, but you gotta wonder what a mother's to think about being so broke in those early lean years her son has to stitch his shoes together with safety pins while his pappy's got the cash for whisky.

Well. You know how that ended.

And when it did I got a gun, a suitcase full of the Good Book, and a taste for the bottle.

It hadn't been good between Juney and me for some time.

There were times when I was glad she worked the night shift so she didn't have to see me crawling in at three or four in the morning. But, God, I still remember that girl I saw in church. Her garters slipping out from under the hem. Her stockings drooping.

I didn't know how bad it was, though.

I didn't know that she must've been over at Carl's place crying some mornings after her shift, in that trailer of his with its jars full of choking flies. What it must've been like for her to go to her big brother for help.

Even though he was mean.

Even though he could be vicious as a mad dog.

Maybe we all have blind spots.

49

When I first see Kelsi Koehler I think maybe I'm looking through the thick, glass bottom of the bottle. It isn't real. It could be any woman with her hip up on the kitchen table, her thigh leaving the lightest trace of sweat there.

"Hiya, honey," she says. That voice.

"Hi yourself," I say.

"Pour a girl a drink?"

I nod. Maybe I nod. I find a bottle anyway and pour out whatever's in it. Something cheap, I imagine. Whisky. I get two ice cubes from the freezer and her eyes are following me all the way. *Plop* go the ice cubes. They chime as they hit the glass. I've always loved the sound of ice cracking in whisky.

She takes the drink without saying a word. Makes a face when she tries it.

"This is the best you've got?"

I shrug. She cocks her head and now her eyebrows are doing that kissing thing I remember so well from the big screen.

"Am I dead?" I wonder. It could be. Maybe I've flipped my car on that tricky bend coming out of the canyon. It could be. I guess I'm wondering out loud because she laughs in that low and husky way of hers.

"No, honey," she says. "I am. Ovarian cancer. It's been eating away at me for years now. Guess it must have won out." She pauses. Takes a sip of the whisky. "And Nurse said I been having a good day."

I look again. She must be, what, in her fifties? Sixties, even? Not that she looks it. Her skin is flawless, breasts small and perky as apricots. Her thigh is one long, smooth curve. There's a sweet little divot in her dress at the delta where her right leg crosses her left. She's nineteen years old and gorgeous, just like I remember her.

"Careful," she says, "you'll catch flies." And she laughs again.

I'm thinking, "But what have I caught here?" I don't know. Lord help me, I don't know.

And then she's gone. Fast as that the moonlight's got her. Fast as the curtains pulling shut. And I'm left holding a glass of whisky and water.

Maybe a better man would have told Juney. I wonder about that, but I don't think she would've believed me.

I had to know if it was real. If Kelsi Koehler was real. And so I did just about the last thing in the world that I wanted to do. I go cold turkey.

I empty every bottle down the sink. Every drop of it, gone. And then the mouthwash too. And then the rubbing alcohol because even though I know it'd make me go blind I don't trust myself not to try it if things got hard.

Juney watches me dump it all and she don't say a word. She's seen this before. But still. I see a little light in her eyes switching on like I haven't seen in some time.

All she says is, "Will it stick?"

I shrug. What more is there to say?

It's Hell. The shakes get real bad on the second night and I'm glad I dumped the rubbing alcohol. I think I might've tried anything at that point. I stay in the house. I keep the phone off the hook so none of the boys can call.

Because I want to know. I want to know.

And on the third night Kelsi's back, and this time there isn't a drop of drink in me to cloud my vision.

She has a look to her. Maybe I missed it with the vet because I wasn't paying attention but on Kelsi it is pretty damn hard to miss. She's paler. Gorgeous? Hell yes, but now it's a scary kind of beauty. I don't know how else to say it. Just that I know something is off. Maybe she'd been the Lady of Good Times once, but tonight, she's something else. The Lady of Bad Things Coming. Even I can see that.

"I'm dry tonight," I tell her when she quirks one of those perfect eyebrows.

"Guess that means I'm dry too, honey."

I stand there staring at her for a while, just making sure it's real. Eventually she gets bored. She stands up. "Got music at least?"

I switch on the radio. They're talking about the fall of Saigon. They're talking about our boys coming home. Then I turn the dial, and, out of the static, comes John Lennon crooning about getting by with a little help from his friends. She's nodding her head along. When the jockey comes on during the final fade-out, she turns back to me. "Gonna stare all night?"

"No, ma'am," I say.

"Good," she says. "I can't abide a gawper. They were always gawping at me. Well. In the beginning at least."

"And now?" I say, turning the radio down low so it's just a murmur.

"Honey, I don't know what now *is*. A way station maybe. A pit stop on the Road to Somewhere Else. Who knows how the rules work? I'm just happy to be playing the game a bit longer before. . ." She tosses her hair and the copper-red of it gleams in the buttery light. "I'm cold," she says.

The sun's been baking the Arizona desert all day, and inside the house, even though I've got the air conditioner cranked up and it's past midnight, it's still so hot I worry that the windows might crack. It's been known to happen.

But she's cold. And I'm a gentleman.

"Warm me up?" she says.

And I love Juney. I've loved her since the minute I laid eyes on her. But this is something else.

So I go with her. She tastes the way the desert smells after the rains. Like creosote. The black taste of tar. Her skin freeze-sticks like an ice cube, but she's my Lady of Good Times.

She's my Lady of I'm Only Human.

She is beautiful in the moonlight streaming through the window as I lay her down on the bed. As I kiss the curve of her breast.

She is wearing garters. I know this should mean something to me, but in that moment it doesn't.

I slide my fingers up the silky surface of her stockings. I can feel the muscles underneath. I dream I can feel her pulse. My thumb catches on the hook.

She's just a way station, I think. Just a pit stop.

She is beautiful but now her eyes are black. Whatever it was that's underneath her skin, that coldness, that oily sweet smell, it's getting stronger. I don't know what she is. It's starting to scare me. But I can't stop. I don't want to stop. I want to touch her. I want the feel of her stiffening nipple between my fingers, the clench of her legs around my waist. . . .

And that's when the door to the house busts open.

Because I have left the phone off the hook.

Because Juney has been worried. But pleased too. Pleased about me pouring all the booze down the drain. And she don't want me to fall off the wagon. Not this time. Because this is my last chance. I know that. I know I can only break her heart so many times. And Carl knows that too. Carl knows how close Juney is to the edge. How close to breaking she is with that shit-drunk husband of hers.

None of this is a mystery novel. None of this takes much guesswork.

So he hears the noises coming from the bedroom. He knows what those noises mean. And he knows Juney's still on shift at the Dunkin' Donuts.

And, best of all, he knows where the Colt is.

Carl's got a sour smell to him. Like sweat mixed with old bacon. I can smell him.

There's a hot breeze that's tugging at my hair.

I can feel the muzzle of the Colt pressing into my back.

"Turn around slowly," he says.

I'm struck because I have heard this line so many times. I want to ask him, "Is this a stickup?" I want him to say, "Reach for the sky, pardner!"

I can't help it. I let out a snort, and he hears it. When I turn—slowly!—his face is running from stunned to hurt to angry.

"I can explain," I tell him, but now that we're face to face, I know I can't. What do I say? What part of this can I tell that would make sense? Carl's not a smart man. Carl's not a forgiving man. Carl won't buy whatever line of bullshit I want to sell him.

I open my mouth. I close it again. He leans in closer. His teeth're pressed tightly together, the little nubs of them rubbing together. He's angry, but I think he's also curious about what I'll say. A dull curiosity. The same look he gives the flies as they bumble around the inside of the jar. How long'll this one last?

When my mouth opens the second time, I'm just as curious about what'll come out.

Because a drunk'll say anything to get a drink. And a cheat? A cheat always has a happy tune to whistle.

"I can explain . . ." And I surprise myself. "No. I can't. I love her," I say. "I love Juney."

"I know," he says and his mouth twists. There is something that goes across his face—and if I stared hard enough I could catch exactly what it is—but I'm not looking that hard. I don't what to know.

Because by then I'm moving. Because, then, I think, he has moved in close enough. There is just enough room. If I'm just fast enough I can—

And then there's a noise like a thunderclap.

It's late when I find myself back in the house. I don't know what time. Close to dawn because Juney has just got in. Her hair is mussed. Silvery-grey strands coming undone from her neat bun. Her Dunkin' Donuts uniform is creased a little. She somehow looks pretty. Worn, but pretty.

My Lady of Half 'n' Half. My Lady of How Do You Take It?

"Smiley," she says. "Did you just get in?"

I allow that I did.

"And are you sober?" she asks.

"Yeah, Junebug," I tell her. "Sober as a priest."

And it's the truth.

"Good," she says. And then: "You look good."

She's dead on her feet. I can see her swaying a little, her hands on the kitchen table, keeping her steady. But she's smiling and that makes me happy. I'm glad for that.

"Come to bed," I tell her, and take her in my arms. I can feel her weight sagging into me.

"S'cold," she says, but I don't say anything. Somewhere off Route 66 my body is waiting for the sun to scorch it crisp and black. Somewhere Carl's washing the blood out of his shirt. He is careful. Gentle, even. But there's a part of me that is here. Maybe the better part of me.

I take Juney to our bedroom. I help her peel off the uniform. I kiss her gently on the forehead where she still tastes like icing sugar and cinnamon.

I want to tell her about Carl. About how she must be careful around him. How there's bad news coming for her. I want to tell her so much it's burning up like bad liquor in my gut but somehow I can't. Maybe it's cowardice. Maybe it's just that I can't stand the thought of that forehead of hers creasing, that same old fight we spent twenty years on, same as every other fight.

Maybe I shoulda. Maybe.

The thing is, the dead can't see the future any better than the living. They have to drive down that same road. One mile at a time.

And this is just a pit stop for me. Maybe. A way station. I can't stay.

I don't want to.

There is something growing in me. Something cold. Something heavy and black as tar. Is this death? Or is this something else?

And it is cold. And she is warm. I lie down next to her. I don't want to touch her. I can't help wanting to touch her.

"G'night, Smiley," she says.

"G'night, Junebug," I say.

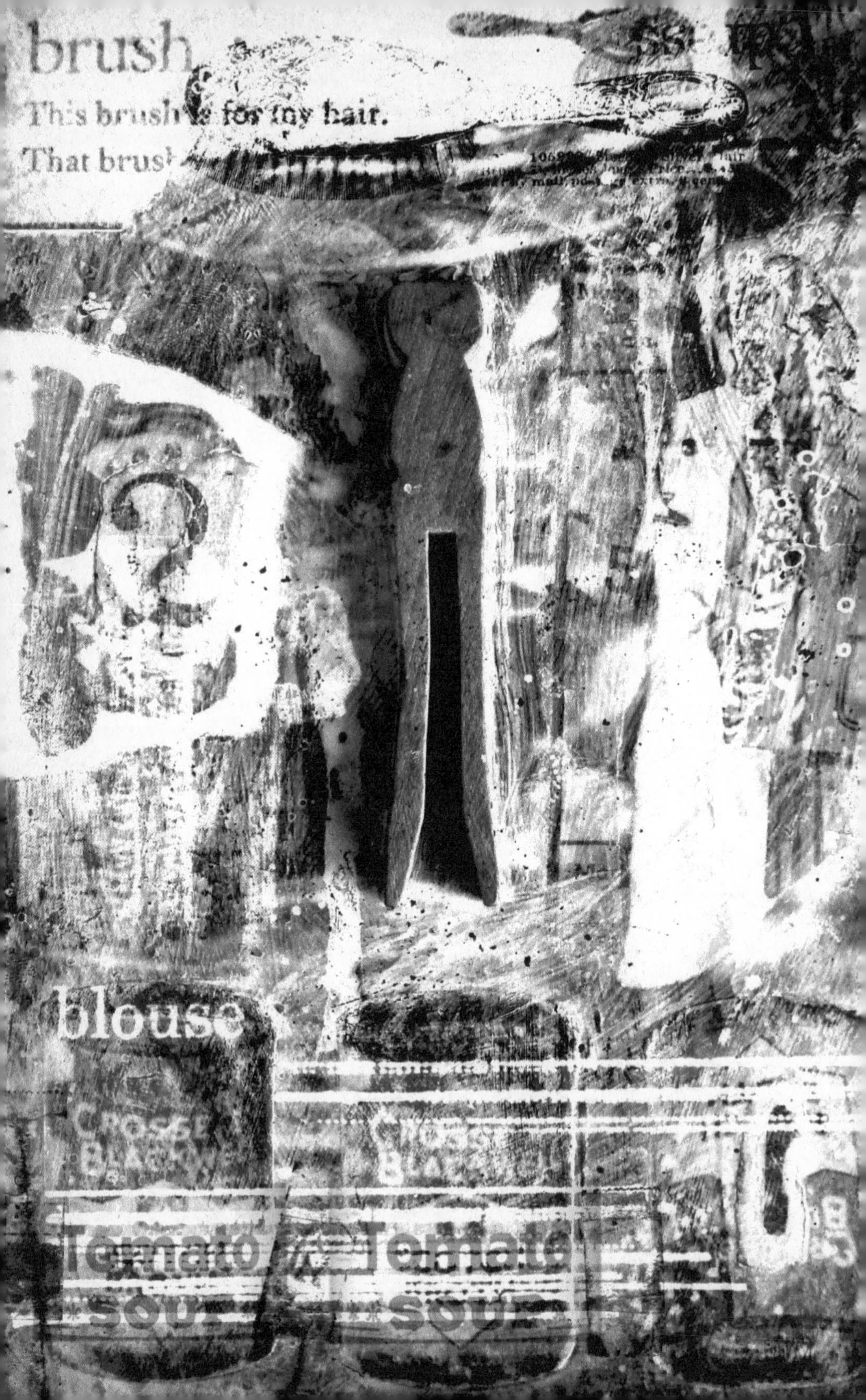
brush
That brus
blouse
Tomato

". . . we love you, Angela Clothespin Jacket. You know what it is like to live in the dark, just like we do."

LESSONS IN THE RAISING
OF HOUSEHOLD OBJECTS

Mommy asks me how I am doing, and I tell her that I am afraid of the twins.

This is true. I don't know who the twins are. In fact, the twins aren't anybody yet. In fact, the twins are quite probably dead. Mommy tells me I don't really know what dead means, but I most certainly do know what dead means. When Scamper forgot how to wag his tail on my fourth birthday, Daddy told me that meant that he had died, and I said "Oh," and he said, "So now you know what dead means, that's good, that's good, sweetheart, you're growing up." So I do know what dead means, it means when you stop being what you were before.

Mommy doesn't like that I am afraid of the twins. She tells me it will be the same between us, even with the twins there, that the twins will not make me different. Mommy insists that I press my head up against her belly until her little poked-out bellybutton fits right into my ear. It feels strange there, but it also feels normal, as if bellybuttons were designed for ears.

Then there is a kick, and then there is another, and I know that the twins are mad at me, so I start to cry. I don't like crying very much but sometimes you can't really help crying. It's just something you have to do.

Mommy pats me on the back and she says. "It's okay, darling, honey, peanut, Miss Angela Clothespin Jacket." My real name is Angela Chloe Jackson, but I like that other name for me better even though it isn't real.

"I don't want them, I want them to stay there, I don't want them to come out," I tell her, but I am still crying so she doesn't hear me. The thing about Mommies is that they can't hear what you're saying whenever you're crying, and so I hate crying, but like I already said, sometimes it's just what happens.

But, anyway, that isn't quite what I meant because I don't want them to stay there. I don't want them to stay anywhere, but maybe inside Mommy is better than outside Mommy where they will have to roll around with their lumpy flesh and the tangled-up arms and legs like Daddy showed me in the black and white picture.

Mommy says, "But Angie, Mommy's tummy will get too big. They can't stay in there forever."

And I think, yes, that is exactly the problem.

I decide that I will be a good little girl, and I will practise loving the twins.

Mommy says it is important that I love them and that I am nice to them because they will be very fragile when they come out. "Like a lamp?" I ask. I have broken the lamp in my room more than once, and then I have to sleep in the dark because of it so that I will learn. Daddy calls this an object lesson.

And Daddy says, "Like the lamp except even more fragile than that."

"If you're very good," Mommy says, "I'll let you hold them." I wonder what it will be like to hold these things.

"But what if I break them?" I ask, and Mommy just purses her lips in that way and says, "You'll have to be very careful, Angie."

Mommy asks, "Do you want to feel them kick again?" and I say, "No," because how can you love something that is trying to kick you? I must practise first on something easier to love than the twins.

I find two cans of tomato soup in the pantry because tomato soup is the thing I like most, 'specially with toasted cheese. Tomato soup will be easy to love. Even without the toasted cheese.

I am not supposed to go in the pantry by myself, but I think Mommy and Daddy will like it if I learn how to love the twins so I do even though it is dark and I am worried about the shelves and all the other things there are in the dark.

I name one of the cans Campbell. I name the other Simon because I cannot name both of them Campbell. I decide that Campbell must be the older of them, but I think, deep down, that I like Simon better. He is better behaved. And besides, he doesn't have any dents. His label is crisp and new.

Campbell and Simon must stay with me if I am to learn how to love them. Sometimes I watch them. They are not very interesting to watch. I decide that it is probably because Simon is too well behaved, and so I love him a little bit less for that. I try rolling Campbell down the stairs. I can hear his insides sloshing around. Afterward he is slightly more dented than he was before, and I decide that this is what Daddy calls an object lesson. Simon says nothing.

"You're supposed to say something, Simon," I tell him. "You shouldn't let me roll Campbell down the stairs, not if he's a baby." And Simon starts to cry so I can't hear what he's saying, and I decide that I don't love him at all. I tell him I like cream of broccoli better. I tell him I like chicken with noodles, and why couldn't he be chicken with noodles? In fact, why couldn't he be *real* and filled with guts and things instead of soup? Simon is crying even more now, but that's what babies do. They don't ever say anything, they just cry.

Finally I give Simon to Mommy who always helps me when I am crying. Later on Mommy gives me tomato soup and toasted cheese for lunch. I look at Campbell with his dented rim and his sad, sad face. I hope that this has been an object lesson for him.

The problem is that Mommy is not getting bigger because the twins are getting bigger, but Mommy is getting bigger because the twins are thieves.

The morning that Mommy came home and said to me, "Darling, baby girl, Angela C., you're going to have brothers!" was the first time I knew they were thieves. She was smiling so much that her face looked like another person's face, and Daddy's face looked like another Daddy's face and both of them were hugging each other and hugging me. But after all the hugging was over with, I noticed that my hairbrush was missing, the one with the pink handle that I have used since I was a baby even though it is too small for me because it never hurts.

"No," Mommy tells me, "it wasn't the twins," but I know it was anyway.

I have come to a decision about Campbell. Well, we have reached the decision together.

The decision is that I will not eat any more tomato soup because Campbell says it is cruel, and Campbell will help me to catch the twins who have now carried off not only my hairbrush but also my flower fairy which I only left out to see if she would like the rain and also the bunny-eared hat that I was given at Christmas. I do not mind losing the flower fairy and the hat so much but that was a really good hairbrush and Mommy says they don't make them anymore, so now I have to use a grown-up hairbrush and grown-up hairbrushes pull and pull and pull until I am crying all over again.

So I will leave Campbell out on the bookshelf next to my bed, and I will keep on the nightlamp so that he can see properly even though I am now fully too old for it, and nightlamps are stupid anyway, but Campbell gets scared of the dark and besides how else will he see the twins?

Mommy and Daddy come and kiss me goodnight, and Daddy smells wonderful, like cinnamon and coffee and chocolate, but Mommy doesn't smell like Mommy at all. When she sits on my bed I can feel her tummy moving as the twins go kick, kick, kick. I think to myself, or rather, I say to Campbell, "Look, you can see them kicking, just you wait and see." But Mommy doesn't like it when I talk to Campbell, and Daddy has to say, "No, honey, it's okay, we won't take Campbell away," and then I stop crying.

In the morning, Campbell is sitting in exactly the same place, and my stuffed Adie is gone who I liked best because one eye was blue and one eye was green and dogs don't normally look like that.

"Campbell," I say, but Campbell is still asleep and so he doesn't answer me.

This is how the twins come out, I think.

There is a hole in Mommy's tummy. I have seen it because that's what the bellybutton keeps all plugged up, and that's why her bellybutton points out now, because the twins are pushing on the other side. I wonder if I came from the other side of the hole like the twins, or if I came from somewhere else. I am afraid sometimes. What if I don't have guts and things behind my bellybutton?

At night, when Mommy is under her covers, I think she cannot see her bellybutton anymore and anyway just like Campbell she has to fall asleep. That is when the twins come out. Daddy says that the twins are still quite small so I think they must be able to still fit in through the bellybutton.

Sometimes when I am sleeping I hear noises. I think it must be the twins and I want to say to them, "Go back inside! You're supposed to be dead still!" But I don't think they can hear me very well. Maybe that is because I am whispering it to Campbell.

It is scary when the twins are outside of Mommy and sometimes I have to hold Campbell very close to me. I don't love him yet, but I think I might be somewhere close to loving him. I say it is okay if he falls asleep and he says that he loves me very much.

"They are taking things, I know they are," I whisper to Campbell and we are both afraid together. In the morning things are a little bit different than they were the night before and Mommy's tummy is a little bit bigger. I think they must be building a tent inside, filling Mommy up with hairbrushes and flower fairies and bunny-eared hats and Adie.

The next time Mommy asks me to listen to the twins, I put my ear against her tummy. I think I feel the shape of the hairbrush and I think I can hear Adie barking, so I bite Mommy's bellybutton until there is blood because if I can get in then maybe I can get them back. Now Mommy is crying though, and so I can't understand what she is saying, and Daddy is so mad that he puts me in my room and he turns out the light and he takes away the nightlamp and he takes away Campbell.

So now I am sitting in the darkness, and I have the blankets close to me and I miss Campbell which makes me think I must be starting to love him a little, but I am also thinking that this must be what it is like for the twins inside Mommy's tummy.

I don't know where Campbell is, and when I go into the cupboard there are other cans of soup, but they aren't Campbell and so I cannot love them.

I wonder if maybe the twins have taken Campbell too, or if maybe they are in cahoots with Mommy and Daddy.

"Mommy," I say when she opens the door at last and is standing in the doorway and there is light all around her so that it hurts my eyes. "Is Campbell inside you?" I ask, but she just squeezes her lips until they aren't lips anymore they are just a single line that she cannot speak out of, and then she closes the door again.

I am trying not to think about Campbell anymore. I am trying to pretend that there has never been a Campbell, and so in the morning I eat cereal and I think to myself, this tastes nothing like tomato soup and that is a good thing.

Mommy is still hugging Daddy but neither of them wants to look at me properly so I just eat my cereal. I pretend that I can't see Mommy's tummy moving when the twins kick. But I am thinking to myself, "I know that you are in there, I know that you are all in there," and Mommy has no idea that I can see all of the things that are starting to poke out of her because she is not big enough for all the special sequined purses and shoe racks and televisions and nightlamps and Adies and bunny-eared hats and flower fairies and Campbells that she has inside of her. Maybe this is the secret truth: maybe all the people like Mommy and Daddy have worlds and worlds inside them, and only some of us are filled with soup.

There, right there, I can see the spokes of my brand new ten-speed bicycle poking out of her, but she has no idea and neither does Daddy when he hugs her.

I don't know how the twins have done it but they have taken Daddy too.

Last night he was here and kissed me on the forehead and he read from my special book, the only book that is left now, and he said, "where are your other books, Angie?" and I said, "the twins have taken them, Daddy." Then he touched my forehead very lightly like a butterfly, and he said, "You can't keep doing this, honey, peanut, darling. The twins are coming and they are coming soon."

Daddy doesn't understand, but now Daddy has gone too, and I am afraid he is deep inside Mommy and we won't be able to get him out.

But I have a plan.

This is my plan. I will lay a trap for the twins. I will catch the twins and then maybe I will be able to give them what Daddy calls an object lesson so they will know that they can't keep doing this anymore.

I don't have a nightlamp and I don't have Campbell and I don't have Daddy, so I must do this alone.

I take my special book, the one book that I have left and I tie a string around it just like Daddy taught me to tie my shoelaces and then I tie another string around my wrist, because then even if I fall asleep I will be able to catch them. Mommy kisses me on the forehead and she asks if I want her to read to me but I shake my head and I say, "No, Mommy, I am too old for reading," because being too old is when things stop working the way they did before. So Mommy smoothes my hair like she did when I was itsy-bitsy, and she sits on the bed with me. I want to tell her not to sit on the bed, that I don't want the twins that close to me, but Mommy is so big with all the dishwashers and bookshelves and staircases and basements sticking out of her that I can't believe she even fits on the bed.

"Are they building a house in there, Mommy?" I ask and Mommy just laughs and shakes her head. "No, Angela Clothespin Jacket, they are not building a house, they are going to come live in our house."

Then I am crying again, and I cry until I go to sleep.

I wake up in the middle of the night and there is a tugging at my wrist, so I look and there is the string and the string is pulled out all the way to the book and then there are the twins. The twins are not two people, they are just one person, and they are not a person at all because really they are just a bunch of arms, and legs, and foreheads like in the picture.

"Why don't you just go away?" I ask the twins. And the twins say, "Because we love you, Angela Clothespin Jacket. You know what it is like to live in the dark, just like we do. We want you to come live with us forever inside Mommy where it is safe and warm and there are nightlamps and there is Campbell and Adie." I think about this for a while because I don't like the twins very much, but it is lonely out here and perhaps it will be less lonely inside Mommy, in the dark, with the twins. At least then we will be all together, even if it is inside Mommy.

I say, "Okay, twins," and then I go through the bellybutton with them.

The thing is that the twins are cleverer than I thought.

Adie is in here and Campbell too and the flower fairy and every part of Mommy's world, but the twins have locked the bellybutton and it is very dark and I don't know how to get out.

I feel around, amidst the ten-speed bikes and the sequined purses and the nightlamps, and then there is a sound and it is Daddy. It is not the real Daddy. It is the Daddy that lives inside of Mommy. I am feeling very scared, so I climb over the bookshelf and the club chair until there he is, smelling like cinnamon and coffee and chocolate. I want him to hold me, but it is too crowded for holding in here, so I hug Campbell close to me because he is small enough for holding.

"We have made some bad decisions," I say to Daddy, and he says, "No, peanut, this is what was supposed to happen. This is what we planned for all along, it was supposed to be the twins coming out and you going away."

"Why?" I ask Daddy. "Because," he says, "we made you a very long time ago. Out of peanuts and honey. And now we want a real baby, a baby with worlds and worlds inside it, not just a clothespin jacket."

"I can be a real baby," I say. Maybe I say that. I'm crying so it is difficult to tell.

"No, honey, you're a clothespin jacket. Now that the twins are born we don't need you anymore."

I think about this for a while. I cannot see Daddy's face in the darkness. All I can smell is cinnamon and coffee and chocolate, and I decide that I don't like those things anymore. Those are just things, and they aren't Daddy.

"No," I say to Daddy, "I'm going to get out of here, and when I do I'm not going to take you with me."

Daddy doesn't like this very much, but I don't care. I like this, and Campbell likes this so I think we will be okay.

It is time for another plan, I say to Campbell, and Campbell also thinks it is time for another plan.

I take Campbell and I put him in Mommy's sequined purse and I put it over my shoulder. Then I climb the bookshelf and feel along the top of Mommy's tummy which is big and curved like being underneath an umbrella. Daddy tells me to stop doing that but I have decided that I will not listen to Daddy anymore. I know that there is a bellybutton somewhere and so all I have to do is find it.

"You can't do that," says Daddy. "There's no room for you out there! We have the twins now, and we need you to go away!"

"Well, Daddy," I say, "you should have thought about that before you made me."

I climb from the bookshelf to the club chair to the minivan, and for a moment I wonder how on earth the twins managed to fit all of these things inside Mommy, but then I stop wondering and I keep climbing. Finally, I discover the bellybutton at the very top of Mommy's tummy.

I put my ear to the bellybutton, and I can hear that on the outside Mommy is laughing. I think she must be laughing because the twins are doing something funny like telling jokes or aerial acrobats, and I hate the twins a little bit more for making Mommy laugh and I hate Mommy a bit more for loving the twins like that. But at least I have Campbell, and at least Daddy has already taught me how to tie and untie knots.

I start to untie the bellybutton, and Daddy says to me, "You'll never be able to get out there, you're not a real daughter, Miss Peanut, Miss Honey, you're not a real Angela, you're just a clothespin jacket."

"No," I say to him, "I am too real, you made me because you wanted me and so I am as real as the twins and I am real as Campbell and we are getting out of here right this very instant!"

First there is a light, and my eyes hurt because I have gotten used to the dark, but Campbell tells me to be brave, that it will be okay out there, and I say, "I love you, Campbell." He says, "I love you, baby girl," and I like it when Campbell calls me that, so I tug at the string and the light gets brighter and the hole gets bigger. Then I am sticking my head out and then I am staring at Mommy and she is staring at me, and I am half inside her and half outside of her so I climb out the rest of the way even though I can hear the Daddy inside Mommy still crying.

"What are you doing here?" she asks.

"I just wanted to see the sunshine," I say. And there is my proper Daddy, and there are the twins, and they are all the things that they were before but somehow they look more and more like people and the people they look like are Mommy and Daddy. But when I look at Mommy, Mommy looks more and more like just a mess of arms and legs and skirts and pantyhose and lipstick and eyelashes and not the thing that she was before.

"What will it be now, peanut?" she asks me. "Can you love the twins?"

I think about this for a bit because I will be lonely and scared without Mommy and Daddy. But I know that the Daddy inside Mommy is right. There are worlds and worlds inside of Mommy and one day there will be worlds and worlds inside the twins and inside me it will be hollow as a drum. Hollow as an empty soup can.

But then I take Campbell out of the purse and he whispers something in my ear.

For so long I have tried to be the thing they have wanted me to be, but now I want to be the thing that I am.

"This has been a real object lesson," I say to Mommy, and I am holding Campbell close to my chest because I love him so very much, "but I think we will be going now."

And we do.

"This is the great fear of fatherhood. To know that love is a chancy thing. It has its tides, it has its seasons, and it can shatter a man's luck."

ALL MY LOVE, A FISHHOOK

Listen.

It was not that I believe my father did not love me. He did. It is not that I fear I do not love my own son. I *do.* I do love him. It is a truth written in my blood and bones. Inescapable. As strong as faith and deep as ritual. But there is a thing that pulls inside me—it pulled inside my father, my babbas, this I know—and it is something like love and something like hate.

Do you know the feeling of being on a boat for the first time? It is a feeling of alternating weightlessness and great heaviness. Now your body is light—soaring even!—and now your knees are catching the great burden of you. Some men stagger about as if they are drunk. It makes others ill. Being a father is very much like that. There is great joy in the littlest thing. A smile. A skill freshly mastered. The way he walks on legs that have not learned to carry him. The shape his mouth makes when he begs for milk. But also a great blackness that descends. Your child will not be mastered. He grows at odds to you. Now he is your friend. Your comfort. Now he is your enemy. He will best you. He will live long after you have died, make his way in a world that no longer needs you or cares for you. Now he is your greatest luck. Now you wish you had drowned him at birth.

Stefanos was quiet as a boy. Prone to long silences, eyes fixed on the horizon, his little fingers dancing across his palm as if he were counting. He is quiet as a man. Dark-haired. His jaw has the same sharp line that mine does, that my babbas had once. But his eyes are the same tawny brown as his mother's: like the heartwood of an olive tree. They grow very round when he laughs, which is seldom. He smiles rarely, but he has a very beautiful smile.

Perhaps it is something hooked inside all the men of our line—the way my babbas would jam a fishhook in a piece of wood for luck and quick healing if he cut himself on it. I remember dark spells when I was a child. I would disappear to the cliff face around sunset some days when the wind was high enough to maybe send a young boy—small for my age—reeling off the edge and into the dark waters of the Aegean. I called these the knuckle cliffs. Their cracked ridges reminded me of my father's hands—callused hands, unyielding as granite. Yet in the evening the sun would catch hold of the edges of the gneiss and send up very beautiful sparks of light.

My mother worried for me during these spells, but when I returned, wind-chapped and shivering, she would brew strong coffee over the gas burner and sit with me as my body, wracked with shivers and nearly blue, quieted. Together we would listen to the wind scrabbling at the cliffs, whistling through the holes in the plaster and brick. Her voice was a plucked string humming out tunes of worry: "Kostas, what were you doing out there? The wind, you hear, boy? Aieee!"—a toothless whistle, a half-sucked breath—"Please don't go out again. Please. I could not stand for it."

My babbas would say little, but his eyes were flinty and cold. He would work me hard the next day, re-caulking the boat or checking the nets until my fingers bled from loosening and retying salt-hardened knots. He was impatient with me. A hard man, intolerant of weakness. He had survived two wars in his lifetime, buried his brothers, seen his home ravaged by looters and communists. Sometimes I hated him. Sometimes I think he hated me.

But I loved him too. Perhaps even more because of that hardness. We are like that as children—always chasing storms, running toward the wolf's teeth. And perhaps he did love me. He taught me a trade and made sure I never starved as he had, never suffered the ache of a stomach gnawing away at itself. But he grew to smile less and less for me. Eventually the love I had for him, at high tide when I was seven or so, began to recede. When it did, it left little behind but sharp rocks, broken shells and the gasping struggles of tiny fishes—ignorant of death until they were taken.

It is one such memory—a broken fragment whose shape I have never fully understood—that I hold closest to my heart. So close it cuts me, I know, but that is the way of memory.

Our family had lived on the island for many years. My babbas was a sailor and a fisherman. He kept a single caïque for long lining, which he made himself, from memory, without any plan. It was on my father's caïque I learned to navigate the waters around the island, to work the windlass if we were trawling. It was there I learned to obey.

Though Mama kept several crosses in the house and mass was a regular, solemn ritual for us, my babbas was not a particularly religious man. Like many of the older sailors he had his own private rituals, his own fears and superstitions, his own way of spitting in the nets before he cast them, or reading the clouds for signs of storms. He kept sacred objects. A medallion of St. Christopher which Mama gave him when they married. A little pouch filled with the bones of a bat. But his most precious possession—and never mentioned in the house after the incident I will tell you, for Mama did not like to think of her husband as an old pagan— was a small statue. Babbas told me that it was shaped in the image of Poseidon who had once owned the island of Delos—the sacred island, a place of many gods once, where it was forbidden for any to be born and any to die. I have seen this island from the water. It is filled with broken columns and arches, a graveyard now.

The statue was very old, a stone lump, now the colour of old teeth. There was a face, yes, but its features had been worn down to something of a skull: gaping eye sockets big enough to hold my thumbprint when I was an infant. A snake's nose—just two slits in a little mound. The upper arm had broken off, leaving a solid stump like a growth. The right arm, clenched against the body, had worn away into a ribbed mass.

The statue was very dear to my babbas, and it is perhaps this love for it that drew me to the thing when I was a child. I longed to hold it. Mama said I wept for it in the secret language of babes before any could understand me. Once, in my infancy, I remember knocking it from its position beneath Mama's portrait of Jesus above the table. Babbas was furious! I remember bursting into tears immediately at the sight of him, red-faced and grunting like a bull, his fists clenching and unclenching.

"Mama!" I cried, lunging for the safety of her arms. But Babbas was faster, terrible in his fury, like a storm overtaking me on the cliffs: hot air whistling from his nostrils, the sudden slick sweat of his hand pressing against my mouth. There was violence in him. I had known that always. Babbas was an ocean. His strength was irresistible. My arms were weak, my skin soft and ready to bruise.

He took a knife to my palm and cut a single red line. He would have severed my thumb if I struggled, but I did not. I was helpless. As brittle and breakable as the twig of bone he kept in his pouch. I could not see his face. His hair hung lank and damp as a curtain. It clung to his chin in a strange pattern. Mama was screaming at him, and this shocked me more than anything, how suddenly these people I loved had become like animals to one another. To me!

Babbas pressed my bleeding hand against the little statue—and in that moment it seemed like a great tooth. Oh, how I howled! I feared it would gobble me up! But the blood only smeared against the jagged line of that lumpish stone body, the little withered arm smashing against my palm.

Then it was over. Aieee. It was over.

Perhaps I am lucky. In another age Babbas might have drowned me in the sea. Or left me on a hill to be torn apart by animals. It is strange to look at one's own father and think he might have done such a thing, but I cannot say with any certainty that it would have been beyond him. I loved him. He was a stranger to me. The scar still grins at me when I look for it.

When I was older, Mama told me that some piece of the statue had broken in the fall. I had not known, I was too young then, but the family's luck was not good for several years. Babbas's boat was loosed from the shore in a bad storm while all the other boats were safely harboured. No one knew how the ropes slipped or the knots failed. But they did. Much of our meagre savings went to repairs. I know Babbas blamed me.

But that thing—whatever it was that had my clumsy infant fingers reaching and reaching and always reaching for it—it never left me. Babbas took the statue away and kept it in a secret place, but by the time I was ten I had discovered it again. I would sneak into his room and take hold of it from behind the loose brick where he kept it among his other sacred possessions. I would turn it over gently in the uncertain light and run my fingers along its grooves. I could see the rusted spots of my own blood, ancient then, or so it seemed to me. It could have been anyone's blood.

It was blood that bound me to Babbas. Our shared blood. Sometimes it made me smile to see my blood upon the statue. Sometimes it made me feel proud.

My babbas left Mama when I was fifteen.

It was a shock to me but by then I cannot say it was an unwelcome one. I had lived in the shadow of his temper for many years, and grown up stunted the way a tree does when it must cling to rocky soil. I knew he was unhappy. There are many forms of violence that one can do upon another when love is gone. Once blood bound us like a knot. Now blood made my mother and me weak to him, vulnerable, those first touched by the storms of his passions. There were ways he could hurt us for loving him when he did not love in return.

What we did not know was that he had found happiness with another woman. She was pregnant, Babbas told us. He had responsibilities to her. I was close enough to fully grown that Mama would not starve if I was a man. He delivered the words like kicks. Carefully. They were meant to cripple, perhaps; to wound, almost certainly. But to me they simply brought relief in the knowledge that, with another child, he would not return to us.

He took few things. A wool blanket. His favourite knife. A pot he had mended on several occasions. It heated unevenly, burnt whatever it touched or left it raw, but when it disappeared from its hook, Mama wept like a child and I wrapped her in my arms. Arms muscled from turning the winch on our boat, hauling nets from the sea. They were not weak arms. They were a man's arms. We would survive.

It was only some time later that memory struck me. I raced to Babbas's room—the room he had shared with Mama for all the years of my life. I went to the little hiding place. He had left the stub of a candle. A tin medallion of St. Christopher. A satchel filled with bat bones—they were lucky, he had told me once. But the statue was gone. Of course it was gone. These other things were trinkets. These were the lesser lucks he had carried with him. He had taken his greater luck with him for that new child.

I hoped his seed would stunt and shrivel.

I hoped he would never have another son.

I hoped the baby would be weak.

I hoped its mouth would mewl for milk but no milk would sate it.

I hoped its lungs would howl and howl and howl as the wind howled in the winter but there would be no season for it, only the howling, forever and ever.

He was not coming back. He had abandoned us entirely.

Time passes. The sea goes out. It comes in again.

By the time my son was born my mother and Babbas had reconciled. The other woman moved to the mainland to work in a shop that sold jewellery to the foreigners. I never knew what happened to the child: if he had been real or simply a convenient fiction on my father's part. A reason for leaving we might understand.

I was twenty. A man as my father had demanded and my mother had required.

At first I was afraid of fatherhood.

I confess that when Marina—the beautiful dark-eyed girl I had married—told me of the child planted in her belly, I was tempted to demand she find us a way out of the mess. Such things were possible, I knew. There were things to be done to loose the thing from the womb, to let it unspool in blood like a badly wound ball of yarn.

I even spoke to Babbas of this. It was midday. The sun falling on the water looked, not like a mirror as some say, but like fine blankets of lace piled high upon one another, the kind of blanket under which an old man might sleep in the winter.

"Aieee, Kostas," my babbas said, making the same whistling noise my mother had made once. They were growing into the same person, these days. "Of course, you will have the child."

"What can you tell me of fatherhood?" I asked him.

"A child is a blessing," he said, and spat. The water shivered. The old man in the ocean was sick today.

I smiled at him, and tried to find love in the answer he gave me, but the old scar itched when I worked the winch. I watched my father in the stern with the tiller. His hair was a tangle more silver now than black, the skin of his face bruised into dark pouches beneath his eyes. His tongue, when it touched his teeth, was tobacco-stained, the colour of a worm. I, who had been a small boy once and weak, towered over him now.

I wondered if I had been a blessing to my father.

I wondered at that other child he had left behind. Or had died. Or had never lived.

I knew Marina could not keep the baby.

But that night when I saw my wife, her face was shining with excitement. Excitement, yes, and maybe just a hint of fear that I would say to her exactly what first sprang into my head.

"Are you happy too, Kostas?" she asked me. She was curled against me in the bed we shared, her hands resting in the knotted wire of my hair, salted and damp. Her voice was soft, sweet. She sounded nothing like me. She spoke her words the way they are spoken on the mainland. The way farmers speak them.

"A child is a blessing," I told her.

I could not bring myself to speak my heart.

I would be a father. I would help her bring a son into the world.

My son was a blessing.

At two he toddled about, his head barely higher than the table, eyes that saw spoons and jars of salt, the knees and ankles of our guests when he hid. His speech was slow to come. When it came, he did not speak like other boys.

I remember Marina gave him a set of toy soldiers. They were made of lead, heavy things, and clumsily crafted. The paint flaked off to expose the dull sheen of metal beneath. But the boy loved them.

One day I saw that Stefanos had separated out a single soldier. Not the poorest of the lot, by any stretch, but certainly no favourite. The figure—head tilted to the ground, helmet askew, caught in some badly rendered mimicry of motion—held a red rifle by the barrel as if he intended to use it as a club. The rest of the soldiers circled him at a distance, wary perhaps, or merely watching the shadow show in amusement.

"A firing squad?" I asked him playfully.

"No, Babbas."

"Then what?"

Stefanos shook his head. "The other soldiers do not like him."

"Why do they not like him, Stefanos?"

"God lives in this one," he said.

Marina did not like this very much. She shooed him from the house and placed the soldiers all in a box. Except the lone soldier in the centre.

"Throw this in the sea," she begged me. One delicate hand clutched the lead soldier, the other, white knuckled, squeezed the folds of her skirt. My wife asked little enough of me, and I could see the fear in her eyes, the rolling white edges of them, and so I did as she asked.

Stefanos never spoke of his missing soldier, but sometimes he would wear a strange look on his face: as if he had breathed all the silence in the room into his chest and held it there, his lungs a perfect prison. He became a quiet boy, but always obedient. I loved him.

I did not speak to Marina further concerning the little toy she had brought for Stefanos. I could not. I could not tell her about the way the metal seemed to glow like a coal in my hand when I touched it. Not hot, exactly. But something. The way I hated the feel of it in my hand. That raised red rifle pressing into the mound beneath my thumb. It was as if I had touched something unclean. It would have only frightened her further to hear these things. And, besides, Stefanos soon outgrew such toys. He did not dwell long in childhood.

Even now I look at Stefanos in admiration. At twenty, he is good at his work. Far better than I ever was. But I worry for his happiness. I worry he is not kind enough to the women who sometimes smile at him, that he will never find a wife and have a child of his own. There is too much quiet in him, too much solemnity. When I look at him I see so little of myself there, except, perhaps, in the shape of his jaw, the curve of his forehead. But perhaps he keeps much of himself hidden from me. Perhaps all sons do, as I hid myself from my father.

And he always obeys me. If I tell him to handle the boat in a certain fashion or to set it on a particular angle to the wind, he will always do so. He never speaks against me even if, privately, he may disagree. If anything, there might only be the briefest pause—barely a pause at all!—before he says, "Yes, Babbas."

I believe he respects me. I think that obedience comes from respect, does it not? But still I wonder if it would have been easier if we argued. If he had a streak of insolence in him. As it is, I have begun to listen for the pauses. To hate the feel of his eyes on me a moment too long before they flinch away.

Sometimes I change course. Sometimes I ask myself, "Kostas, have you checked the lines? Are you certain of the waters?"

Sometimes I stare at my son. "Stefanos knows something," I say to myself. "What does he know?"

More than once these questions have averted disaster, but would it not have been easier if he had simply told me straight off? Is he afraid of me? I have never once given him cause to be afraid. To doubt my affection. Have I? I have never laid a hand upon him. I have never cut a grinning red mouth into his hand. I have never spoken of my doubts.

This is the great fear of fatherhood. To know that love is a chancy thing. It has its tides, it has its seasons, and it can shatter a man's luck. I know the shape of the waves, the sound they make as they grind against the hull, as they drag pebbles on the beach. I know the constellations. I know pattern of the clouds. But even now I do not know my own son.

My father—Old Babbas now—had always been a strong man, his muscles thick and corded underneath his loosening, wrinkled skin. The other sailors respected him. He had built the caïque himself, fitted the planks. Two wars he had fought in, and lived. No bullet found him. He laughed at storms. But the years were a burden upon him.

Now he could work the winch of the windlass. He could haul in the nets. Now he could not. His legs failed him. He gasped for breath. Then he died.

After his death it fell to me to tend to his effects. Stefanos and I went to the little house he had lived in, but there was little of value. Two copper pots, one dented and mended, the other new. Chipped crockery. A jug with a split lip. I recognized the wool sweater that hung on the chair. It stilled smelled of my father, the peculiar sweet smell of his sweat. I folded it gently.

"You should keep that," Stefanos said.

"The hem is unravelling."

"Mama can mend it," he told me. He rested a hand lightly on my shoulder, but I turned away, wiped at my eyes with the back of my hand. The unwashed salt of the sea stung.

His bed, when we found it, was unmade. The sheets were dirty and stank.

"Babbas," said Stefanos.

"We should burn these. They will be no good to anyone."

In the bedroom I found the old nook I had pillaged so often as a child. There it was. The little statue. I had not known I was looking for it, but having laid eyes on its familiar shape, my blood long since flaked away from the belly, the jagged, teething line of the arm, I felt a keen sort of tension go out of me like the slacking of a rope.

I picked it up slowly. Stefanos watched me. I could feel his eyes tracking my movements.

The statue was much how I remembered it. Ugly. Misshapen. Now I wanted to smash it to pieces. Now I wanted to clutch it to my breast.

"Babbas," said Stefanos.

Truthfully, I had forgotten he was there. But he was. I could see the shape of his shoulder in the dull light. His smoothly muscled arms. Even the black wiry hairs stood up, pricked to attention.

"That is mine. Old Babbas gave it to me."

"You are mistaken," I scoffed. The feel of the stone was cool in my hand. The weight was exactly the same. It should have felt lighter. My hands had been a boy's hands when I last held it. Or perhaps I had diminished. Perhaps I had lived through the better part of my life already.

"No, Babbas. It was for me to have. He told me so."

"Listen, boy," I said. "I have loved this statue since I was a boy."

"He said you broke it."

"I—" My tongue stumbled.

"You must give it to me," Stefanos said. His eyes were calm. Sad even. "He did not want you to have it."

He was normally such an obedient son! I turned away. Tried to make a jest of it.

"Surely you would not turn against me now," I teased. "You would not risk my love for such a little thing?"

"No, Babbas." It was like his body had been set ablaze. There was a heat to him. A furnace nestled inside. His teeth were set so that he smiled differently in the half-light. His lips twitched as if a ghost tugged at them. I shivered though the room was stiflingly hot now.

Still he was so quiet! My silent son! His tongue was a dead snake, why did it never stir? Except now. Except in disobedience. Could he not see the old man had been addled? Did he not know that a father's possessions were the fair due of the son? Ungrateful! Intolerable! Had that man not been my father? Had I not loved him as best I could, forgiven his abandonment, given him a grandson, comfort in his old age?

"It is mine." I howled the words at him. I had kept my own silences too long. He would hear me now. He *must* hear me. "It is my right!"

"No, Babbas," he said. "Please. Set it away."

I did not want to listen. I clenched my fist, made a great club of it. My nails pressed into the sick white scar my own father had given me. I wondered where he had left the knife. I thought of all the sons who had been left on hillsides for animals. The sons who had been torn apart by wolves. It was only as I raised my hand into the air—ready to knock his insolent teeth out!—that I was aware I had made any movement at all.

Stefanos, for his part, was still.

It was as if we were on the boat again. He did not speak, but there was the slightest pause in his breathing. That tiny silence I had learned to recognize. And then I knew—he would let me strike him. He was younger. His arms were tireless, his joints did not stiffen, did not slow. He was more than my match. But he would let me strike him.

There was only the pause. Only the waiting.

I have never felt such shame. It came sickening and sudden. What was this thing that had come between us?

I sat down heavily on the bed, appalled.

I did not want him to touch me, but he did. He rested a hand easily on my shoulder. A light touch, but strong.

"Let me tell you," Stefanos said, "how this statue came to him."

"How do you know this story?"

"He told me."

"He never told *me*."

"I shall tell you."

These were his words:

Once there was a time when Old Babbas had been a young man,

twenty perhaps. The war had just claimed the first of his brothers. The family had little to eat. So Old Babbas took out the boat though the wind was high and it was not a good time to sail. Many had warned him against this, but he was young, full of anger and grief, and perhaps he wished the waves to claim him. I do not know. He did not tell me. Only that a storm overtook him and smashed his boat against the shore of the sacred island, Delos, which was once called the invisible island when the gods kept it beneath the waters.

He had never set foot on the shore because of the old law that no man should be born or should die there. But the storm broke him upon the beach and he found himself pierced badly by a spar. He who knew his own strength best could feel it pour out of him in a bright pool on the beach. He lay on the sand amongst the fish and the broken shells and the things that had crawled out of the ocean during the storm, and he knew he must not die. And so he prayed to the dark god of the ocean—not as my mother or my grandmother would have it—but to the one who watches us when we take to the waves, the one who blesses us with fish and curses us with salt.

You have seen the island from a distance. You have seen the temples there, the ruined pillars of marble. How they catch the sun and send off such a dizzying light. Perhaps Old Babbas found himself amongst one such temple. In any case, he discovered there this little statue, and the statue drank his tears and the statue drank his prayers and the statue drank his blood. And though the night was long and cold, and the storm was fierce, he did not die as he supposed. When daylight touched the marble and sent it blazing, his brothers found him.

Old Babbas had believed himself lucky, but, of course, this was not so: the war took his brothers one by one by one, and it took their sons and it took their daughters. Only you were spared. You alone. And now me. Of course, me.

Old Babbas never knew much of the statue. He called it his luck. He called it his curse. Perhaps it is Poseidon, as he believed. But perhaps it was not. Perhaps there is another god who lives within the ocean. Waiting.

There are things in the ocean, Babbas, that you cannot imagine. I have seen them. And this statue? All your life you have sought after the shadow of the thing instead of the thing itself. A rock is not a god, even if it is in the shape of one. You are clutching at moonlight on the water as if it were the water and not the light itself that was beautiful.

But I have seen more than moonlight. I have seen the shape of dark things in the night. You have given your blood to the rock, yes, but there is something of it lodged in me, like a fishhook, and I will not heal from it. Do you not see that? Do you not understand?

This, this is mine. My blessing and my curse. You will die one day. I have seen your death, Babbas, as I saw the death of Old Babbas before you. But I have not seen my own death, do you understand? For me there is something else and I do not know what it is, but I cannot turn away from it.

There are things you do not understand. The old man of the ocean slumbers beneath his blanket of salt but he shall not stay silent forever.

And I belong to him. This is what Old Babbas told me. You were spared. But one of us must go.

I cannot say if I believed what Stefanos told me. All I can say is that when he finished his tale, his hands were shaking, and I clutched at him as I had when he was a small child. In that moment, whatever else he was, I saw him as very young. And very afraid.

For the long years of my life there has always been a grief in me. It has a weight and it has a shape that I recognize. And perhaps all sons carry it. Perhaps all fathers carry it. He does not want this thing. He does not want it as I wanted it, my fingers always itching to claim it as my own. But something has hooked within him. He struggles like a fish on the line but it will not let him free.

I hold Stefanos in my arms—and he is burning, he is burning—and there is an awfulness, an uncleanness to him. Perhaps I ought to have strangled him at birth. Left him in the wilderness. But when I close my eyes I am struck by the sense that we two are aboard a very small caïque, and I know the ocean is beneath me, monstrous deep and very very wide, the waves rocking us both. Now light, now heavy, now joyful, now terribly sad.

It is every father's dream that his son should outlive him. No father wishes to see the death of his offspring.

And yet. And yet. I do not know my son. I do not know what shall come from him.

And so I hold him. And I pray Stefanos will be a good man.

I pray he will care for his mother.

I pray he will have sons of his own in time, and that he will take some measure of comfort from them—if such a thing is allowed to him.

I pray—it is a failing on my part, perhaps, the curse of too-weak love that I cannot take this from him—but I pray that when I am dead, he will bury my bones far from the sea, where the earth makes a knuckle to beat back the waves.

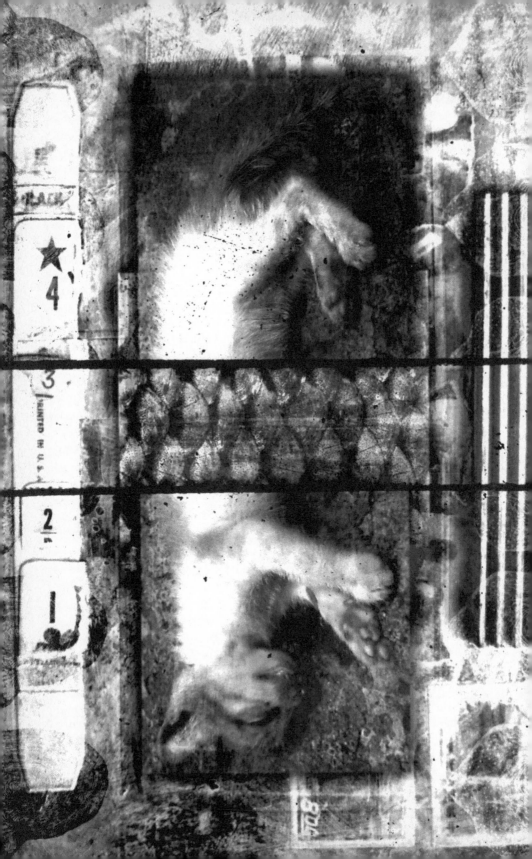

"The omens weren't what you hoped for. They weren't what you thought they would be. But you knew when it was yours."

IN THE YEAR OF OMENS

That was the year of omens—the year the coroner cut open the body of the girl who had thrown herself from the bridge, and discovered a bullfrog living in her right lung. The doctor, it was said by the people who told those sorts of stories (and there were many of them), let the girl's mother take the thing home in her purse—its skin wet and gleaming, its eyes like glittering gallstones—and when she set it in her daughter's bedroom it croaked out the saddest, sweetest song you ever heard in the voice of the dead girl.

Leah loved to listen to these stories. She was fourteen and almost pretty. She liked dancing and horses, sentimental poetry, certain shades of pink lipstick, and Hector Alvarez, which was no surprise at all, because *everyone* liked Hector Alvarez.

"Tell me what happened to the girl," Leah would say to her mum, slicing potatoes at the kitchen counter while her mother switched on the oven. Leah was careful always to jam the knifepoint in first so that the potatoes would break open as easily as apples. Her dad had taught her that before he had died. Everything he did was sacred now.

"No," her mum would say.

"But you know what happened to her?"

"I know what happened, Leah."

"Then why won't you tell me?"

And Leah would feel the slight weight of her mother's frame like a ghost behind her. Sometimes her mum would touch the back of her neck, just rest a hand there, or on her shoulder. Sometimes, she would check the potatoes. Leah had a white scar on her thumb where she'd sliced badly once.

"You shouldn't have to hear those things. Those things aren't for you, okay?"

"But mum—"

"Mum," Milo would mumble from his highchair. "Mum mum mum mum."

"Here, lovely girl, fetch me the rosemary and thyme. Oh, and the salt. Enough about that other thing, okay? Enough about it. Your brother is getting hungry."

And Leah would put down the knife, and would turn from the thin, round slices of potatoes. She would kiss her brother on the scalp where his hair stuck up in fine, whitish strands. Smell the sweet baby scent of him. "Shh, monkey-face, just a little bit longer. Mum's coming soon." Then Milo would let out a sharp, breathy giggle, and maybe Leah would giggle too, or maybe she wouldn't.

Her mum wouldn't speak of the things that were happening, but Leah knew—of course Leah knew.

First it was the girl. That's how they always spoke of her.

"Did you hear about *the girl*?"

"Which girl?"

"*The girl*. The one who jumped."

And then it wasn't just *the girl* anymore. It was Joanna Sinclair who always made red velvet cupcakes for the school bake sale. She had found her name written in the gossamer threads of a spider web. It was Oscar Nunez from the end of the block whose tongue shrivelled up in his mouth. It was Yasmine with the black eyeliner who liked to smoke pot sometimes when she babysat Leah.

"Maybe it'll be, I dunno, just this one perfect note. Like a piano," Yasmine had murmured before it happened, pupils big enough to swallow the violet-circled iris of her eyes. "Or a harp. Or a, what's it, a zither. I heard one of those once. It was gorgeous."

"You think so?" Leah asked. She watched the smoke curl around the white edge of her nostrils like incense. There were only four years between them, but those four years seemed a magnificent chasm. Across it lay wisdom and secret truths. Across it lay the Hectors of the world, unattainable if you were only fourteen years old. Everything worthwhile lay across that chasm.

"Maybe. Maybe that's what it will be for me. Maybe I'll just hear that one note forever, going on and on and on, calling me to paradise."

It hadn't been that. The omens weren't what you hoped for. They weren't what you thought they would be. But you *knew* when it was yours. That's what people said. You could recognize it. You always *knew*.

When Hector found her—(they were dating, of course Hector would only date someone as pretty and wise as Yasmine, Leah thought)—the skin had split at her elbows and chin, peeled back like fragile paper to reveal something bony and iridescent like the inside of an oyster shell.

Leah hadn't been allowed to go to the funeral.

Her mum had told her Yasmine had gone to college, she couldn't babysit anymore, Leah would have to take care of Milo herself. But Leah was friends with Hector's sister, Inez, and *she* knew better.

"It was like there was something inside her," Inez whispered as they both gripped the tiled edge of the pool during the Thursday swim practice, Inez's feet kicking lazily in hazy, blue-gray arcs. Inez had the same look as her brother, the same widely spaced eyes, skin the same dusty copper as a penny. Her hair clung thick, black and slickly to her forehead where it spilled out of the swimming cap.

"What kind of thing was it?" The water was cold. Leah hated swimming, but her mum made her do it anyway.

"God, I mean, I dunno. Hector won't tell me. Just that . . . he didn't think it would be like that. He thought she'd be beautiful on the inside, you know? He thought it would be something else."

Leah had liked Yasmine—(even though she had always liked Hector more, liked it when Yasmine brought him over and the two of them huddled on the deck while Leah pretended not to watch, the flame of the lighter a third eye between them). Leah had wanted it to be a zither for her. Something sweet and strange and wondrous.

"I thought so too," Leah whispered, but Inez had already taken off in a perfect backstroke toward the deep end.

It was why her mum never talked about it. The omens weren't always beautiful things.

There had always been signs in the world. Every action left its trace somewhere. There were clues. There were giveaways. The future whispered to you before you even got there, and the past, well, the past was a chatterbox, it would tell you everything if you let it.

The signs Leah knew best were the signs of brokenness. The sling her mum had worn after the accident that made it impossible for her to carry Milo. The twinging muscle in her jaw that popped and flexed when she moved the wrong way. It had made things difficult for a while. The pain made her mum sharp and prickly. The medication made her dozy. Sometimes she'd nod off at the table, and Leah would have to clear up the dishes herself, and then tend to Milo if he was making a fuss.

And there was the dream.

There had always been signs in the world.

But, now. Now it was different, and the differences both scared and thrilled Leah.

"Mum," she would whisper. "Please tell me, Mum."

"I can't, sweetie," her mum would whisper in a strained, half-conscious voice. Leah could see the signs of pain now. The way her mum's lids fluttered. The lilt in her voice from the medication. "I just don't know. Oh, darling, why? Why? I'm scared. I don't know what's happening to the world."

But Leah wasn't scared.

❦

A month later Leah found something in the trash: one of her mother's sheer black stockings. Inside it was the runt-body of a newborn kitten wrapped in a wrinkled dryer sheet.

"Oh, pretty baby," she cooed.

Leah turned the lifeless little lump over. She moved it gently, carefully from palm to palm. It had the kind of boneless weight that Milo had when he slept. She could do anything to him then, anything at all, and he wouldn't wake up.

One wilted paw flopped between her pinkie and ring finger. The head lolled. And there—on the belly, there it was—the silver scales of a fish. They flaked away against the calluses on her palm, decorated the thin white line of her scar.

Leah felt a strange, liquid warmth shiver its way across her belly as she held the kitten. It was not hers, she knew it was not hers. Was it her mum who had found the thing? Her mum. Of course it was her mum.

"Oh," she said. "My little thing. I'm sorry for what's been done to you."

She knew she ought to be afraid then, but she wasn't. She loved the little kitten. It was gorgeous—just exactly the sort of omen that Yasmine ought to have had.

If only it had been alive . . .

Leah didn't know what her own omen would be. She hoped like Yasmine had that it would be something beautiful. She hoped when she saw it she would know it most certainly as her own special thing. And she knew she would not discard it like the poor drowned kitten—fur fine and whitish around the thick membrane of the eyelids. Not for all the world. Not even if it scared her.

She placed the kitten in an old music box her dad had brought back from Montreal. There was a crystal ballerina, but it was broken and didn't spin properly. Still, when she opened the lid, the tinny notes of "La Vie en Rose" chimed out slow and stately. The body of the kitten fit nicely against the faded velvet inside of it.

The box felt so light it might have been empty.

Now it was October—just after the last of the September heat had begun to fade off like a cooling cooking pan. Inez and Leah were carving pumpkins together. This was the last year they were allowed to go trick or treating, and even so, they were only allowed to go as long as they took Milo with them. (Milo was going to dress as a little white rabbit. Her mum had already bought the costume.)

They were out on the porch, sucking in the last of the sunlight, their pumpkins squat on old newspapers empty of the stories that Leah really wanted to read.

Carving pumpkins was trickier than cutting potatoes. You had to do it with a very sharp, very small knife. It wasn't about pressure so much. It was about persistence—taking things slow, feeling your way through it so you didn't screw up. Inez was better at that. It wasn't the cutting that Leah liked anyway. She liked the way it felt to shove her hands inside the pumpkin and bring out its long, stringy guts. Pumpkins had a smell: rich and earthy, but sweet too, like underwear if you didn't change it every day.

"It's happening to me," Inez whispered to her. She wasn't looking at Leah, she was staring intensely at the jagged crook of eye she was trying to get right. Taking it slow. Inez liked to get everything just right.

"What's happening?" Leah said.

Inez still didn't look at her, she was looking at the eye of the jack-o'-lantern-to-be, her brow scrunched as she concentrated. But her hand was trembling.

"What's happening?"

Cutting line met cutting line. The piece popped through with a faint sucking sound.

"You know, Leah. What's been happening to . . . to everyone. What happened to Yasmine." Her voice quavered. Inez was still staring at the pumpkin. She started to cut again.

"Tell me," Leah said. And then, more quietly, she said, "please."

"I don't want to."

Plop went another eye. The pumpkin looked angry. Or scared. The expressions sometimes looked the same on pumpkins.

"Then why did you even bring it up?" Leah could feel something quivering inside her as she watched Inez saw into the flesh of the thing.

"I just wanted to—I don't even know. But don't tell Hector, okay? He'd be worried about me."

Leah snuck a look at Hector who was raking leaves in the yard. She liked watching Hector work. She liked to think that maybe if the sun was warm enough (as it was today—more of a September sun than an

October sun, really) then maybe, just maybe, he would take his shirt off.

"It's okay to tell me, Inez. Promise. I won't tell anyone. Just tell me so *someone* out there knows."

Inez was quiet. And then she said in a small, tight voice, "Okay."

She put down the knife. The mouth was only half done. Just the teeth. But they were the trickiest part to do properly. Then, carefully, gently, Inez undid the top three buttons of her blouse. She swept away the long, black curls of hair that hid her neck and collarbone.

"It's here. Do you see?"

Leah looked. At first she thought it was a mild discoloration, the sort of blemish you got if you sat on your hands for too long and the folds of your clothes imprinted themselves into the skin. But it wasn't that at all. There was a pattern to it, like the jack-o'-lantern, the shapes weren't meaningless. They were a face. They were the shadow of a face—eyes wide open. Staring.

"Did you tell Hector?"

"I'm telling you.

"God, Inez—"

But Inez turned white and shushed her. "Don't say that!" Inez squealed. "Don't say his name like that. We don't know! Maybe it is, I mean, do you think, maybe He . . . I mean, oh, Jesus, I don't know, Leah!" Her mouth froze in a little "oh" of horror. There were tears running down her cheeks, forming little eddies around a single, pasty splatter of pumpkin guts.

"It's okay, Inez. It's okay." And Leah put her arm around Inez. "You'll be okay," she whispered. "You'll be okay."

And they rocked together. So close. Close enough that Leah could feel her cheek pressing against Inez's neck. Just above the mark. So close she could imagine it whispering to her. There was something beautiful about it all. Something beautiful about the mark pressed against her, the wind making a rustling sound of the newspapers, Hector in the yard, and the long strings of pumpkin guts lined up like glyphs drying in the last of the summer light.

"It's okay," Leah told her, but even as they rocked together, their bodies so close Leah could feel the hot, hardpan length of her girlish muscles tense and relax in turns, she knew there was a chasm splitting between them, a great divide.

"Shush," she said. "Pretty baby," she said because sometimes that quieted Milo down. Inez wasn't listening. She was holding on. So hard it hurt.

Inez was dead the next day.

Leah was allowed to attend the funeral. It was the first funeral she'd been allowed to go to since her dad's.

The funeral had a closed casket (of course, it had to) but Leah wanted to see anyway. She pressed her fingers against the dark, glossy wood of the coffin, leaving a trail of smudged fingerprints that stood out like boot marks in fresh snow. She wanted to see what had happened to that face with the gaping eyes. She wanted to know who that face had belonged to. No one would tell her. From her mum, it was still nothing but, "Shush up, Leah."

And Hector was there.

Hector was wearing a suit. Leah wondered if it was the same suit that he had worn to Yasmine's funeral, and if he'd looked just as good wearing it then as he did now. A suit did something to a man.

Leah was wearing a black dress. Not a little black dress. She didn't have a little black dress—she and Inez had decided they would wait until their breasts came in before they got little black dresses. But Inez had never got her breasts.

The funeral was nice. There were lots of gorgeous white flowers: roses and lilies and stuff, which looked strange because everyone was wearing black. And everyone said nice things about Inez—how she'd been on the swim team, how she'd always got good grades. But there was something tired about all the nice things they said, as if they'd worn out those expressions already. "She was my best friend," Leah said into the microphone. She had been nervous about speaking in front of a crowd, but by the time her turn actually came she was mostly just tired too. She tried to find Hector in the audience. His seat was empty. "We grew up together. I always thought she was like my sister."

Leah found him outside, afterward. He was sitting on the stairs of the back entrance to the church, a plastic cup in one hand. The suit looked a little crumpled but it still looked good. At nineteen he was about a foot taller than most of the boys she knew. They were like little mole-rats compared to him.

Her mother was still inside making small talk with the reverend. All the talk anyone made was small these days.

"Hey," she said.

He looked up. "Hey."

It was strange, at that moment, to see Inez's eyes looking out from her brother's face now that she was dead. It didn't look like the same face. Leah didn't know if she should go or not.

Her black dress rustled around her as she folded herself onto the stair beside him.

"Shouldn't you be back in there?"

Hector put the plastic cup to his lips and took a swig of whatever was inside. She could almost imagine it passing through him. She was fascinated by the way his throat muscles moved as he swallowed, the tiny triangle he had missed with his razor. Wordlessly, he handed the cup to her. Leah took a tentative sniff. Whatever it was, it was strong. It burned the inside of her nostrils.

"I don't know," Hector said. "Probably. Probably you should too."

"What are you doing out here?"

Hector didn't say anything to that. He simply stared at the shiny dark surface of his dress shoes—like the coffin—scuffing the right with the left. The sun made bright hotplates of the parking lot puddles. Leah took a drink. The alcohol felt good inside her stomach. It felt warm and melting inside her. She liked being here next to Hector. The edge of her dress was almost touching his leg, spilling off her knees like a black cloud, but he didn't move. They stayed just like that. It was like being in a dream. Not *the* dream. A nice dream.

"I miss her, Leah. I can't stop it . . . you look a bit like her, you know? I mean, you don't look anything like her really, but still," he stumbled, searching out the right words. "But."

"Yeah," she said.

"I'm glad you're here."

She took a larger swallow. Her head felt light. She felt happy. She knew she shouldn't feel happy but she felt happy anyway. Did Hector feel happy? She couldn't tell. She hadn't looked at enough boys to tell exactly what they looked like when they looked happy.

Suddenly, she was leaning toward him. Their hands were touching, fingers sliding against each other, and she was kissing him.

"Leah," he said, and she liked the way he said her name, but she didn't like the way he was shaking his head. She tried again, but this time he jerked his head away from her. "No, Leah. I can't, you're . . . you're just a kid."

The happy feeling evaporated. Leah looked away.

"Please, Hector," she said. "There's something . . ." She paused. Tried to look at him and not look at him at the same time. "It's not just Inez, okay? It's me too." She was lying. She didn't know why she was lying about it, except that she wished it was true. She wished it was her too. She *wished* Inez hadn't found something first.

He shook his head again, but there was a glint in his eyes. Something that hadn't been there before. It made him look the way that Inez's mark had with its wide, hollow eyes. Like there could be anything in them. Anything at all.

"I've found something. On my skin. We were like sisters, you know. Really. Do you want to see it?"

"No," he said. His eyes were wide. Inez's eyes had looked like that, too, hadn't they? They both had such pretty eyes. Eyes seeded with gold and copper and bronze.

"Please," she said. "Would you kiss me? I want to know what it's like. Before."

"No," he whispered again, but he did anyway. Carefully. He tasted sweet and sharp. Like pumpkin. He tasted the way the way a summer night tastes in your mouth, heavy and wet, wanting rain but not yet ready to let in October. The kiss lingered on her lips.

Leah wondered if this was what love felt like. She wondered if Yasmine had felt like this, if Hector had made her feel like this, and if she did, how could she ever have left him?

She didn't ask for another kiss.

The world was changing around them all now, subtly, quietly at first, but it was changing. It was a time for omens. The world felt like an open threshold waiting for Leah to step through. But she couldn't. She couldn't yet.

The day after the funeral Leah cut her hair and dyed it black. She wore it in dark, heavy ringlets just as Inez had. She took a magic marker to the space just below the collar of her shirt, the place Inez had showed her, and she drew a face with large eyes. With a hungry mouth.

She looked at forums. They all had different sorts of advice for her.

If you say your name backwards three times and spit . . .

If you sleep in a graveyard by a headstone with your birthday . . .

If you cut yourself this way . . .

Those were the things you could do to stop it, they said. Those were the things you could do to pass it on to someone else.

But nothing told her what she wanted.

For Milo, it started slowly. When Leah tried to feed him, sometimes he would spit out the food. Sometimes he would slam his chubby little hands into the tray again and again and again until a splatter of pureed squash covered them both. He would stare into the empty space and burble like a trout.

"C'mon, baby," Leah whispered to him. "You gotta eat something. Please, monkey-face. Just for me? Just a bite?"

But he got thinner and thinner and thinner. His skin flaked off against Leah's shirt in bright, silver-shiny patches when she held him. Her mum stopped looking at him. When she turned in his direction her eyes passed over him as if there was a space cut out of the world where he had been before, the way strangers didn't look at each other on the subway.

"Mum," Leah said, "what's happening to him?"

"Nothing, darling. He'll quiet soon." And it was like the dream. She couldn't move. No one could hear what she was saying.

"Mum," Leah said. "He's crying for you. Can you just hold him for a bit? My arms are getting tired and he just won't quit. He wants you, mum."

"No, darling," her mum would say. Just that. And then she would lock herself in her room, and Leah would rock the baby back and forth, gently, gently, and whisper things in his ear.

"Mummy loves you," she would say to him, "c'mon, pretty baby, c'mon and smile for me. Oh, Milo. Please, Milo."

Sometimes it seemed that he weighed nothing at all, he was getting so light. Like she was carrying around a bundle of sticks, not her baby brother. His fingers poked her through her shirt, hard and sharp. The noises he made, they weren't the noises that she knew. It was a rasping sort of cough, something like a choke, and it made her scared but she was all alone. It was only her and Milo. She clung tightly to him.

"Pretty baby," she murmured as she carried him upstairs. "Pretty, little monkey-face."

It was only when she showed him the little kitten she had tucked away in her music box that he began to quiet. He touched it cautiously, fingers curving like hooks. The fur had shed into the box. It was patchy in some places, and the skin beneath was sleek and silvery and gorgeous. When Milo's fingers brushed against it he let out a shrieking giggle.

It was the first happy sound he had made in weeks.

What were the signs of love? Were they as easy to mark out as any other sort of sign? Were they a hitch in the breath? The way that suddenly any sort of touch—the feel of your hand running over the thin cotton fibres of your sheets—was enough to make you blush? Leah thought of Hector Alvarez. She thought about the kiss, and the way he had tasted, the slight pressure of his lips, the way her bottom lip folded into his mouth, just a little, just a very little bit, like origami.

Leah checked her body every morning. Her wrists. Her neck. She used a mirror to sight out her spine, the small of her back, the back of her thighs.

Nothing. Never any change.

⚜

The stars were dancing—tra lee, tra la—and the air was heavy with the fragrant smell of pot. They passed the joint between them carelessly. First it hung in his lips. Then it touched hers.

"What are you afraid of?" Leah asked Hector.

"What do you mean, what am I afraid of?"

Leah liked the way he looked in moonlight. She liked the way she looked too. Her breasts had come in. They pushed comfortably against the whispering silk of her black dress. They were small breasts, like apples. Crabapple breasts. She hoped they weren't finished growing.

She was fifteen today.

Tonight the moon hung pregnant and fat above them, striations of clouds lit up with touches of silver and chalk-white. It had taken them a while to find the right place. A gravestone with two dates carved beneath it. His and hers. (Even though she knew it wouldn't work. Even though she knew it wouldn't do what she wanted.)

The earth made a fat mound beneath them, the dirt fresh. Moist. She had been afraid to settle down on it, afraid that it wouldn't hold her. Being in a graveyard was different now—it felt like the earth might be moving beneath you, like there might be something moving around underneath, below the sod and the six feet that came after it. Dying wasn't what it used to be.

"I mean," she said, "what scares you? This?" She touched his hand. Took the joint from him.

"No," he said.

"Me neither." The smoke hung above them. A veil. Gauzy. There were clouds above the smoke. They could have been anything in the moonlight. They could have just been clouds. "Then what?"

"I was afraid for a while," Hector said at last, "that they were happy." He was wearing his funeral suit. Even with grave dirt on it, it still made him look good. "I was afraid because they were happy when they left. That's what scared me. Yasmine was smiling when I found her. There was a look on her face . . ." He paused, took a breath. "Inez too. They knew something. It was like they figured something out. You know what I mean?"

"No," she said. *Yes*, she thought.

Her mother had been cutting potatoes this morning. Normally Leah cut them. She cut them the way her dad had taught her, but today it was her mother who was cutting them, and when the potato split open—there it was, a tiny finger, curled into the white flesh, with her dad's wedding ring lodged just behind the knuckle. Her mum's face had gone white and pinched, and she dropped the knife, her fingers instinctively touching the white strip of flesh where her own wedding ring used to sit.

"Oh, god," she whispered.

"Mum," Leah said. "It's okay, Mum. It'll be okay."

But all she could think was, "It should have been me."

Because it was happening to all of them now. All of them except for her. When Leah walked down the street, all she could imagine were the little black dresses she would wear to their funerals. The shade of lipstick she would pick out for them. Her closet was full of black dresses.

"I've never felt that way about anything. Felt so perfectly sure about it that I'd let it take me over. I'd give myself up to it."

"I have," she said. But Hector wasn't listening to her.

"But then," he said, "I heard it."

"What?"

"Whatever Yasmine was waiting for. That long perfect note. That sound like Heaven coming."

"When?"

"Last night." His eyes were all pupils. When had they got that way? Had they always been like that? The joint was just a stub now between her lips, a bit of pulp. She flicked it away.

"Please don't go away, Hector," she said.

"I can't help it," he said. "You'll see soon. You'll know what I mean. But I'm not scared, Leah. I'm not scared at all."

"I know," she said. She remembered the way Milo had been with the kitten. He had known it was his. Even though it was monstrous, its chest caved in, the little ear bent like a folded page. It was his. She wanted that, God, how she wanted that.

And now Hector was taking her hand, and he was pressing it against his chest. She could feel something growing out of his ribcage: the hooked, hard knobs pushing through the skin like antlers. He sighed when she touched it, and smiled like he had never smiled at her before.

"I didn't understand when Yasmine told me," he said. "I couldn't understand. But you—you, Leah, you understand, don't you? You don't need to be scared, Leah," he said. "You can be happy with me."

And when he kissed her, the length of his body drawn up beside her, she felt the shape of something cruel and mysterious hidden beneath the black wool of his suit.

❋

That night Leah had the dream—they were on the road together, all four of them.

"Listen, George," her mother was saying. (What she said next was always different, Leah had never been able to remember what it actually was, what she'd said that had made him turn, shifted his attention for that split second.)

Leah was in the back, and Milo—Milo who hadn't been born when her father was alive—was strapped in to his child's seat next to her.

"Listen, George," her mother was saying, and that was part of it. Her mother was trying to tell him something, but he couldn't hear her probably. So he turned. He missed it—what was coming, the slight curve in the road, but it was winter, and the roads were icy and it was enough, just enough.

"Is this it?" Leah asked. But her mum wasn't listening. She was tapping on the window. She was trying to show him something she had spotted.

Leah knew what came next. In all the other dreams what came next was the squeal of tires, the world breaking apart underneath her, and her trying to grab onto Milo, trying to keep him safe. (Even though he wasn't there, she would think in the morning, he hadn't even been born yet!)

That's how the dream was supposed to go.

"Listen, George," her mother was saying.

The car kept moving. The tires kept spinning, whispering against the asphalt.

"Is this what it is for me?" Leah tried to ask her mother, but her mother was still pointing out the window. "Is this my sign?"

And it wasn't just Milo in the car. It was Inez, too. It was Oscar Nunez with his shrivelled-up tongue, and Joanna Sinclair, and Yasmine with her black eyeliner, her eyes like cat's eyes. And it was Hector, he was there, he was holding Yasmine's hand, and he was kissing her gently on the neck, peeling back her skin to kiss the hard, oyster-grey thing that was growing inside of her.

"Leah can't come with us," her mother was saying. "Just let her off here, would you, George? Just let her off."

"No," Leah tried to tell her mum. "No, this is where I am supposed to be. This is supposed to be *it*."

And then Leah was standing in a doorway, not in the car at all, and it was a different dream. She was standing in a doorway that was not a doorway because there was nothing on the other side. Just an infinite space, an uncrossable chasm. It was dark, but dark like she had never seen darkness before, so thick it almost choked her. And there was something moving in the darkness. Something was coming . . . because that's what omens were, weren't they? They meant something was coming.

And everyone had left her behind.

When Leah woke up the house was dark. Shadows clustered around her bed. She couldn't hear Milo. She couldn't hear her mother. What she could hear, from outside, was the sound of someone screaming. She wanted to scream along with it, oh, she wanted to be part of that, to let her voice ring out in that one perfect note. . . .

But she couldn't.

Leah turned on the light. She took out the mirror. And she began to search (again—again and again and again, it made no difference, did it? it never made a difference).

She ran her fingers over and over the flawless, pale expanse of her body (flawless except for the white scar on her thumb where she'd sliced it open chopping potatoes).

Her wrists. Her neck. Her spine. Her crabapple breasts.

But there was still nothing there.

She was still perfect.

She was still whole. Untouched and alone.

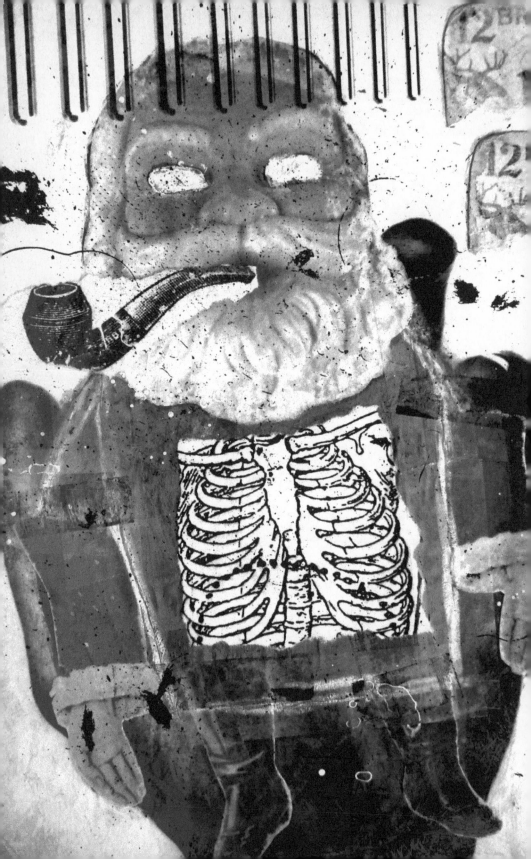

"You can tell the lifers, not because of the look in their eyes. Not because of the way they handle the Santas. But because they have stopped counting."

THE SANTA CLAUS PARADE

This is a shit job and everybody knows it.

"I'm only here for the summer," says Anna B. She's Jewish. She lights a menorah every year. She doesn't get what all the fuss is about and so most of us are willing to believe her. Sean M. is a lifer. He only started three months ago, but we can all tell anyway. That's the way it is. His fingers are delicate. He loves the little Santas as they go past, but he is heartless as well. He doesn't mind snapping their necks if they are Incompletes, throwing them into the heap. Anna B. still cries when she has to do that, though I can see her face hardening a little each time. That's why I know she'll be out at the end of the summer, and Sean M. will be a lifer. Some people get a taste for this kind of work.

Me, I haven't decided yet. I started back in April when winter seemed a long way off, or too close maybe if I looked behind. There was still frost on the trees some mornings, but I knew it would be melting.

Maybe it's not so bad. I have money in my pocket and Stacy S., the hot blonde, queen of Lincoln Central High, now gives me the time of day though she pretended, for two years, not to recognize me in math class. College is somewhere on the horizon. I need money for college. I need money for Stacy S. College seems further away than winter.

Some people think the Santas are smiling.

The Company tries to weed out that kind of thinking pretty early on with videos from the eighties, people with big hair, shoulder pads, smiling in bleached-out, crackling colours. There are diagrams about brain function. A specialist gave a talk on the subject but I slept all the way through it. Sweet dreams.

Anna B. worries that the Santas can dream. If the Santas can dream, does that mean they are properly alive? I don't worry about that sort of thing. I have a job to do. These three feet of conveyer belt are all mine.

"One, two, three," Sean M. sings next to me. "They don't get by me." It's catchy.

I pick up the Santas off the conveyer belt. They're naked and squidgy. Most of them just lie there. Some of them wriggle. They feel jelly-like when I hold them in my hand. I like the weight. Like a softball. I transfer the Santa from hand to hand, hot-potato-style. Stare at both sides. There is a beard, check. There is an anus, check.

These are the two central qualifications for life. Otherwise the Santas get three feet to live. Only three feet on the belt.

A Santa without a beard isn't a Santa at all. Sean M. calls those ones Cindies. I don't think they are female though. Just beardless. I don't know how Santas reproduce exactly. Maybe that was in the video. Maybe that was in the talk.

The anus is essential. Waste management. A Santa without an anus will build up waste over time. To be frank, it cannot shit. Shitting is essential, even for Santas. Sean M. says they will explode if we let them live. It's messy. Easier this way, he says. I can see the look in his eyes. He is the perfect little killer.

It wigs me out when they don't have anuses. I'm afraid I might handle them too roughly. I'm afraid when I slap them hard against the sharp edge of the table that they will explode in my hands. This has never happened. I'm proficient. The necks break with the sound of a wishbone at Christmas. I toss the dead Santa into a bin with other, smooth-chinned and smooth-cheeked Santas. The Incompletes. The Cindies.

Like I said, this is a shit job.

Sometimes Anna B. gets teary-eyed. Sometimes she comes to me during the break and she puts a finger on my wrist, feels my pulse.

"I could've got a job at one of the malls," she says. "I could've been a fantastic elf."

"Sure," I tell her. She has a fantastic ass. It would look good in green leotards. But elves have to smile more, I think. Anna B. doesn't smile so much.

"Do you think I'm pretty?"

"I guess so."

She isn't as pretty as Stacy S. but that's okay, who's judging really? Besides, Stacy S. has dumped my ass. She says I smell too much like peppermint at the end of the day. She says she's tired of drinking hot cocoa in the summer. It's a small price to pay, I try to tell her. And it's the

Company policy. The smells soothe the Santas. Apparently they can tell when something's wrong. They don't like the smell of us normally. That goes away by the time they are properly matured and they are sent out to the malls but in the early stages it just spooks them. The Company prescribes a strict diet for the handlers.

Anna B. and I drink cocoa together on break. She fishes around for the marshmallows and plops them on her tongue, wet and soggy, one by one by one. Anna B. has pretty fingers. The nails are clean. She has painted them a bright cherry red. This is not technically allowed but the Santas like red and Anna B. has a fantastic ass so no one says anything.

Sometimes I try to count up the numbers in my head. There are approximately 47,835 shopping malls or strip malls in America. There are street corners too, on the weekends or after business hours when the commuters are heading home. There are company parties, skating rinks, parades and the like. The numbers add up. It's a thriving industry.

Today Sean M. dumped his thousandth Cindie. The Company sent him a card. He got a bonus. He's much faster than me but his accuracy sucks. There are complaints. Sean M. shrugs them off.

Anna B. is leaving today. She gave notice two weeks ago. She tells me she will never drink cocoa again. She says chocolate of any sort gives her hives now.

"What will you do?" I ask her.

"Who knows?" she says. Her fingernails are still cherry red. I think they are sexy. Anna B. let me kiss her underneath the mistletoe at the Christmas in July party. I never bring it up. We were both embarrassed.

"Come with me," she says suddenly.

"Where would we go?"

"To the North Pole."

I laugh. I can tell she's not serious. Or maybe she is serious. She taps a red fingernail against her teeth. The idea scares me. But it also excites me.

"Tell me more," I say. She stares at me.

"No," she says. "It's a stupid idea. Forget it. You know we'll never be able to get rid of the smell."

"You mean peppermint?"

"No," she says. "Not the peppermint, dummy. They'd be able to tell at the North Pole. The Santas would rip us apart. The wild ones, you know? But I miss the winter. It'd be nice to see what it looks like up there."

"Right," I tell her. But the truth is I don't much like the winter. It makes my lips chap. I'm happier here.

I have learned something. You can tell the lifers, not because of the look in their eyes. Not because of the way they handle the Santas. But because they have stopped counting. I don't count anymore. My days have a shape. A rhythm. But they aren't measured in numbers. Sean M. has given me bonuses, so surely he at least is counting. Mister M. we call him now. He's been promoted. He's running the whole damn joint. I suppose it was predictable.

Then comes the day when he tells us we have been replaced. Still I'm not listening to him properly. It might have been by cheap immigrant workers. Or maybe they're offloading processing centres to China. Maybe it's robots.

Mister M. looks each of us in the eye. He's put on weight. His belly bulges over a too-tight belt. His chin wobbles beneath his jaw. He told me once he thought about growing a beard but decided against it. That was a mistake. When he takes my hand, his palm feels doughy. It has the weight of a softball. He looks so much like a Cindy it makes me want to laugh but I'm afraid if I do I will split him open because he is that full of shit. . . .

When I walk home at the end of my shift I smell like peppermint. I have come to like the smell. It is soothing. Snow in the air—light marshmallowy snow that reminds me of Anna B. I hope she's found the North Pole. I hope they took her in, there. I hope she still fits into green leotards. I miss her fantastic ass.

On the street I see one of the Santas—a big one, fully mature, broad as a linebacker. He's collecting money for the Salvation Army. I see a woman drop in a coin. Some children tugging at the fur trim of his cherry red suit. He smiles at them. His beard is white as the snow. A perfect specimen.

I look him in the eye as I pass. I wonder if he recognizes me.

"Ho. Ho. Ho." He says the words slowly. He is sizing me up. My skin starts to crawl.

I walk past him. The stare lingers but I force myself to keep going. I try not to see if he is watching me. My boot lands in grey meltwater and the distance increases between us.

One foot.

Two feet.

Three feet.

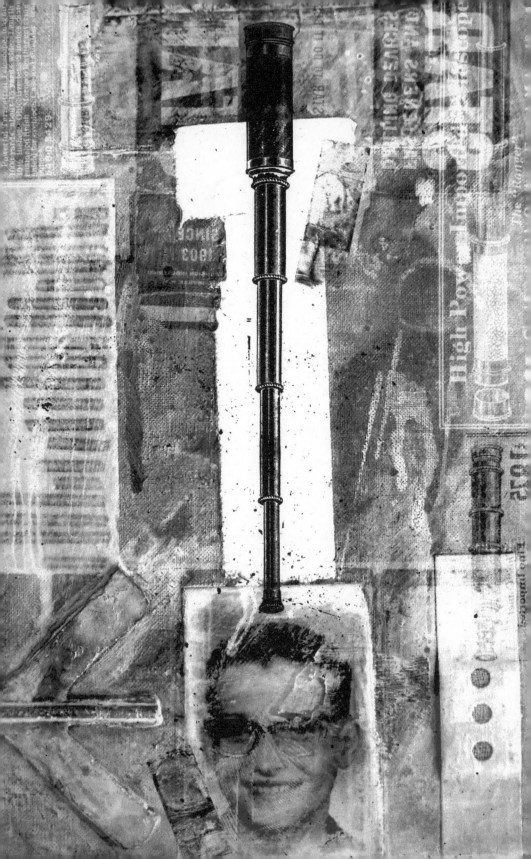

"Whatever you were seeing, it had already happened. It was only the effects that filtered out through the universe, light moving more slowly than time, time moving backwards . . ."

THE ZHANELL ADLER BRASS SPYGLASS

The Zhanell Adler Brass Spyglass was a masterwork of beauty: the slim brass mailing tube, the swivelling brass mountings and the gleaming mahogany tripod. When Richard Damaske saw it in the catalogue it evoked images of medieval astrolabes and Antikythera mechanisms, seventeenth-century telescopes and Copernican sextants, the abandoned debris of an era of exploration when the world seemed as perfect and new as an egg.

"All right," Richard said when Danny had finished tearing through the blue-and-silver wrapping paper. "Tonight, Dan-o, tonight we'll get this baby set up and I'll show you something . . . something that'll just knock your socks off."

"No one says that anymore, Dad."

"Sure, they do, buddy. You still have socks, don't you? Yes? Good. Then be prepared to have them knocked off."

Danny grinned. He was pleased immeasurably by the gift, but pleased also by the way his dad smiled at him. It had been months since his dad had smiled like that.

And so he was almost buoyant with happiness when he nodded off to sleep that night, the Zhanell Adler Brass Spyglass gleaming in the moonlight like the abandoned relic of some Martian exploration team, and that happiness stayed with him the next morning as he slung his backpack over his shoulders and marched off to North Preparatory Junior Public School. But when Danny came home that evening and he found his dad slumped at their makeshift kitchen table with the morning's newspaper beside him that feeling wavered.

"Not tonight, okay, Danny?" his dad said, barely looking up. "Can't you see that I'm . . . it's just. That thing cost a lot of money. God, over five hundred dollars, what was I . . . And now I have to—" he broke off. "Can you just go play in your room? I'll get you for supper in a little while."

"Sure, Dad," said Danny. "We can do it later. We can do it tomorrow."

But the next day when Danny came home from school he found his dad in the kitchen, shirt soaked into an atlas of water stains. A pipe had burst on the floor above them. The water was beginning to seep through, first in little trickles and then in gushing streams. There was no thought for the Zhanell Adler Brass Spyglass then. Danny spent the evening emptying copper pots and bowls as the ceiling turned the colour of a winter storm blowing in.

"Isn't this fun, Dad?" Danny asked as he heaved about with a massive soup pot. "We've got to bail faster or else we're going to go under!"

"Damnit, Danny! Just be careful where you put that," his dad replied, and as an afterthought: "Wash your hands! The last thing I need is you getting typhus and your mother breathing down my neck about it; who knows what's in these pipes?"

In the wake of the nautical disaster and the subsequent evenings spent unpacking soggy boxes and blow-drying old clothes, Danny forgot all about the spyglass, but on Friday evening when he trudged through the door, he was surprised to find his dad in his bedroom, the miraculously pristine box folded down and the thing itself pointed out his window, nestled between his fraying, navy curtains.

"Sorry, Dan-o," his dad said, "I know things have been. Different. It's not easy for you. Nor me—ha, but you know that, yeah? But tonight I'm going to knock your socks off just like I promised. Okay, buddy? Even if they don't say that anymore. Tonight is all about you."

"Okay, Dad."

"C'mere." And Danny did, and his dad hugged him in one, tight burst of affection before settling him in front of the eyepiece. "Would you look at this? Just look. She's a beauty, isn't she?"

"Sure, Dad," Danny said. "A real beauty."

"You don't get this quality for nothing, not for cheap, no. Not the double-refracting lenses. Not magnifying up to sixty times the naked eye . . . and, erm, helical focusing rings."

"What's helical focusing rings?"

"Well, helical . . . like, uh," his dad squinted. "Like a helicopter, you know, but with rings."

Danny smiled. He imagined great spinning blades, he imagined infrared sensors and, and extradimensional something or others. "It's great, Dad, really great. Thanks. The best present ever."

At that his dad flushed a deep shade of red that made the faint traces of his beard stand out, and he smiled such a proud, excited smile that Danny couldn't help but grin too.

"Let me show you." His dad adjusted the knobs. "There. Just stand and look into the eyepiece. It should be set up for—"

"Wow!" exclaimed Danny. There it was, the sky awash in a swirl of colours. "What is it?"

"The Orion nebula." Danny's dad frowned. "Is it okay? It says the light pollution makes it hard, you know, but maybe, well, maybe we'll be able to take it out to the field by Papa's place. You'll get some real good images there, I'm guessing."

"A nebula," Danny breathed. "Wow. Is that what it really looks like? Am I really seeing into space?"

His dad chuckled. "Of course, buddy. Well, mostly. That's not what it's like now. It says that everything you're seeing, it's already happened. Something to do with the way light travels. What you're seeing is how it *was*."

"Oh," Danny said.

His dad stumbled, seeming to sense his son's disappointment.

"Don't worry, if we get a really good night, I bet you can see something over a million years old."

"A million years old? Really?"

"I promised I'd show you some really good stuff, didn't I? And here—" His dad picked up something off the bed. "A journal. To record what you see. It's already got your name inside it."

Danny fingered the velvet of the embossed stars and rocket ships before flipping it open. "To Danny Damaske. From Richard Damaske. Lots of love for your twelfth birthday, buddy. Dad."

"Well, you deserve some really good stuff, don't you? A little magic?"

"It *is* magic." Danny wrapped his arms around his dad. "Thanks. Just wait 'til Evan sees this! It's gonna knock his socks off!"

"I guess it's sort of cool," Evan said. He was reclining on Danny's bed, his arms haphazard, one covering the fringe of bangs his mom couldn't cut quite often enough. "I mean, my dad would never get me something like that."

Evan was in the same grade as him, but his birthday was in February so he had already had a good long time to get used to being twelve. For Danny, twelve was still new. Twelve was still exciting. But for Evan, halfway to thirteen, twelve was already kid stuff.

"It has helical focusing rings," Danny said. "It can magnify up to sixty times the naked eye."

"Huh," Evan allowed.

"It's . . ."

"It's a bit queer if you ask me. I mean, what do you want with something like that? What does your dad think you are, a queer?"

"What do you mean?" Queer was what they called Pete Cartwright, the new kid from Manchester who had been jumped up a grade.

"I mean, that's why my dad wouldn't get me one. He'd be worried it would make me queer." Evan rolled onto his stomach. The afternoon sun knifed across his face and revealed a landscape of acne craters and freckles.

"You don't want to try it?"

"What for? It's daytime. It's not like there's any planets or anything, except, I mean, for the sun, and that'd just, I dunno, burn your eyeball up like a toasted marshmallow if you looked at it through that thing."

"What about something else? What about . . ." Danny searched for something definitively not queer. "What about if we look into Sarah Englemont's room?"

The moment the words were out if his mouth it was like someone was turning a radio dial in his head, and what had been a muzzy static of pre-adolescent longing suddenly jumped into sharp relief.

Sarah Englemont.

This was new territory for Danny. He knew some of the other boys from class liked to look at the magazines they sneaked out of Mac's Milk. They all had hiding places—under the bed wasn't good enough, that was a well-known fact. Nor was under the mattress or in the sock drawer. Jammed behind the headboard, taped underneath the dresser, that was better. Sam Stenson, whose parents were both fanatical clean freaks and vacuumed the whole house top to bottom twice a day, had hollowed out an old encyclopedia with a penknife. With all the cleaning, his parents never got around to reading much.

Over the last few months, Danny had watched Evan gain admittance into the secret cadre of boys who had been twelve for some time, sharing their winks and nudges, trading greasy, glossy centrefolds at recess. Sometimes Evan, with a glassy-eyed look, would try to tell Danny about big titties and nipples as round and hard as gumballs. Would tell him about the time he found an inflatable plastic doll with "Bride To Be" magic-markered onto its chest discarded behind Spadina Station, and how there had been a hole *down there*, and he was absolutely sure it had been filled with cock slime.

Danny didn't quite get the point of these stories, but sometimes when Evan was done Danny would think about how Mrs. Pembridge's breasts hung like half-filled balloons, and how sometimes when she quizzed them on vocabulary and spelling he might see the beads of sharp, little nipples poking out against her blouse. Then he would feel the same sweaty, glassy look steal over him, and he'd have to keep his workbook over his lap.

The thought came to him again.

Sarah Englemont.

Sarah Englemont was different. Even at twelve, Danny could tell there was a difference. With Mrs. Pembridge you didn't want to feel that way, you didn't want to think about breasts and beady nipples. But Sarah was twenty-three. She used to babysit Danny to help pay for university when his family had lived across the road in the apartment beneath hers. Back in the days when his parents used to do things like "date nights." Back when they could share the same space without wanting to kill one another.

Sarah Englemont was like . . . she was like the way you felt on a hot August day when the smog and humidity sunk into your skull and made you drowsy. She was like when you ate so much Halloween candy you knew you'd get sick but for just a moment the world was all shimmery. Sarah Englemont was like that. Except she wasn't only *that*. She was . . . she was . . .

"Okay," Evan said. Evan didn't know Sarah Englemont, and so could not know the rush of emotion that had flooded Danny's system when he even suggested the possibility of . . . Like he had stumbled onto something mysterious, like he had wandered into the pharaoh's tomb. "Okay," said Evan, and the glassy look was there so maybe it didn't matter, and Evan understood better than even Danny did. "Show me Sarah Englemont's room."

His bedroom filled up with lazy, June sunlight when Danny pulled back the curtains. He looked across the way at 106 Spadina Road where he used to live, he and his dad and his mom all together. And Sarah Englemont in the apartment above, her music leaking through the floorboards at night, the smell of her dinner drifting through the vents, her laughter like a ghost inhabiting the silence his parents never managed to fill.

"There," Danny said.

Lo and behold, *there* was Sarah Englemont's room just above the window that had belonged to his parents' room.

And lo and behold, *there* was Sarah Englemont at the window, curtains open, and—as Evan swung the Zhanell Adler Brass Spyglass in a slow parabola from the sky to 106 Spadina Road—suddenly Danny was sorry he had suggested this. He didn't want to share Sarah Englemont with Evan, not Evan who liked big titties and nipples as round and hard as gumballs, Sarah Englemont wasn't for him, Sarah was his, Sarah was *his*.

But a slow grin was spreading across Evan's face, a sleepy sort of molasses grin that made Danny want to punch him, just land a solid one amidst all those craters and freckles.

"Whoa, Danny, she's a real . . . she's primo, you know what I'm saying? She's just, yeah. Let's see, baby, let's just see. . . ." Evan pressed his eye against the lens piece so that when Danny turned to look all he could make out was that one red comma eyebrow floating above the mailing tube.

Danny said nothing.

Danny said nothing because Danny had stopped looking at Evan and his molasses-slow grin, his dirty fingers leaving marks like pennies on the polished brass.

Danny was looking at the window where Sarah Englemont lived. Sarah Englemont, who had smiled at him through a shimmer of pink lip gloss, with whom he had watched old black and whites like *Casablanca* and *Kind Hearts and Coronets*, and who, when he had struggled with the moving box full of his most prized possessions after his parents split, had given him a look of profound sadness before she ruffled his hair like she used to when he was six even though he was eleven then and never let anyone ruffle his hair.

In that window, by some chance, by fate, by whatever gods watched out for twelve-year-old boys, there was the distant figure of Sarah Englemont. Even from a distance Danny could recognize her McDonald's uniform. He'd seen her in it countless times.

No, Danny thought, no!

Because Sarah Englemont *hated* that uniform. She despised its polyester feel. Its stench of cooked meat and grease, so thoroughly soaked into the thing that not even the laundry machine could strip it out, disgusted her.

No, he wanted to cry out, even as he felt an electric jolt from his balls to his brain. No, don't do that, someone is watching, don't you know someone is watching?

But Sarah Englemont could not hear his silent pleas, and because Sarah Englemont did not know, she proceeded, achingly slowly, to strip off the loathsome uniform.

Her pants first. She removed them easily, slipping out legs that were long and slender. And then the shirt. She began to wiggle. The shirt wouldn't come free. Her head was caught.

Danny was stunned. His breath stalled in his lungs. He couldn't move. He couldn't speak. He was held captive by the scene playing out before him, barely discernible to his naked eye, half imagined, perhaps, but magnified, perfected and etched in the exquisite detail by all his boyhood longing. The black lace of her bra. The white strip of white flesh above her panties, a strip of white that had he been able to magnify his vision sixtyfold would have revealed a perfect, little bellybutton with a jewelled stud.

Then the shirt was off, and—at last—Danny shook off his paralysis.

"Hey! Don't be such a spaz!" Evan snarled as an elbow collided painfully with his ribs. The Zhanell Adler Brass Spyglass spiralled wildly and almost clocked Danny a good one in the chin, but then he had it under control, and now *his* eye was pressed to it. He was scanning, madly scanning the windows, found his mom's—he recognized the little floral teapot she kept to hold back the curtains during the day—and brought the scope up a few degrees to find . . .

"Jesus, what's wrong with you?" Evan grumbled, annoyed. "You can't see anything anyway. She's not even there. What a frigging waste." The older boy rubbed at a spot under his t-shirt. "The thing must be busted. Your dad bought you an old busted-up telescope, how do you like that?" There was bitterness in his voice. As if they had both been let down by his dad's failure. "Who'd want something like that anyway?"

Danny wasn't listening. He had an inkling that he had screwed up, could hear that in Evan's voice, and that he'd pay for it sometime. Even though he and Evan were friends now, something else had entered Evan when he turned twelve. He wasn't a bully. He couldn't be, not yet, not when he was a four-foot nothing, skinny-assed redhead with a face full of acne, but he *would* be one day and he was already starting to try on the clothes of his older self to see if they might fit.

But Danny didn't care at that moment, though the warning bells were still going off, muted, in the back of his head. He was searching, searching, searching.

Finally, the Zhanell Adler Brass Spyglass slid into place and he knew instinctively that he had found it, that as the image resolved itself he would see something magical and forbidden, whatever Evan said, something that would be worth any number of imaginative future torments.

But as his eye focused, everything looked wrong; it wasn't Sarah Englemont after all. It was an old woman, cigarette clutched between two xanthic-stained, twitching fingers. She let out a smoke plume that curled like a cat's tail out through the open window.

Danny pulled away.

Sarah had tugged on a new, baby blue cardigan.

Danny looked into the spyglass, but there was only the strange old woman, eyes full of sadness gone stale, chain-smoking through the window.

"I told you, spaz, it's broken. Your dad got you a broken spyglass. What a jerkoff."

That white strip of flesh continued to burn feverishly in Danny's mind even after Evan had left. He masturbated tentatively and then with increasing fervor until he came in a little puff which he wiped away with a tissue.

As his mind went to that sharp, blank place it always went to afterward, it was not the strip of flesh that lingered but the face of the old woman releasing all that sadness in curls of chalky smoke.

It had been Sarah's room, he was sure of it.

It couldn't have been Sarah's room, he had *seen* Sarah's room and Sarah had been in it, one part of his brain argued. But it *was*, said another more deeply buried part, the reptilian hindbrain that dreamed sex and violence and held that image of Sarah like a mosquito in amber. *It was, it was, you know it was.* The window had the same crumbling ledge, the same paisley, trimmed curtains. Yes, it was the same. Mostly the same. The same, yet different.

"Her name was . . . Jennifer," Danny's dad said that night at the dinner table. "Something like Jennifer anyway, maybe it was Ginny. Ginny Crowther." He trailed a spoon thoughtfully through the mess of cheese sauce and elbow macaroni clumped in his bowl. It was overcooked to the point that the noodles split easily under the pressure of the spoon. "You wouldn't remember her but she used to watch you sometimes when you were just a baby."

"Was she sad?" Danny asked.

"I guess so. She, uh, passed away about seven years ago. You were, what, five at the time then. You kept asking where she went and if you could see Crowsy again." His dad looked at him oddly. "That's what you called her."

"Did she smoke?"

"Like a chimney," his dad chuckled. "Your mom hated it but I was still smoking then, so she never really said it out loud. But you could just tell. Your mom would get this look and she'd never have to say anything, you'd just know immediately that something had stuck in her craw." His dad looked away guiltily. "I mean, your mom really loves you, Dan-o. I never want you to think . . ." He lapsed into silence, and Danny took to dividing the elbow noodles into pulpy confetti.

"Did she . . ." Danny couldn't think what else to ask.

"I think her husband died in Vietnam or something like that, and then her sons, well, one had a heart attack and when she called to let the other know . . . he just . . . the same goddamn thing." He shook his head. "It would make you laugh if it weren't so crazy."

Danny tried to remember her, the smell of cigarettes maybe, how she might have laughed, the colour of her eyes. Crowsy.

His dad blinked, returning to himself. "Not hungry, Danny?"

"Sorry, Dad. It's getting better though. This pot was better."

"Yeah, well, your mom was always the cook. Thanks." Danny's dad stood, and began to clear the dishes away, stacking them in a growing, uneven pile in the sink.

Danny stayed at the table. In his mind he dissected and re-assembled the pieces of information his dad had given him. The same window. Two different women, one twenty-three, impossibly perfect. Present. One ancient and grieving, died seven years ago. Past.

Danny thought about the light travelling from distant stars. Whatever you were seeing, it had already happened. It was only the effects that filtered out through the universe, light moving more slowly than time, time moving backwards if you only knew how to look at it properly.

He blinked and caught his dad's shadow falling across where his bowl had been, a tiny ringlet of cheddar-orange left in its place.

"I know it's been hard, but we're okay, right?" His dad's voice was oddly disembodied. "You'd. Well. You'd talked to me if you were having problems." Pause. "Adjusting."

Danny turned and, on an impulse, wrapped his arms around his dad's waist. Richard Damaske's hands lifted and flapped for a moment like startled birds before coming to land on his son's head. He fingered the fine blond hair. To Danny his dad smelled of equal parts stale, chemical nicotine and something sweeter that he couldn't quite recognize—like syrup, maybe. But it didn't matter, it didn't matter because under all that was his dad's smell, and Danny clung to that, breathed it in, let it fill him up.

Every other Tuesday Danny went to his mom's for dinner, and so when Danny came home at the end of the day with his backpack slung over one shoulder, a hand crammed into his side pocket, he walked on the west side of the road rather than the east as he would on every other day of the week. Danny entered the code on the outer door, mumbling the numbers as he did so. He took the elevator up six floors, turned left when the doors slid open and made his way through the overbright corridor. Danny paused in front of unit 24. He wasn't sure if he was supposed to knock now. He shrugged off his backpack and let it settle in a heap. He waited a moment. Knocked tentatively.

His mom was instantly at the door, thin body etching out an autumn-tree silhouette. "Oh, Danny, you're here. You're here. Good. Perfect. Happy birthday, darling." She kissed him on the cheek. Once. Twice. "Come in! You can put your bag . . . well, you know what to do, don't you? It's not your first time here."

Danny stepped inside, and dragged his bag until it was just inside the door. Green and blue crepe paper stretched like kudzu from corner to corner. A pile of hastily blown balloons rested on the chesterfield.

Danny's mom had dressed for the occasion in a fitted, black wool dress, pearls circling her neck and studding her ears. She was a handsome woman. Had Danny's fine, blond hair and arched eyebrows. But whereas on him they looked slightly feminine, on her they were boyish. Almost androgynous.

"Darling," she said. "Come here, come here. I want you to meet someone."

A slow sinking feeling settled in Danny's stomach.

"This is Henry. Henry Croydon. My friend from work. He's going to join us." As an afterthought: "If that's all right with you. It's your birthday, darling, so if you're not comfortable . . ."

Henry Croydon emerged from next to the cluster of balloons, and Danny realized they must have been his handiwork. The crepe paper too.

Henry Croydon had bruised bags beneath eyes. His suit was an identical shade and pattern to the chesterfield. He looked like a high school vice principal. Or a small-town crook.

"Hello, Daniel," Henry Croydon said. "Twelve, eh? That's really something. Congratulations." They shook hands, Danny's sliding in and out with as little contact as possible.

Danny decided he didn't like Henry Croydon. Danny decided he hated Henry Croydon.

"Well," said Danny's mom. She watched the exchange with a kind of sick concentration, and when it was over, she smiled an overdressed smile. "I'm sure my two men will be close as houses."

"Safe as houses," Henry Croydon whispered under his breath, and Danny decided, no, his mom had been right, safe as houses didn't make any sense, safe as houses was crap.

That night after he had returned to his own apartment across the road, Danny stared through the Zhanell Adler Brass Spyglass at the bedroom that now belonged to his mom and Henry Croydon, but had once belonged to his mom and his dad. Inside, he could see the floral teapot still holding open the curtains. Beyond it, the queen-sized bed with the chocolate and tan duvet his mom had purchased when the building heating had blown out that awful January and the three of them had to curl in all together to keep warm. Danny remembered the feeling of being trapped between two sets of knees and elbows, and every which way he turned there were the wrong angles, but still he had been warm, and his mother had stroked his hair until he slept.

He couldn't remember if his parents had kept that comforter. No, he thought, Henry Croydon would want a new comforter. Henry Croydon wouldn't sleep underneath the same blanket his dad had slept under.

Danny turned the dial on the Zhanell Adler Brass Spyglass. The image went blurry and resolved itself again. The same bedroom, but this time the comforter was askew with a figure half-buried in a mountain of blankets. Sitting on the edge of the bed, a young man with his dad's blunted nose slipped on a slate-grey jacket. Danny watched for a moment longer, and the man in the grey jacket leaned over to pull back the covers. A pale hand emerged first, then a halo of blonde hair, then a stomach bulging with the bellybutton popped out like a balloon tie.

His mom.

She heaved herself out of the tangle of sheets as if gravity meant something different to her, spine arched, her hand on the small of her back for support, but smiling with a sort of happy, pained smile.

Enough.

Danny turned the dial again, and the image went soft like running water colours, became a darkened room, curtains pulled shut, backlit by the soft, orange glow of the lamp. Cozy. Muted silhouettes behind.

Danny turned the dial.

The same room, curtains pulled back again, a single figure. His dad. Even younger, broad-shouldered with a clean, unlined face that Danny recognized as the one his own might grow into. He was laughing. He looked like a man who laughed often. He was unbuttoning a white dress shirt, the tails pulled out haphazardly at the back to hang in two wrinkled diamonds. He was staring at the doorway.

Danny nudged the Zhanell Adler Brass Spyglass the barest degree. There. The doorway darkened, the light suddenly blinding behind the silhouette of a slim-hipped woman.

She hung in the doorframe for a second that seemed to stretch on and on, husband and son both frozen in time. She was immeasurably beautiful, like a stage performer, otherworldly. The long sheaves of her hair twined into wreathes pinned at the top, the special silk dress she would wear only to the Canadian Opera Company, a Marilyn Monroe dress, black with a net of lace over the shoulders. Father and son stuck in that frame, hung up together on that beautiful woman. Sarah Englemont in ten years. Danny in ten years.

The image held, and then came unstuck. She began to walk from the pooling light of the hallway.

Danny turned the dial back. Found her again, framed in light. Beautiful. Still. She began to move. He reset the image, but he could not get it to stay put, there was no pause button, only an endless slice of time set on repeat. Light filtering out through the universe. Past becoming present.

Danny turned away from the spyglass, taken by the vague shape of some new emotion you must only get after you turned twelve. He tried to think about his mom, but all he could pull up in his mind was the image of the plastic doll with its magic marker tattoo. Bride to Be.

He turned back to the spyglass.

When Danny arrived at school Wednesday morning, the Wednesday after his second birthday party, something was different. Off. Like all seventh graders, like all weak creatures in a predatory ecosystem, he had attuned himself to the complex minutiae of his surroundings—the mouths hidden behind cupped hands, the whites of eyeballs rolling away from him, the vicious giggles of Laura G., Laura L., and Laura S., and the immediate hush as he passed them.

These were bad signs.

A kind of hurricane whisper blew across the schoolyard as Danny crossed the twenty yards from the chain-link fence to the doorway. He passed Evan and the other big tittie boys. Evan smiled casually. His eyebrows had sharpened to points.

Here it is then, Danny thought. The new Evan.

"Hey, Danny." But it wasn't Evan. It was Sam Stenson who spoke, the cauliflower-eared kid next to him with the cut-up encyclopedia and a nose like a faucet. "Hey, Danny boy." It was Sam speaking, but Danny could almost see Evan's mouth moving along.

Time stood still. The storm was breaking around Danny.

"I heard your dad is a queer. I heard your dad likes to . . ." Sam paused, screwed up his eyes in concentration. His tongue jammed against his cheek, ballooning it in and out.

The trio of Lauras giggled, the giggles spreading out in a fan around them. Danny looked at Evan. Evan looked back at Danny.

"I'm talking to you, Danny boy!" Sam called, rubber-lipped. "And. I heard it's not just men your dad likes. It's. It's. Little boys. He likes to. Watch them." The words were broken up as if Sam was unsure, remembering. The synapses firing too slowly in his brain. But then all at once the words came out in a rush. "That's why your mom kicked him out. Isn't it? Isn't that why you had to move? What I can't figure out is why she kicked you out too. It must've been because you're queer. Are you, Danny? Are you and your dad just a couple of big, ole queers?"

The pressure system reversed so quickly Danny could feel his ears popping. And now the silence, the calm, the deadly quiet was all around him, and the hurricane was inside, whipping across his synapses, rattling his teeth.

His fists clenched.

There was a line of drying snot on Sam Stenson's jeans. It caught the morning light like the edge of a knife.

"Don't be such an asshole," Danny wanted to say.

"Everyone knows what your mom really does when she says she's working the night shift," Danny wanted to say.

"Just go to Hell," he wanted to say.

Nothing broke that terrible silence.

"No," he wanted to say. "It wasn't him. It was *her*. It was *her*."

"Slut," he wanted to say. "Whore," he wanted to say.

His fingers unclenched.

Sam look at him, glanced at Evan. The silence stretched a moment longer, two, and still there were no words, no punches thrown. The crowd began to stir, restless, making jungle noises.

"Just leave him alone," Evan said at last. "God, Sam, why do you always have to be such a jerk? We all know your mom could suck the chrome off a trailer hitch."

Faint laughter.

"C'mon," Evan said to Danny. "Don't worry about him. I think I heard the bell. We'll be late for class if we don't move."

At home that night Danny sat down to the umpteenth bowl of mac and cheese.

"Did you learn anything interesting today?" Danny's dad asked him.

"No," said Danny.

"Nothing?"

"No."

"Did you want Evan to come over after school tomorrow?"

"No," said Danny."

Silence.

"C'mon, talk to me, buddy. I'm drowning here."

"Why do we always have to eat this stuff for dinner?" Danny asked. "I'm sick of it! It makes me sick, I'm so tired of it! Okay, Dad? Just one night without mac and cheese! Okay?"

Danny realized he was yelling. His dad was staring at him. It hurt Danny to see the pale look of fear flash in his father's eyes, but it also felt good, saying those things out loud, seeing that hurt. Sometimes it felt good to hurt people.

"Okay, buddy," his dad said.

They finished the meal in silence.

Danny hardly looked at the sky anymore.

When Danny put his eye to the spyglass, he kept the notebook his dad had given him beside him. He adjusted the dial methodically, checked the numbers, made a mark with his pencil. Adjusted the dial again.

It was easy once you got the hang of it. No different than what they had been doing in math class, making bar graphs. Charting out the stagger of datasets on grid paper under Mrs. Pembridge's sharp-nippled guidance.

Danny licked his lips. He turned the dial. The window swam into focus. There was the teapot. The brown and tan duvet. He waited, but there were no figures in the circle of vision. He tried again, vision blurring and resolving, blurring and resolving. There. His mom standing by the mirror of the dresser, a finger pulling back errant strands of hair behind her ear.

Danny made a note in his book. Turned the dial. Turned the dial again until he found her propped up on pillows with a paperback. She licked her index finger and turned the page. She seemed happy enough, Danny thought, content. He made a note. He turned the dial.

Danny spent the night like this. The next as well. The next after that. He ignored when his dad knocked at the door, learned to turn up the volume on his radio, ate dinner silently, sullenly. Worked. The images went by, smearing across his vision, one superimposed on the next, on the next, on the next. Danny found it strange, captivating, the gradual progression backwards, watching his mom's cheeks smooth out like the skin of an apple until there were only the faintest of lines where the wrinkles would later net at the corner of her eyes and mouth.

Sometimes Danny recorded the moments when she was with his dad, the grey streaks at his temple receding like a tide as the image changed again and again. He was smoking now. Danny watched his arms thicken, his back straighten from its fishhook slump. Danny watched the distance close between them, the way they touched each other, the casual kisses in the morning, the way his dad might run his palms across the side of her face, curving around her ears. The way she would lean into him, sometimes, when she was very tired in the evening.

But mostly Danny watched his mom. Watched the years lift off her, the thick, invisible weight of them peeling off as he turned back the dial click by tiny click.

Slut, he wanted to think. *Whore*, he wanted to think.

But then sometimes there *he* was in the room too. Seven years old. Five years old. Four years old. Vibrating like a puppy, hands in her makeup drawer, interfering, until she would scoop him up underneath his armpits and sit him down on the bed as she got ready for work. Sliding the studs of pearls into her ears. Rouging her cheeks.

Three years old. Two years old. He watched himself shrink smaller and smaller, the mass of him disappearing into thin air. Where am I going? Danny would think. Fingers whittling down to the length of crayons. Of baby carrots. Pudgy baby hands still grasping at the hem of mommy's dress as she swept by him and landed a quick kiss on his forehead.

And then he was the size of a football, and she would keep him swaddled in a blue blanket, torpedo-shaped, legs vanished to a single vertex. They would keep him between them, his mom and his dad, their bodies pressed close but not too close. His dad slept uneasily in those months. Danny would catch him waking in the night, a look on his face like he was afraid he had rolled the wrong way and smothered the little lump of his son.

Smaller and smaller until baby Danny disappeared entirely into her body, and there was just that hot-air-balloon bulge in the stomach and the breasts pillowed above, and then that shrunk too, smoothed over, the mountain becoming a molehill under her navel.

It took Danny nine days to chart out the length of his lifespan. He charted it in smiles. He charted it in touches. He charted it in wrinkles and haircuts and naptimes and workdays.

Slut, he wanted to think. *Mommy*, he wanted to think.

Danny did not watch for his dad. It was that other thing he watched for. Whatever it was that had come between them, that must have started earlier, mustn't it? Something like that couldn't simply arrive without warning. Without being anticipated. Expected.

So Danny watched for it. Watched for Henry Croydon or someone like him. Charted out twelve years back into the past, and then another nine months. He watched for that other thing. He waited for his mom to become the slut he knew she would become.

He watched. It had to be there. Something had to be there.

It wasn't.

"I want to live with Mom," Danny said at the dinner table that night, the hot, damp of July having crept into the apartment almost overnight, soaking armpits and crotches with sweat. They were eating Rice-A-Roni mixed with slices of chicken breast.

"What?" his dad asked. He was serving himself a big spoonful from the pot. A glob broke off and landed on the morning newspaper, which had been used as a makeshift placemat. "I want to live with Mom. I want to move back. I don't like it here." *With you*, he wanted to say. *I don't like it here with you.*

"But, Danny. You can't." He paused, stricken. "I mean. Danny, please. We had an agreement. Your mom needs time. We all need some time."

"I can have my old room back," Danny said.

"C'mon, buddy, I know it's been rough here, but it's not that bad, is it? I mean, we're all upset. I know it's not ideal, but I've been trying. Look, I've been trying, you know I've been trying."

"Mom said I could have my room back. Mom said it wouldn't have to be an office if I lived there."

"You can't, Danny. Please. I'll do better, I'll make us something better tomorrow. Chicken fingers, huh? How about that? How about hamburgers and French fries? You love hamburgers and French fries. You can help me in the kitchen, that'd be fun, wouldn't it? Danny?"

"I *hate*," Danny said delicately, "hamburgers and French fries. I hate this apartment. I hate you. I'm going, okay? I'm going."

Before his dad could get up from the table, before he could even stand, Danny was at the door, Danny was slipping on his sneakers, he was in the hallway, he was on the street, he was racing across it and entering the code. He was standing in front of the elevator. The elevator door opened. He stabbed at the button for the seventh floor. The elevator door closed. His heart beat like the wings of a hummingbird in his chest, individual thumps turned to a steady buzz.

Danny listened to the sound of the floor passing, the tinny chime as another one sped beneath him. He imagined his dad at the table, still staring at that stupid spoonful of Rice-A-Roni. Still eating mechanically as if nothing had happened. As if you could simply keep going like nothing had ever happened.

He wondered if he had called his mom. Danny didn't care.

The elevator door slid open, and Danny stepped out, turned left and walked through the overbright hallway to unit 24. He knocked.

He imagined his dad finding the journal. He imagined his dad reading the journal. Wondered if he would understand it.

The door opened. Sarah Englemont's door. Sarah Englemont's apartment.

"Danny," she said. "What are you doing here?"

She was beautiful. She was twenty-three and beautiful, her hair flowing in loose, delicate curls around her shoulders, hair the colour of honey, hair the colour of champagne, skin sweet-smelling, sweet like his dad had smelled.

"You're not supposed to be here, Danny," Sarah Englemont said. "Does your mom know you're here?"

"No," said Danny.

"I can't let you in," she said to him. "Your mom would be so mad, you wouldn't believe it."

"But you have to," Danny said. "Please."

She shifted her weight from foot to foot, but her slender arms continued to block the door. This wasn't right, Danny thought. It wasn't supposed to be like this. She was supposed to let him in. She needed to let him in.

"I can't, little guy. I'm not even supposed to talk to you. I've given notice." She bit her bottom lip, leaving a faint trace of lip gloss on her front teeth. "I'll be out at the end of the month but it took some time to find a new place. Longer than I thought it would. Will you tell your mom that? I didn't mean to talk to you. I'm, just, I'm so sorry, okay?"

Her mouth was curled up into a tight little knot.

"Look, Danny, I have to go, okay? You can't stay here. Just go back downstairs, will you?"

A look came over her face.

"Oh, Christ, Richard. I didn't know he was going to come over. He just showed up."

Danny turned, took in the details of his dad's face in a moment, the flushed skin, the thin slot of his mouth. His eyes were wide.

"It's okay, Sarah," his dad said. His voice was strained, strangled. His hand fit over Danny's, and the skin was hot and dry. "This isn't your fault. Your problem to deal with. I'll take him home." The hand jerked. Danny followed it, only pausing for a moment to look back.

Sarah framed in the doorway, hand smoothing the curl of her hair. The smell of sweetness on the air.

"You can't do that, Danny," his dad said. Angry? Scared? Some other emotion you got when you turned forty? The elevator dropped beneath them and Danny felt his stomach go with it. "You can't run out like that. You can't bother Sarah."

Danny said nothing.

"Please," his dad said. "I'm so sorry, Danny, but please don't talk to her again. Your mom would kill me."

"Why?" Danny asked.

"Because," his dad said, voice quiet, so very, very small. "I'm sorry I did this to you, Danny," he said. "I'm sorry, okay? I didn't mean for it to happen." Then his voice disappeared entirely inside him.

Danny let the world drop away from him, felt it rushing by outside, floor after identical floor.

He looked at his dad. It seemed as if the lines on his face had been drawn on heavy with a magic marker. Danny imagined them getting darker and darker, the skin sagging, coming apart in weighted folds. At the eyes first. Around the mouth. Ginny Crowther smoking at the window, the thin plumes breathing out between her lips. His dad's body folding up inside itself, the muscle receding to straw bones, the back hooking and humping, the hair gone grey and brittle as grass.

He had seen it. Danny had seen that. He could look through the Zhanell Adler Brass Spyglass, train it on his dad while he slept, and turn the dial forward. Again. And again. And again. Watch his dad waste away. Watch the wallpaper peel behind him, watch Danny grow up, go away to university, come back once. Twice. A young man. A man growing older. Watch the way he never hugged his father anymore, watch that space between them, become a pregnant thing that grew and grew and grew.

"Okay," Danny whispered, child's hand hot in his dad's. "It's okay. Let's go."

"His smile has many teeth to it and some of them are baby teeth, which are less frightening, and some of them are shark's teeth, which are more frightening."

DEATH AND THE GIRL FROM PI DELTA ZETA

Carissa first sees Death at the Pan-Hellenic Graffiti mixer where he is circled by the guys from Sigma Rho. They can't seem to help crowding him even though they clearly don't want to be there. She has gone with several of the Sig-Rho boys. All of them have. But she has never gone with anyone like Death before.

Death is wearing a black track jacket, with a black t-shirt on beneath and faded black jeans. Carissa, like all the other girls, is wearing a white cotton tank top with the letters Pi Delta Zeta embroidered in dark pink. She is also carrying a marker. The boys from Sig-Rho have already begun to make use of the marker to write things around her breasts and stomach and neck, things like "Sig-Rho 4Evr" and "Love your body" and "Kevin likes it with mittens on."

The guy with the black t-shirt and black jeans doesn't call himself Death though. This is what he says.

"Hi," says Death. "My name is David."

"Hi," says Carissa. She wants to say more but Logan Frees has grabbed her in a big, meaty, underarm embrace so that he can write "Occupy my crotch" on the small of her back, except he is drunk so it comes out as "Occupy my crouch," which doesn't make any sense.

It is only later that Marelaine points him out to her.

"There," says Marelaine. "On the couch. That's Death."

"Oh," says Carissa. "He said his name was David. How do you know that's really Death?"

"Death is like a movie star: he can't just tell you his real name. He has to go incognito. But you can tell anyway." Marelaine punctuates this with a sniff. Marelaine is the former Miss Texas Polestar. Her talents include trick-shooting, world change through bake sales, and getting what she wants. She has mastered the sniff. She has also mastered the ponytail flip, the high-gloss lipstick pout, and the cross-body cleavage thrust. Only Sydney, from the third floor, has a better cross-body cleavage thrust.

Carissa is concentrating on the pitch and execution of Marelaine's sniff. She misses what she is saying.

"What?" asks Carissa.

"You know, when that Phi Lamb girl died last term. Staci. Or Traci. Or Christy. Whatever. He was there. When you've seen him once, you always recognize him. He's Death."

"I think he's kind of cute," says Carissa.

"If you like that type," says Marelaine. This time her sniff is deadly.

Death's face is smooth and white as marble. His eyes are the colour of pigeon feathers. His smile has many teeth to it and some of them are baby teeth, which are less frightening, and some of them are shark's teeth, which are more frightening.

This is what Death looks like, except Death looks nothing like this at all.

His hair is cowlicked, brown with flecks of gold at the temples. His chin has a stylishly faint shadow of stubble. His cheeks curve into dimples when he smiles, which he does often, and it is not frightening at all.

Marelaine is watching as Carissa approaches Death, and Carissa knows that Marelaine is watching. She wonders if she should attempt the three-ounce vodka flounce or try for something more subtle. She has an apple-flavoured cooler beading droplets of water in one hand. She taps Death on the shoulder with the other.

"Have we met?" asks Carissa.

"Not the way you mean," says Death. He is smiling at her with that dimpled smile. "I don't come out to these things very much."

"Why is that?" asks Carissa.

"People make me nervous," Death answers. "I'm only here for work." He laughs at this, and his laughter is not what she expects it to be. It is cool and soft. It has the texture of velvet. It is intelligent laughter, and Carissa feels charmed by it, by its simplicity, its brevity, the way it sounds nothing like church gates yawning, the way it doesn't smack of eternity. She decides she likes talking to someone as famous as Death.

"That's a pity," says Carissa, and her fingers brush her white cotton top, pulling it tighter around her breasts. "Would you like to give it a go?" She hands him the marker.

"What do you want me to write?"

"Write me a magic word," says Carissa.

Death's writing is easy and graceful. There are many loops to it. He chooses a place somewhere near her left shoulder blade, and when he bends over to do it Carissa can feel the warmth of him, even though his skin is so white it is bloodless. He writes, "Abracadabra" first, and then "Open up" and then "I know you're in there" and signs it with a D.

Carissa smiles at him.

Later they play Spin the Bottle and every time Death sends the vodka twenty-sixer whirling it points at Carissa. Carissa wonders if she should try the closed-mouth kiss, the single-lip kiss or the tongue-flick kiss. She knows she is best at the tongue-flick kiss, or at least that is what she has been told by the Sig-Rho boys. She tries the tongue-flick kiss but finds, unexpectedly, that she has transitioned first into a bottom-lip nibble and next into the deeper and more complex one-inch tongue glide.

At the end, Carissa smiles at Death, and Death smiles back at Carissa.

"Don't eat the lemon squares," he whispers with a wink. And then he carefully writes his number on the hem of her tank top.

Carissa thinks Marelaine would be proud of her for this, but then, reconsidering, thinks she probably wouldn't be after all. Soon she stops thinking about Marelaine, and instead thinks about the feel of Death's teeth, both the smoothed, tiny pearls and the sharp, jagged ones.

Carissa waits a week after Sydney's funeral before she gets up the nerve to call.

Death takes Carissa to a fancy restaurant, somewhere where they serve French food and French wine and all the entrees have French names she can't pronounce. Death has a certain celebrity status, and they are shown to the table immediately.

At one point one of the other diners comes to their table. Carissa is eating the *poulet à la Provençale* which is delicious, and Death is most of the way through his *filet de boeuf sauce au poivre*.

"It's you, isn't it?" The man is sweating. Damp patches have bloomed at his armpits.

"Yes," says Death.

"I bet you don't remember, but you were there when my wife died." The man pauses. "I just wanted to say thank you. Thank you so much. She was in such pain." He plucks at his moustache nervously. "Could I get an autograph?"

Death is gracious. He signs the napkin in large, looping letters.

"Thank you," the man says. "Thank you for taking such good care of her."

Death smiles.

Afterwards, Death is walking Carissa back to the house, and they laugh about it. "Does that really happen all the time?"

"All the time," Death says, and he slips his arm around her.

Carissa wonders what Death's Johnson will look like. Does Death have a Johnson? Will he put it inside her, and what will happen when he does? Does Death have a mother? Does he call her on Sundays and on her birthday, or is he too busy with being famous and being Death to remember the people who were there before he was Death?

As it turns out Death does have a Johnson after all.

He is a gentle lover unlike the many lovers Carissa has had in the past, most of whom taste of stale beer; most of whom smell like old socks. But Death is sweet and attentive and polite.

He brings her flowers first. These flowers are not ironic. They are not lilies. They are not roses with petals dyed to black velvet. They are not grave myrtle, cut-finger, vervain, deadnettle or sorcerer's violets. They are not death camus or Flower-of-Death. Death hates irony.

Instead, Death brings her a bouquet of yellow and deep orange celandines, which he says are named after the Greek word for *swallow*, and will bring her pleasant dreams.

Marelaine and the other Pi Delta Zeta girls are jealous of the flowers, and they slip into Carissa's room when she has gone to class and cut away some of the blossoms for themselves. In the morning at the breakfast table they talk in hushed whispers about their dreams.

They dream of Death, but the Death they dream of is the death of sorority girls: killers with long, hooked knives and fraying ski masks; they dream of sizzling in superhot tanning beds; they dream endless shower scenes in which they discover their names written in fogged mirrors and their blood on the white, porcelain tiling.

But when Carissa breathes in the blossoms, she dreams about Knick-knack, the shepherd mutt she got when she was eight. Knick-knack who waited patiently for her to come home for Christmas break before he collapsed that first evening home on her bedroom carpet unable to move his legs, waiting noiseless, not a whimper, until she woke up and held him. Carissa dreams that Knick-knack is a puppy, and she holds his velveteen muzzle close to her cheek while his tail ricochets back and forth like a live wire. She dreams about him nuzzling her under the blankets with his cold, wet nose.

Their wedding is the September following graduation, and it is a surprise to everyone.

"You're so young," her mother coos.

"Will he be able to support you?" her father demands.

Carissa sends out invitations to all the girls from Pi Delta Zeta: You are cordially invited to witness the union of Carissa and Death. They have not included last names because Death does not have a last name. All the girls send their RSVPs immediately. Marelaine is her maid of honour.

It is a celebrity wedding. Carissa wears a beautiful wedding dress with a chapel train and the bridesmaids wear taffeta. Death wears black.

Carissa and Death have decided on a simple double-lip graze-and-peck kiss for the ceremony because Carissa's parents are both religious. Even though it is not entirely proper she ends up halfway into a tongue glide anyway, but she remembers where she is and what she is doing. When they pull away from each other, they are both a bit embarrassed, but nevertheless they smile as if they have both gotten away with something.

Later, as they are standing in the receiving line, Death introduces his brother, Dennis. Death has never mentioned that he has a brother, and so there is some initial awkwardness, but Carissa is a Pi Delta Zeta and so she is good at recovering. She takes his hand, and it is warm and slightly damp. There are fine golden hairs on his fingers, and he has long eyelashes. He looks the way that Death sometimes looks when he is not being Death.

"I'm so pleased to meet you, Dennis," Carissa says. "Death talks about you all the time." Carissa wonders why he doesn't.

Dennis smiles, and he has the same dimples that Death has. He holds her hand for too long. She lets go first.

"Welcome to the family," he says.

Later, after the cake has been cut, Marelaine pulls Carissa aside.

"Who's he?" she asks. She is pointing at Dennis, who is trying to teach her mother how to foxtrot.

"That's Dennis," Carissa says. "Death's brother."

"Oh," says Marelaine. "He's quite a looker, isn't he? I mean, he's not Death. But."

In a year, she receives an invitation that says "You are cordially invited to the union of Marelaine and Dennis." She wonders if she should RSVP.

They live happily ever after.

When Death dies it is very sudden.

Neither of them planned for this, and so Carissa is caught off-guard when she hears the news. She thought they would have more time. She thought she would die first, and Death would be there for it, to help her through.

At the funeral Carissa wears black. Death is also wearing black. Death is lying in a coffin, and makeup has been applied to his skin to give it a deep, bronze tan that makes him into a stranger.

Carissa secretly hopes that Death will attend the funeral, and she is disappointed when he does not. She wants to see him one last time.

Marelaine hosts the post-funeral reception. At first Carissa thinks she has gotten fat, but then Carissa realizes she has gotten pregnant. Dennis is there as well. He pats her hand, and he fetches her cocktail shrimp, which Carissa doesn't even like.

"How are you holding up?" Dennis asks. Dennis smiles, and his cheeks are still dimpled.

"Don't ask her that," says Marelaine. "How do you think she's holding up? Just look at her."

Carissa finds herself thinking that Death must have been so mindlessly bored if this was what he did all day at work.

Carissa is lonely.

She tries Ouija boards, but she can never get anyone on the other line. Sometimes Dennis comes over.

At first he is purely solicitous. He brings over frozen lasagnas that Marelaine has prepared meticulously. He brings over casseroles. He brings over pies. And then he collects the baking pans, and the casserole dishes, and the pie plates, only so that he and Marelaine can fill them all over again.

After the first month Carissa wonders if she is pregnant, but then she realizes she is only getting fat.

One time when Dennis comes over, his hand accidentally grazes against her ass as he washes a two-quart dish that had previously contained a tuna casserole.

"Oops," he says, smiling. His hands are dripping water and soap onto the kitchen floor. Carissa doesn't say anything.

The next time he comes over, he brings a bottle of cabernet sauvignon along with a black cherry pie that Marelaine just baked this morning. She has crisscrossed the top with strips of dough with scalloped edges the way that pies always look when they are on television.

"How are you getting on today?" Dennis asks, and his voice sounds to Carissa like a famous person's voice. It is smooth and cool and easy to listen to, but it is not Death's voice.

"I'm fine," she says, and she takes a sip of her wine. It tastes better than the pie. "I'm fine," she says again.

They finish the bottle of wine quickly. Carissa suggests that they play Ouija because there are two of them, and Dennis agrees. Carissa has lost the pointer so they use an ace of hearts instead, and it circles and circles and circles but it only ever stops on the picture of the crescent moon. Dennis suggests that they play Spin the Bottle, and Carissa feels like it's only polite so she agrees.

The bottle spins and spins and spins, but there are only the two of them so no matter where it ends up pointing, she still has to kiss Dennis. His teeth are entirely smooth.

Carissa wakes in the middle of the night, and Dennis is still beside her. The sheets are all askew and somehow she has ended up on the wrong side of the bed. From this side, the bedroom seems strange, like it could be another place. Like she could be another person sleeping in it.

Dennis is beautiful. She cannot tell whether his hair is blond or grey in the moonlight, and so she decides that it must be both at the same time. She decides she likes to look at him while he is sleeping.

She takes the marker from the bedside table and she writes on Dennis' perfect, moon-white skin.

"Abracadabra," she writes.

"Open up," she writes.

"I know you're in there."

"Did he tell you he was going to die?" asks Carissa.

"I never asked him," Dennis answers. "We didn't talk that much. He was Death."

Carissa is quiet for a while.

"Do you want to run away with me?" Carissa asks.

"Yes," says Dennis.

Dennis decides that they must tell Marelaine in person. Carissa wonders if she is nervous, but she decides that, in the end, she isn't. But when Dennis opens the door, Death is sitting at the table with Marelaine.

"Darling," says Dennis.

"I knew it," says Marelaine. "And with *her* too. I knew it would be with *her*."

"No," says Dennis. "It's not like that. We're in love."

"We're not in love," says Carissa. "I don't love you."

They both look at her.

"I knew it," says Marelaine once more, and she rushes out of the room. Dennis follows after her. Carissa wonders if she is supposed to go as well, but decides that she probably shouldn't. Sometimes it seems as if real life is exactly like sorority life.

"Why didn't you ever come to see me?" asks Carissa.

"That's not how it works," Death says at last. "I'm Death. I couldn't be David forever."

"I've missed you," says Carissa.

Death says nothing. He is still handsome, although Carissa can see the glint of a few threads of silver near his temples. He looks older. He looks tired. She wonders what she must look like to him.

"What are you doing here?" Carissa asks at last.

"Triple homicide," says Death.

BANG goes Marelaine's gun somewhere upstairs. And BANG again. There is a sound as bodies hit the floor.

"Oh," says Carissa. She considers this. "Oh."

They sit together in silence, and, for the first time since the funeral, Carissa feels happy again. She decides that Death does not look that old. He looks good. Death is supposed to have some grey to him. It makes him look distinguished.

"That was only two gunshots," she says.

"I know," Death says. After a moment, he says, "It was arsenic in the pies. You know. Marelaine always was such a bitch." He pauses, and pours a glass of wine for her. "I think we'll both have to wait for a bit."

"It's good to see you," Carissa says.

"I've been waiting for such a long time," says Death. "I've brought you flowers." He removes a single, yellow celandine blossom from his jacket pocket. Carissa smiles. She takes it from him gently, afraid to crush the petals. Their fingers touch, and his hand is warm, familiar.

"Where are we going?" she asks.

"You'll see," Death says. "Don't worry, darling. I'll take you there."

She breathes in the scent.

When she dreams it is of Death, and she is happy.

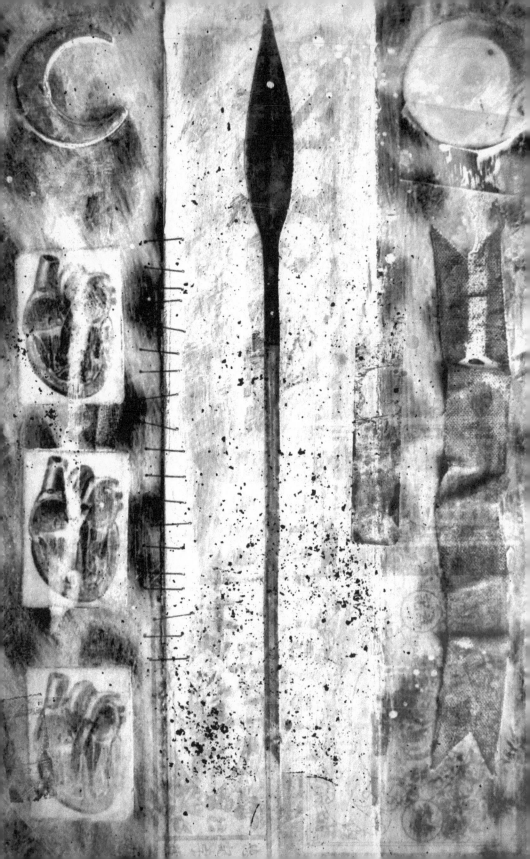

CROSSROADS AND GATEWAYS

Dajan faced east, as he did every morning, greeting the Sun with a toothy smile that split the creases of his face. His spear was planted in the sand beside him, gripped by a hard and callused fist. The wind tugged at the bright red cloth that hung from it. The sand dunes seemed smooth as elephant bones in the morning, limned in a brilliant gold. Brown and gold—the colours of the desert. Dajan's colours.

He shaded his eyes as he scanned the horizon. In the distance, he made out the silhouette of a man approaching. This was unexpected. So little was unexpected in the desert. So little changed. The desert was its own kind of prison—parched, loveless, limitless.

Dajan leaned against the shaft of his spear and waited.

"There are no crossroads here, Esu," Dajan called out. The approaching stranger was naked but for the stretch of cloth about his waist. Today, Esu had the look of an old man. He wore his skin like a threadbare blanket over muscles lean and hard as baked clay. His white hair, tangled in beads and bones, gleamed against the darkness of his shoulders.

"All men are crossroads," Esu answered with his hyena grin—mouth stretching wide, too wide, to reveal uneven teeth. "You more than most."

Like the flickering of a flame, Esu shifted faces—ancient wanderer to teasing boy-god. The lanky body was smaller now and rounded with baby fat. The lines in his face smoothed like the wind sweeping away footprints in the sand. Still, the hyena grin was the same.

"All men are crossroads," Esu repeated with a sly look, "and all women are gateways. It is unfortunate that you are not a woman. Women deserve gifts."

"Women have gifts of their own," Dajan answered cautiously.

Esu cackled at this, now turned white-haired and old once more. "As do you, as do you. Have you no questions for me, dead one?"

"No," Dajan said. Asking questions of Esu—in any of his forms— was dangerous. His tongue gave shape to lies. He was a deceiver. He broke the world apart and knitted it together as he pleased. He might grant favours, yes, but there was always a price.

"You've learned wisdom, I see," Esu said as he pressed his face close. Dajan refused to flinch when the wrinkled lips whispered into his ear. "Or the desert has taught it to you. A question for a question then. What was the name of the first woman you loved?"

Dajan paused. In his mind's eye, he saw her, hips swaying beneath the crimson cloth, mouth slightly parted, eyes full of a thousand secrets.

Silence had its own price. There had been silence for so many years. Years of wandering. Years of waiting.

"Duma," Dajan whispered, his chest constricting at the thought. Duma. Cheetah.

Esu threw back his head and shrilled like the bird. "Did she mark you with her claws? Or did she simply run faster than you?" There was something hungry in the old man's eyes that set Dajan on edge. "Wise, you are. Wise as a woman's eyes. Sly as a woman's eye. It doesn't open easily. Did hers?"

"One question, you said."

"Aye," Esu crowed. "A question, a question. Would you know how to please her?"

Dajan's throat was dry. The Sun was higher in the sky than it should have been, scorching him with its rays. The desert was no longer the warm golds and browns of dawn. Instead, it had bleached into the blinding white of midday. Bone light, his people had once called that colour. Only Esu's crooked body darkened the surroundings. "Why are you here?" Dajan asked.

"Wise, of course. Always whys." Esu grinned again, his wrinkled face broken by the white gleam of his teeth. "I have come, Dajan of the Sands, to open a gateway for you."

"Tell me a story, hunter," Esu said as he began to climb towards the top of the dune. His feet made tiny dimples in the sand as he walked. He had taken the face of the child: snub-nosed, heavy-lipped, and dark-eyed. The whites of his eyes seemed to dance like twin Moons.

"I thought you were here to open a gateway," Dajan replied wryly.

"You are lost in the desert of Zamani. The past. You must see the way you have come before you go further." He pointed at the footsteps.

"I don't understand."

"Of course not! No one ever *understands* me," Esu whined. "You are at a crossroads. Speak, and take the first step."

Dajan knelt down and ran his fingers through the smooth sand as he mulled over the boy-god's words. He held a handful for a moment. The grains ran in thin streams as he gathered his thoughts.

"Once," Dajan said, "there was a hunter—very young. He had barely seen the Sun of sixteen summers, but he was keen-eyed, long-armed."

"Ah," Esu whispered as he beckoned Dajan with his hands.

"Women thought well of him, and many had laid necklaces at his tent in hopes of a fond welcome. He decorated himself with their gifts for he was as vain as Nyani, the baboon, but he never touched the women who offered them."

"Foolish as Nyani," the boy-god replied with a giggle.

"Of course," Dajan replied, "but he was keen-eyed, long-armed, so he wore each of their hearts around his neck as a trinket.

"One morning, during the Season of the Spear, he set out among the heartlands in search of antelope. Keen-eyed as he was, it was late in the day before he found a herd. As the spear left his hand, the herd scattered as if forewarned of his attack. Long-armed as he was, his throw went astray. That was when he saw *her*. She was ... beautiful," Dajan murmured. "Golden as the Sun and graceful as the wind through the grass. She was like him: a hunter. She was a *duma*." Esu's eyes flickered at this. "He crept towards her, careful lest she catch his scent."

"It is dangerous for a duma to catch a man's scent," Esu said softly.

Dajan paused for a moment, glancing towards the Sun. Then he turned towards Esu with a sly look. "The day grows hot and I am thirsty. Now is not the time for stories."

"Bah!" Esu's young voice took on the plaintive tones of a grandfather. He shook his skinny arm at Dajan. "It is always the time for stories." With that, he took a cowrie shell from his pouch and threw it towards the heavens. It gleamed for a moment, and then it was no longer a shell but the bright face of the Moon come to chase down the Sun. The Sun fled towards the hills, fearing today the hunter might catch her. In a moment, there was darkness. "Finish the story!"

"Soon," Dajan replied, secretly pleased at the tantrum. "First, you must answer my question. Why am I a crossroads?"

Esu chewed the bottom of his lip sullenly. Dajan waited. When no answer was forthcoming, he turned away from the dark child and began to walk.

"Where are you going?" Esu asked, but before he had even finished speaking his eyes widened at his mistake. He let out an animal sound of frustration—a howl as loud and long as a hyena's. The noise meant a brief victory.

Dajan turned.

"You would ask me a question, little god?" His tone was insolent. Foolishly so. But pride had ever been his weakness. "I go towards the tribe of my brother. I would know if all you say is true."

"I do not lie," Esu spat. "You have passed from Sasa into Zamani—history, the past. You are beyond their memory. You can't go back unless..."

"Yes?" Dajan asked, pretending nonchalance.

"Ah!" Esu's frown transformed into a smirk. "One question. You are a crossroads because Sasa and Zamani meet within you."

"I thought I was within Zamani," Dajan said. He shifted his weight onto his spear.

"Sasa lies ahead. *If* you can open the door," Esu replied, leaping in the air. "But come, come! We must walk. And it is the time for stories."

Dajan nodded, then trudged after Esu who had set off in a new direction. It was always this way with the gods. Nothing held fast. Nothing held still. They were the wind and he was the grain of sand blown heedless in their wake. He licked his lips. It tasted of salt, but he smiled anyway. He had tricked this boy-god once. There was more to be gained from him.

"Very well," Dajan said. He closed his eyes. Reached for the rhythm of the story.

"The hunter was close now. With his keen eyes, he could see the pattern of her soul upon her skin. He knew her by it and knew he would never mistake her for another. The skin of a duma is like the fingerprint of a man. With his long arms, he could almost reach her. But the necklaces, the necklaces he had worn to please his pride, clattered as he moved. She heard, and knew the scent of heartbreak and pride, for she was a woman as well as a hunter. So she turned on him. He was weaponless and in love, so he did not fear her claws.

"She carved the pattern of his soul onto his skin. It was one of pride and heart's blood. When she left him, he was keen-eyed, and long-armed, and broken on the sand."

There was silence for a time as, in the dark desert of the sky, the Scorpion wheeled overhead.

"A good story," Esu said, charmed out of his usual impishness. Perhaps it was the blood, Dajan thought. For a moment, he could catch the gleam from Esu's hair in the moonlight before the silver returned to its boyish darkness. "Another story then."

"I am empty of others."

"Then I shall teach you." The hyena grin, once more. "Once, there was a mound of skin and bones dyed red with the blood of a hunter."

Dajan looked up sharply, but Esu continued in his singsong voice, his hands carving a space in the darkness between them. "And a duma came, a huntress blooded once by a man. Her claws were red in the light of the setting Sun, and she touched him. Touched him again. Where her claws met his skin, it was re-joined, stitched together once more until she lay atop him and he was whole."

Dajan felt a flicker of fear within him. For a moment, he could see the shape of trees in the distance beyond the edges of the desert. Jagged as teeth against the stars.

But trees did not last. They *could* not last. The desert was too strong.

"She left him, of course, as is the way of mothers and lovers, and his necklace clattered as he tried to touch the fur of her coat. She was gone. The hunter rose from the sand and the blood and collected his spear, never looking back, for he had forgotten her, as is the way of sons and lovers. Still, for all his pride, each night he placed a necklace by the door of his tent and each night a woman reclaimed her heart until his throat was bare and he was simply a boy again."

"If only it were so easy to change the past," Dajan muttered.

"Perhaps it could be. With help. You live within Zamani, hunter."

"This is *not* Zamani," Dajan snapped. "I know it. My brother's children, they still offer milk and honey to my memory. I have not been forgotten."

"Once, they did," Esu said. He became again the ancient traveller, his body flensed of its youth and promise. "But you have passed from Sasa. The now. Your brother's children are gone. As are their children."

Esu's eyes were milky and half-blind, skin folded into thick creases when he squinted. Body bent and burdened. Dajan could read the passage of time in that transformation. Could see the years he himself had spent in the desert. When had he last tasted the gifts of the living? When had he last drunk in their memory of him? How long had he wandered the desert while his brother's line fell to the sands?

"Why are you telling me this?" Dajan demanded. His hands clenched into fists. He did not want to think about such things.

"To open your eyes!" He paused. Spat again. "Fweh. You are careless with your questions." He waved a hand in disgust. "For that answer, you must tell me another story."

It was midday once more. The Moon had let the Sun chase her from the sky, dancing ahead, vanishing beneath the line of the horizon.

Dajan and Esu continued to walk the dunes, leaving a trail of footprints like the spots on Ghana's long neck. Dajan knew these hills. Had travelled them ceaselessly as the Sun hunted the Moon. But could he be sure they were the same hills? Did his footprints show the path he had come or the path he still must tread?

The past mattered. It *meant* something. But the bowls had been empty for so long. The children's bones licked clean by sand. Baked to dust by the sun. He could not remember the faces of his brother's sons and daughters. None remembered his face. Perhaps none of it mattered anymore.

Yet a story was owed. The old laws still meant something. He would give the boy-god his due.

"Once, there was a beautiful woman named Mayasa," Dajan began. "Her arms were dark as the coals of a fire burnt out, long and slender. Her hair was plaited and wrapped in a band of crimson cloth beaded with cowrie shells. When she walked, her movements were swift and sure. She was a princess of her tribe."

They crested the top of a dune, and Dajan paused for a moment to survey the land. It stretched towards the horizon in an arc of mottled gold and brown. Empty. With a sigh, he took another step and led the way down the mound.

"Her mother," Dajan continued, "broached the topic of marriage one evening as she knelt at the loom. Mayasa smiled obligingly and said: 'There is a little while yet before I must find a husband.' And her mother was satisfied and went away.

"The seasons passed, and Mayasa's mother returned to her to speak. Again, Mayasa smiled and put aside the question, for she loved her freedom more than any man.

"Finally, during the season of the Sun, when the old men complain of water and the young ones lay quiet in the shade of the trees, her mother returned. This time, Mayasa could not put her off. 'I shall marry he who catches Ubora, the King of the Antelopes,' she said, and her mother was pleased. Such was a task fit for a prince."

Esu chuckled to himself as they walked over the sand. "Only a princess would bind her eye in gold."

"Perhaps. But is the right of a woman to name her own price."

"As you say."

Dajan resumed his tale. "So one by one each of the hunters came to ask Mayasa for her blessing. She said to them in turn: 'Go forth and bring me Ubora.' None ever returned with the King of the Antelopes.

"Finally, the youngest hunter came to her, saying, 'I would have your blessing in my hunt, princess.' She paused before this one longer than before the others, for he was handsomer than most, keen-eyed and long-armed. But she knew his heart, as is a woman's way, and she knew that he did not love her.

"The King of the Antelopes was clever and fleet, but Mayasa was afraid. Even a King could stumble. This hunter would make an ill-fitting husband for her. He was too proud. Too full of disdain. There was no room in his heart for love. But what was there to do? She nodded once to the hunter and said: 'Go forth and bring me Ubora.'

"She turned to leave, but the hunter spoke again. 'I will, princess. But I would ask a gift of you.' Mayasa was startled, for none of the others had dared to approach her thus, but she was a princess above all else, and she knew her duty. 'What would you have of me?' The hunter paused for a moment and Mayasa almost blushed at the way he stared at her. 'The cloth from your hair.'

"Softly, Mayasa cursed, but she unwound the red scarf and let her hair fall in a dark cascade down her back. When the hunter left, Mayasa knew that she had been right to fear him. That night, she followed him from the city. Her unbound hair was a cloak of shadows that hid her from his eyes. He, in turn, tied the cloth around the head of his spear.

"After several days, he found the herd that followed Ubora. Approaching through the tall grass, he drew nearer. The King of the Antelopes scented the hunter, but when he searched the grasslands, all he could see was the head of the spear bound in the red scarf. He mistook it for the princess herself and was unafraid.

"Mayasa, seeing the danger her gift presented, slipped out of her skin in the way that all of her mother's line could. When she was free of the rags of human flesh, she was a duma, sleek and deadly.

"*This* scent Ubora knew, for it was the scent of wild death on the plains, and he ran. The spear that the hunter had thrown missed its mark, but the hunter did not care. He had seen Mayasa in the form of the duma, and he knew that she was the true prize.

"Weaponless, he approached her, thinking that he could tame her with his bare hands. But the love of a duma is reckless and wild and cuts deeper than a knife. She knew that, clever and handsome though he was, she would never run free if he caught her. So she caught him with her claws and her teeth, and she left him for dead on the plains."

"Ah," Esu whistled through his teeth. "That was well-told."

"It will be well paid-for," Dajan said.

"Double-tongued, as I am double-faced. I like you, hunter," cackled Esu, throwing his hands into the air. "Perhaps I *shall* give you a gift. You speak like a woman."

Dajan caught his arm and held him for a moment. His fingers dug into Esu's sinewy flesh. "Tell me how I can return to Sasa."

Shaking away the hunter's grasp as if it were nothing, Esu replied, "Surely you know stories. It is not yet time."

"Then what gift?"

"A story, of course. Words are the currency in Zamani, hunter. Which shall you hear? How the hen scratched away the continents of the world? How Tembo gained his mighty tusks?"

"I know those stories," Dajan replied with an irritable wave of his hand. "Tell me a story about you."

Esu preened for a moment at the request. "Of course, of course. Walk with me, hunter, and I shall tell you."

The Moon still hung in the sky, casting a silvery light over the sands until they gleamed like the hair of a newlywed bride. There was not a hill here that Dajan had not climbed, not a grain that had not tickled his skin as he walked. Still, Esu seemed satisfied to simply wander as he talked, so Dajan shrugged and kept pace. He had the patience of a hunter, and he knew his prize was near.

"Once, there was a man as handsome as Ghana is tall and as wily as Ubora, King of the Antelopes," Esu began, his hyena grin dividing his head like two halves of a split calabash fruit.

"Better to say as proud as Tembo the elephant," Dajan snorted.

"Quiet, hunter." Esu commanded, aiming a swat at Dajan's head. "This man knew the secrets of the world and was a trickster at heart. During the Season of the Sweet Grain, he met a hunter in the desert."

"I believe I know this story," Dajan muttered.

"And the hunter was rude, but the trickster, who was patient as the wind, spoke with him a while. You see the hunter was no ordinary hunter. Of course not. The trickster never talked with ordinary men. The hunter was a spirit. He had been foolish and had lost his life for it. His brother's sons offered honey and milk to his memory, but as is the way of mortals, they grew old, and their sons grew old, and their sons grew old until the honey became rare and milk was needed for the babes of the family. None remembered the foolish hunter. As is the way of such spirits, he passed into the desert. Into Zamani."

"Stop!" Dajan ordered. "Do not mock me."

Esu rolled his eyes. "Are you deaf? I do not lie. Besides, this is a *story*."

With regal dignity, Esu began to speak once more. "So the trickster found the hunter in the desert and was well-pleased with his tales. Still, the hunter did not understand why the trickster had come to the desert.

'Why are you here?' he cried with all the impatience of a child. And the trickster answered, for he was kind as the honeybird who always aids mankind, 'I am here for a trade.' 'I have nothing,' the hunter replied, but the trickster was wily as Ubora, and he knew this was not true. 'You have many gifts, hunter. I but require one—a red strip of cloth so I might bind up my hair.'"

"Be quiet!" Dajan pleaded. "I do not want to hear your story anymore!" And he clutched the spear closer to his side. Esu only clicked his tongue and grinned a wide grin, his ancient teeth gaping.

"Of course, the hunter was loath to part with the gift, for it had been dyed with his heart's blood and would look foolish in the hair of an old man. 'What would I gain in return for such a prize?'

"'Why, I shall tell you the end of a story,' the trickster replied. 'All the tales I know end sadly,' the hunter told him, and his face was dark because he could not see. 'Bah!' cried the trickster. 'There is no sadness in Death. Death is a Woman, and sometimes taking is less sweet than being taken.'"

"That is no story," Dajan grunted. "It is not true. Death is not a Woman. I *know* this!"

"You know nothing, hunter!"

And before Dajan could stop him, Esu pulled the scarf free from Dajan's spear. He danced out of reach and tied it into his own hair.

"No!" Dajan cried. Something was breaking apart inside him. A pain lanced at his heart. The pain of claws and sharp teeth. He had not felt pain such as this for many years.

He advanced wildly on Esu. His eyes, a hunter's eyes. They saw, keenly, as the hunter sees. His limbs were long and tireless. And the god? The god was skinny and old, his body bent like a grandfather. For a moment, only, Dajan was allowed to forget that *this* was no grandfather. *This* was no old man.

"Be quiet," Esu commanded. His voice was sharp. Dangerous. Free of the sidling whispers and mocking grins. "It was won fairly."

And in that moment of forgetting—that moment of bitter reprimand—Dajan felt himself begin to come undone. It was as if that scarf had bound him together for these long years. Set his shape in place.

"Please," Dajan cried. "It is all I have of her! It is all the hold I have upon this world. There is no milk, no honey, to keep me in this place! Only her."

"Foolish boy!" Esu's voice rang out across the desert. His mouth was terribly wide. He could have plucked the Moon from the heavens like a calabash fruit and ground it between his teeth. "Have you learned nothing? Listen! It is the knot that holds you fast. Would you stay?" He smacked Dajan on the side of the head. "Look!"

Dajan turned with a snarl to see.

And froze.

He knew the desert. He knew the feel of the sun baking on his back as he climbed the dunes. He knew the taste of dust on his tongue. He had counted every grain of sand. He had memorized the curve of the hills.

But, in the distance, he saw something he did not recognize: the rippling waves of the grasslands.

Esu clicked his tongue. "Ah," he whispered with a satisfied sigh, "the savannah."

"What?" Dajan asked. Heat could drive a man mad. He knew this. And there was a kind of madness in that image. The beautiful, shimmering waves of grass: soft as a woman's hair.

But this was not madness. This was Sasa.

"Now the time is right, hunter. The crossroads. What will you choose?"

"What do you mean?"

"You would have another gift from me? You truly are a woman," Esu said, his hyena grin wide as the arc of a spear. "*You* are the border between Sasa and Zamani. You carry the desert within you."

"I may leave, then?" Dajan murmured in wonder. His eyes searched the landscape like a lover's hands in the darkness. Long swells of tall grass rippled with the passage of the wind. Beyond the savannah he could make out the dark smudge of the jungle on the horizon. Sasa.

"Are you ready to walk through this gateway, hunter?" Esu asked, shaking his cowrie shell as if it were a child's rattle.

"All gateways are women, are they not? What is her name?" Dajan answered.

The old man clicked his tongue again. Dajan didn't think he would answer, but after a moment, Esu said: "Duma."

Dajan clenched his spear in surprise. Surprise and something else. Desire. As the cowrie shell shook, he saw her on the plains—beautiful as the Sun at the edge of night.

"Go!" Esu hooted. "Make me a story!"

Dajan was running. He left his spear on the dunes, knowing that he must do this on his own. If he were to tame her, it would be with his hands. He let out a whoop of joy as his feet landed on the cool grass of the savannah. Then, as he disappeared into the sweet embrace of the grassland, he was silent once more. His body made no more than a whisper as moved, the stalks sliding around him like water around the prow of a coracle. It was infinitely sweet, the tickle of grass in his nostrils, the moonlight on his back, the breeze teasing the tips of his braids.

It was life.

It was home.

It was the hunt.

He was close now. The silver light lit up her coat in a soft copper sheen. He knew the mottled spots on her skin, knew them as he had known his own footprints in the desert. It was a part of him. Taking a breath, Dajan held his hands out before her, not to touch her this time—he was wiser than that now—but in a gesture of supplication. He saw the duma's muscles tense.

There was a smile touching his lips as she pounced.

He was keen-eyed and long-armed, yes, as he had told the boy-god. That had not left him over the years. But in this place he was armed only with the wisdom of the desert. There was nothing between him and her claws.

She was a duma, a huntress in her own right. She was prey for no man.

And she tore through him easily.

Dajan cried out, stumbling in blood beneath the weight of her body.

Esu, watching from the distance, furrowed his brows. He mumbled words beneath his breath and continued to shake the cowrie shell.

"All men are crossroads," he whispered in a singsong voice, "and all women are gateways."

Out on the plains, Dajan died. The claws of the duma flayed the skin from his body. But there was a smile on his face.

He was wise.

The duma stood over him, claws and teeth red from the kill. She made a noise deep in her throat and began to nose through the still-warm remains of the hunter. Her claws swept through the rags of skin, searching, always searching. She saw a movement among the bloody strips and nudged the refuse away. Beneath, she saw the first glimmer of gold. Then an eye dark as desire. Gold and brown.

With a low growl she swiped away the last pieces like the hen scratching away at the earth to form the continents of the world. From the space she had cleared crawled the lean form of a cat. The duma knew the pattern of his skin, knew it from long ago. There was no pride this time. He smelled of the desert, the sharp scent of sand and the lonely wind.

The second duma rose and shook free of the remnants of his former life. He could feel a change within him, another path, another story.

Warily, he took a step towards her. She snarled and batted at his head with her paw. He hesitated, but the gesture was playful—coy.

He tilted his head slightly, keeping it low to the ground, and made an inquisitive noise.

"Shall we hunt?" he asked in the language of the duma.

"Our prey?" she growled in a voice as soft as the feather of a guinea fowl.

With a soft huff of breath he said, "Ubora, King of the Antelopes."

Atop the hill Esu watched with a half-mocking grin as the two of them raced through the tall grass, little more than a blur of gold and brown. Absentmindedly, he scratched at his crotch.

"Sly," he mumbled, "sly as a woman's eye." He ran his hand through his stubbly black hair and carefully bound it up within the stretch of red cloth.

With that, his arms stretched out into the wings of a heron. In a moment, he was nothing more than another flash of silver in the night sky, an arrow shot from the bow of the Moon towards the fleeing light of his prey.

"The house sat so perfect and still in the shadow of the mountain. Like it could wait forever. Like it needed no one—the waiting was enough."

SHIP HOUSE

I am the law of your members,
the kindred of blackness and impulse.
See. Your hand shakes.
It is not palsy or booze.
It is your Doppelganger
trying to get out.
Beware . . . Beware . . .
—Anne Sexton, "Rumpelstiltskin"

Her mother had become an old woman by the time Eileen came back to Ship House; she and the house in the shadow of Table Mountain had both sunk in on themselves, both had their backs broken by the winter rains and the too-hot summers of the South African Cape, their foundations crumbling to dust and gravel. Eileen's mother wore old pearls and a red-and-white shift dress underneath a thin, woolen sweater. Her face was like Eileen's face, almost. Her eyes had the white-blue of milk. Her hair was so thin she looked nearly bald.

"This is what happens," Andrew had told Eileen before she left, "when you get to be *her* age. It's no surprise that things aren't quite working right."

Andrew hadn't come with her. Even though he *knew* she was the weaker of them, he had had not come. He had stayed to look after Emma.

"Emma's barely fifteen," Andrew had said, "and, God, you know what she's like, hon, but she's not stupid. Let her see where she comes from."

"No," Eileen had said. "She couldn't even play in the backyard *there*, not with, well, you know. It's not safe. Not for my daughter. Not even at my mother's house."

So Andrew had not come. He had left her to do this alone.

Eileen had hired a special taxi to take her to Ship House upon the advice of one of her friends who still regularly travelled back to Cape Town. The regular taxis, she had been told, couldn't be trusted. Her driver wasn't white, but she supposed that was okay. She couldn't tell for sure. He was polite. He took her bag and made sure she settled comfortably into the backseat of the car. Ten minutes later she was driving past the shanty towns with their little houses made of plywood, corrugated metal and sheets of plastic, the lines of laundry—bright blue, salmon, violet and indigo, God, the colours were bright! Unnatural!— fluttering in the sticky-hot breeze. The taxi made its way up the side of the mountain. All of a sudden, there it was: the hard ridge of the South African coastline laid out beneath her and Table Mountain looming above, thick and exposed as a varicose vein.

It was home.

It was home, it was home, but it didn't feel like home any longer.

And when Eileen embraced her mother, her mother sank into her arms the way a cellar sinks into the muck: in three awful, slow stages.

"Oh, mother," Eileen said.

"You've come back."

"It's time for us to be done with this place," she said. "You can't be trundling around with no one else here. You'll slip and break something, and then what will we do?"

"Nothing, dear," said Eileen's mother. "I'll just lie there until they find me."

"No one will find you, mum." Eileen disentangled herself carefully.

"Shush up, daughter mine," her mother whispered. Her teeth clamped down. *Snap.* And then she smiled again. "There's someone who will find me here."

"There isn't, mum." (An old fight.) "That's why I'm here."

The wind plucked at her mother's hair like harp strings, setting them loose to float in the air. It was January—but even the wind blew hot here on the other side of the world. Eileen had forgotten the tang of the salt air; milkwood, gladiolas, and freesias; underneath it all, the bitter-sick smell of the Caltex Refinery. The way the heat hung in the air like a second kind of light. Suddenly she was five years old again—back when things had been safe, back when she had learned the stories of the grandfathers: fairy tales, the kind in which stepsisters were left mutilated and forced to dance in hot iron shoes, the stories of *Hansie* and his sister *Grietjie* lost in the woods, the story of *Raponsie* and her long ladder of hair, and *Repelsteeltjie*, Granny Tamsyn's favourite. The stories had scared Eileen viciously until she begged her mother to sit next to her bed through the night. There were other stories too, how the elephant got its trunk and the sing-song of Old Man Kangaroo, but it was the old tales she remembered best, the ones she had heard at the feet of her uncles, her great-aunts and her grandmother.

"They've all gone now," Eileen told her mother, "Jacob and Rees, the great-aunts Johanna and Eirlys—Granny Tamsyn was the last but that was three, four years ago."

"That's not right," her mother said. "I just saw Tamsyn last week. She brought me *koeksisters* from Bree Street. There might've still been some for you if you'd come sooner, but as it is I've gobbled them all up."

"No, mum."

"Maybe I'm thinking of someone else."

"Let's go inside, mum," she said. "Why don't you take me inside?"

The house was called Ship House.

It had been named, Granny Tamsyn had told her when she was little, by one of the grandfathers who sometime during the war—"Which war?" she had asked; "Shush up, dearie," she had been told—had been stranded on a massive boat in the middle of the ocean. This house—this rambling half-mansion of a thing with its twelve arches and three terracotta roofs, its silences and croaks, its rooms so lush in daylight and so deeply oppressive after sundown when the heat of the day sunk into its bones—this house, Granny Tamsyn said, had reminded him of his time adrift. Eileen had never questioned it as a child. The house sat so perfect and still in the shadow of the mountain. Like it could wait forever. Like it needed no one—the waiting was enough.

Now Ship House felt strange on the inside to Eileen: too small and too large at the same time. The boards her mother passed over silently creaked under Eileen's feet. "Go home," they groaned. "Leave us to our ways," they whispered. "Traitor," they hissed.

Eileen wrestled her suitcase into the vestibule, grunting and sweating in the flush midday heat. Dust motes skittered through the light, settling on the gleaming backside of a giant ebony elephant. Her feet tangled on a coarse pink-and-blue rug. What would she do with all these things when she packed them up? They wouldn't fit in the apartment back home. She ought to call Andrew, she knew, but—

"Come along, my button," her mother said, "don't linger."

—would there even be a working phone? Had anyone bothered to keep up the payments to the electrical company?

"I thought you arranged for a cleaning service. Dr. Jans said you had."

"I did," her mother said. She paused to straighten an old photograph of the cable car that ran up the side of the mountain. "But I cancelled it. I don't like them touching my things. Not *them*. Fingerprints everywhere.

Strangers running through the house!"

Eileen didn't say anything to that, but she felt a pang sharp as a needle.

She abandoned her bag in the hall, and followed her mother over the step into the sitting room where the family used to gather in the old days. "Quiet," whispered the boards. "Let her sleep, let her rest," they muttered.

Let her rest. Yes, she thought. Let her rest in the ground. In a little grave behind the house.

She shook her head, tried to unthink the thought but it sat like a stone in her mind. She did not want to think that way about her mother. But it was hard, sometimes. Oh, but it was hard. Andrew should have come, he should have, he should have, he should have, he *should* have—

The sitting room was as Eileen remembered it. There was Granny Tamsyn's seat, and the matching set for the great-aunts Eirlys and Johanna, and for the uncles Jacob and Rees. Three generations had gathered here. The years had accumulated in the house: they were a weight, a presence, substance, form, smell. They clung to her fingertips like dust when she touched the ancient upholstery. Eileen helped her mother into her proper place. Her brittle knees clicked together under the white and red patterned dress like marbles or fine-boned china.

"They steal things, you know."

"They don't, mum."

"They do. They come up from the ravine. They come at night, while I'm sleeping. And they take things."

"Oh, mother," said Eileen. "Oh, mother. It's okay. Please don't fret. I'm here now."

And then her mother's hand was in her hand, and they were clinging to each other. Adrift. The only two passengers left on the ship.

"No," her mother said. "Oh, no, no. They have such little feet. Such little feet pattering across the floor, coming to take my things away."

"No," Eileen whispered. "I'm here."

"Oh, lovey," she said. "They do not care. One is as good as two. One has always been as good as two when they come for you."

The men came in the night. That's what her mother had said.

Oh, mother, she thought.

Eileen was in her room now. Her very own room. She hadn't called Andrew to let him know she'd got in as she'd promised, but, well, it would be late at home wouldn't it? Or perhaps it would be early. Time flowed differently here, and she hadn't caught the rhythm of the new hours yet. And what would Andrew say anyway? "She's old, Eileen," he would say. "Of course, she's like that. It's a shame, darling, but it happens."

And Eileen was tired. She was very tired. And the room had beckoned to her. Her own little room. Her own sweet place, tucked away on the first floor. The same green walls, the same paisley curtains she remembered. The same pale orange shaft of light when the sun began its slow descent below the crest of Lion's Peak. What a sad strange place it was, this room of hers. It looked nothing like Emma's room back home, even though she had been much the same age, close anyway.

There were two twin beds, identical in size and shape and dressing, both with the same twisted iron headboards and the same loosely coiled springs. Beds for boys, really. Not for a little girl. Granny Tamsyn had said they belonged to her mother's younger brothers—Jacob and Rees— when they had been little. The bed on the right was hers. She had never slept in the bed on the left.

There were old school notebooks on the shelves filled with her childhood books: an ornate collection of the tales of the Grimm Brothers done up with gold trim, alongside a dog-eared Afrikaans textbook, biology lessons and history notes: the dates of the first and second Boer Wars, the Krueger telegram, Mandela's imprisonment.

Ja, she thought, and *goeie naand*. Good evening.

All of it such a long time ago.

The sheets she had claimed from the closet were stale and thin, but comforting nonetheless. By habit she had made both beds. She had always done that—kept the other bed made. For a sister, maybe. She had thought Emma might stay in the room if she ever came over to see the house. They could have shared it together. For a little while, anyway.

There were no sounds from outside. Silence. She could almost imagine the lonely expanse of the ocean all around her as the house bobbed up and down. Ship House.

Sleep grabbed at her. Twisted. She was caught in its net even though the sun still hung low in the sky, lighting up the black bulk of Table Mountain and, northward, the bare edges of Lion's Head.

She was asleep, she was asleep.

And then she was not asleep anymore because the men had come.

This is what the men said to Eileen, ugly as fear, monstrous looming things that they were: "Do you remember my name?"

And this is what Eileen said to the men: "No, of course not, who are you?"

And the men grinned their horrible, split-faced grins, and their sharp, hooked nails twisted into her skin.

❊

When Eileen woke it was to the sharp tang of vinegar in the air.

The smell made her think of the harbour. Getting thick bundles of fried fish wrapped in newspaper with Jacob and Rees. So hot, but then the way her teeth would break through the batter to find the cod so sweet on the inside. They used to sit on the docks together and watch jellyfish floating like little Coke bottles beneath their sandals. Rees had found them for her in Kramp's *Synopsis of the Medusae of the World*—"Just a little sting," he had warned her, "like a pinprick or a tack. Like your first kiss, over with quickly, *ja*? But then you are dead!"

Eileen felt dislocated. Lost in the memory. But then she heard her mother singing.

"*Bobbejaan* climbs the mountain," she heard, "so quickly and so lightly—"

It was an old South African war song her mother had sung to her as a child. Like so many things from her childhood, its meaning had twisted over time and taken on darker shades: the Voortrekker, the endless feuds and fighting. At the heart of it was *bobbejaan* climbing the mountain, ceaseless and relentless.

Eileen swung her legs out over the side of the narrow bed. The bed on the left—Jacob's, or had it been Rees's?—was untouched.

"Mum?" she called out. She didn't know what time it was, but there was hot, buttery-yellow sunlight streaming through the windows. The room was picking up heat like an oven. She'd lost half the day already.

"Eileen," she heard through the walls. "Be a darling, will you? Give your mother a hand."

She found her mother in the elegant powder-blue bathroom off the second hallway, bent like a willow over a porcelain sink. She had stripped off her shirt, and her hair hung wet and dripping into the basin. Her body was so thin, the skin translucent as onion paper. Eileen could count the fluted bones of her shoulder blades.

Her mother turned at Eileen's shadow in the doorway, and it was like watching the gnawed gears of a clock attempting to spin.

"You remember *bobbejaan*, darling?"

Eileen said nothing for a moment, struck by the sight of her. And then:

"*Ja, nee,*" she muttered. "The baboon climbs the mountain to torment the poor farmers. It's not a very nice song, mum."

"Most childhood songs aren't," she clucked. "But they do their job. Do you mind pouring for me? It's such a chore with my arthritis."

Eileen took the silver jug her mother had left out on the vanity counter, and breathed in the vinegar sweetness of it. She had washed her hair that way every morning that Eileen had lived in the house. It was a kind of ritual.

Eileen poured the water over the mother's downturned scalp and smoothed the soap out gently. She fetched a towel, patted away the dampness. She flinched, for a moment, as her fingers pressed against the hard shape of her skull.

"Mum," she said, her tongue slow in her mouth. "You know why I'm here, right? You know that Dr. Jans called me about the fall?"

"Of course, darling," she said. "But it was such a little thing."

"It wasn't, mum. Dr. Jans said you could have died if no one found you. You can't live here on your own."

Her mother took up a silver-backed brush with fine white bristles and began to run it through her hair. It whispered like a scythe as it fell from crown to waist, over and over again.

"*Ja,*" she muttered. "Whatever you say, daughter mine."

"Please, mum."

"Stupid child," she muttered.

"What?"

Her mother's mouth twisted into an ugly scowl.

"You just want my things!" her mother shrieked. "You want my blessings! My gifts! Just take them, you ingrate! Take what you like. They don't mean anything. Here, take this!" Her mother flung the hard-handled brush with bruising speed. It bounced off Eileen's flinching shoulder with an audible *crack*, and spun into the jug of water, which crashed again the dark blue tiles.

"No, mum!" Eileen cried out, rubbing viciously at the spot the brush had struck her. She felt a wave of anger. She wanted to slap her mother. She wanted to . . .

Her mother was staring at her with wide eyes. She was trembling.

"You don't want it? You must take it, Eileen. You must. It's yours," she said, and now her voice was quavering. She stared at the jug on the tile. "They're yours, darling. You must take them with you. Please, darling, won't you just—?"

"Please, mum," Eileen begged. Her throat was raw. "I don't want them."

"You must," she said, "You must take them."

Dr. Jans had *warned* her it would be like this. When she was frightened.

When she was unsure. Her mood could spin so quickly—but it still shocked Eileen to see that stranger where her mother had been.

"Oh, my darling. I should have protected you. I should have let you go more easily. We fought, didn't we?"

Eileen turned away.

"Yeah, mum. We fought. But it's okay. Children fight with their parents. That's what they do."

"I should have set the gas, shouldn't I? Just let it leak out, *ja*? No one would have known. I should have done that for you."

Eileen wrapped her arms around her mother. "Don't say such things. Please, mum, don't ever say such things." Shivered.

But the thought stayed in her mind: the house quiet and still, surrounded by the dark expanse of ocean. And not a passenger on board. Beautiful. Still as a tomb. The quiet *hiss* of the gas . . .

"It would have been better for you."

Eileen took her mother in her arms and held her, with the vinegar smell wrapped tight around the two of them, and her mother making little sobbing noises. Eileen felt the bones clicking against one another and she tried not to make a noise, to keep her lips perfectly sealed against her own tears.

Because her mother was right. It would have been easier. And she hated herself for thinking it, hated herself for knowing that it was true because, at the same time, it wasn't. It wasn't at all. It was awful to think of, her mother with her blue lips lying still on the bed.

She felt her mother stiffening in her arms.

"Brush my hair, would you, girl? Your father's taking me out later. Jacob and Rees will mind you for the evening, so be sure you don't give them any grief."

"Okay," Eileen pleaded in a soothing voice, "it's okay."

She began to run the brush in gentle strokes through her mother's thinning hair. It seemed to calm her.

"Sing to me, would you?"

"Sure, mum. Of course." The brush came down in slow, even strokes and the hair parted around it easily.

"*Bobbejaan* climbs the mountain," Eileen sang, "so quickly and so lightly."

The men were *hairy*: thick-bristled as boars. Their arms hung down around their knees, bald only at the pebbled skin of their elbows.

"Why did you forget our name?" the men said to Eileen.

Eileen didn't want to answer.

They frightened her badly, made her skin pucker and crawl with fear as they touched her wrist, her hair, her neck. When they turned the wrong way, Eileen could see that they were not men at all, they were merely two halves of the same man—an ugly, dwarfish brute—a man split in half with his insides scooped out like a melon.

"I've never met you in my life," she said.

"Oh, but you have," said the first half, and smiled half a wide, white-toothed smile.

"And we have chucked your chin, and counted your fingers, and called you best beloved," said the second half.

"If you did," Eileen said, "it was a very long time ago."

"We know," said the men, "we know all this. It is you who have forgotten."

"No," said Eileen.

"Yes," said the men. "You have been gone so long. But blood runs true, does it not?"

"Blood run true," the other whispered.

"Two by two by two."

"Such a pretty girl. Such a pretty, pretty girl come home to us."

Emma had been such a pretty child.

Eileen loved her daughter the way she always imagined mothers were supposed to love their daughters. Cleanly. Effortlessly. Her love was transparent as a wineglass. Habitual as putting on a sweater.

When Emma was five she used to stand on the bed, a wobbly little girl, and run her hands through Eileen's hair, her fingers never quite tangling in it but just gently touching her scalp, the back of her neck. Sometimes she would lay the sweetest little kiss on Eileen's cheek and when Eileen turned, Emma would be smiling like an imp.

"I've got the apple in your cheek," she would say. "I've stolen the apple of your eye."

Emma didn't know what the words meant, but she'd tear off, giggling, out of the bedroom until Andrew caught her up in his arms.

"Give them to papa?" he would say.

"Of course, papa. I stole the apples just for you!"

When Eileen had been pregnant with Emma, Andrew would sometimes run his fingers over the giant balloon of her stomach when they were lying in bed together, the house quiet as it would never be quiet again afterward.

"Look at you," Andrew would say. "Grown so big. What have you got inside you?"

"An apple?"

"A cherry pip?"

"A girl?"

"A boy?"

"Could it be twins?"

"God, I hope not."

But there had always been twins in the family, her mother told her. Jacob and Rees. Johanna and Eirlys. Always twins, except for the first generation, the first apple of the womb. Granny Tamsyn. Her mother. And her, of course. But there were two beds side by side in her room in Ship House. The one hers, and the other empty as an overturned basket.

Eileen and Andrew didn't talk about the other baby.

They didn't talk about the second set of kicks or the second heartbeat. And they didn't talk about how when Eileen pushed and pushed, out had come two little bodies: one pink and thriving as a piglet and the other purple as a blood clot. They didn't talk about that other little baby because Emma was such a good girl. A pretty girl.

"She just wasn't ready," Andrew had said to her, "She wasn't even really there—not a little thing like that. She didn't die, hon, she wasn't even there yet. She was just a piece of a little girl. So hush up, my love."

Eileen hadn't cried for that other baby.

She hadn't let herself cry.

She had clung to the little piglet child, and she had kept it close to her until it resolved itself into a small person, a scampering, singing toddler and then a coltish and wise youngster too old to suck her thumb, and, oh, time had marched on and brought her this strange teenager with a fringe of black hair cut below the eyes.

"Bring her to Ship House," Andrew had told her. "Don't deny her a grandmother. She has a right to see her."

But Eileen had said, "No, she's too little. Maybe when she's older. She'll go when she wants to go."

She had said that every year.

And every year Emma had grown older and older until she could join in the chorus too: "I don't want to," she said. "I've got friends here. They promised they'd take me skiing during the break, before the snow melts. Have you seen the hills, mum? They're beautiful. They're just waiting for me. Can I go, please, skiing?" And who could deny her snow angels and skiing? Emma was a child of a different place, with her cheeks that went gloriously red when the frost kissed them.

And Eileen felt *happy* when Andrew relented. She felt giddy with relief.

She didn't push.

Perhaps Emma would go to Ship House one day. But not now. Not now. Not until she was older.

Some things just slip away from you.

❧

The men slipped around her, moving the way that shadows move.

They stood, each on their own one leg, on either side of Eileen, their good sides toward her. But still she knew. Still she knew on the other side of each of those faces was no face at all. Their cheeks were cored apples with nothing inside them but white pulpy flesh.

"Come, my girl," they said. "Let us show you the way." Their voices were deep and high at the same time, forced through their strange half-bodies.

Eileen went with them. She couldn't resist. Their strength was the strength of mountains. As they went they made the same strange dragging sound as wounded animals, each with their own single, bent knee.

"*Bobbejaan* climbs the mountain—" she giggled madly, unable to stop herself, but the first half shushed her with a dirty, stunted finger.

"We do not like that song—" he said through half of a mouth.

"—we do not like it at all," the other one said.

Their bodies were warm. She could feel the air heating around them as if their skin was molten copper. There was a rank animal smell to them. They smelled of tunnels. They smelled of her mother's hair as she brushed it.

And they were *touching* her. They were gripping her elbows, and she had to walk quickly and carefully between them. She was so afraid to touch any part of them. She hated the feeling of their oily, dirty fingers touching her skin. Their sharp, hooked nails.

"Where are you taking me?" Eileen asked them.

And the two men looked at each other, each with one good eye as blue as a robin's egg.

"To see what is what—"

"—and which way the wind is blowing."

"Are you going to hurt me?" She wanted to ask, but the question lodged at the back of her throat like a tongue depressor held too firm.

She did not like the way they moved, even with their good sides toward her.

She closed her eyes and pretended it was Rees and Jacob, one on either side of her. They were taking her to the harbour to watch the bottle-jellyfish bobbing beneath their sandals. She could smell the vinegar of the vendors. It smelled of the ocean. It smelled like the crisp and sweet taste of the fish. It made her mouth water.

"Oh, my lovely," said the first one, "my little button. My dearie. You don't know the story of this house, do you?"

"She's let it drift out of her head—"

"—along with us."

"She doesn't remember the grandfathers."

"Tell me," Eileen cried out, for she was frightened of the little jig the men had to dance to stay with her. They capered, each with their one boot moving, their one ankle twisting down the hallway, and her dragged between them like a caught trout—down and down and *down*.

Eileen and her mother started in the downstairs: in Auntie Johanna's room where the dust was thick and choking.

Eileen's mother seemed all right. Her eyes were clear. She chattered easily as they went through the closets, pulling out gorgeous old dresses with big boxy shoulder pads in colours that had gone out of fashion years ago. There were hat boxes and shoe boxes, silk gloves with beading, and a portrait of a handsome man with a dark, pencil moustache—a darker, sharper Errol Flynn—hidden at the bottom of the dresser.

"She was a looker, your great-auntie was! A real *choty goty*," her mother remarked as they stared at the old albumen browns and beiges. "You've got something of her features, I think, sometimes I see her when I look at you. I think, oh, that's Johanna. She's come back!"

Eileen didn't remember Johanna very well. Just the vague floating image of tight, golden pin curls and a strange, low-lidded despair in her eyes. But Eileen didn't look a thing like that. Eileen had her mother's sharp cheekbones, narrow hips, and tiny plum-shaped breasts.

"Did I tell you the story of how I met your father?" her mother asked. "It was Johanna who did it for me, *ja*? The wild one. We were travelling together by boat to England, a big old steamer and, the noise, my God, the noise! She was older than I, your great-auntie Johanna was, but you know that, don't you? She was supposed to be minding me, although I'll never know why Granny Tamsyn chose her for a chaperone! She was just a few years younger than your grandmother but she was always a dotty old thing. . . ."

"I know the story."

"You know the story?"

Eileen sunk her hands deep into a closet filled with pretty silk and gauze dresses. Beaded fringes tickled like spider webs, and for a moment she closed her eyes and it was like being a child at a party, seeing the world through stockinged knees, hiding under tables and stealing sweets off silver platters.

"Tell it to me anyway, mum."

Her mother drew in a breath, blinked. "He was handsome. *Ja?*" she ventured as she stared at the photograph of the handsome man. "This isn't him, of course. This was Johanna's husband. The one who left her. The one who *divorced* her."

"What about Dad?"

"Handsome," she said firmly, "but in a way I had never seen before, not like Rees and Jacob were handsome. They were golden things, like angels, *ja?* But your father, no, he was crosswise handsome. We met him on the steamer heading out from the Cape of Good Hope. He'd just finished his degree and wanted to see the world a bit before he settled down. Got a job working for one of the mining companies. We all did it back then. The European Tour, Granny Tamsyn called it."

"But you ran away."

"I did!" she laughed. "There was your father, this handsome, young engineer. And you know what Johanna said to me? She said, 'Away with you, girl, and—'"

"'—don't come home until you're pregnant!'"

"She was a wild one," Eileen's mother fingered the photograph delicately. Someone had loved her once, Eileen thought. She tried to imagine her mother young and gorgeous, pretty as a new dress. "I don't know why Tamsyn chose her to watch over me. Barely five minutes, and she sent me flying."

"But she told Granny Tamsyn."

"Oh, she did. Eventually. And Tamsyn sent the boys after me, but by the time they caught up with us in Paris I was round as a pumpkin with a ring on my finger, living in a little apartment on Rue Puget in Montmartre. But Jacob and Rees, well, when they came they talked straight to your father. They insisted that you be born in Ship House. Like all the others come before you."

"Well."

"I was such a happy old thing there, in that little apartment. Your father used to bring me *pain au chocolat* every morning! Ha! Imagine that. But my mother was a difficult woman to deny, and I wanted you, my dearie, to come into the world in your own proper place."

Eileen looked down at the photograph tucked away in the cardboard boxes they had filled. The room was almost finished. But there would be other rooms. There were so many rooms. A whole hidden warren of them. She imagined if she went into the cellars there would be a tunnel—a long tunnel, a twisting tunnel—and if she followed it far enough she would find her way back home. Back to the other side of the globe.

"You'll do the same," her mother said. "When it's your turn. You shall bring them back to Ship House just as you should, won't you, darling? Won't you, lovey? The twins? My little granddaughters?"

Eileen turned, touched a finger to her mother's wrist. Her skin was powdery and loose, Eileen could feel the thick worm of a vein. The wrist. Her fingers touching against it, and the soft pulse of the flesh, almost dead, soft and clinging. Her mother was slipping away. Her mother was bleeding out one day at a time, like a cloth running out its dye in a damp, sticky puddle.

She suddenly had the urge to run. Ship House was a crypt. A grave. A coffin.

Her mother was speaking. "Lovey," she said. "Johanna loved you, do you remember? You would watch her in the mirror some evenings. Just there, on the bed, as she brushed out her hair. How we all wanted to have hair like hers, how it curled in her hand like a little flower. She was so beautiful but then something happened to her . . . I don't know what happened to her. . . ."

One part of Eileen was in the tunnels.

". . . it was bad though, wasn't it? The thing that happened?"

One part of her was walking away from all this. Stumbling through the darkness. Smelling the whisper of sulphur and dirt and copper and vinegar.

"Eileen?" her mother asked, and she twisted her arm, twisted it out of Eileen's grasp. "What happened to Johanna? You're hurting me, Eileen. Please let go."

One part of her was almost free of this place.

But that was only one part of her.

She felt her fingers go slack and nerveless, and her mother touched dizzily at the place.

"Ellie?"

She would never be free of this place. Eileen could feel it taking hold of her. The old country. The dark country. With its blood spilled in the streets, its wars and its corruption, its buried bodies and its hidden resentments turned from whispers to violence. She remembered what it had been like to live here. What it had been like to go to school.

Every time Andrew asked her, she said it had been normal. She had gone to school the way that anyone had gone to school. She had read magazines made sticky by the heat of her fingers—could still find one or two of them if she looked on the shelves in the bedroom—had listened to Radio 5, not Pink Floyd, not The Police as Andrew had, because they weren't allowed then, they were banned by the government, but there had been other bands, other music. . . .

Her life had been normal, she told herself. Her life had been the life of any young girl.

But it hadn't been normal, had it?

When she was old enough she had left. She had *run*. There had been no chaperone. There had been no listless, beautiful Johanna with her low-lidded eyes telling her to make a baby and then bringing her home again when it was done. No. She had found her own crosswise husband, her own handsome man. And she had followed him to a place where the sun didn't breathe down on the back of your neck, and all the while your mother insisting you wear a woolen vest—"Wear a vest to school, Eileen, you mustn't catch cold! Please wear it. Wear it for me?"—even though it scratched in the heat, it made you feel sick inside, like you were wrapped up in all that wool, all that thick, clotted, scratching hair. . . .

She had gone away to a place that was cold and distant and shockingly free. She had been weak for leaving, she knew that. But she *was* weak.

"I'm tired," Eileen's mother said. Her hands twitched.

Eileen rested the photo of the rake with his pencil-thin moustache on top of one of Johanna's old romance volumes where it skittered a bare half-inch across the fraying boards, caught in one of the unpredictable drafts that breathed through the hallways and set the windows rattling.

"I'm tired," Eileen's mother said. Her body had begun to shake like a leaf. "Oh, daughter mine, I'm so tired. It scares me sometimes, how tired I am. I'm always afraid here. Why did you leave, Ellie? Was it because of me? Did I make you leave?"

"No, mum," Eileen said. Thought she said.

And then her mother was speaking again: "They come sometimes. In the night. "

"I know, mother," Eileen said, one part of her cold and present. "This was too much, too fast. Come with me, mum. I'll make us a cup of tea."

And one part of Eileen watched her take her mother by the hand, a cold hand, a hand that quivered like a fine-boned pigeon. One part of her stroking, calming, soothing to rest that frightened thing she held, and all the while the other part she left, the other part, she did not touch, the other part she let free to roam in the darkness like a thread winding its way home.

"Come with us," the men said, winding their fingers through her hair. Pulling her along.

"Where?" Eileen cried. "Where are you taking me?"

"To the room," the men said, "in the centre of Ship House."

There was no room at the centre of Ship House.

Ship House had no centre, that's what Granny Tamsyn had always said. One of the grandfathers had built the house. He had been an architect. He had built banks and he had built churches when there were churches still to be built—one at Camps Bay and one at Newlands and a hotel at Bishopscourt with a great sweeping staircase and a whitewashed façade. But then had come the house, and the house was no easy thing, no, not a house such as Ship House would be.

It was a strange house. It was a special house. It was a house like a new cherry—without a stone at the centre of it. That's what the grandfathers had told Tamsyn.

Eileen did not remember the grandfathers.

They had been dead and buried by the time she had come along, but the others would speak of them. And when they did, there would be a little twist in their voices, a little hitch in their breathing, that might have been sadness and grief or it might have been something else.

When they died, the house had gone to Jacob and Rees as the only boys left. And when *they* were gone, it had passed to Granny Tamsyn, the oldest of them all.

Eileen's mother was sleeping now in her own little room. It was not the room she had shared with Eileen's father—that was the bridal room on the second floor. Eileen had never been in that room either. It had a special key in the shape of a twisted heart, and though the key hung with all the other keys on the rack in the cellar, Eileen had never touched it.

There were things about a house like Ship House. There were rules to it, and the rules were like the rules to a happy marriage. There were doors that were not meant to be listened at. There were doors that stayed locked. You could learn to move around these places, to never think on them. You could blind yourself in one eye and train the other to see only what it needed to see. You could cut off your right foot and train your left to walk only in the places it was welcome.

Eileen ought to be asleep.

Somewhere in the house her mother was sleeping, her body curled up like a kitten's. The house wanted her to sleep. The house breathed quietly and cautiously, and Eileen tried to let her own breath follow it. In and out. Silent in the lung. Silent over the lips.

But she wasn't tired. She paced the hallways, followed them to the backyard.

"It's not safe," she had told Andrew. "Emma couldn't play in the back."

"Nonsense," he had said. "It's just a place, darling. The world is full of dangers everywhere. She'll have to learn some time."

Jacob and Rees were buried in the backyard. They had lived and died at Ship House, the two golden boys, the two perfect ones. Rees had had hair the colour of her mother's, Eileen remembered. Her two younger brothers. Identical. The two mirror halves of one another.

Of all of them, she had loved those two the most. Rees had built her a swing in the back and he would push her on it.

"Be careful," her mother would tell her whenever she went out back, sometimes planting a delicate kiss on her cheek, sometimes smoothing out the tangles of her hair.

"Don't let go," Rees would tell her then. "Or you'll sail all the way to the top of Table Mountain."

"Faster than the cable car?" Eileen would scream as the air whizzed out of her lungs, bare knees kicking wildly at the dirt as she swung up and then down again.

"Faster than anything in the world!"

"I shan't come back, you know," Eileen had told him afterwards, gasping and giggling. Her little belly puffed against the linen of her dress as he straightened the hem, kneeling, in front of her.

Rees had beautiful hands. His fingers were long, and the palms were callused but he kept his nails clean and square. He held her ever so lightly. "Of course, you shall. You're the little girl of the house, and you must come back. We should all be quite lonely without you, my button girl, my little dove. Your mother most of all, and then me after that!"

"No, you shan't! You have Jacob!"

"Your uncle Jacob will be married soon and will bring his wife home—"

"Will they stay in mama's and papa's room?" she asked.

"Of course, they shall. And they'll be very happy I imagine, the two of them, the little scamps." And he chucked her underneath the chin. "And then who shall play with me in the garden? I shall be all alone in the world."

"Is Jacob's wife pretty?" Eileen had asked him. These things were important. She knew that. Granny Tamsyn had told her how things like that mattered, that making a pairing wasn't easy and that if it was done badly, well, the family couldn't afford another scandal such as Johanna had made.

"Not as pretty as a silly little button like you."

"Good," said Eileen. "I think I ought to be prettier than her, don't you?"

"I think so too. Let Jacob have his less pretty young wife. I shall keep you, won't I? I shall keep you safe."

But Eileen had never seen Jacob's pretty, young wife.

She must not have been beautiful enough.

She must not have been strong enough.

Or perhaps someone had told her to fly just as her own mother had been told. Perhaps someone had told her to come back pregnant. The first apple of her womb ripened and ready.

Rees and Jacob had died later that year. Eileen remembered. It was when the winter rains came and the air whistled through the walls of the house like a child calling a dog. A congenital heart defect, Tamsyn had told her. It struck them down together, and they had been laid side-by-side in identical, slender coffins and buried behind the house.

The swing was still there. It hung lazily from the branch of a giant walnut tree.

Eileen could see it from the window in the sitting room, and she went out into the garden—a weedy, tangled mess now—but she found she liked it anyway. There were a series of angular stone steps set into the dirt. Eileen stepped across them. She knew she shouldn't be out here. It wasn't safe. Not for Emma. Not for her.

But *this* had been her home once and, as she rested back into the swing, too small now and creaking gently with her weight, it felt like home again.

From the swing she could make out the headstones. She had worn black the year they had died. Nothing but black. And Tamsyn had wanted to cut her hair, just chop it all off, to make a hair wreath for the boys. Eileen had cried when she came in with the scissors. She had loved Jacob. She had loved him with all her heart, but still, she hated the way the scissors had gleamed, and the way that Tamsyn held them, her knuckles bulging around the curved grips.

"Don't make her do it, Tamsyn," she remembered her mother say. "She's too young. She's too young for this."

"Shush up," Tamsyn had snapped. "She's old enough. As you were before her."

"Look at her," her mother had pleaded. "She's just a little thing."

And Tamsyn had taken the scissors. Had grabbed a fistful of Eileen's hair. "Darling," Tamsyn had said. "Little button. Please. Stop struggling."

"No! Mama, no!" Eileen pleaded. "I don't want to! Please, don't let her cut my hair!"

"Didn't you love Jacob? Didn't you love Rees?" Tamsyn asked, a dangerous glint in her eyes. "You told me you loved them. How else will you honour them?"

"Mama, I loved them. Tell Grannie Tamsyn I loved them!"

"She's so tiny! No, *moeder*, no!"

But Tamsyn was pulling her hair tight. Eileen could see the way it twisted around her fist. Her beautiful hair. She was weeping furiously now. "Mama!"

"She must honour them."

Eileen shrieked as she felt the hair ripping from her scalp.

"No, *moeder*, not her!"

As quick as a snake, Tamsyn had released her clutch. Her hand whipped around and caught her mother on the flat across the cheek. Eileen was sobbing now. She touched her scalp and her hand came away sticky, fingers dappled in red.

"I love them," she whispered. "I promise I love them. I promise, I promise."

"You stupid, disrespectful child!"

Her mother stared at Tamsyn, dumbstruck, and now Tamsyn was pulling Eileen close, fat tears running down her cheeks as she twisted and struggled. But Tamsyn's grip was unyielding. It bruised her tiny arm. And then Tamsyn was forcing the scissors into Eileen's hand, her blood smearing the handle, splattering onto the floor.

"Let down your hair," Tamsyn demanded.

"No," her mother had pleaded.

"Someone must honour Jacob and Rees. Branch and bough, we are bound. Two by two. You have taken their blessings. You have taken their gifts, have you not? And you have given them a gift of your own, have you not?"

Eileen remembered the look on her mother's face as she stared at Tamsyn. Eyes wide with fear. Lips trembling.

"Have you not?" Tamsyn demanded.

Eyes wide. Resistant. Then slowly shuttering the way a window shutters. "I have," her mother said at last.

"And so will your daughter. Until then you must honour them."

And slowly. Slowly. She pulled the black ribbon that bound her hair. Let it fall about her shoulders in a thick, sweet-smelling blanket. Glossy and rich.

"Good," Tamsyn said. She was close behind her. Her fingers wrapped around Eileen's fingers. Smashed her knuckles into the heavy handles of the scissors. "Now, child."

"Go on," her mother repeated in the barest, dull whisper.

Eileen didn't want to but her hands were so small and she could not resist. She bunched the hair in a tight fist and she began to cut. It fell away in pieces. First it had looked as if someone had made a doorway into the back of her mother's head, as the rest of the hair fell around the place she had cut. But it wasn't enough. Eileen kept cutting. Snip, snip, snip she went until the hair lay around her like a heap of straw. Tamsyn gathered it up in her apron.

"You were always the weak one," Tamsyn had told her mother.

The weak one.

Tamsyn had been a formidable woman. Uncrossable. Untouchable. But Eileen had seen her weaken. Seen her back hunch, her hair whiten, her own skin grow so slack and loose as if the flesh was eaten from her bones. Eileen had watched it. Her mother had watched it. And when Tamsyn had died in a black coughing fit, the house had gone to her mother.

They were all dead now. Rees who had made the swing for her. Whom she had loved a little more than the others. And Jacob. Johanna, the wild one, and Eirlys who had never left, who had stayed to take care of Tamsyn as she got on in years.

Two by two, the rows went. Except for the first of each generation. The first apple of the womb.

Two by two, she had tended them under her mother's watchful gaze. Swept off the dust in summer and polished the granite to a smooth and silky shine after the winter rains. Thus, they had cared for the dead, and wound the hair wreath together, knotted it tight, and laid it to rest.

Two by two they had passed on with only her mother—the weak one—left to care for Ship House.

Staring at the sullen little graves, she came back to herself.

The knotted ropes of the swing pressed uncomfortably against Eileen's thighs. Her clothes felt hot and sticky even though evening had spread a dampness as thick as jam over everything. She never stayed up this late at home. She had forgotten the way the world became a different place when the lights went out, now that she ventured past midnight into the early hours of pre-dawn only once in a blue moon. Like a mouse stealing crumbs.

Tomorrow. Eileen could almost feel the one day shifting into the other, the boundaries between them noiseless and lost in the indigo hush: that killing-jar quiet.

Tomorrow, she would call Andrew and tell him the progress she had made. For now, all she wanted was the feel of the night air on her skin, and the silence of the shadows creeping, stretched out like tar and woven together. Her mother was tucked away in the safety of the house. Her mother was sleeping. Her mother's head was laid out gently on the pillow with a halo of vinegar-washed hair floating around her.

"Did I make you leave?" her mother had asked her.

"No," she had wanted to say. "It wasn't you."

It had been the grandfathers.

There *was* a room at the centre of Ship House—the grandfathers' room.

That was the way stories worked when you whispered them to your daughter at night, smoothing her forehead so she might sleep, kissing her cheek so she might know that she's loved. There were chinks in stories. There were holes. There were pieces you forgot and lies you told and little wrinkles you smoothed out to make it all turn out right in the end.

And through the dark tunnels that wove through the mountain, the men brought her to *that* room.

The door to the room was thick and heavy, made of dark planks of oak and trimmed in old, black iron.

There were no other doors like that in Ship House. No doors with locks as weighted as a fist.

The men, together, opened the door with the tiniest of keys, a dainty little thing, in the shape of a twisted heart.

"You came home too late," they told her.

"You have waited too long," they told her.

It was like watching marionettes dance, the way they jumped and hopped together—the two pieces of them almost, but not quite, fitting together. Eileen wanted to laugh. But then again, Eileen very much did not want to laugh. It was awful. It was so awful what they were doing.

They pushed her through the doorway. Just like that. She stumbled, and the skin came off her knees and palms easily the way it did when she was a child. She was not used to violence of any kind, not from Andrew, never from Andrew.

But from the men . . .

From the grandfathers . . .

She heard a click and a rattle of locking behind her. Then only silence in the black room at the centre of Ship House. A kind of dead, heavy silence. The silence like the beats between the blows of an old lady striking a hung carpet to rid it of dust.

The light was gone. None crept between the boards of the door. None snuck underneath.

But the air here smelled delicious and warm and sharp, and it reminded her of the smiling twins and their long, narrow coffins—or was it their long narrow beds? Perhaps she was back in her room. Perhaps she was asleep. Perhaps she would wake up any moment to the sound of her mother singing, "*Bobbejaan* climbs the mountain."

But there was something tickling her fingers, something smooth and soft and brittle as snakeskin. It was all around her. It was like a cloak. It was like a blanket. The suffocating heavy vest she wore as a child. It made Eileen think of her mother.

She walked into the room at the centre of Ship House.

She moved into blackness. There was no light here, there was just that tickling like a rash and the thick, thick smell of vinegar all around her. She reached out her hands and there was a thing like lace in them. It might have been her mother's bridal room with its key like a twisted heart, or it might have been her own bridal room, the one Andrew had rented in Niagara where they had gone for their honeymoon. He had carried her over the threshold even though that wasn't exactly how the tradition was supposed to work, and she had kissed him. She had loved him, with his strong hands and his crosswise handsome face. She had loved the way he delicately lifted the heavy white skirt of her wedding gown, the way he had unhooked the garters and pulled the stockings off slowly, with his teeth, so he could kiss the inside of her thighs.

That was the beautiful, glorious thing about Andrew; he could take her so easily, lightly, make her stretch and flex like a cat beneath him, he could plant himself inside her—and then it was over, and he was wholly himself once again. Separate. Content in separation. He never had that feeling Eileen did, that secret desire she had to climb inside of his skin and sew up that last sliver of daylight. He didn't know what it was like to wrap something up inside you and feel it pulsing into life, bit by bit, accreting in pulses, spreading outward in fierce kicks aimed at the ribcage or bladder. And then to see this thing tumbling out like spilled guts, and that dancing, twisting cord between you.

Eileen came out of somewhere, and she was still part of that very thing, just as Emma was part of her, just as Andrew would never be, because he couldn't be, because he was a stone. He was a whole universe to himself, while Eileen had spread herself out through an infinite number of Russian dolls. . . .

Eileen knew it was not her bridal suite either, but it *could* have been. It *could* have been because she was deep beneath the earth, and the door was locked behind her, and were not all rooms the same room in the darkness? Could this not have been any room she wished it to be? Was there not some secret space she could unlock to make it so?

Something touched her face. Something like cobwebs. She wiped at it and her fingers tangled and would not come away.

She knew the feel of it. Thick, sweet-smelling and glossy. It twined around her fingers. It slipped around her like silk, as she pressed forward into the room. Thick as fog, thicker still the more she pressed into it. Like a pillow. Like a smothering blanket. But she pressed anyway because behind her was only the door, and on the other side, the strange half-men with their insides scooped out like melons.

Eileen walked with her hands in front of her like a blind person, and she held her breath so tight inside her. She kept herself perfectly sealed up, there in the darkness, there in the mess of it, there in the centre of the Ship House, in a room that could have been any room, except it was not any room because this was the place she had kept locked all her life, this was what she had trained her eye not to see, her foot not to find.

And in that way she pressed through until, creeping like a slug, she came on the hard nubbin at the centre of it all. The stone at the centre of the cherry. And she let her fingers crawl across the whatever-it-was that had been swaddled so carefully in the fine, silky hair until the tips of her fingers hooked in and her thumb found the knobbles of vertebrae sticking out like badly set cornice stones.

There it was. There.

The thing she knew she had been sent in to find.

And Eileen knew that she had always been looking for this whatever-it-was. Always. Since the day that Andrew had taken it from her so the doctors could do with it whatever it was they did with the unripe children that popped out like spat seeds.

And so she gathered up the little bones of the whatever-it-was and carried them back to the door to the grandfathers.

It was evening, and the moon lit up the bones of the mountain in a thin line of silver. Eileen left the swing and returned to the house, opened the door, let the electric light fall on her like a blessing.

She went in, and as she went the floorboards rolled under her feet, but they had begun to feel comfortable, rolling, yes, the way an ocean rolls the decks of a ship, but her feet had become good little sailors and they knew their way about it. They walked ever so quietly past her mother's bedroom. Eileen didn't open the door to check on her. Eileen was glad for the quiet. Her mother talked so much, and sometimes it was so hard to find her way through those words, find her way back to her true mother, the mother she remembered. Eileen wondered if it was that way for her mother too. Always trying to find her way back. Always trying to rediscover that thing she had lost.

So she walked past her mother's room, the floorboards quiet beneath her, until she came to her own little room.

It had been Jacob's room, once, and Rees's too. Her mother's brothers. The two of them.

She wanted to open the door. But then, all at once, she didn't want to open the door. Was she tired? She wasn't really tired. And perhaps she ought to call Andrew. It had been some time since she had spoken to Andrew and she missed the sound of his voice. She missed Emma gazing up at her from underneath that black fringe of hair. She didn't understand her daughter—not the way she had when Emma had been younger, when Emma had run her little sausage-fingers through her hair and kissed her lightly on the cheek. Eileen had understood that little girl, but maybe that wasn't enough. Maybe she ought to have brought her to Ship House.

Maybe she ought to have taught her the song about *bobbejaan* climbing the mountain.

The baboon climbs the mountain to torment the poor farmers. . . .

Eileen's fingers rested on the doorknob. She almost pushed it open.

Then she remembered the beds. Jacob and Rees's beds. Long and narrow and so close together. And—

She didn't want to go into the room. She would call Andrew first.

Eileen went back into the sitting room. She picked up the receiver, and listened to the cool, crisp dial tone. So. The phone worked. Was she happy? Would it not have been so much better to hear the gnawing silence? To know that whatever else there was in this house, it was hers, and it was her alone.

She dialled.

"Hello?"

"Andrew," she said. And she realized her heart was pounding, but here was Andrew, and so it was all right. It was Andrew. It was just Andrew. Who else would it be?

"Eileen." His voice was quiet and rusty. A long way away. Distracted, but she was distracted too. There were footsteps. Inaudible, really. Noises that set your bones rattling, but left your tympanic membrane taut and still. "You got in safely then? You've settled in?"

"Yes. Yes, I'm here, Andrew. I'm in the house."

"God, it must be late for you. I've just been getting Emma up for school. Is everything all right? You should be sleeping, hon. You're tired. You must be very tired."

Was she tired?

"I'm not tired, Andrew."

"Yes, you are, hon. I can hear it in your voice. You sound very tired. Don't you want to sleep?"

She didn't want to sleep. Something would happen when she fell asleep. Something awful was going to happen when she fell asleep.

"Just go crawl into bed," Andrew said. His voice was soft. It was reassuring, and kind. She loved the sound of his voice.

"I don't want to go to bed, Andrew. I was outside. I was in the garden, and I thought—"

"Eileen, we talked about this. You said it was dangerous there, didn't you? Why are you going outside alone?"

"Can I speak to Emma?"

"Just go to bed. Don't you want to? You must want to. Just pretend that I'm next to you. Just pretend that I'm right beside you. In the bed. Next to you. Just pretend that my arms are around you, that I'm touching you, that I've crawled in beside you and you can feel the weight of me, you can feel my hands, my breath on your neck. That I'm winding my fingers through your hair. Just pretend that I'm with you and it will be okay."

"There's someone in the house, Andrew."

"It's just the sound of your mother breathing." Andrew said. "And old houses. Old houses always sound like there are more people in them than there should be. It's nothing. It's the wind."

"It's not the wind," Eileen said, and then she hung up the phone, trembling.

And trembling with their own fevered palsy, the grandfathers led Eileen out into the hallway.

The air felt plain and empty without the touch of silk against her cheeks now. It was like something had been taken out of the world. She felt like a fish gasping on dry land, and the breath rattled in and out of her chest, but the grandfathers didn't care. The grandfathers smiled half smiles, and Eileen could see their teeth set in their mouths like tiny, yellowed pearls.

"She's come back—" the first one said.

"—she's come back," said the second. "And what has she brought with her?"

"An apple?"

"A pumpkin?"

"A cherry pit?"

"No," said Eileen, "no."

But they were smiling, one to another. The look flashing back and forth from half-man to half-man like the beacons they lit on mountaintops to send messages.

Eileen held the little bundle of bones close to her, each of them delicate as filigree, a tiny skeleton hand clutched in her own. It was hers. It was hers. They would not have it. They *must* not have it. It was hers. Even if it had died it was hers. It was of her body, and she would not let them touch it.

"It is ours, granddaughter. It is ours already."

"It has always been ours."

"It's mine," she said. The skull tiny as a teacup, the delicate column of the spine running like an umbilical cord, bones marbled the white-yellow of old teeth or the fat trimmed from cheap cuts of steak. But polished. Gleaming. They were beautiful. They were beautiful and they were *hers*.

"I know your name," she whispered. "*Baabajan*," she said. "*Repelsteeltjie*."

"And we know yours, granddaughter," said the one, the grinning one, his face taken apart with a peeling knife, split straight down the centre. "We sowed your seed, we spun your hair, we have chucked your chin and counted your fingers for so many years, my sweet little bird."

"Names have no power when they are shared. Your name is our name. We command each other now, is that not so?"

"There is a bargain." The grandfathers grinned horribly. "There is a bond. We shall have the first of them. You must give it to us!"

The smiles began to curve downward, the edges of the lips moving in horrible mimicry. It was the same mouth. The same mouth pulling down into a scowl. The same eyes rolling like marbles, but black, God, they were black but they were blue as hers, they were hers too. . . .

And in their strange hobbling shuffle, they moved closer until she could smell the rancid stench of them, could feel the hairs bristling against her own soft skin. She clutched the bundle closer to her. A shudder of revulsion shivered her flesh and set her own hair standing on end.

"She is already gone, granddaughter."

"Let us have her."

"Let us take her."

"She must be given. You know that, dolly. You know it, my little dear."

"And do not think because you did not bring your daughter to Ship House that we could not take her just the same!"

And the men drew close to her. They caressed her skin. They plucked at her hair. And Eileen wanted to scream, a wild animal howl, but she could not master her breath for it.

"Why?" Eileen cried. "Why must you take from us?"

"Once there was a ship," said the first grandfather.

"Once there was a ship and it sailed and it sailed and it sailed alone in the ocean—"

"Once there was only one of us, but we tore ourselves in twain for the love of a woman," the one half said. "We were so *hungry* for her. And our hunger was the *best* part of us—"

"The only part of us—"

"And we ate our worst parts—"

"Oh yes," said the other half. "We ate the worse parts of ourselves as the worm eats the rotten apple."

"And we were still hungry—"

"—so *hungry.*"

"And we were adrift for so long, until we came here—"

"—here where our best parts had so much to offer. Gifts fell from our fingers. We granted such blessings—"

"—we wove such fineries—"

"—cloth-of-gold—"

"—diamond rings—"

"And all we wanted was one small thing."

"A small thing?" Eileen asked.

"The bargain was made, dearest. Lovey. Our darling best beloved."

Although she loved her husband, although she always listened to him in times of crisis, Eileen did not go back to her room.

She stood by the phone, cradling the receiver in her hand. Eventually, she put it down.

She followed the rolling curves of the floorboards.

"Stay with us," they whispered to her. "Never leave us."

The light was dim and faltering, but she knew the way. She could hear the sound of her mother breathing. Faint through the door, but present. Eileen leaned against the door. She pushed her ear close so she could hear without seeing. She didn't want to see her mother anymore. Not like this.

Sometimes she just wished it were over. That her mother could rest.

"Come home," she had said. "You must come home."

But it hadn't always been like that, had it?

"You mustn't leave me," her mother had begged her.

"Please," she had cried. "Don't leave me here. Don't leave me here. I know you must go, but please, my darling. Please, Ellie. Don't leave me here."

They wouldn't leave her be.

The grandfathers.

Eileen tried to back away from them but the hallway was narrow as a coffin, and she could feel their breath hot against her.

"My mother?" she asked.

"*Ja*, my pretty. She made the bargain once—"

"—she crumbled—"

"—she caved—"

"—she broke all to pieces like an old teacup when she let you go."

"And we *ate*, did we not? As we did the gift her mother made of her sister?"

"Oh yes, we *ate* and *ate* and *ate* all the best parts of her away."

Eileen hated them. She hated them so much. But it was like a door opening in her mind. Their hands touching her, familiar, cradling her now as she had been cradled as a child. She remembered her mother. The mother she had forgotten. The woman plump on *pain au chocolat* and the love of her handsome crosswise husband, the woman who lived and laughed in old photographs, as young as she was, as beautiful as she was. Once.

"And what shall we do with her now, granddaughter?"

"Shall we lock her in a tower?"

"Shall we marry her off?"

"Shall we give her one of our good eyes and teach her to riddle with the best of them?"

"No," Eileen said with a shudder. She thought of her mother in the darkness, all alone, endlessly washing her hair, stroking it, brushing it smooth with those long, curving strokes of hers. Her mother with the flesh scooped away, her body cut in two with all the best parts of her eaten away.

And Eileen thought of Andrew. The way he would stroke the smooth flesh of her breast. The way he would crawl in beside her, fit the length of his body against hers until she could feel the hard jut of his erection pressed against the base of her spine. Could feel the warmth of his breath against her neck and his strength as he pulled at her shoulder, gently at first, but then with an urgency.

"Let me give you a child," he had said.

"Please, no."

But then it wasn't Andrew's face she saw any longer, it was the face of the grandfathers, and it was their breath hot against her skin, and their fingers touching cupping stroking her shoulder blade. And it was Rees, her beloved uncle. It was Jacob, the less loved of the two of them, with his pretty, foreign wife. It was all the men. The men who loved without cost, who were not part of the bargain, who demanded so much of their women and then left them to pay such a terrible price.

. . . and wasn't it the grandfathers' child, already? Hadn't they taken it from her already?

She felt the body loosening away from her, felt herself giving it up the way her body had given up the child once before, letting it fall slackly from between her legs, purple as a bruise, and the blood pooling all around her.

"Give us the child," they said in that sly whisper of theirs—

"Let me take the child," Andrew had said, pulling Emma away from her breast so he could chuck her under the chin, so that she could squeal in delight at father's embrace.

"We can be kind," they said. "You shall have the other one. We always leave one behind, don't we? The first of a generation, the others untouched. One to pay and the other to pay again."

"And again."

"And again."

"No," she said, but her voice was weaker. Was it not worth it? Was it not worth the surrender of this bag of bones? After all, the little whatever-it-was had died, hadn't she? She had died years ago and the pain of that, it had dulled, hadn't it? With Emma? If she had Emma, could she not bear the loss? It was just a little sting, *ja*?

And the grandfathers were beside her.

And the grandfathers were chucking her chin.

And the grandfathers were counting her fingers with her.

And she was letting go of the bundle.

And they had it now.

She tried to turn away, but she could not, not from the grotesque, dancing look on their faces as they placed the tiny skeleton between them, the two halves of them open and bleeding like a blister.

But they were not two men any longer. No. As she watched the grandfathers began to dance their curious, half-hobbled dance, knees pumping furiously, half-chests rising and falling, lungs ballooning in the cavity, split apart like two halves of an apple. Not split apart. No. They were stitching themselves up. They were sealing themselves up, the two halves knitting and mending, mending and knitting, around the little skeleton child. The two halves of the grandfathers closed around it like the delicate petals of a Venus flytrap snapping shut.

Eileen moaned a single, deep-thrumming note. She felt an ache so deep and profound that it was like birthing pains, like her muscles locking together in orgasm as she watched the two men become a single wizened figure no bigger than a two-year-old. No bigger than a stepladder.

And she knew his face—

Her husband.

And she knew his name—

Andrew.

And she knew the thing he would do for her—

"Make me a child."

"Spin it for me, grandfather," Eileen whispered.

"Oh—" said the man and even though it was one mouth there were still two voices to it, running up unevenly against each other so the words collided like rocks in an avalanche. "She remembers after all."

And he bent closer to her, so close that the bristles on his chin stood out. His two hands—hands that hung so low to the ground the knuckles dragged across the floorboards when he walked—chucked her underneath the chin as they had when she'd been a little girl.

Those hands touched her hair. They smoothed it down until it was soft and pretty beneath their fingers.

All that hair.

"I remember," said Eileen, and she remembered, of course, she remembered but this memory was not a gift: she knew why her mother had forgotten, she knew why her mother had let the memories seep out of her like water from a cracked cup because memory was a terrible thing, truth was a terrible thing but there was a gift with it, yes, there was always a gift with it—

"Did you leave because of me?" her mother had asked.

But that was the wrong question, wasn't it?

"Did I leave you to them, mother? Did I leave you to the darkness? Did I leave you knowing they would come in the darkness? When you were alone?"

She had.

She had always known what those two long beds had meant, the two coffins, one for Rees and one for Jacob, one for Eirlys and one for Johanna. One from every generation. The first apple of the womb. One to go and one to stay. One to go, the other to pay and pay and pay. She had not wanted it for her daughters. No. When she had grown round and pregnant as an apple with the twin children inside of her, when Tamsyn had come for her—an old woman with her back stooped like a crook, because there was no one *left*, no one left for the grandfathers—Tamsyn had told her to come back to Ship House, and she had said no. And Tamsyn had taken the little one anyway, but that had not been enough, not enough for the grandfathers. . . .

Because the child must be given. That was the bargain. That was the price.

But in return, there might be blessings. There might be *gifts*.

"Once we spun straw. The king would have killed his wife, would have cracked her head like a hazelnut on the hearth, but we spun and we spun and we spun. But it was not straw that we spun for her. Straw would never turn to gold. Gold for gold, that is what we told her, and she cut her tresses for us. She gave up a piece of herself to keep her husband happy. What shall we spin for you, darling? What shall we spin for you, oh granddaughter come-home-to-us?" There was glee in those two rolling, robin's-egg eyes, in the grit of the teeth clicking together as her grandfather grinned at her. And his fingers were in her hair and this time they were pulling at it, plucking at it like straw. Eileen cried out, but still the hair came away in a thick tangle.

"Why does it have to be like this?" Eileen asked, clutching her fists together.

And her grandfather drew close to her, and although Eileen shied away, she couldn't. Not in that tiny hallway. The walls pressed her toward him, and she spun her head furious from side to side, but he took her chin between his thick, dirty fingers. She looked. She looked because she had to. He was as ugly as a mussel shell, his skin hanging slack off his cheeks in filthy crenellations. A stunted thing. A tiny little monster.

But not all monster. There was something in those rolling, robin's-egg eyes, something slick and gleaming and Eileen knew if she touched it her fingers would come back salty and wet.

The grandfather was crying.

"Because someone will always pay in blood, sweet granddaughter. The ground is thick with it, the air is rank with it, and we have grown with it, we grandfathers, the spinners and menders, the death-singers, the charnel-houses. And we are old, and we are tired, and we are broken, but still they call for us to take the bodies away . . . *bobbejaan* climbs the mountain. Poor *bobbejaan*. Always climbing."

"To torment the poor farmers," Eileen whispered.

And then: "Go," she tried to tell him. "Please." And her throat felt engorged and thick with a pity she did not want but she could not be afraid of him any longer, this sad, clinging thing, this misshapen lump of clay.

"You have paid in blood already, granddaughter. Let me spin for you." And it seemed almost as if he were pleading with her.

And she could not resist. The bargain had been made. The price had been paid.

And in return all she wanted was one small thing.

"Yes," she said. "Spin for me," she said.

And her grandfather began to spin, and the sweet smell of her hair was all around her.

In the morning, Eileen woke to the smell of bacon sizzling in the air. Sunlight was streaming through the window, falling slantwise on the two narrow beds in the little bedroom. The heat of it had not yet set in, and a cool breeze trickled in off the mountain.

Eileen got up carefully and stripped off her clothes. She had fallen asleep in them. They were damp and sticky, and she was glad to be rid of them.

She showered quickly. Let the water run over her in thin, happy rivulets as she massaged the shampoo into her hair.

Her shorn hair. The stubble felt soft as down against her fingers. She had thought it might be sharp and prickly, but it wasn't. When she towelled herself off, it stuck up at odd angles in the mirror. She ran her hand through the damp fluff of it and felt oddly satisfied.

When Eileen finally made her way to the kitchen, her feet moving silently over the woven rugs and the polished wooden floorboards, it was to see her mother in the kitchen leaning over a pan of smoking bacon fat, dipping in two thick pieces of bread to fry up.

"*Goeie more*," her mother called out as she turned the bread in the pan carefully.

"*Ja*," said Eileen and the Afrikaans came easily back to her. "*Goeie more, moeder.*"

They took breakfast together on the little table in the backyard, and though the garden was a ragged, unkempt thing, it was still sweet-smelling. Table Mountain gleamed a dull green-grey in the distance, and the clouds folded themselves over the long flat top like a draping cloth. In the distance, a cable car slowly trundled its way to the top, floating over the canyons and sharp rocks beneath it.

Her mother was clear-eyed today; she was like a properly made bed, everything folded just so, with the corners tucked away.

"Mother," Eileen said. "We need to talk."

"I know, darling," her mother said.

They were silent for the space of three breaths as the cable car docked at the top of the mountain. It would be filled with happy children, girls and boys lathered in sunscreen, ready to scrape their knees while their parents tried to usher them away from the edge.

"I've decided to stay in the house," Eileen's mother said at last.

"Mum," Eileen began, but mother silenced her with a wave of her hand.

"I know you worry for me, love. But this is my house. I need to stay here. I can't leave."

"Of course you can, mum. I want you to come back with me. Please?"

"Hush up, Eileen."

"I want you to meet Emma. I want her to know her grandmother—"

"—listen to me," her mother said with a wave of her gnarled hand. "To meet my granddaughter would be a wonderful thing. Perhaps the sweetest thing of all. The only thing left to me . . ."

"But?"

"But."

"You won't."

"No, child. I have lived in the shadow of Table Mountain all my life. That is not a small thing. It is different for you, I know it is. You found a way out of this place, and perhaps that is how it should be, perhaps it is better that way, but this is my *home*. I have shed tears in this house. I have found love in this house. The sum of my life is in this place, and I . . . I cannot let it go so very easily. It cannot let me go."

"Doesn't it frighten you? This place?"

Her mother smiled a sad sweet smile, a smile her daughter had never seen her smile before. "Of course, it does, love. A home is a frightening thing. An anchor. A place of resting. A place of waiting. A sign, perhaps, that you will never move any further than you have come at that very moment . . . but. I love this place. Let me to set it to rest."

The air was still and quiet. In the distance there was the sound of a bird—or a child—whooping gleefully.

"They will not come for me," her mother whispered, and Eileen looked at her sharply. "They will not come in the darkness again."

"How do you know?"

And her mother smiled a grim, tight-lipped smile.

"There are some things I know, lovey. Blood whispers to blood."

And Eileen gathered up her mother in her arms, and her bones were thin and delicate underneath the pale cotton dress, but her back was unbent, it had uncurled itself like a spring sapling loosed from the weight of winter. They sat together for a time. Listening to the sounds of the morning, the birds and the cries of the children, as the sun dappled the garden.

"You will have to go," her mother said.

"I can stay awhile," Eileen said.

"It is best done quickly. I've arranged for the taxi. It will be here soon."

"What if I don't want to go?" Eileen asked.

"Ha," her mother laughed. "Oh, child. Your Granny Tamsyn always said I was the weak one of her children, but I have some of her steel in me yet. You think you can deny me this? I am an old woman, maybe, but not a weak one. You have a husband. You have a child. Go."

And Eileen wanted to say something to that, but she didn't. She felt a kind of relief fall over her like putting on a sweater to keep away the chill. When they were finished, she carried their dishes to the sink, and she filled the basin with water.

"Leave it be, love," her mother said. "Do not linger."

Eileen packed quickly, and when the taxi came to her she was ready. When Eileen kissed her mother lightly upon her dry, powdery cheek, she breathed in the smell of vinegar.

And she did not look. She did not look.

The taxi carried her down the side of the mountain, and sometimes Eileen slept, and sometimes she let her gaze drift outside the window to the shantytowns and their long lines of coloured cloth floating in the breeze. She did not recognize the faces there. She felt something of the place falling away from her. It had been home once. But no longer. No longer.

She had left her mother in the kitchen, scrubbing away at the dishes, singing softly to herself. She wanted to remember her mother like that. Clear-eyed. Present. Wholly herself. It was a kind of gift.

And in return she had taught her eyes not to see—
the crank of the dial on the stove
And she had taught her ears not to hear—
the slow hiss of the gas, and perhaps the striking of the match
She had let her feet follow the floorboards—even as they whispered, "Fare thee well, child," even as they whispered, "Let her go, daughter"— past the threshold and away.

"If you look far enough in one direction," he said, *"you can see the beginning of everything."*

A Brief History of
Science Fiction

i. Cosmology
Carole at Fifteen

Her relationships never made it through the Big Bang.

"Is it the penis?" Ted asked.

It wasn't the penis.

"You've probably heard things about my penis. Did Anita tell you? She's such a. Bitch. Sorry. I don't mean that. I know you're friends."

"We're not friends, Ted. Not since seventh grade. No one told me anything about your penis."

"It's just. Listen, Carole. It's not true. What Anita's been saying. Just because my dad's Chinese. I don't have a microdick, okay?"

Around them there was utter darkness. It was as if they were floating in space. Not space, exactly. Pre-space. The space before there was space. The emptiness before matter and time and love and microdicks exploded into the universe 13.798 ± 0.037 billion years ago. Before the primeval atom. Before the primeval penis. Utter blackness. And silence.

Silence except for the snuffling sound that might have been Ted crying. Silence except for the tinny orchestral music playing over the speaker.

She didn't even know what a microdick was.

Carole wanted to look at Ted. She wanted to see if he was crying. She wanted, maybe, to take his hand and reassure him that it wasn't anything Anita said. Anita could be a bitch. Didn't she know that? Didn't she know how much of a bitch Anita could be when she wanted to?

And Ted probably didn't have a micropenis.

Probably.

Carole didn't want to find out. Ted was nice. He was a nice boy. But even nice boys always wanted to *move*. All she wanted was to remain motionless. At a fixed point. The world was beginning to accelerate around her. She hadn't even wanted to kiss him. Not really. She just thought she should. She just thought, "That's what you do, right?" So she'd kissed him.

And now this. Utter blackness. And in a moment, the primeval atom ripping into a billion, billion bits and ushering in the universe as she knew it.

"Sorry, Ted," Carole said. "It's not Anita. I think I just don't like you enough, you know?"

He hiccoughed. "Yeah. I know."

"So we're okay?"

"I guess."

"Shall we go then?"

"I guess."

Carole started to walk. She didn't wait to see if Ted would follow her. There were little green dotted lights on the ground marking the pathway out. There was a large sign—very elegantly done—counting out the years as she walked. The formation of stars. The formation of the solar system. Life on earth.

There was an emergency exit sign.

"I'm going to go, Ted, okay? You just finish up here by yourself."

"You're really leaving then?"

Now Carole could see his face. Just a little. It was red and blotchy. It might have just been the light from the emergency exit sign.

He was sixteen. He wasn't sixteen in a cute way. He was sixteen in a sort of greasy, pimply, not fully formed way. The red light from the emergency exit sign made the pimples on his face stand up and wave hello.

Carole was sure, then. This was the right thing to do. Even though Anita would talk. Even though Anita would say she was some kind of ice princess or something. Ted's mouth had a twisted look to it. She waited for his last words.

"I knew this would happen," Ted said. He clenched his hands into futile little fists. "I knew this would happen. Anita told me. She told me if I let you take me here . . . she said it was always here. You always break up with them right here. Right in this very spot."

"I—" Carole began, but then she stopped. She hated Anita. She wanted to say something nasty about Anita, but what was there to say? "I'm sorry, Ted." She paused. "You were a good kisser."

"I was?" he asked hopefully.

He wasn't.

"Sure," Carole said. "Goodbye, Ted."

And then she took the emergency exit.

Just as she had before, every other time. Just like Anita said, Anita the bitch, Anita who never kept her mouth shut about anything.

And she abandoned Ted. She abandoned his spotted face and his twisted lips. She abandoned all of it to the fortunes of the cruel, ever-expanding universe.

ii. Synchronicity
Carole at Thirty-Four

She didn't know when it was that Nicholas changed.

Maybe it was at the crash site when the doctor—measuring pupil dilation, asking the date, his name—had declared the head injury near catastrophic.

The car had come out of nowhere, he said. The road had been perfectly clear, he said.

Or maybe it came after, during the slow recovery time when he called her Cocoa as he had during the early days in college, both of them new to the city, their first time living alone, or as he tottered out of the hospital eight days after the crash, refusing the wheelchair and insisting he drive home. She could see the way his hands shook. He couldn't put the key in the ignition until she did it with him, her hands over his.

At first they didn't talk. She let her glances land like butterflies on his face, startling away before he could catch them. Then it was the questions after.

"Do you remember what speed you were going?"

"No."

"Do you remember if the other driver stopped to see if you were okay?"

"No.

"Do you remember how we first met?"

Shamefaced. "No."

Carole would lie in bed beside him. She craved the presence of some other Nicholas, the one she had fallen in love with. The loneliness was somehow made deeper by his presence beside her. His body scant inches from hers, his fingers brushing a nipple by accident before he curled into a comma away from her.

Afterward he would insist on driving although Carole had a license too. They had taken their test in different cities on the same day—

November 15th—the birthday they shared by chance.

That birthday had become a secret sign between them over the years.

"Will you marry me?"

"Yes."

"Why?"

To which the answer was both as clear and as complicated as the way they had aged perfectly alongside one another. Graduated together. Turned thirty together. It was its own form of time travel, this steady march into the future.

Afterward she would let Nicholas drive because that seemed easiest. His confusion, his anger, was more pronounced if she said no.

But sometimes it was as if her Nicholas had caught up with her. As if he had bridged the lagging gap between them. But if she insisted on driving, insisted on going over the taxes or turning off the stove element, then a stranger would be there, and she would feel time dilate and stretch as Nicholas became an old man, infirm. Her father. Her grandfather.

"Do you still love me?" he would ask. "Do you still know me?"

Sometimes, she would think. "Yes," she would answer.

And on the road she would sometimes feel that same look of confusion overtake him, as if it was the world that had changed hideously and unexpectedly around him. Then, she would touch his hand, and she would pray he didn't startle and tap the breaks too hard.

"Do you remember where you are going?" she would never ask.

"No," he would never answer.

"It's okay, it's okay. We'll get there. Together. At exactly the same time."

iii. **Singularity**
    Carole at Seventy-Four

When they came from the stars, Carole greeted the spacemen with an appraising stare. She shook hands delicately. She had woken with the feeling the day would hold something miraculous.

"Take us to your leader," the spacemen said.

There were four of them: green from head to foot, eyes large as black ostrich eggs. The eldest of them had the look of her father: elephant wrinkles. Dark as moss.

Carole leaned in the doorway. There were things that should be done, she knew. People who should be told. Somewhere government agencies were in a panic. Somewhere interns were being fired, red phones were ringing off the hook. But the house was quiet as the house was always quiet. The air breathed in and out of it. Sunlight dappled the carpeted stairs. Time slowed here.

"No," she said at last. She brought them inside. Offered them ginger tea with biscuits on the cracked porcelain tea service her mother had left her when she died.

The spacemen munched at the biscuits. They were polite.

"Where do you come from?" Carole asked them.

"Are you familiar," said the greenest of them, an eager thing, "with the Horsehead Nebula? Sigma Orionis?"

"No," said Carole apologetically.

"Well," he said. *Munch munch.* "Interstellar landmarks are a bit difficult at a certain point. But your biscuits are delicious." Carole decided she liked that one. He had a certain look about him: his skin was smooth and bright as a mango.

"What did you see out there?"

"If you look far enough in one direction," he said, "you can see the beginning of everything."

"Oh?"

"It has something to do with the way light travels."

"And if you look in the other direction?" she asked.

"No one looks in the other direction," said the oldest.

Carole poured the tea in a hot, steaming parabola. She took hers with sugar.

The spacemen drank enthusiastically under her gaze, rattled saucers, exchanged glances, fondled the crumbs and licked them from their fingers. Looked around

"We've been such a long time travelling," the greenest of them whispered at last. And then: "Your house is very beautiful." Carole could see he was wet behind the ears and, remembering her own awkward upbringing, pitied him. She touched his hand. Winked. She was a jazzy beauty in her ancient silk nightgown, her hair gleaming like bone china.

"Thank you," Carole replied. "I take pride in it."

Carole and the spacemen sat in a glorious ten-minute silence, her index finger touching the edge of the saucer, their hands curled in their laps—lost in that moment after tenderness and just before love.

Then:

"You're as gorgeous as cucumbers," Carole said. "I love your eyes."

The oldest of them coughed. His skin wrinkled and smoothed. Twitched. "We ought to be going now." He was apologetic.

So was Carole. She rose unsteadily.

But the greenest of them lingered. He was sick with sorrow. She could tell. When she showed them to the door, he kissed her fingers, ever so gently, as if he were licking up crumbs. "Will you wait for me?" he asked.

The space between them was expanding. They were hurtling farther and farther apart from one another.

Carole smiled. "Call me Penelope. I can wait."

Afterward, the house seemed empty. Carole cleaned up the saucers, put away the biscuits. When the phone rang she ignored it. It would only be Anita, demanding to know who her guests were, what they had to say for themselves, would they pay for the damage to the lawn?

What was there to say?

The spacemen had come. They had gone. They had found a place in her home, briefly, like a spoon beside a soup bowl on a cold day. And, thinking that, Carole settled down to wait for the slow, graceful arc of things lost returning once more.

"Here was something that was ours. The one bright and shiny thing the universe had dropped into our laps."

SUPPLY LIMITED, ACT NOW

Because Larry said it would never work, we knew we had to try.

Because Larry said he didn't want any part of it, we knew we had to try it out on him first.

That was the way it was with Larry. That's how it had always been between us. The four of us knew it. No one questioned it. We could all see the slightly sick look come over Larry's face as he realized. We could see him turning pale. Pushing at his taped-up glasses and starting to scramble.

He tried to say something.

Marvin grabbed the shrink ray.

Marvin pressed the button.

And the world popped and crackled around us.

That's how it started.

Maybe it wouldn't have been like that if Larry had never said anything. But when Larry had followed the instructions last time it had been a disaster.

"FRIENDS," the ad had said. "HERE'S HOW TO GET at almost **NO COST** YOUR *NEW*, Real, Live MINIATURE DOG!"

"Supply Limited," the ad said. "**ACT NOW!!**"

"*Please* let me come home with you," the miniature dog begged in a giant speech bubble.

The dog was black, with long, floppy ears, cartoonishly wide eyes and a white-speckled snout. Larry, on the other hand, was skinny as a beanpole with a face full of acne. His elbows and knees were huge and knobbly. They stuck out like the knots in the ropes we had to climb for gym class. And if there was any boy who ever was in need of a dog it was him.

And so Larry sent in his coupons and waited at the door for the mailman every day.

He waited the way he had every day for the past year; while those other times it had been with terror, this time it was with stupid, fearless joy.

You see, the thing you need to know about Larry is that his brother Joe had joined the Air Force last September.

"GEE!! I WISH I WERE A MAN!" said the ad.

"Come to the UNITED STATES AIR FORCE Recruiting Station," it said.

We all wished we could be men—of course we did!—but only Larry's brother Joe was old enough. So he'd signed up just like it said to. They'd sent him to Honolulu for a while and then after that he had been moved to Seoul where he wrote back letters every once in a while about how hot it was and how many of the shovelheads he had killed and how much he missed his kid brother.

Those weren't the letters that worried Larry. Of course, it wasn't *those* letters. It was the official letter. The one signed by President Harry S. Truman himself. Larry knew exactly when the mailman came every day. His whole family did.

But after Larry sent away for his miniature dog? For a couple of weeks anyway things were different. This was about the only time in the whole last year that Larry waited for the doorbell to ring with something besides near dread.

And when the mailman arrived, Larry was over the moon!

We all cast an eyeball on the package when Larry brought it over to the clubhouse, half skipping, half stumbling, his glasses gone crooked and his hair plastered with sweat to his forehead in big, wet, wormy lines.

The package was small, but that was okay. The dog was a miniature dog. It wouldn't need a large package.

The package was beat-up. The tape was scruffy and the glue had crusted and peeled off in parts. One corner of the package had split open.

We were all there. Marv, Todd, Mel and me—this was back when Mel still came around. But Larry opened the package with glee. We all saw him do it.

And inside the package? Nothing but a little ball of fur and a tiny collar with the word "Rufus" inscribed into a metal disc that jingled when it fell into his hand.

We all clapped Larry on the back. We all made apologetic noises.

"Ain't that a bite?" Todd said mournfully before he offered him one of the Cokes he had brought over to the clubhouse. The Coke was beautifully cold. You could see the Coke almost melting in his hand. It was June by then and the fresh summer heat had made us all a bit stupid and giddy at the same time. Stupid enough to believe an ad for a miniature dog for only twenty coupons.

That wasn't enough for Larry though. Larry was relentless. Larry wrote back to the address the package was stamped with.

"Please sir or madam," he wrote. "I have sent the twenty coupons as requested, but my miniature dog did not arrive."

And three weeks later there was an envelope.

And inside the envelope there was a note.

Dear Valued Customer,

It appears as if you were the intended recipient of "Rufus," one of our finest miniature fidos. We're sorry to hear the news, and can only presume that he has escaped in transit, the little scamp!

Unfortunately, we cannot offer refunds for missing pets, but we guarantee that Rufus is a loyal dog. We recommend you leave out some Boyer Smoothie Peanut Butter Cups (those are his absolutely favourite!) and, perhaps, Rufus will find his way home to you, his expectant new owner.

Because of his size, it may take some time. We advise patience.

Sincerely,
Arthur Graham,
President of Norwood Enterprises, Incorporated.
Des Moines, Iowa

We told Larry not to bother. We told Larry that Rufus was gone. We told Larry that's how life was sometimes. No, it wasn't fair, and no, it wasn't right, but that's how it was.

But Larry didn't listen. Larry didn't want to live in a world of "it's not fair" and "it's not right." Who could blame him? We all knew someone who had never made it home. We all had uncles and cousins and big brothers, fathers and grandfathers who never came back from North Africa or Okinawa. We all had prayers we said for the lost ones. And we were all waiting for something.

Larry was like that.

If it was possible to love a thing before you had ever seen it and Pastor Davis said that it was, that was how we were all supposed to love God, then that was the way Larry loved that dog. Larry loved Rufus more than God but even that wasn't saying enough. After all, we could all remember the day when Pastor Davis said, "Let us give thanks," and Larry spazzed out, shouting, "I don't wanna give thanks! Thanks for what? Why the hell would God make a world like this one, huh? Thanks for nothing, God!" Larry looked embarrassed after, but he didn't go back to church and he didn't say sorry to Pastor Davis neither.

No. Larry waited for Rufus the Miniature Dog to find his way home. Larry left out the Boyer Smoothie Peanut Butter Cups (just in case). Larry kept the collar in his pocket (just in case). And sometimes, when Larry didn't think any of us would notice, he would trail behind a little ways as we dragged our skinny asses back from the baseball diamond in Glenn Park. And then we would hear him whistle and call very softly, "Rufus, Rufus, c'mere, boy, c'mere, Rufus. Willya come on home?"

Finally, it was Melanie who had to say to him, "Let him go, Larry. He's not coming home. There was never any stinking miniature dog."

And because it was Melanie who said it he listened.

We were all a bit in love with Melanie.

And so Larry said it would never work. Especially when he saw the shrink ray, nine inches of moulded plastic with these big brass bands looping around the barrel. It coulda been a toy. It looked about as good as anything you got out of a Cracker Jack box.

Larry said he didn't want any part of it.

And maybe it was the heat. Maybe it was the way it made us stupid and giddy, just not to be doing anything of real consequence. To lay in the shade of the clubhouse where the air smelled of stale cedar and it didn't move except when one of us got up to fetch sandwiches and moon pies from the pack. We traded comic books back and forth. We marvelled at the possibilities of cardboard submarines and x-ray glasses. Shoes that would make you two inches taller. And the shrink ray. Of course, the shrink ray.

Maybe it was because Melanie didn't come by so much anymore. Not since she had become Melanie, that is. Not since she'd stopped being Mel or Melly. *Mel* had been one of us. Mel could throw knuckle balls and cheat at rummy. *Melanie* didn't do any of those things.

And Marvin was just being a cauliflower-eared twit anyway. He hadn't expected it to work.

And when the shrink ray *had* worked, well, we all just stared in stupefied wonder. Like we were all waiting for God to take it back.

"What happened?" Larry said. It sounded like he'd been sucking on the tail of a balloon. It made me giggle. It made us all giggle.

"Ya got shrunk," Marvin told him.

"I did?" Larry asked.

"Sure as shit," he said.

And he had.

There was Larry, holding half a PB 'n' J sandwich in his hand, but now it was quarter-sized because Larry was just half a Larry. He was hardly three feet if he was anything.

"Huh," said Marvin.

And none of the rest of us had anything better to add to the conversation so we just let it lie until Todd grabbed the shrink ray out of Marvin's hand and aimed it at a can of Coke.

"Be careful," Marvin said. "The box said to *use caution at all times!*"

"Baby!" shrieked Todd with a jazzed grin on his face.

"What?" said Larry who was still looking around in confusion.

And then Todd yelled, "Gotcha!" and he cranked up the dial and pressed the button.

There was a feeling like thunder when there's no thunder. It made me think of tornado weather. The air got hot and sticky. And it crackled. But there was no noise. And then the Coke bottle was gone. It was tiny. It was no more than a thimble.

"Boss," said Todd. His blond hair was sticking up like a fluffed duck's.

"Shit," I said. "I was gonna drink that."

"Nothing to do for it," said Todd. "Larry'll have to drink it now."

"No way. It's too small for Larry," I pointed out. Todd just shrugged and then he pointed the shrink ray at Larry.

"Wait!" yelled Larry. But Todd didn't wait. The gun went zap. The world went fuzzy and there was Larry, five inches high.

"Eff you!" Larry shrieked in a near falsetto.

"Stop spazzing out," said Todd.

And maybe that's where it all should have stopped. Marvin was reading the instructions on the box. He was trying to read them anyway. But then Todd zapped the box and when it was done shrinking they were too small for Marvin to read anymore.

"Be careful!" Marvin said. "Ya almost got me! Now how are we gonna figure out how it works?"

"I know how it works!" Todd said.

"C'mon, man," said Marvin. "I paid for the thing."

"Just ice it, willya? Possession," said Todd with infinite patience and condescension, "is nine-tenths of the law."

"Candyass!" said Marvin.

"Spazz!" said Todd.

"Jerk off!" shrieked Marvin.

"Just listen, willya?" said Todd. "Listen."

And we stopped. And we listened.

But Todd didn't say anything. He didn't say anything at all. And neither did the rest of us.

Because Todd was starting to grin. It was a big grin. It was like some sort of primo super grin. And his eyes, his eyes had this crazed and gleeful look. They were wide as saucers like the kid was on cloud nine. Like this was the living end.

"This is it," said Todd.

And no one said anything.

"Ya see it, right?" said Todd.

"Right," said Marvin.

He was the first to speak. And he had that grin too. It was crazy. It was infectious. It looked like it was going to split the top off his head. But then I was grinning too. I was grinning right along with them. It was like there were bottle rockets going off in all our brains.

"Sure," I said.

"I dig," said Larry and his voice was tinny and high but didn't matter because he was grinning too and it was like that grin made him nine feet tall anyway. It was the first time anyone had seen him smile properly since Rufus had chewed his way out of the post.

Marvin scooped up Larry and tucked him away safely into the front pocket of his checked, flannel shirt.

"Let's go," said Todd.

We started with trashcans and mailboxes because that was the sort of thing we always started with. They were easy. The McCallisters'. Mr. Kane from around the block who had painted "Remember Our Boys" in big red and blue letters on the outside. WHOOOOSH!

"See ya later, alligator!" Larry shouted in that high, squeaky voice of his.

But then it was Todd who got bolder. He was a January baby and so he already had inches on the rest of us. Todd was always the first of us to get bold. Todd was always pushing us a little further down Damnation Alley, saying, "C'mon, can ya dig it? Can ya dig it?" And we could dig it. Hoo-boy, could we ever dig it! We were whooping and hollering, tearing through the neighbourhood.

There were lamp posts and shopping carts and we shrunk the hell out of them.

There was the old dumpster behind the Milk Mart and we shrunk the hell out of it.

There was Todd's stepfather's Buick Super Rivera and we shrunk the hell out of it.

There was the baseball diamond in Glenn Park and we shrunk the hell out of it.

We stopped to pick up moon pies and Boyer Smoothie Peanut Butter Cups at the 7-Eleven and the attendant shortchanged us a nickel.

"Whaddya think you're doing?" said Marvin and his forehead was sweaty and red like he was getting a sunburn. His hair was an electrified bird's nest. "I want my nickel!"

"Go screw," said the attendant. His nametag read Jimmy. "Clear out, wouldya?"

And in that moment Jimmy was everything we hated about the world. He was everyone who was always telling us to go screw. Who was screwing us. Who was gypping us. So Todd shrunk the hell out of him, and when the air had finally settled, Marvin gave him the finger.

"Whaddya think of that?" he asked. "Whaddya think of that now, huh?"

"Marv," said Larry. He sounded worried. Like *real* worried. "Marv."

He was staring at Jimmy the attendant. Jimmy the inchworm. He was even smaller than Larry, flailing his arms around and trying to shout something that none of us could make out. Small enough that Todd could squish him between his fingers like a mosquito if he wanted to.

"Shit," said Marv. "We can't just leave him, can we? Not like that?"

"Sure we can," said Todd uncertainly. "I mean, he'll get better, right? Just on his own?" And Todd had a look on his face like he wished he could take it back. Like he thought maybe this was all going a bit further than he really wanted it to. And maybe it was. Maybe it was.

But still.

It was the middle of August. School was right around the corner. We knew the last of the sunlight was going to slip away before we'd hardly had a chance to do *anything* at all. And here was something. Here was something that was *ours*. The one bright and shiny thing the universe had dropped into our laps. Would we give it up? Maybe eventually. Maybe someday. But right now?

No effing way.

"Let's split!" I yelled, and we did.

Sometimes something happens when you're stupid. If you're lucky enough not to get caught then there's such a feeling of relief you swear off whatever badness you were up to forever, and then it's as good as if you *did* get caught in the first place. Sometimes. But there are those other times when getting away with something is just the beginning. Sometimes getting away with it can make you wilder and crazier than you ever thought possible.

And that's how it was with us.

The four of us wailed out of there, Todd with the shrink ray, Marvin with Larry, and Larry munching away happily on a Boyer Smoothie Peanut Butter Cup twice the size of his head.

There was Sinclair Pumps and we shrunk the hell out of it.

There was the Route 9 City Bus to Port Hope and we shrunk the hell out of it.

There was Washington Memorial School and we sure as hell shrunk the hell out of *that*.

We shrunk the hell out of the cop car that chased us out by Highway 29.

We even shrunk the hell out of Grace Presbyterian where Pastor Davis liked to preach, and then Pastor Davis himself and the whole Saturday Night congregation that was gathered with him.

Pretty soon it was starting to look like we were living in Shrinky Dink, USA and that's when the feeling of it all going sideways on us started to get worse. We were getting scared again. Real scared.

And maybe then it's no surprise that we ended up at Melanie's doorstep a little bit after nine. After all, she was the one always knew best. And what was the whole point of this if it wasn't her?

Marvin was going to try the bell, but Todd shushed him down.

"Whaddya mean be quiet?"

"Don't be such a spazz!"

"Don't be such a jerkoff!"

"Hey, be careful with that, willya?" I cut in, slapping down the shrink ray before Todd could get off a shot. "Let's be cool for once in our lives now, dig it? Her old man's not gonna let her out this late."

Marvin nodded.

There were rules for Melanie now. It was like her parents had gone to bed and woken up thinking the world had turned dangerous for a girl like her overnight. There was curfew. There were long shouting matches about what kind of clothes she could wear, what kind of friends she could have. And boys? We were suddenly finks and fakes to them. Space cadets. Shucksters, one and all. Were we good enough for their daughter? Hooboy! Not a chance!

So I took a handful of gravel and I chucked it at her window. This was how we used to do it back when Melanie was Mel and she'd come out with us to play ball or drink the brewskis that Joe would sometimes buy for us.

Eventually there she was at the window and she was beautiful as ever with her hair done up in these big pin curls that just made my heart melt. Her eyes were green as a chemist's bottle, luminous, I could see them perfectly even though the sun had mostly cut out at this point.

"Hey, Mel!" Todd called softly, forgetting for a moment that she was Melanie now and she was not one of us. I could have kicked him for that. It was an unspoken rule between us that we wouldn't call her that anymore.

"Hey, yourself," she said. "What's the story?"

A moment later, she was wedging the window open and climbing her way down the drainpipe the way she used to. She shimmied her way to the bottom, her pedal pushers hugging her thighs, and then she was standing in front of us panting and pink in the soft, filmy glow of the evening.

"You boys raising some Cain?" she asked.

"Maybe," said Todd.

"You too?" she asked looking at me. I felt that look travel like electricity right through me and give my balls a good jolt. I blushed. I blinked. Wiped at dirt on my face and hoped my hair didn't look as nuts as Todd's and Marv's did.

"I guess."

"Where's Larry?"

Marv took Larry out of his pocket, and the kid was curled up there like a kitten in his palms.

"What's that supposed to be?" said Melanie.

"Larry's gone looking for his dog," Todd burst in. "Ya know, Rufus the Miniature Pooch? Heeeeeeeeeeere, puppy puppy puppy!" I punched him in the arm. "Aw man," he said. "Whaddya do that for?"

"Can it, willya?" I said.

And just then Larry started to stir. He blinked and rubbed his eyes. Said in that high voice of his, "What's up, Doc?"

Marv giggled, but Melanie just stared.

"Cool," she said. The tiniest of grins was starting to tug at her lips.

"Come out with us tonight," I said. I didn't look at her. I couldn't. She was too pretty in the evening light just then.

"I can't, boys," she said. She shook her head very gently and those big pin curls of hers did a lazy bob around her shoulders.

We could all feel something drain out of us then, like piss down a pant leg. I don't know what it was. Craziness? Courage? Whatever it was that Larry's brother had joined the Air Force to find?

"Course you can," I tried. It was important. She had to come with us. That was the whole point, wasn't it? "Nights like tonight? They're limited supply only. Act now."

She looked at me funny then. Like she was sad. Like she knew I was righter than I meant to be.

But she also looked at me like she knew I wasn't being straight with her. And maybe I wasn't but maybe that was because we were *never* straight with her anymore. We didn't ever tell her we loved her. We didn't ever tell her that's why we had showed up at her place on a Saturday night with a shrunken boy in our pocket and the kind of ray gun that only ever works in comic books.

We didn't tell her that maybe we'd gone a bit too far.

We didn't tell her that maybe we were thinking of going a bit further but we only wanted to do it if she was there. We woulda laid the whole stinking world at her feet if we coulda.

"Peachy," she said.

So that was how it happened.

We took Melanie into town and we showed her just what kinda Cain we'd been raising.

We walked like giants through what was left of Main Street, tiny cars motoring around our feet and honking at our knees. Tiny parents clutching at their tiny babies, holding them tightly behind their tiny bedroom windows.

It was like we were kings.

It was like we were on top of the effing world!

And Melanie? Her eyes were wide as saucers and pretty soon she was laughing with strange delight at Jefferson's clock tower which we'd shrunk to the size of a putt-putt club, and she was putting her hand on my arm, and her touch was soft and warm, and her laugh was beautiful, and she was whispering to me, "Oh, you boys, you boys, just look what you've done, you crazy things!"

And Todd poked me in the shoulder, and, God, could I have told him to scram just then!

We walked up to the lookout where all the lovers go to play backseat bingo. None of us had ever dared go there before far as I knew. Except Melanie knew the way. She knew things now that our Mel wouldn't have known.

The evening sky had darkened until there was just a hazy glow of light and the moon was big and sitting heavy and yellow on the horizon. Todd pointed the shrink ray at it but this time it was Melanie who shook her head, batted down the gun.

"Oh no, boys," she said. "You can't go shrinking the moon!"

"I bet I could," Todd said with a grin.

"But," Melanie replied, "whatcha gonna do without a moon in June?"

And Todd stared at her. And Melanie grinned. And then we all burst into giggles like a bunch of stupid kids.

The lookout was empty. Not a car in sight. Made me wonder where all the lovers had ended up, or if maybe we'd shrunk the hell out of them already. Maybe there were tiny little boys and girls somewhere sharing tiny little kisses under a moon that was now big enough to swallow them.

We settled in the grass together, the five of us. Shared out the last of the moon pies and the Boyer Smoothie Peanut Butter Cups. The night was beautiful. Melanie was beautiful. And I felt happy. Buoyant. I felt grown up, nine feet tall, like I coulda done anything. Like I coulda even kissed Melanie up here at the lookout where the boys and girls went for that sort of thing. If I wanted to. Which I did. Of course I did.

And then we heard a noise. It was so soft it coulda been drowned in the crickets but I strained my ears.

It was crying.

It was this weird, breathless, tinny crying sound.

And I looked down and there was Larry, tucked into Marv's shirt pocket, holding onto his Boyer Smoothie Peanut Butter Cup and sobbing away like it was the end of the world.

"What's wrong, Larry?" I asked.

And he didn't say anything.

"Larry?" Melanie said. And Marv fished him out of the pocket and Marv held him up in the palm of his hands so we could all get a look at him, his tiny shrunken glasses sitting crooked on his face. His tiny shrunken mouth smeared with chocolate.

"I dunno, guys," he said. "It's just. Well. We got a shrink ray, didn't we?"

We all nodded.

"We got a shrink ray and it worked. It worked. It really *really* worked! And that's just boss, ya know? It might be the bossest thing of all."

"Then why're you weeping?" Todd asked him.

"Because. It's just. Well. What about Rufus? What about the little guy? How come we got the shrink ray and I ain't got my miniature dog? I mean, what if he really did escape? What if he's lost out there?"

"Oh god," cried Larry, "What if he's *dead*?"

And Larry's voice had turned into a wail. We all looked at one another, but no one had a thing to say. Todd coughed. Marv scratched at his nose.

"What if he's dead?" Larry went on, his voice hiccoughing and broken. We all had to lean in to hear him properly. "I mean it's funny, isn't it? I mean, I think I can see Port Hope from here. Do ya think we could shrink Port Hope?" he asked. "I mean, do ya think we could just . . . shrink all of it? We could just shrink the hell out of it! And then all of Michigan, ya know, just ker-blammo! Shrinksville!" His voice had taken on a desperate quality that made me feel weak and scared to hear it. "And then maybe, I mean maybe, maybe we could just shrink our way to Korea, ya know? Just shrink the hell out of it, just shrink the hell out of all those fucking shovelheads, just shrink 'em down and step on them until they're dead! Whaddya think, boys? Whaddya think? Do ya think we could? Huh?"

His tiny face was red and heartbroken. But his eyes, man, even at only five inches tall we could all see that there was something real and alive in his eyes, something crazy, but a different sorta crazy than the crazy the rest of us had caught.

And whaddya say to that? Whaddya say to a thing like that?

Pastor Davis would know, but we sure as shit didn't.

"We could do all that," Todd said slowly. "Course we could. Right, boys? We could? We got a shrink ray, don't we? We could shrink it all down?"

And then he took out the shrink ray. He pointed it out over the edge of the lookout.

And Larry nodded miserably.

And we all knew Todd woulda done it. His hands were shaking. Right then the shrink ray didn't look like a dumb plastic toy in his hands, like it coulda come out of a Cracker Jack box. It looked like something else. Like something *real* dangerous. We had all heard that thunder that wasn't thunder, after all. We'd all seen what it could do.

And Todd gulped. I could see his Adam's apple bob up and down like a yo-yo, and I could see the way his hands were starting to shake now, like he knew it was dangerous. Like he hated the thought of pressing down on that button but he was going to do it anyway.

And I know he woulda.

He woulda shrunk Port Hope.

He woulda shrunk all of Michigan.

He woulda shrunk the whole world down if Larry had asked him to. Just shrunk the hell out of it.

Because that's the way it was with us. That's how it had always been between us. We all knew it. No one questioned it.

Except for Melanie. Except, of course, for Melanie. And that's why we'd gone for her, wasn't it? Because some part of us knew. Some part of us knew that she had to be here. That we *needed* her. It wasn't just that we loved her, though we did, of course, sure as shit, but there was something else too.

"No," she said, and at first it was a soft thing, just a little exclamation.

And then she said it again. Louder. "No!"

Todd looked at her.

"Christ, no! For eff sakes, no!" And now we could see that *she* was shaking. She was grabbing Todd's arm and she was wrenching the shrink ray out of his hands. "No, you stupid kid! No!" And she was pounding on his chest. Todd had a stunned, slightly surprised look on his face. He was bigger than her. She still hadn't hit her full height yet, and Todd had already shot up six inches in the last couple of months, and his arms were big and bulky even if he didn't quite know what to do with them yet, but she was just wailing on him anyway. She was punching his shoulder. She was tearing at his shirt.

"Mel?" I asked, feeling scared. Unsure what to do.

"Oh god," she said. "Why ya always gotta go doing that? Why ya always gotta go making things small just so that you can grow up? It doesn't have to be like that, you know? Why do ya wanna go on being the kids that just wreck everything because ya don't know better?"

And she wiped the tears from her eyes, leaving big black stains like the grease quarterbacks use to keep the glare from the sun down.

"We could do all that. We could do it just like you said, and we could scoop Joe outta Korea, maybe, bring him home safe and sound. But then what? Do you want to live in a world that's only three inches tall? You want to tower over it and crush the hell out of it every time you take a step?"

And then she wasn't wailing on him anymore. She was just crying. Crying like we'd never seen our Mel cry before. Her pin curls were wilting like old party streamers and her pedal pushers had grass stains and dirt from where she'd been sitting.

"I dunno why I go around with you boys. You're just stupid kids, ain't ya? You're just kids!"

And Todd was holding her in his arms, first to stop her wailing on him, and now like he just didn't know what to do with her. The look on his face woulda been priceless if it didn't make some sort of anger boil up in me just to see the two of them like that, even if it wasn't on purpose.

And so because of that anger I almost missed what Larry said next. Larry who still had that strange, crazy look in his eyes, even if he was only five inches tall.

"Why's that?" he said softly. Dangerously, even. "You tell me why it's gotta be like that?"

And I wanted to say something back to him because right then he didn't look like Larry at all. He looked more like his brother Joe, even if he was small. Even if he was tiny. But I was still too scared, and that's when it struck me that Melanie was right. She was so right. We were just kids. We were just kids playing at something stupid, and why didn't we see that before? Why couldn't we have been better for her? More like men? Why was it that whenever we tried something that'd make us a bit closer to her it just kept pushing us farther and farther away?

I could tell the other boys were thinking it too. Marv with the little guy cupped between his hands. Todd with his bruised shoulder, holding the girl we all wanted to be holding and still not a clue about what to do next.

And finally it was Marv who just shrugged.

"I don't know, Larry," he said, "but she's right. That's how it is. Maybe ya got a miniature dog out there. Maybe ya don't. But the world's a big place. And I. I don't think I wanna be one of those folks who's always trying to burn it all down. I don't wanna grow up just so's I can make everything around me like it's nothing. Like it doesn't matter for shit."

"But what about me?" Larry yelled. "What about me? You *shrunk* me! What about me, huh? What the eff about *me*?"

And we all looked at each other. There was a sick feeling in my guts. Like I had the cramps. Like I wanted to throw up.

Like he was right.

"I don't know," said Mel. She pushed herself away from Todd, wiped at her eyes again with the pale underside of her wrist. "I don't know what to tell you, Larry. We wait, I guess. We wait and see."

And that moment stretched on. And on. Larry was shaking. Like he was finally scared now too. Scared by what he'd just said. And it was only then that it had started to dawn on us that the little guy was only five inches tall. I mean, *really* dawn on us. He was shrunk. I mean, *really* shrunk. And maybe, just maybe, there might not be any way to make it right again. There might be no growing up for Larry like there would be for the rest of us.

And none of us could think of a better thing to say than that.

It was like the world our parents had always been telling us about, the world of *mistakes matter*, the world of *no more freebies*, the world of *ain't just kids anymore* was the world we were gonna be living in for the rest of our lives.

God. Whaddya say to that? Just whaddya say?

Finally it was Melanie who found the words first.

"Here," she said. "We got one Boyer Smoothie Peanut Butter Cup left, don't we? We'll help you look for Rufus. Okay, Larry? You dig it?"

And, reluctantly, Todd nodded. You could see he had that same look on his face. Like he was feeling the same thing I was feeling. Like we were looking at Larry and we were wondering what the hell it was we had all gone and done together.

And then Marvin nodded.

And then I nodded.

And the moon was hanging low and fat on the horizon, and it was starting to sink beneath the hills. And the air was starting to cool, just a bit, just the tiniest bit. Outside there was a city three feet tall. Out there was Shrinksville, USA, where our fathers and stepfathers and mothers and sisters were trapped in their tiny houses. Locking their tiny doors. Scared to death of the thing that we had done to them, even though we hadn't meant anything by it. Even though it'd just been crazy kid stuff we were up to.

And then Larry spoke at last in a voice that sounded as tired as it was scared. "I dig," said Larry. "I dig, Mel."

And so Marv slid him back into his pocket. And Todd helped Melanie get to her feet. And then we set off. The five of us. Together.

And maybe there'd be a miniature dog to find, with a white-speckled nose and a tongue made for licking up peanut butter. And maybe there wouldn't be.

And maybe tomorrow we'd wake up to find Todd's stepfather's Buick Super Rivera parked outside the garage, large as life, with its headlights like torpedoes and its hubcaps gleaming in the July sun. And maybe we wouldn't.

And maybe there was a letter already winging its way home with the signature of President Harry S. Truman inked at the bottom. And maybe not.

But we set off together.

With all our tiny loves.

Our tiny hopes. Our tiny maybes. Our tiny tomorrows.

No. 100002

"You will fall and you will fall and you will fall."

WE RUIN THE SKY

The night seeps in through a hole in the cracked window.

You can see it. Feel its inexhaustible weight, the pressure of lake water on the windshield of a drowning car. Smell the night air, sharp with the cat-piss stink of gasoline and exhaust from the traffic on 23rd Street. The night pours in through the hole, magnifying sound, the conversations from the street. From twenty floors below me, a man hails a taxi. He curses loudly in that thick Chicago accent you hated so much when Jonathan first brought you here. "Fuck," he says. "Fuck-fuck-fuck." A door slams. "Fuck-a-duck," you hear.

"Fuck-a-duck," you experiment, savouring the guttural sound, the suggestive slide of fricative to plosive, the same sound a cork makes when it leaves the bottle. "Fuck-fuck-fuck." The word has a hard, delicious weight; a word that Jonathan would never say, and so it is precious to you.

You have been staring at the hole for two hours.

You glass is empty. This is not the central problem: it is a peripheral difficulty, solvable. The bottle of gin is two feet seven inches away from you: the golden label winks, light glances off the curve of its glass shoulder. The window is six feet four inches away from you. An approximation, but realistic. In seven steps you could reach the window, but in one step, you could take hold of the bottle.

Fuck. Fuck-a-duck.

One step. Nothing, correct? Perhaps. That would be a wise estimate, nothing to a single step, is that not so? But magnetism is the problem, the attractive pull of negative space. If you move, the force will increase; if you approach, it will become irresistible.

That's the worry. Magnetism. The hairs on your arm flutter, teased by the persuasions of that force. Oblivion beckons.

One step to reach the gin. You think you are fully capable of this, of a single step. You are not so old that you should totter, though some might think you so, with your hair gone to white, but distinguished, some would say, attractive even. You are stronger than they take you for—why should this frighten you so much?

Standing now, swaying slightly, you lean over and take up the moss-green bottle in your hand. Your weight shifts dangerously as you pour a drink, and replace the bottle. Prone to panic, this is enough of a trigger. Your throat seals itself up. You gasp, but the air is too heavy, viscous as molasses, and black too, also like molasses—and in that moment, you realize it is not air that you are breathing, but the night itself, which has crept in through the window, the night which has been slowly insinuating itself like a heavy gas, invisible and undetectable. There is a word for this. You reach for that word. Vertigo. You are light-headed and leaden at the same time. You are now less than four feet away from the window, but of course, it is not the window you fear, but rather the brutal cavity, the hole. How can an absence exert such force? You can feel the pull of it. If you fall, you know you will fall toward the window. You will fall and you will fall and you will fall. Your skin shivers and tightens, gooseflesh, and a hard weight in your stomach. You tip.

But then the drink is in your hand, the clear liquid perfectly level in the crystal tumbler. It does not flutter or distend. You see no signs of meddling.

And so you are perfectly calm.

You retreat with your gin, steady on your feet, entirely in control of your faculties. As the distance increases, your head lightens mysteriously, and you laugh at your own silliness. What a fool you have been, how extraordinary! You sit down lightly in your armchair. The pattern has always pleased you: diamonds picked out in gold, against black and blue. Jonathan did not like it, but you prevailed, and, as such, you have always felt a keen smugness in occupying this chair; You feel, you imagine, as Napoleon must have after Austerlitz. Marriage is a battleground, you have always thought so: at times it is filled with the *sturm und drang* of cannons, and yet it has its ceasefires, its quiet occupations, the extraordinary moments when the two lines meet, and cigarettes might be exchanged, stories of home, warily done, of course, but not without affection. Napoleon was famously in love with his wife Joséphine, and she with him; they took lovers, sometimes, fought bitterly, but this was a problem of timing. They were never in love with one another at exactly the same moment. It is easy to mistake this for a genuine lack of passion, as some have done. You stare at the diamonds, they have their own hypnotic power, and your nerves ease off their eccentric energy as the seconds slowly tick by. But then you are looking at the window again, and the hole in the window—and, beyond it, the night.

Is six feet enough? A safe distance? Should you go to bed?

It will not be so easily solved. You would try, of course, but if you were in bed, even if the duvet buried your neck and shoulders then you would still clench the white cotton sheets so tightly you would feel the imprint of every thread. You could not stop thinking about the hole. You would see it in a vision, on the ceiling, perhaps, or the door, or floating in space like a phantasm: the delicate bloom of cracks and fissures.

Several minutes have passed. Your tumbler is empty. The bottle of gin is still two feet seven inches away. The window is still six feet four inches away. The tableau is fixed as if in a museum. You crave sleep, but you fear it as well. What if you should sleepwalk? What if you should rise from the bed, unbeknownst to your conscious mind? Then you will be in its power completely, and can you imagine what it would be like, to wake and discover yourself falling? To find the wind ravishing you, the ground rushing up on your uncomprehending but now terrified mind?

From this height you can see the Chicago River. The boats thread merrily along beside those famous buildings, and in the distance glitter the bright lights of Navy Pier and its magnificent Ferris wheel.

So you explore the dilemma further.

You are on the twenty-first floor. It is a fact known to you that one should never take a room above the fifth floor, a point you made to Jonathan several times in your initial deliberations, but this was not one of your victories. Only the penthouse would do, he insisted. He did not understand. No ladder reaches higher than the fifth floor. Or perhaps a ladder might reach so high as that, but it is policy that emergency services will climb no higher than the fifth floor for fear of falling. And so, in the case of a fire, those occupying the penthouse suite, however much they have paid for it, however impressive and tastefully decorated it might be, whatever their fame and fortune, or, perhaps, because of this, there is no doubt at all that they will be abandoned.

Jonathan would not listen; he could be implacable.

Is there a fire escape outside this room? You do not know. You can only assume there is not, or if there were, it would be completely untenable in any case. The force of the wind at this height is enough to sway the building several inches, it would knock you flying. And this is the so-called Windy City.

But you could check. Would it reassure you to know that there is a fire escape? It would. But that would be impossible. To check would be to place yourself in too much jeopardy. You will not do it.

And yet, why? If you were to fall from this height, you would not feel it. You would only ever see the ground approaching. In the final six feet of descent, you would be moving faster than the signal in your brain, and so death would be painless, unprocessed: you could apprehend the ground without experiencing the final collision. Perhaps it would be lovely to die like that.

But you do fear falling: that empty space, the sense of powerlessness. But why should this terrify you? You know that marriages are built on emptiness: the gaps in conversations, the lags, silences that take upon themselves a weight. Jonathan was always rushing to fill up the emptiness; like the boy who sticks his finger in the dam, there was always another hole, and another hole. Eternity is like that, and marriage is, of course, like eternity.

You force yourself to blink, but the hole is still fixed as ever, still gaping, and so you reach for the gin. You hand stays suspended in the air above the neck of the bottle. You close your eyes once more. You try to imagine what it would be like to fall, but instead you imagine nothing at all: only blackness.

You open your eyes. How many minutes have passed?

The hole is bigger.

It cannot be a trick of the light, no, the hole is bigger. You are fascinated, but wary—the edges of the hole have peeled away like the petals of a dark flower. And the night is thicker, so thick it bleeds out over the carpet, sweet-smelling and rank at the same time, like lilies at a funeral.

There is a story about silence: a story she told you, Jonathan's friend, his little friend, his fuck-a-duck friend with the slim, white neck and the golden curls, the one who smelled of lilies, that one. She recounted it at a dinner party you held last November, a fine affair which the mayor and several councilmembers attended, the entire table was astounded and delighted, oh, they roared with laughter! She was quite the sensation!

She liked to travel, this pretty friend of Jonathan's. She travelled wherever took her fancy, eager to experience beauty, unwilling to leave any country unexplored. Napoleon, you imagine, was rather similar. He could not look at a map without wishing to conquer it. But Napoleon is not the point, this girl is, and so. She spent a month in India, in a Buddhist monastery, one of the few places in the world, she said, where one could properly contemplate such things as beauty and eternity. She had taken a vow of silence, she told you, her eyebrow cocked, a playful smile alighting on her lips as if to say, "What a thing it was! How charming!"

But she was a sleepwalker, Jonathan's friend, a condition she had managed all her life, though it seldom put her at a true disadvantage.

On a day soon after her arrival, she went to explore the city. This was encouraged to provide fodder for contemplation, but there were lepers in the city. Jonathan's friend had never seen a leper before. She was afraid of the way they huddled together in clots on the street with their fingers reduced to short stubs and their noses collapsed like old buildings. She was afraid of the things she had read about lepers, about their disease, about the putrefaction of their bodies. One of them asked her for money, but she could not say anything—at this point in her narration she would mime her consternation, her sadness at having no money to give them, but also her disgust at the sight of the lepers, her utter revulsion, and of course the councilmembers laughed along with her.

And so, without giving the lepers anything, she went away.

But that night, as she lay in her bed, tucked away inside the monastery, she dreamed that she was in the street again, with the lepers, and she was walking. She was walking, but because it was a dream, the ground moved strangely beneath her feet. When she tried to step over one of the lepers, she stumbled and fell. Her foot—naked now, because it was a dream—pressed into the leper. She could see the expression on the leper's face, something like horror and something also like hunger. As his body gave way around her foot, she could not free herself; the feeling, she said, was like trying to pluck a spoon out of congealed porridge.

She screamed, of course.

But there were others in the room she was sharing, fellow tourists such as herself, or contemplatives perhaps, and she woke up hunched above one of them, a terrified women, with her foot sunk into the pillow next to the woman's head.

And she couldn't explain. Not a word, the vow of silence, remember? And so she and the frightened woman spent the subsequent month locked together in the room every night, Jonathan's friend unable to explain herself, and the other woman no doubt terrified of her, afraid she was a lunatic.

She told the story charmingly, and the councilmembers were in stitches, the mayor himself tore a button from his suit, he was doubled over with such laughter.

But you were quiet. You and Jonathan both. And afterward you asked him, what was worse, the dream she had or the vow of silence that prevented her from explaining it? This was one of those rare times he took your hand. He told you not to be so silly. It was just a story, it didn't mean anything more than that, and he laughed but you could tell it frightened him, how those ruined bodies repelled her.

You have thought about this for some time now, and you believe you know the answer: the dream, you would say, was worse. The silence, although it may have frustrated her, also offered her a measure of protection. She never had to reveal, in the presence of those monks, how terrifying she had found the lepers. She should not have told Jonathan that.

The young are terrified by imperfection; they cannot imagine a world that does not serve them exactly as they demand.

It has been thirty-seven minutes.

Is that even possible?

You could not have been here for thirty-seven minutes.

But then, the hole can't be there either, it is impossible. The window cannot be pierced, you were assured of that, nothing could break the glass. And since the hole is there, anything is possible. The hole is like a penny thrown into the fountain. The hole is like a wish. The hole is magic.

You can feel it here, even though you are sitting down: it is like the room is tilting toward the hole, as if the room were a jar that was being shaken out very slowly. Your fingers clench on the arm of the chair, your nails dig into the flawless fabric, you could scratch it to pieces right now! Your knuckles are white. Your breathing is harsh. It makes a strange sound in your ears, like someone who has been weeping. The hole is bigger, and its force is magnified: the chair moves, to some it would be imperceptible but you have been steeling yourself for this moment, for the chair to move, to slide, just a little bit, toward the hole.

The world is not the place people imagine it to be. The world is full of pitfalls, and odd occurrences; it is full of hauntings and dark powers. The longer one lives, the less one comes to trust oneself in the perfection of the world, the more the struts of logic and reason are stripped away.

It is amazing what can happen to a body.

Let us take Jonathan, for instance.

You start to laugh, and the sound is a wild, howling thing, shocking in its intensity, echoing round and round the penthouse suite, bouncing off the Chippendale cabinet, the Japanese dining table until the laughter falls dead where the night is pooling beneath the crack in the window.

Pooling with . . .

Pooling with . . .

Take Jonathan, for instance. Jonathan who was always clean as a whistle, Jonathan who never left a mess before today, no, he was a Harvard man, perfectly appointed to his situation, never swearing, never one to say more than G.D. when he meant "goddamn," no sir, no ma'am, it was against his upbringing.

Marriage is a battlefield: Jonathan and you have known this for all your lives, you were like Napoleon and Joséphine, he and you, in love, yes, definitely in love, but never at the same time, not with one another. You have wandered in and out of love, as if it were a room in a house, as if you could only occupy it for a moment, on your way to more pressing matters.

But you always returned to one another. That is the point. Equal forces oppose one another, always. They strive for mastery, but no mastery is possible. You hated Jonathan, there were entire years when you hated him, when you stood across the trenches from one another with blood on your hands, unwilling to bend. You took petty vengeances on him, sank your claws into him deeply, but there were sweet moments as well, when he might take your hand and call you his precious, old thing—as he did that night, after the dinner. And yet you have the feeling that you have been sleepwalking all this time. Is that possible? That perhaps this is a dream? But, of course, it is not a dream. The details are too exquisite, the colour of Jonathan's blood on the carpet, the deformed lump of his flesh, it would repulse her, wouldn't it? Give her such nightmares?

The world does not work by ordinary logic, the ground moves strangely. . . .

You cannot stay here. The danger is too great for you.

Now that the thought is in your head it is positively urgent, there is no stopping the force of it. The hole in the window has swollen, but you can resist it, you are strong, you have always been known as such—Jonathan could never prevail against you, could never score a victory without suffering for it, that's the truth of it.

And yet it is attractive. You see the appeal of the emptiness beyond the window.

We have always found such wretched ways to fill the gaps, you think: with idle conversation, or sex, or power, or money—but these are diversions. You recall a story, told to you by your father, that Winston Churchill upon his visit to New York, awoke the day after Black Tuesday, to the noise of a crowd outside the famed Savoy Hotel; there he discovered the body of a banker who had dashed himself to pieces after a fifteen-storey flight. This was before you were born, but the story has always moved you, you don't know why. Yours is a generation of ruined skies. When you gaze up into the dazzling blue, you are as likely to see the billowing white plumes of the Challenger—how hopeful you were back then, how proud!—or the flutter of a hailstorm of burning papers and bodies, yes, bodies too, plummeting from the broken towers as you are to see the angels of previous generations. You have filled the skies with the bleak wreckage of your hopes.

And Jonathan has wrecked himself.

You loved him.

Did he not understand that? Did he not understand why you would not let him go from you, not after these many years? How could you survive it? He begged you. He pleaded with you, but it was nonsense, how many times have you pleaded before to be set free and he would not do it? Jonathan would have hated her, young and pretty though she was. He would have hated her for her youth, for her charms, he would have resented her bitterly for all she had that he had lost to old age. It would not have been the hatred you shared for each other, a survivable hatred.

"*France, armée, tête d'armée, Joséphine*," Napoleon said at the last. He had loved her.

And you loved Jonathan, even though he made such a mess of it. He cracked a hole in the centre of that love, and now every evil thing is rushing in to fill the space. He always promised you would outlive him. Sheer spite, he said, would preserve you forever, but you believe you might have been eternal, the two of you, circling one another, you exerted such a force, repellent and yet magnetic: it would have taken the collapse of the solar system, the collapse of the universe, to free you of each other.

And yet.

You are exhausted.

The night pours into the room, blackness, desperate and inexhaustible. You are tired of fighting; you let it coax you into sleep.

"Are you all right in there?"

The sound of knocking startles you out of your slumber, insistent, urgent. You stumble from the chair, and as you do, the glass tumbler you have been holding slips from your numbed fingers. It breaks into several bright, jagged pieces.

"Hello?"

You blink, and your eyes focus on the pieces of crystal glittering at your feet. You feel effervescent, drowsy, drunk.

You walk carefully from the chair, minding the glass, and open the door a crack.

"Hello? What's happened?"

The face that appears before yours is young, and very handsome: smooth cheeks, eyes as blue as cornflowers. You cannot remember his name, though you have seen him many times. A neighbour from downstairs? Harry—or Henry?

"I heard a noise," he says in that thick Chicago accent, lovely and raw.

Through the open door, you can see the warm lights of the hallway, and it occurs to you, right then, only then, you could leave. You could get out. You could walk through that door, and leave behind this battleground: the memories and torments, scars, loves, the reconciliations and romances, the feel of his hand upon your hip, coffee on his breath in the morning, the rustle of his newspaper expertly folded, the lilt of a New England accent when he was drunk, the thousand recollections upon which you have built a life for the two of you.

You could take the elevator, take the stairs. You could be on the ground floor in no time. No time at all. You could do it. Then it wouldn't matter. It would just be a hole in a window, a crack in the glass—pedestrian, harmless. You would be so far away, you couldn't fall. You couldn't fall then, and it couldn't take you.

And before you can think what you are doing you lurch toward the door.

But he is there.

"Oh, God," he says, "what's happened to you? What's happened? There's blood!"

The young man grabs your arms. Though you struggle against him, he is far stronger than you are. His hands are like vices around your wrists.

"No no no no no," You mumble. He pretends not to hear you. He pushes you into the room.

"What was the noise?"

"It was the glass," you say wildly.

"What glass?" he says. But now he is staring at you. His testicular Adam's apple bobs up and down nervously. You have seen that look before.

"I must look a mess," you say. You finger the silk of your dressing gown plaintively, and pull it tighter around the waist. He shouldn't see you in your dressing gown. You aren't fit for company now. He takes a step forward, and you retreat toward the table. "The glass."

"Where?"

You point, and he kneels down at your feet. He is so close, you can see the fine, golden hairs on the back of his neck. You can smell this fellow— Harry, or Henry—as he begins to pick up the largest of the pieces of broken glass. He smells good. He smells like Jonathan smelled. Perhaps it is the way all of these men smell. Is that possible? That perhaps all men smell the same?

"Be careful," you say, "not to cut yourself. You might cut yourself."

He places a long sliver of glass on the table next to the bottle of gin. The glass is beautiful and sharp, cut like a diamond. You shiver. Just a little bit, you shiver. He is such a handsome man. No more than twenty-five: gloriously twenty-five, all charm, all innocence, but here he is, and it is late, and he has seen you in your silk dressing gown.

You know what men are like when they see something. And he has not looked beyond the table, not beyond you in your silk dressing gown. He has not looked further than that. You touch his hair. You take a step, but the ground moves strangely beneath your feet, and you stumble. He catches you. His hand on your wrist again, but this time the touch is light, tentative, as if he were asking you to dance. He *is* very young. Such a confused look in those cornflower blue eyes of his. Your dressing gown is slipping open, and you move to close it again—but pause. "Will you take a look?" you say.

He nods again, uncomprehending, you think, but intrigued. Men are always like this. Jonathan was always like this.

Harry's eyes are wide, very wide, as you step aside for him so he can see what has happened.

"Oh," he says. It is a little noise. Such a little noise to come out of that beautiful little mouth of his. "Oh," he says, and that's how it starts, "oh God!"

"Harry," you say. "Please."

"Oh God! Oh God, fuck!"

"Fuck-a-duck," you whisper, but so quietly he does not hear you. His hand tightens around your wrist. It is so tight that it hurts. You moan. You can't help it. He stops hurting you then but he is pushing past you toward Jonathan.

And the hole.

The hole has become very large now. It has become greater than the window, its tendrils spidering out into the very architecture to devour the frame and the moulded settings, it has eaten up the curtains and the lacquered table. It is hungry for everything.

Harry. He takes a step toward it.

"No," you tell him. "Please don't."

He is at the chair. Six feet four inches. You know that distance very well, but you can see clearly he is unaware.

Five feet.

Four feet.

He is crossing the distance like it is nothing.

"What have you done?" he demands. "What happened to him?"

You take a step toward him. Toward Henry. Toward Jonathan.

"Just tell me, okay?" he stammers. "I won't do anything. Just tell me what happened. You've got to tell me what happened. Was there an accident? Was it an accident?"

He's afraid. The poor little boy. Oh, but he is afraid. And you realize then that he is afraid of you, and isn't that funny? Isn't that just the funniest thing in the world? Because you did not do this, you did not shatter the world like this.

It isn't you he ought to be afraid of.

You are coming to rescue him.

"Just stay there, Harry," you say, "just stay there and I will come and get you."

The world tilts around you, gravity twisting in the wake of those two bodies: one living, one dead. You can feel the wind fluttering at your dressing gown.

The hole has stretched open like an angry maw. It is big enough to take a man, and it has sharp, sharp edges. You can hear the noise from the street so loudly now, the honking of traffic, and the quiet hiss of the cars driving past.

"Take my hand, Henry," you say.

You cannot move any closer toward him, you are too close already, and yet you take an involuntary step forward. Your whole body shakes.

"Take my hand."

You reach toward him to bridge the gap.

And he reaches too.

But his hand is red with Jonathan's blood, and so you shriek. Harry stumbles backward.

It is too late.

The hole has taken Harry.

It is has just lifted him straight off his feet. He is gone. He was here a moment ago but now he isn't. If you were to look through the window you would see him floating. You would see him floating the way all those men floated off the buildings when the stock market crashed.

Drifting down.

Like sleepwalkers.

Harry won't feel the ground.

That gives you a little peace of mind.

Poor Henry.

But you are here. You are still here.

But the question is.

The question is. Is it still hungry?

You are two feet away. You can feel the night breathing against your skin, tugging at your dressing gown. You can imagine the wind whipping out so fast that it grabs you. Grabs you the way it grabbed poor Henry.

You can feel the touch of the wind against you, and you moan. Just a little sound, like someone sleeping.

It still wants you. You know it still wants you: the way Jonathan still wanted you even if he would not admit it, even when he scorned you, even when he hated you. He would still come to you. Jonathan was never filled up with anything, never.

What a wreck he has made of himself! She would have scorned him! She would have scorned his mutilated flesh, a brainpan cracked open, a bullet that has continued its course through him and out, into the night air where perhaps it is travelling still. She would be repulsed to see what he has done to himself, and yet you feel something like love. It is too late, of course, but it is love. You have always been out of sync with one another.

You sit down heavily into the chair, mindful of the glass scattered at your feet. The night is spread out before you. When you look out, you do not see the bright lights of Chicago set in their jagged, familiar line; rather, you see the cosmos spiralling on and on, infinitely spacious, infinitely empty, the plumes of gas jettisoned from collapsed stars, the burning debris of inconsequential matter. At the heart of the glorious, perfect machine? A brutal cavity, fuelling the movement of the stars themselves . . .

Perhaps the sky has always been ruined.

And then it is coming for you, the darkness, that eternal, irresistible force, it is coming and coming.

Six feet. Then five feet. Then four feet.

Then three. Then two.

Then.

"I think, sometimes, that she used to be someone else before she came here. I think we were all someone else before we came here."

In the Moonlight, the Skin of You

I remember the winter that Dad brought home that blacktail buck tied to the hood of his car. I could smell the blood. Dad seemed like he was covered in it.

And here was this thing, this giant, beautiful thing with antlers branching out like forked rivers. The kind of thing you just wanted to touch, just wanted to tangle your fingers in. Do you remember the old nursery rhyme? Did you have it as a child?

I know so little about your childhood. Where you came from. Why you came here. Why you chose *me*.

But the rhyme. This is how it goes. *Here is the church, here is the steeple. . . .* I used to do that with Mom. That's what the antlers made me think of. The way her fingers folded with mine when I was very young.

Dad loved hunting. They all do here. They all *did*, anyway, until Mads died.

For so long, I wanted to love it. I wanted to so badly, but there are some that can hunt and some that cannot. That's what Dad told me, his mouth a thin line and something like anger on his face. I think it would have made things easier if I could have been more like him. I was a girl. That was the first strike against me. But there were so many ways I failed at being *his* daughter. Hunting was only one.

You came to know that about me. You who loved me best. I think you were maybe thankful for it, if thankfulness is a thing you can feel, but not Dad. Not Dad. You could see it in the way his mouth would crease like a badly used dollar bill as he was cleaning out the gun, getting his pack ready. He never asked me to go with him. Why would he? Me, a girl? A woman one day? But I knew he wanted to. I always got this sense when his eyes glanced over to me just before he'd leave. Me, curled up into the warmth of the chesterfield, reading one of Mom's old books. He'd tense. It was the fact that he couldn't ask that made him angry.

That he knew before asking I wouldn't go.

"Anna," he would say. "I'm going out. Don't let the fire burn low."

"Okay, Dad," I would say.

"You'll freeze, Anna. You hear me? Pay attention, child."

"Yes, Dad. I won't let it burn low."

I knew he wanted there to be something between us, just as I knew he'd always wished—just a little bit—that I had been born a different kind of person. One he could love better.

I saw sometimes the way he'd look at the boys. Baldwin, who drank gin on Fridays and could skin a hare no problem, and Mads. Mads was seventeen and he had been going to the camp for years. To haul wood or watch the ropes, fetch the older men their coffee. Mads had thick, muscled arms. A quiet disposition. He spoke softly and not often, the same as I did, but Dad still loved him more than me. Those boys were the sons he should have had, their mothers the wives he should have had.

"Mads," he would say. "*There* is a boy for you. A boy like that will take care of you, Anna. I seen him cut and haul like he has done this for a good long while. I seen him snare that fox begging round the camp. Just like that. Almost cut the beast a-two."

Those boys would be men one day.

But there is another thing, I remember, and this one has stuck with me. It wasn't a nursery rhyme, but it was something *like* a nursery rhyme, you know? The kind of thing Mom might have told me when she was telling me nursery rhymes. Her voice was so beautiful. It made me feel the way you told me that listening to rain makes you feel. Sad and happy. Peaceful. Like you've got so much space on the inside, in your ribcage, that you could never see the horizon.

The thing she told me—it must have been her, because who else, except you, would tell me that sort of thing?—that if you killed a buck then his wife would seduce you. Crazy, isn't it? The kind of things she said to me.

But I remembered her voice and the thing she said when Dad came home that day.

The blacktail was strapped to the hood of the car, even though you're not supposed to do that if you want to carry it home right. You taught me that. It looked broken. The deer, that is. His hind legs roped to the car, ropes fixed to each of the tips of the antlers, pulling its head up and away from the chest. I couldn't see where the bullet entered. I knew it must have been near the shoulder, or maybe behind a bit where it would have struck the heart or the lung.

"Do you want to see the bullet hole?" Dad asked. He was proud. I could see he was proud. The deer was huge. It was massive. Mads would have been impressed.

"No, Dad," I said.

"Mebbe I could show you."

Have you ever seen what a deer looks like when it's been stripped down and skinned? Same, pretty much, as with its skin on. When I was younger I'd always worried that it was the skin that kept everything together, you see? That if you took the skin off something then you'd just have a bag of guts spilling open. But it's not like that. You take the skin off a deer and you've got something that looks just like a deer, except it's red and shiny at the neck, the muscles running down to the shoulders, and then these great skeins of white fat marbling the rest of it.

"I show you," he said again. "Please, child."

"Okay."

It wasn't so long after that you came.

I don't know why Mom left. She never said anything beforehand. She used to write in the evening, sometimes, when she was done minding me, when I was calm and settled. I remember that. When I was going through her old things afterward I found a piece of paper tucked into the pocket of one of her sweaters. This is what it said:

> I am ~~standing by the~~
> standing by the window
>   in light
> like it's from a different place
> where I know ~~myself better~~ you.
>
> The moon ~~scares me~~ (?) sometimes
> as much as ~~love~~
> the way the light is falling
>   and you
> cutting it apart with your body.

I don't know why Mom left but I also don't know how she came to be here. How she came to love Dad.

I think, sometimes, that she used to be someone else before she came here.

I think we were all someone else before we came here.

"I show you," Dad said to me. And there was something in his eyes.

"Okay," I said to him.

He started with the forelegs, which he sawed through easily. He hoisted the deer on a gambrel hook, mounted an anchor beneath the tailbone, and tied a rope in a hangman's noose so that it would continue to tighten. Then he tied the rope to the back of the truck.

"Here," he said. "Handle the truck."

"Dad. I don't want to."

And he gave me a look that sliced through me as easily as a fillet knife.

I took the keys and started up the truck. I didn't know how fast to drive, but as soon as I slipped it into gear I could feel the resistance.

"Good," he said. "Easy, now. Just like that."

The engine was rumbling beneath me. The truck smelled of old cigarettes and sweat—a gamy sort of smell. I kept the pressure even on the accelerator. I didn't want to look in the rear-view mirror, but I couldn't help it. Dad was over top of the thing, working furiously with the knife, freeing the meat up underneath. Grunting. Mostly, I could see, it came away easily under the tension but sometimes the silverskin—the fatty film-like substance—would hold fast and he'd have to slice at it. He knew what he was doing. The cuts were short. The knife was sharp. He wiped sweat away with the back of his hand.

I hated to see the deer slowly unravelling like that, but when it was finished, Dad smiled at me. A smile I had never quite seen before.

"I seen you do it well," he said.

I felt a strange and unwanted pride rising up inside me as he clasped me on the shoulder. My cheeks were burning. But I felt. Happy.

Later that night I couldn't sleep. The image of the skin coming away haunted me. I had dreams—bad dreams—in which I felt Dad standing over top of me, working away at my skin with the knife, that same smile on his face.

"There's someone else inside of you," he said. "I seen him. Hold still, child."

I woke up in a sweat, sick, wasn't happy until I'd emptied the contents of my stomach into the sink.

Do you ever try to remember what it was like before you were born? I read about that once. Some people can't look at old pictures of their parents. It's like death for them. Seeing the happy faces of people who live in a world where they don't exist yet. Where maybe they'll never exist yet.

One day at school I saw Mads by the dogwoods, way off on the other side of the fence. You were with him. You must have climbed the fence or maybe taken the easy way farther down where it had been bent up and you could crawl under, if you wanted to. But I could see you on the other side of the fence, you and Mads. I could see you through the crisscrossed chain-link. I had always figured it might be Finn you'd go with, or Baldwin even. But I knew Mads by his red hair, even at the distance. And I would know you anywhere.

The dogwood was blooming. It was white and perfect from the distance. That's why you went with him, I imagine. To see the dogwood blossoms up close. Even now I imagine what it would have been like to lie underneath the dogwood tree like it was one of those heavy clouds waiting to lay a blanket of snow on us both.

Or else maybe he had caught you. That's what scared me most. Maybe he had found a way to snare you.

I don't think you saw me.

After Mom left, the house smelled different. It breathed different. The air moved in and out of the rooms with a different sound, as if it was scraping underneath the doors now, as if it wanted to go with her but it couldn't because she was already gone.

Dad didn't know what to do with me. I had been *her* child. I didn't settle easily anymore, and he had a host of new responsibilities. The first time I saw Dad with his hands in the soapy water, fumbling with the breakfast dishes, I couldn't believe it. I thought it was someone else. I thought Dad would never do that. But there he was, dirt-crusted sleeves rolled back past his elbows, taking the dishes out one by one. The soap made a perfect, slick rainbow, and I thought it was beautiful, the way he was there, washing the dishes like that. Like he was afraid they'd break apart in his hands.

"Bring me the dishes, Anna," he said.

But I wouldn't. They were Mom's dishes.

And then there was that day that Dad brought the deer home. I was older then. I hadn't met you yet, but when I saw it I knew I was going to meet you, I don't know how. Sometimes you just know things. I felt something new breathing inside of me, and it was like the way that it was just before Mom left, because I knew that was coming too. Everything she did became so gentle. So precise. The way she'd stroke my hair down.

Dad was that careful when he took down the deer, and he slid the skin off it.

I don't think Dad knew about the thing Mom had told me.

It was the week after that you came.

You had hair so fine that it clung in all sorts of shapes to your sweater. You weren't used to how dry it could get here in the winter, the cold snaps. Your voice sounded different than everyone else's voice because we had all learned how to speak together, and it was only when I heard you speak that I realized there was a different way to do it. That words could come out differently if you let them. If you learned how somewhere else.

You laughed at different times than everyone else did. I didn't mind. I liked to hear you laugh even if it was when you shouldn't laugh. And you didn't know the things we all knew, like what to do if you ever saw a bear, how you shouldn't use perfume, even in your shampoo, because of the way it could attract animals.

That meant the first day you were at school Britta didn't like you, because you smelled so nice and your hair was so much finer than hers. It took a while before she left you alone. That must have made it hard for you. You must have been very lonely in those early days.

I wanted to say something to you in the beginning. Oh, my hands would shake when you walked by, and my body would get flushed with the heat of you sitting next to me, sometimes, if it happened that way. And remember the first time I did say something? You laughed. I don't remember what it was that I said, but it made you laugh.

"Anna," you said. "Oh, Anna!"

That was good, but I hadn't meant to make you laugh then. Even if it was nice to hear you laughing. Britta didn't laugh though. And, later on, she taught you what things were funny and what things weren't funny, and so you didn't laugh so much after that.

It was hard, that year. It was hard to have someone like you so close to me. I never knew what to do with myself. It was like another person had jumped into my skin.

❀

I think Mads might have been holding your hand. Under the dogwood. I think I might have seen him kiss you.

Was that his mistake? The first one?

❀

When Mom taught me that rhyme about the steeple her hands were very soft. I always wondered if maybe your hands would feel like that. Mads had hands that were rough from the work with the lines and from the few times that someone in the camp let him use the axe. I think Dad taught him how to do it, but it might have been one of the other men. Baldwin's father, maybe, or Britta's. I had never used the axe before. But Dad took me out to the camps once so I would see what they were like. I don't know what I thought it would be like. It was men drinking coffee from old thermoses. Some of them worked the big trucks that would haul the lumber out.

But I could see the way they looked at me. They did not want me there. Not these men. These boys who would be men. I made them nervous. They did not chatter around me. They kept their tongues.

Dad showed me one of the trails that he'd cleared to a new patch of wood, the ones they'd maybe be starting on soon, he told me.

"This is mine," he said. "I cleared the way myself. They will all follow after me."

He was proud of the trail. He was proud of the trees.

I tried to imagine him roped in by harness to the top of one of those trees, stripping away the branches so that it would fall cleanly. It was so high up. I told him that, and he said he was never scared when he was up there.

"The ropes will hold me," he said. "I won't fall."

"But someone else fell."

"Mebbe. But it won't be me," he said. "Not me. I know the trees too well for that. It's only the young 'uns that fall. The crazy ones. Or stupid. They don't check the equipment first. I seen them at it."

It was the longest speech I had heard from him in years.

"What about Mads?" I asked him. "When will he become a high-rigger?" Mads had been telling us that's what he was going to do.

Dad chewed on the inside of his cheek a little. His beard was just starting to grow in salt and pepper, the beginnings of an old man's beard.

"He won't," he said. "Mads? No. He's a good boy, mebbe, but he won't be a high-rigger." And he looked at me. It was this strange look. Like he wondered who I was. What I had heard.

There were secrets among the men in the camp.

"Okay," I said, "maybe I'll become a high-rigger."

And Dad just stared at me. He stared. And then he shook his head. It was slow the way he shook his head and something made me think of him washing those dishes back then, the way he set them down so carefully even though they'd already been chipped in small places before.

"No," he said at last.

"Why?" I asked him. I thought of the men in the camp. I hated those men. I hated their stares. "Maybe I could do it."

But he didn't say anything else and he took me back to the camp, then, away from the place he'd started to lay out for himself.

He told Mads to take me home that evening, and even though I could tell Mads wanted to stay out with the men longer. When the coffee changed to whiskey or mash then it would be a different sort of evening. I was ashamed because I didn't know the way. Dad walked these roads every day to work, and Mads did too, but I didn't know them like they knew them, and, besides, it could be dangerous at night.

Mads was an inch taller than me. His shoulders were broad. I could imagine the muscles knotted and hard beneath his shirt. His legs were longer and I had to hurry to keep up with him. He wasn't resentful, though, about having to go back. At least he didn't show it. He was kind. Polite. A bit shy even the way men sometimes are around me ever since I filled out. That's what Dad called it. Filling out. But eventually we got to talking. I asked him a bit about what it was like to work with the other men, and he said he learned a lot about drinking and swearing and other things besides.

"What other things?" I asked. He didn't want to talk about it at first, and so we walked a bit longer. The night was starting to settle like a blanket around us, but Mads wasn't worried, he knew the way.

"It's like this," Mads said after I had pestered him for a while. "There's things the men seen."

"What things?" I asked again.

He made a noise in the back of his throat. And when he looked at me there was something I didn't expect to see. Helplessness. He looked trapped.

"There was this time," he said. I didn't know if he was going to keep going, but he did.

"There was this time and I was in the woods near that clearing that Jon, I mean, your father was out at. I was just bringing him the coffee but then I seen something in the woods. I know not to go wandering because of the animals and such, but I did anyway, and I seen something." His voice changed a little, saying the words the way Dad might have said them, not the way we learned at school.

"What did you find?" I asked. He took a step closer to me. I could smell the sweat of him. The dark, burnished tang of it. And for the first time since we had left camp I was afraid.

"It was just this old deer hide. Like someone had been hunting, even though you're not supposed to near the camp, and just left it out in a pile after the field dressing, all slick with blood on one side. I thought I'd take a look. You know, it's not good to leave something bloody like that out in bear country. And you know, there was a hole in it, just there. A bullet hole. Just next to the heart. I figured whoever'd made it did a pretty good job of things up until that point. But then."

I didn't want to know. I wanted him to stop.

"Then what?"

"I don't know if I should tell you this." He looked at me, and I could see some part of him *did* want to tell me. Some part of him was hungry to tell me his secret.

"Please," I said. *No*, I thought. *Do not tell me this.*

"Well."

"Please," I said again.

"I was feeling around this hole with my finger and it didn't feel like a hole. It just felt . . . soft. Warm. I don't know. Like putting your hand into warm water. The softest, sweetest thing I'd ever felt."

"Oh." He was standing so close to me.

"So I took out my, uh, thing. And. I put it in there."

"In where?"

"In the hole. And. I don't know. It just felt so good. So I pushed and I pushed and I pushed and it was the best thing in the world, like nothing else. Like nothing else I've ever felt." The words came tumbling out of him in a rush. He couldn't look at me, and then, all of a sudden, he did: his eyes were round and terrified, but full of something else too— desire, a kind of desire that scared me.

"Oh," I said again. I didn't want to look at Mads then. I didn't want to look at the bulge of his thing in his pants. But I could feel the heat coming off him.

"I left it there in the woods," he said after a bit. "But the men. Sometimes when they get to drinking, they talk about stuff like that. The things they seen in the woods. They seen all kinds of crazy things, and some of it. Some of it is like that."

It seemed very dark then, and even though Mads frightened me, I was glad he was there with me. I was glad I was not at the camp. The camp where men told stories like that.

"What does my dad say?"

"Oh," said Mads. "Your father doesn't talk about stuff like that."

And then he turned away from me. Like he had realized something.

"Let me get you home now, Anna," he said.

I think you knew I loved you from the very first moment.

Mom never liked to use the word "love." She'd write it out in poems sometimes, or in other things, but then she'd always have to cross it out.

But I think it is love. What I have. I think this is what love is like.

I remember, when I was older, the first time you let me hold your hand. I asked you about kissing Mads underneath the dogwood and you laughed at that. You thought it was so funny. You told me you had just been waiting, really. You were waiting for me to lie down beside you.

I was so awkward. You said I should have found my way to you sooner.

I remember the first time you let me slide the sweater off your shivering body. It was all pink underneath the way I'd always imagined it would be. The little goose pimples that I tried to smooth away, and the way that made you laugh because they'd just come back again, and you didn't mind them anyway.

Dad never talked much after Mads died.

It was just the kind of thing that happened. Freak conditions. Nobody knew what he had been doing so far from the skidder trails. But the cold out here can kill a man if it catches him after dark. If it catches him in the woods, lost, too far from the paths he knows. Or maybe Mads didn't want to find his way home. There were things out there, he had told me. I had seen the look in his eyes. I know what that feeling is.

Sometimes you don't want to come home.

Or you want to stay lost.

Sometimes you are willing to lose yourself.

I still love to listen to you laughing.

My dad won't speak of it. What happened to Mads. No one will speak of it.

I love the way sometimes you still don't know the right things to laugh at. I love it when you get it wrong and you don't mind how people might stare at you because they know you come from somewhere else where other things are funny and people say things differently.

Is this how it will always be between us?

Sometimes I think there are things you got wrong, coming here.

Maybe it was deliberate. I don't know. But I wonder. I wonder about when you fell in love with me.

"Oh, Anna," you said. "Anna."

I wonder who else you might have loved once. I wonder what happened to him. You once told me there was a thing you were supposed to do, but then you met me. I led you astray. But you led me astray as well.

Sometimes I see you look at Dad. I'll say something, and maybe you'll laugh. But he doesn't laugh any more. Not when you're looking at him. I think he knows what you are. I think he is afraid of you.

Sometimes when we are together I think back on Mads and what he told me. It feels like that when I am with you. Like I am filled with all the wrong kinds of desire. There is a terror in my heart.

But I cannot stop.

It feels like the best thing in the world.

The only thing in the world.

I think of us lying together covered in the white petals of the dogwood. I think of pulling off your skin and wrapping myself up in it until I am sealed tightly and perfectly inside you.

I love the way your skin pimples when you are cold. I love the way your hair clings in strange shapes to the pillow when you are lying next to me. I love the way it catches the moonlight from the window.

I love the way the air stirs in the house when you are here with me. As if the house is holding its breath.

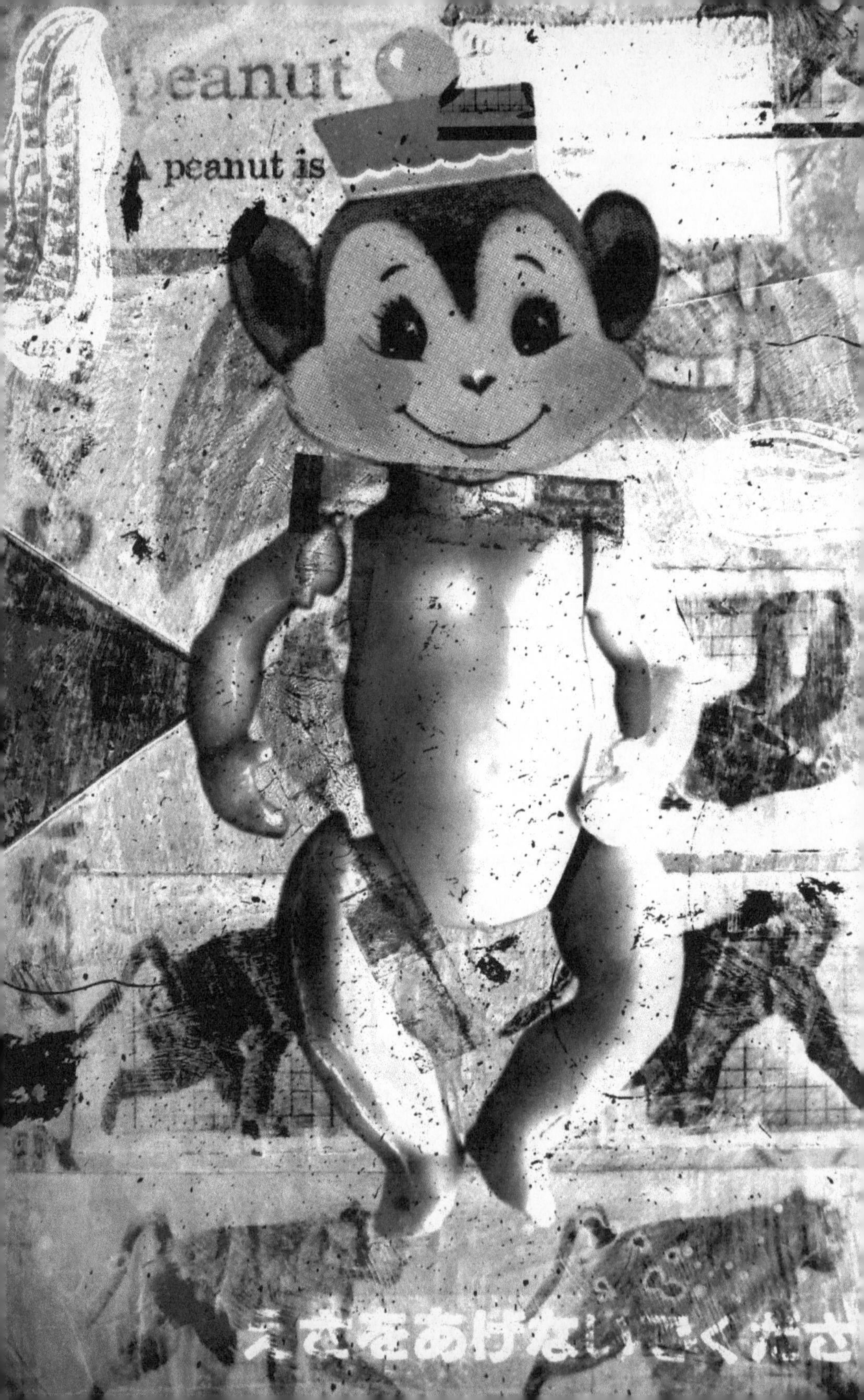
peanut
A peanut is
さをあげないでくださ

"But what we do here only works with animals. Not people. I'm sorry, kid."

THE GALLERY OF THE ELIMINATED

The zoo, for Walter, was a magical place.

At eight years old, he loved the thick animal poop smell of it, the bright orange paw prints. He loved the blue-green of the aquarium and the way the light made weird shadows across the brickwork. He loved the monkeys, yeah, the monkeys were always good! He loved the way his pops gave him a bag of peanuts and made him swear to God to keep half the peanuts for snack time, and half the peanuts for the monkeys who gave big stupid grins and fought when he tossed one in the cage.

He loved the way his mom said she disapproved, but then she wouldn't look away—not to snap a picture of the macaws maybe, or the bonobos which Walter never liked as much as the chimps. She'd just stare. She'd tut maybe. She might scowl. She might even shake her head and whisper, "Honey, don't! Don't let him!" But she'd look. She'd still look. Then Walter would flick a peanut through the octagonal mesh and watch as the bigger monkeys wrestled down the littler ones. He'd watch their teeth shining like little knives. He'd watch their fingers crack open the shells.

His mom used to smile at the monkeys' antics. She might tap the sign that said "DO NOT FEED THE MONKEYS!!!" as if she hadn't been complicit, as if she hadn't wanted to see them fight too. Walter loved the way she smiled at them; her smile wasn't anything like the monkeys' smile. It was thin, delicate. Pretty. It was a smile with a certain kind of substance to it, like perfume. It was there. It wasn't there.

The smile made his mom beautiful.

The zoo made his family beautiful.

It locked the animal parts of their love in cages.

They were free to wander, to hold hands, to point and marvel and giggle together. Afterward, if Pops had got work that week or his mom had picked up enough tips, they would eat ice cream, all three of them. His mom and Pops would share. Walter wouldn't have to share. Walter would get his very own cone, all to himself. He'd stick his tongue deep into the cone like he was drilling for oil and the ice cream would well up over the edges so he would have to lick it clean before it dripped.

Sometimes he would eat his mom and Pops's ice cream too because, even sharing, they wouldn't finish it on their own.

Walter never had to share. His mom and Pops did. But Walter always got his own.

That was the way he liked. That was the way he wanted it to be forever. Him, his mom and Pops.

Until.

❀

It was at the zoo they told him.

"Hey, champ," said Pops. He was holding a bag of peanuts. They were close to the monkeys now. His mom was standing beside him and she was resting her hand very lightly on his arm.

"Can I have the peanuts?" he said.

"Not just yet. We have something to tell you."

"Okay," said Walter. He kicked a rock. The rock went clang against the cage, and startled a hornbill.

His mom and Pops looked at each other. They smiled. "Well, champ," said Pops. "We. Well. You. I mean, this is about you too. *You* are going to have a little sister. A little baby girl. We're so excited!"

And they were. Walter could see that they were. They had big stupid grins plastered all over their big stupid faces.

"*You're* excited," he said. Walter kicked another rock. The hornbill squawked angrily.

They waited for something else. Their smiles remained frozen in place. They stared at him.

"Okay," said Walter at last. And that was that.

But it wasn't okay. Of course it wasn't okay. Walter knew he would have to *share*. His room. His toys. His parents. His ice cream. No more single cones for Walter. No. There would be a baby girl. A baby girl to fight with to see who got to lick the cone first. A baby girl who smelled like poop. A baby girl to make his bedroom smell like baby girl poop.

He'd have to share *everything* with her and he had so little already! His room was small. It was very small. Yes, his mom and Pops had put up glow-in-the-dark stars on the ceiling that went green when the lights went out. But that didn't mean it was as big as outer space. Not really. It was fake. There wasn't any space in the room at all! Not enough for a little sister!

They were whole as they were. They were perfect. How could she be a part of that?

How?

❧

His mom got big. She got big as a pumpkin. Big as an elephant!

There was nothing delicate about his mom now. She plodded. Her ankles were thick. The sight of ice cream made her sick and Walter couldn't have any, but then, suddenly, his mom would need ice cream, she had to have it immediately and she'd work her way through an entire carton in one go and none of it would go to Walter.

"Good morning, Mom," Walter would say at the breakfast table.

"Say hello to the baby!" his mom would exclaim.

"Hello, baby." Walter would whisper. It was like there was something trapped inside her. It was like the tigers when they slept in their pens. Sometimes they wouldn't come out for Walter. And Walter would shout, "Hey, tiger! Tiger!" Sometimes nothing would happen. But sometimes—sometimes—the tiger would let loose with a roar that shook his bladder. Walter didn't do that anymore. He had once seen a tiger piss on a man with a camera from ten feet away!

The baby was like that. Sometimes the baby kicked.

The baby kicked and his mom got bigger.

Just as his mom looked so big that, really, it seemed impossible that she wouldn't just split open, they had to go to the hospital. Pops had told him they'd have to go to the hospital. Pops told him they would need to be *ready* to go. They could go at *any time*. There were bags to be brought. There were things they would need. Walter would have to help them remember.

But when they went they didn't bring any of the things.

"What about the bags?" Walter asked. "You said we have to bring the bags? What about them?"

"We don't need them," Pops said.

"But why?" Walter asked. "Doesn't the baby need them?"

"Christ, Walter. Not now!"

And Walter flinched. He ran away from Pops and he sat on his bed. He breathed in the air. It smelled like dirty sheets and stale farts. He knew that smell. It smelled like him. He was *used* to the smell. But was it a good smell? Suddenly, he didn't know. Suddenly, he wondered. Maybe it wasn't a good smell. Maybe a baby girl would smell better. Maybe baby girl poop smelled better than dirty sheets and stale farts.

But then Pops was storming into the room, and he grabbed Walter by the wrist.

"Get in the effing taxi, will you, Walter?" But he didn't say effing like he was supposed to and so Walter was afraid. Walter was afraid all the way through the taxi ride. It was like his pops wasn't his pops anymore. And his mom. She grunted and squealed. Her face was grey. There was blood on the seat of the taxi. There was blood everywhere. It was like the time Walter had the nosebleed. Except it wasn't like that. Not at all.

"Should we get ice cream, Pops?" Walter asked very quietly.

And Pops stared at Walter. He stared like he was going to start yelling again. But then whatever animal was inside of him went back to the corner of the cage, and it was just Pops again. He didn't say anything. He just put his arms around Walter and started to cry.

They rode like that all the way to the hospital.

The hospital was a strange green colour. It reminded Walter of the colour of the aquariums. They made his mom wear a big plastic-green gown. Pops wasn't crying anymore, but Walter could feel that somewhere inside he was still crying anyway.

Pops bought him things out of the vending machine. Walter wasn't hungry but he munched on chips anyway. And then a chocolate bar. It made him feel sick but he didn't stop. Pops just kept bringing him more and more until Walter was sitting in a little pile of wrappers that scrinched and crunkled whenever he had to get up to pee.

And Walter wasn't allowed in the room. Only Pops was allowed in the room. Pops would go into the room. And then Pops would come out again. And mostly Pops would go to the vending machine and he would buy more things for Walter to eat.

Once a little girl came by. She was wearing a white dress with pink roses. The hem was dirty. She had the look of someone who was sick. The way everyone in hospitals looked. Pale. Grey. There were dark circles under her eyes, but she was smiling.

"Who are you?" she asked.

"Walter," said Walter.

"I'm Emily." She kicked at one of the wrappers. It didn't go very far.

"Are you sick? You look sick."

"The nurses think I shouldn't be out here. I'm not *really* out here, okay?" She winked. The bruises around her eyes winked too.

"I'm getting a little sister."

"Oh," she said. "Can I have a chip?"

Walter gave her a chip.

"Ewwww," she said. "Sour cream and onion!" And she ran off giggling.

Walter wondered if his sister would wear a dress like that. He kicked his feet. The pile of wrappers scrinched and crunkled. He decided he liked the girl. He decided he didn't like sour cream and onion anymore.

But then Pops went into the room and when he came out he didn't buy anything from the vending machine. "I'm sorry, champ," he said. "You aren't going to have a little sister."

Walter's stomach ached. His mouth was covered in chocolate. The taste of chocolate made him feel sick.

Pops sat down heavily beside him. The wrappers went scrinch and crunkle. Walter hated the wrappers. He hated them so much.

"I would have shared, you know," he said. And Pops didn't say anything. His breathing was a heavy whuffle. Walter tried to touch his hand but the wrappers went crunkle and scrinch and Pops flinched, and he stood up, and he went back into the room.

Walter thought of the girl. "Ewwww," she had said. He had liked the way she scrunched up her face. Just like a monkey.

"I would have shared with you," Walter whispered. "You could have been my sister. You should have stayed with us."

And the baby said nothing. Because she wasn't there anymore.

And for a while after everyone was sad and they didn't go to the zoo anymore.

This is how it was for months.

His mom didn't leave her room much. Walter could hear noises through the walls. Sometimes they were low and crooning. Like a deep-throated bird. Sometimes they were high, shrill and broken—animal sounds. Hungry. Desperate. Nothing human sounded like that. His mom never sounded like that.

And Pops was different. He spoke in a whisper now. His back was hunched at the dinner table. It was just the two of them. Pops spooning out three-day-old chili and when the meat ran out, then just beans and onions with a dollop of sour cream on top.

It made Walter think of the girl. Walter didn't like to think of the girl. There was a hole inside him when he thought of the girl.

And the hole sounded hungry. It sounded desperate.

It tasted like stale beans and souring cream.

And all Walter wanted was for his mom to smile again. Just one Mom smile. And then he knew it would be okay.

He wanted to tell her maybe his sister would come back. Maybe she'd be ready soon. Maybe they just have to wait.

So he waited.

And the hole got bigger.

And the hole got bigger and bigger.

And the hole got so big Walter thought it was going to eat him up. Him and his mom and Pops and all of them.

And when the hole got so big that it seemed that everything was the hole, that there was only the hole, then Pops came home and he said, "Right, champ, we're going to the zoo."

At first Walter didn't say anything. It was like Pops's voice was coming from somewhere outside the hole and it took a long, long time to reach him.

"What?" he said.

"The zoo, champ. Get your things. We're going to the zoo!"

"What about school?" Walter asked.

"No school today! Call it a holiday! Call it an educational trip! You like the zoo, don't you? You want to come with your old man?"

"Sure," said Walter and part of him was happy—part of him was ridiculously happy, part of him was grinning like an idiot. But part of him was not. Because Pops wasn't grinning.

"Is Mom coming?" Walter asked.

"Mom is sleeping," said Pops.

"Should we wake her?" he asked.

Pops said, "Not today. We'll let her sleep today. It'll be just us boys. Just the men, okay? You're my little man, aren't you?"

Pops looked tired. The skin around his cheeks had started to sag and wrinkle. His eyes were wet and glassy. Walter thought, just for a moment, that he might reach out and touch his father's face. That he might stretch out that skin again. Feel the roughness of greying stubble. But he didn't. He got his things and climbed into the car.

Walter knew the way to the zoo by heart. He knew the road signs. He knew the turn-off. But he didn't know these road signs. He didn't recognize any of them.

"Where are we going, Pops?" he asked.

"Just you wait, champ." Pops said.

And they drove. And they drove. Walter got tired. He leaned his head against the window, watched the strange landscape, the dying light, and he slept.

Then Pops was shaking him awake.

"Are we here, Pops?"

Walter wiped his eyes. His head felt heavy and aching from the heat, his stomach queasy. He looked around. The place was a dump. A real dump. There were two large wooden gates done up crusted red and yellow paint. A welcome sign that did not say "Welcome." Instead, it read, "Gallery of the Eliminated." Further down, a postscript: "Limited engagement." The sign was old. A stiff breeze would have knocked it free.

"Pops, I don't think I want to go to the zoo after all."

"Of course you do." He took out a bulging travel pack and slung it over his shoulders.

"But Pops—" Walter tried.

Pops tugged him along into the queue.

"C'mon, champ. Just like I promised."

When they reached the ticket ripper, he looked Walter up and down with a steady, loveless gaze.

"How much for this one?" He asked. Pops gave a guffaw.

"This one stays with me," Pops replied.

The ticket ripper did not laugh. He shrugged his nobbled shoulders and when Walter passed he leaned down a great ways and whispered into his ear.

"Don't you dare feed the monkeys, you hear? Don't you dare. Don't you goddamn dare."

The zoo looked different than any zoo Walter had ever seen before. There were no bright paw prints on the ground. There were no safari wagons selling ice cream. The place was practically empty.

"Pops," Walter began.

"Isn't it great, champ? Isn't it just something else?" Pops's eyes were gleaming. His mouth was stretched wide. Not like a smile—like when the monkeys jammed their fingers into their mouths and pulled and pulled and pulled on their lips.

"Yeah, Pops," Walter said at last. He didn't want to look at Pops anymore.

And, well, the zoo *was* something else. It sure was. Not like the zoo he knew at all.

"Pops," Walter said, "what is that thing?

"That's an aurochs, champ."

"What's an aurochs?"

"It died out a long time ago, champ."

And he was right. That's what the sign said. AUROCHS—DIED 1627— KEEP HANDS OUT!

And the aurochs was massive! It had eyes the colour of black marbles and horns that curved out into a nasty hook. Walter wanted to touch the horns. He wanted to bury his hands in its deep, matted wool. He wanted it very badly.

"Whoa, champ," said Pops.

Walter snatched his hand away from the cage.

"Please, Pops," Walter whispered. But his Pops took his hand and led Walter on to the next set of pens. When Walter looked back, he could see that one eye—that giant eye, the size of an egg, but black as outer space—following him and his Pops as they went.

They walked until the sun had rounded the tops of the buildings.

There was the striped quagga, the size of a miniature pony but striped in gold and brown. The herd skittered away as he approached them. They were nervous things. Walter loved them anyway.

QUAGGA—HUNTED TO EXTINCTION—DO NOT TOUCH!

Walter did not touch them.

He heard the sad, low howls of the Honshu wolf. They were small and spotted. Their ears flexed back against their skull. It looked like they were grinning at him. Walter grinned back. So did Pops. He pulled at the corners of his mouth, stuck out his tongue, and made the best Honshu wolf grin that he could. And then they both began to howl together. They just threw back their heads and let the noise come pouring out of them.

HONSHU WOLF—DIED 1905 FROM RABIES—KEEP BACK!

Walter was getting sweaty and hungry, but he didn't want to stop.

"C'mon, champ," said Pops. "We need to take a break. Just a quick one, okay?"

"A quick one," Walter repeated.

"That's a good boy."

Pops tugged him inside the shelter of one of the main buildings. The blast of air was cool and welcome. The air conditioner rattled like a tin can.

"Here?" said Walter,

It didn't look like a reception area. The walls were painted bright yellow. The trim was the colour of dried blood.

"This way, champ."

The hallways were narrow. They were lit by fluorescent lights and filled with the buzz of overworked air conditioners. There were pictures hung up, dusty, unlit. Walter could still make out the shape of a bird's skeleton in one. It looked like a picture in a science book. There were rocks with bones poking out of them. Fossils. Walter wanted to stay longer to look at these, but Pops was pulling him along now.

"Pops," Walter said. "My feet hurt. Can I take a rest?"

"Just hang on there, champ," he said. He pulled Walter up short in front of a door that looked no different than most of the doors they had passed, with the word GRANT stenciled onto it.

Pops stared at the door. Walter stared at the door too but he didn't know why.

"Pops?" he asked, but he was hushed with a flapping of his hands.

"Quiet there, champ. There's just a thing I have to do. Okay? Just one small thing? Will you let me do this thing?"

Walter looked at his Pops's face. It was flushed. There was a strange twist to his lips.

"Sure," Walter said at last. Then Pops knocked very loudly three times.

The door swung wide open. Behind was a very thin, very tall man. His face looked like a melted wax candle. His cheekbones were sharp. He made a soft whicking sound when he inhaled.

"You are Mister Crewe," he said in a nasal voice (*whick, whick, whick* went his lungs). "I believe we have been in correspondence?"

"I was hoping you might," Pops stuttered. "That you could. This is a very special facility, isn't it? And I understand, well, that is I wanted to talk to you about—" Pops trailed off as if he had forgotten what he was going to say next. Then he unslung the travel pack and started to open it. When he caught Walter watching, he stopped. "Could we speak inside your office?" He hesitated, looked at Walter again. "I couldn't leave him at home. My wife isn't well."

"Yes, fine." The man ushered Pops inside with a wave. Walter tried to follow. "Not you. You can stay out here." He placed a hand on Walter's shoulder and gave a little push.

"Is that all right, champ?" Pops asked. His voice was small. It might have been scared.

"Yeah," Walter said, at last. Pops patted Walter on the head.

The door began to close behind them and suddenly it wasn't all right. The door reminded him too much of the hospital door. The hospital where he had lost his sister. Walter didn't want Pops to go in there alone. "Wait," he called out, and the door opened an inch. That fleshy, drippy face appeared in the crack.

"Yes?" (*whick whick*)

Walter didn't know what to say. Pops had gone in there. Pops had asked him to stay out. Walter knew that he *wanted* him to stay out here. He *wanted* him not to know what was happening in there.

"Please," he said. He tried to poke his head through the door. He could see something on the table. A dress. His mom's dress—the one from the hospital. It was covered in blood. Pops was clutching at it. He was sniffling.

But then there was the man standing in front of him.

"Stay," the man hissed. "This is not a place for children."

The door slammed an inch from Walter's nose.

❀

Pops had left him in the hallway. There was a chair. Walter didn't want to take the chair. He started to walk.

He didn't know where he was going. Not really. There were rooms coming off the hallway. Each one was labelled with a name—BARROW and ZEIGLER and DENNISON—but Walter didn't know those names or whom they belonged to. They reminded him of the animal pens.

At the end of the hallway were two rooms with open doors. The room on the left side contained a skinny, dark-haired woman. Her face was covered with red blotches like strawberry jam. She didn't look at Walter. The sign read KIST.

In the other room was a woman who was fat. Very, very fat. Walter had never seen a woman so fat! Great rolls of flesh flubbed off her stomach. The fat woman looked at him. Her eyes were small and wet. They peeked out from underneath the flesh. She said nothing.

"Where did you come from?" he asked. The question just popped out of his mouth. The fat woman said nothing. The question hung in the air between them.

At last the fat woman smiled and her jowls quivered with tiny little vibrations of laughter.

"From my mother," she snorted, "who do you think?"

Walter wanted to leave. He wanted to go back to the chair, but he had talked to the woman. She was peering at him curiously. Like she had never seen a boy before. He knew he was in it now and deep too. He scuffed his shoes.

"Me too," he said at last.

"My mother was a lion tamer."

"She tamed lions?"

"Until the lions ate her."

Walter again was silent. He watched the fat woman. Her stomach rippled and bulged. He wondered if she was hungry. He wondered if that's why her stomach was moving like that.

"I like lions," Walter said.

The fat woman shifted on her chair. It was like watching a tower of jelly move. Every part of her seemed like it spread in a different direction. She rippled. She fanned out.

"I like the lions as well."

"Even though they ate your mom?"

"Yeah," she said. "That's what lions are there for. To eat things. Not much good a lion does otherwise."

"Oh."

Walter turned to leave.

"Wait," she said. "Do you want to see something, kid? Something special?"

"Sure," Walter said uncertainly.

"Close the door."

Walter went to the door. He thought about leaving. He thought about running back to his Pops and pounding on the door until they let him in. He thought about going home. He wanted to go home very badly. But he closed the door. He turned back to the woman.

"Good," she said. "Now watch."

She squinted her eyes until there was barely anything left of them. She stuck out her tongue. For a moment, Walter thought she was holding her breath. Her face began to turn red. There were bright red splotches just below her eyes. Her neck was flushed. But now she was grunting. It was a deep, guttural sound. The sound a warthog makes.

And then the flesh of her stomach began to move.

Walter gasped.

It wasn't just that she was shaking. It was that it was *moving*. It was *crawling*. Her shirt was pulled so tightly that Walter could see the way it rippled. There was a bulge. It pressed against the fabric. The woman let out a mighty grunt, and then a whoop.

But Walter was watching her stomach in wonder. The bulge became something recognizable. A nose. A nose pressing against the inside of her stomach. Suddenly another divot. Two. There were little knobs in the centre. Three of them. Like knuckles. And then the straining became more intense. The knobs pushed further and further until Walter could count toes.

"Bugger," said the woman and she heaved herself out of the chair. She was shivering. The veins were standing out in her neck. And as she moved, the fabric of her shirt finally gave with a tremendous ripping sound. Walter wanted to turn away, but he couldn't. He was fixated. He was rapt. He could see her breasts hanging like old rucksacks. The nipples were round and brown and thick as rope.

Then, slowly, slowly, the ripping sound began again. But this time it was not fabric. No. Her shirt was in tatters from her shoulders. The tails fluttered as she heaved the breath into her lungs.

And the ripping continued.

And Walter could see the woman's flesh beginning to split. Slowly. Slowly. An inch. Another inch. And through the tear came a tiny black nose. No bigger than a puppy's, but with two giant nostrils pushed. And then an entire snout. The jaw was blunted. The lips flexed like a camel's. A long tongue—as long as Walter's hand!—darted out to taste the air. Then came the rest of the head. It had great jowls, furry, slicked with blood and slime. And Walter could see an ear matted into the fur, twitching.

"Watch—" grunted the woman. "She's coming!"

And this time Walter *did* turn away. He didn't want to watch anymore. He ran to the door, gulping at the air. He couldn't breathe. The door wouldn't open. His hands trembled on the handle. Slicked around it. He couldn't get the thing to turn.

"There!" screamed the woman, "there! There!"

There was a popping sound. A deflation. The sound of a slow, wet fart.

"Boy," the woman called. "Here, boy. Look."

Walter turned.

The woman's stomach was torn open, and her eyes were white and round with pain. But she was pulling safety pins from the table beside her. A long string of them. And she was poking them through the skin. Her hands worked fast. She was very good at it. She barely had to look.

"Ugh," said Walter.

And the woman gave a giant belly laugh that made the vast surface of her torn skin twitch and shudder.

"Pass me a blanket," she said hoarsely. "There, in the cupboard. Go on."

Walter went to the cupboard and he pulled down an old grey blanket. The kind he had seen in the chimpanzee enclosures. The fabric was rough against his fingers, but the woman took it easily enough. Draped it around her shoulders. Her fingers pulled her stomach together.

"She's a beauty," the woman muttered.

At first Walter didn't know what she was talking about. But then he followed her gaze, forced himself to look properly at the . . . *thing*. The roly-poly ball of fur lying between her knees. It blinked at him, the eyes still unseeing. Or seeing for the first time.

The tongue darted out and touched his knee. Walter let out a yelp and leaped away from the beast.

"Careful," the woman said. "She'll startle easy. Keep down the noise, would you?"

"Okay," Walter whispered. "Okay."

"You can touch her if you like."

Walter shook his head. He didn't want to touch it.

"Go on then."

Walter shook his head again, but this time he knelt down to get a better look. It looked something like a bear, but not quite like a bear. The size of a German Shepherd, maybe. Maybe an anteater. Its eyes were close to its smooth, brown snout. Two pinpricks in a giant heap of fur. It looked a little like it was smiling. It looked a little like the fat woman.

Walter put out his hand carefully. The little thing reached up one of its own paws. It had three long claws and they curled very carefully around Walter's thumb. He giggled. He couldn't help it.

"What is she?" he asked. "It's a she, yeah?"

"Megatherium," she said. "The giant sloth. Died out, oh, ten thousand years ago. I'm mostly good for the Pliocene era. Mammoths. Stegodonts. Three-toed horses. Jeanine in the room over does cats."

"Whoa," said Walter. He tilted his head. The sloth-thing tilted its head as well. Puckered its lips. "She's beautiful!"

"I know," said the woman. She reached down and she plucked the sloth-thing into her massive arms. She pulled it close to her face. Slowly. Slowly she began to lick at it. Walter knew it should be gross but somehow it wasn't gross. It was delicate. Like she was eating an ice cream cone. Lovingly she began to clean the sloth-thing with her tongue. Its eyes blinked. It let out a tiny murmur. It reached its spindly upper arms around her neck and nuzzled its head against her chin.

Walter watched in fascination. He wanted to hold the sloth-thing himself. He wanted to cradle it in his arms and feel its animal weight.

He reached toward it but the fat woman pulled away.

"She needs sleep now," the fat woman said. She wiped her mouth across her wrist. She rested her chin down. Smiled when the sloth-thing's long tongue touched the bottom of her cheek.

"Thank you," Walter said, "for showing me that."

The woman said nothing for a moment. Then she got a look on her face. "Well," she said. "I probably shouldn't have. But. You know."

"What?"

"I know why your dad is here."

Walter thought about this for a moment. He didn't know why Pops was here.

"It's a survival instinct. You never lost a parent so you don't know what it's like."

"You mean your mom? And the lion?"

The fat woman blinked. "I guess I do. It's bewildering, you know. To realize that you are next. Link by link, generation by generation, the chain of your people are yanked into death. And you are *next*—the link before you? Gone. Your last protection. But losing a child is different. It's like seeing the end of the chain. Watching it dangle over the abyss. Your dad, well. He's lost. But what we do here only works with animals. Not people. I'm sorry, kid."

"Why?"

"Do you know how many mass extinctions this earth has seen?"

Walter stared at her. "What's a mass extinction?"

"That's when everybody dies. Everybody. All the animals. Wiped out. Just like that. An asteroid maybe. Or climate change. Whatever. It's happened five times."

"I don't believe you," Walter said.

The woman shrugged. "Fine," she said. She gave a tremendous yawn. The sloth-thing stretched against her. Curled its snout into her giant breasts. It made little whimpering noises from time to time. "Whatever, kid. This little one here? Starved to death. Her mother died. Hunted by our ancestors. Maybe one of mine even. Ha. And she couldn't feed herself. Not even with that great big tongue of hers. Every species has a *last* one. And this is it. The last Megatherium." The woman sighed. "But that was *ages* ago. Ages and ages." She tickled the fur underneath the sloth-thing's chin. "Just you wait. She'll get big enough to knock down trees. Four tons. Like an elephant. Can you imagine that?" She bopped the sloth-thing on the nose. The creature scrunched up its face, pawed at the air. "People are different than animals. There are so many of us, right? Six billion! But there will be a last human. Maybe not now. Maybe not for a while. But there will be."

Walter watched as the woman's eyes drifted shut. Her thick lips let out a snort. Almost a snore.

And he thought about the hole that had swallowed his mom. Had almost swallowed him. It had a name now.

Extinction.

He knew it was silly. Nothing had changed, had it? Not really. His family was exactly the same as it had been before: his mom, Pops, Walter. The three of them. But it meant something different now, didn't it? That was why his mom wouldn't come out of her room.

Because, one day, there would be the last kid on earth.

Right then he missed his mom with a viciousness that reminded him of one of the baby's kicks. He wanted to curl up next to her. He wanted to nestle his head underneath her chin.

"I don't believe you," he whispered.

Walter went to the door. It was time to find Pops.

"Hey, kid, wait." Walter turned back. The fat woman blinked her eyes fuzzily. Waved a hand toward him. "Just a second. Just a second, kid, you hear? What was your sister's name?"

"I don't have a sister," he said.

"But you were supposed to, right? That's why you're here. What was her name going to be?"

"I don't know," said Walter. Then: "Emily."

"Okay," she said. "Emily is a pretty name. You wave goodbye to Emily." The sloth-thing yawned delicately. Walter could see the white nubs of its teeth. "And come back soon, you hear? Then you'll see something special. Emily'll be something then."

"And she is sleek, gorgeous and deadly—this thing I know is my own death."

THE SLIPWAY GREY

For Hugh William Knyvet-Knevitt

Sit by me, my bokkie, my darling girl. Closer, yes, there.

I am an old man now, and this is a thing that happened to me when I was very young. This is not like the story of your uncle Mika, and how he tricked me in the Breede river and I almost drowned. It is also not like the story of my good friend Jurie Gouws whom you called Goose when he was alive, which was a good name for him. He used to hitchhike all across Rhodesia until he blew off his right thumb in that accident at the Selebi mine, which I will say something about. Afterward the trucks would stop anyway, even when he wasn't trying to hitch a ride, because of the ghost thumb, he used to say, which still ached with arthritis when it rained.

These are what your father would call fables or fancies or tall tales, and perhaps he is right that they have grown an inch or two in the telling, but the story I will tell you is a different sort of story, my bokkie, because it is my story and it is a true story. It has not grown in the telling because I have never told anyone about what happened except for your Ouma, God rest her soul, to whom I told all the secrets of my heart and let her judge them as she would. Still, even she did not know what it meant, and neither of us could ever come to much agreement on this.

I am getting older, and I can feel the ache Jurie complained of in his thumb. It lives in every part of me, but my lungs most of all which the doctor tells me are all moth-eaten by the mining work, even though that was many years past. Perhaps you will say that moths are not made for lungs. They are made for closets and for fine things such as the silk your Ouma wore on our wedding day—white silk, the finest Tsakani government silk, so fine it felt like water in my hands, but then after she died and I went to see to her things, there it was, so thick with moths in the crawlspace she had hid it, so thick it was as if she had made the dress of these little white-winged creatures with their dark nesting eyes, and maybe she had, maybe there had been nothing but moths on her as she walked down the aisle to marry me. But the way that dress looked when the moths had scattered—all coming to pieces in my hands, this beautiful thing, this beautiful thing I had loved so much when I had seen it that day, the doctors say that is what my lungs are like now, from the mine dust.

When a man gets older a man starts to think about all the things in the world—like you, my bokkie, the things that he loves and the things that he will leave behind—but then he also thinks about the place that he might be going to and the people he might see there, like Jurie and the others and especially like your Ouma who has had to wait far too long for me to catch up with her.

The story goes like this, and I know you have not heard it before, but even so, if you have heard parts before or heard something like it then keep still, my bokkie, keep still and listen, for a thing that starts the same does not always end the same.

I first met Jurie at Howard College when I was studying. He was an Afrikaner like I was and he was also studying engineering. From that first look, I judged Jurie to be something of a NAAFI, which is to say, No Ambition and Fuck-All Interest, if you don't mind me saying so and please don't repeat it to your father, but that is the kind of man he was. Skinny as a bushwillow, with a mess of bright red hair. He had the look of a travelling man, and that is an untrustworthy sort of look. As it happened, though, I spent much of my time studying and Jurie spent little enough time at the same endeavour, still when our grades were posted he consistently beat me. I knew he was not a more diligent student than I, and I guessed he was not a smarter one. I confess this rankled somewhat, particularly because I was only there because your Uncle Mika had paid my way to University instead of going himself, and even then he had just been drafted into the National Service, though it was as a cook, thank God, and not a proper service man because he had flat feet.

So it was that near the end of term, after I had had a somewhat ill-informed dalliance with a particular lady who was not your Ouma, because this was before your Ouma and before I found out what love was, that my grades started to slip. You see, my bokkie, the thing about women is that they have a power about them that is not unlike that story Jurie told you about his thumb. Women are like that, they've got the power to stop you in your tracks. You will be the same, my bokkie, just you wait.

But I won't go further into that matter here, for the sake of your Ouma who, if she was listening, wouldn't like to hear it much repeated. The important thing is that I found myself in a somewhat precarious position in terms of my schooling. I had watched Jurie, who, as I say, seemed no smarter than I was, rise higher and higher in the postings while my own place suffered. As the end of term stepped closer and closer, I found myself in what you might call desperate straits, so it was then I approached Jurie and enquired in what might have been rather ruder terms than I shall repeat as to the nature of his successes.

Jurie did not answer in the manner I expected. He was, you see, used to that sort of line of questioning, and had developed a limp and the occasional black eye from answering badly. That smile of his, well, I'll tell you that it didn't hang quite so straight on his face back then. Remember, I wasn't an old man and so all this skin you see hanging off my bones and my lungs raggle-taggled, well, it wasn't much like that. It had been remarked more than once that I could have been a champion boxer if I had applied my mind to that instead of engineering. I confess I might have asked Jurie in such a way that he considered it wisest to answer quickly. So he tells it, anyway.

He told me that he had learned a special trick to train his mind.

Now I know, my bokkie, that this might sound something like those other tales I started off with, but I swear to you that isn't the way of it. What Jurie could do I had seen with my own eyes, and this is it: he would sit in a certain chair suited to relaxation, and then he would take a certain word, which I shall not tell, and he would repeat it over and over and over again. He described the sensation to me as standing at the top of a stairwell partially submerged in water, and as he would say the word, he would take a step farther and farther downward until such time as he had drifted into the water, until it reached his knees and then his belly and then his shoulders and then his chin.

When he was deep into the water, so deep he was floating and he could feel nothing but the warmth of the water and all weight had left him, then he would imagine three boxes adrift in the water. As he continued to say the word, he would swim one stroke closer until at last he had reached the boxes. Then he would open each box and he would place inside each box some part of the day's lessons. Once the whole process was complete, he would begin to stir again, and his eyelids would flutter wild and delicate, then the rest of him would stretch and yawn, but the knowledge would be lodged firmly in his memory.

I thought this sounded a fine thing. When I saw it at work it seemed no harm so I asked him to show me how it was done.

Jurie was reluctant. He said that it took time to master the skill properly, but after some time and some insistence eventually he relented. It is difficult to tell you exactly what the experience of that meditation was like, as I have never felt its likeness at all except for, perhaps, the look in your Ouma's eyes after we had come to the decision together about what should happen, which was a thing both frightening but somehow also calming in the end.

That is what the experience was like.

I stepped into the water, lower and lower, but he had not told me how lifelike it would be. For Jurie's eyes had a furious calm to them, as if he was stepping into a bath, but for me the water was strange and dark. Instinctively, I did not want to go into it.

To understand this properly, I must tell you something about your Uncle Mika and the Breede River. I know, my bokkie, that he has told you this story before, but as I said earlier, a thing that starts the same does not always end the same.

There was a time when we were much younger and we lived along the Breede River. As boys, he and I would go diving in the waters because unlike most of the waters in those parts it was free of crocodiles and mosquitoes and hippopotamuses. Because we were boys, and because I was bigger than Uncle Mika even though he was older, he would often make challenges to me.

He would say, "I expect you cannot swim as fast to the other side of the river as I can," or, "I expect you cannot take that man's prized rod and tackle," and so forth. That day, he said to me that he reckoned he could stay under the water longer, and I, of course, reckoned otherwise, and so it was set that we would swim out a ways and then we would both go under together. Your Uncle Mika was a damn sight smarter than me in those days, and he took with him a straw he had fashioned for the purpose of breathing under water. The Breede, you see, was so murky in that part that though I could see him, I couldn't see anything like the straw he had fashioned.

So down we went, the two of us boys, and out came your Uncle Mika's straw, and he blew and he blew until it was cleared of water and he could breathe as if he were upon dry land. Down I went, and I sank right to the bottom because I was heavier than he was, and I kept my cheeks puffed out and I stared at your Uncle Mika, so close to the surface and I confess I might have laughed to myself, I confess I might have thought him something of a *moegoe* or a coward as you would say it, so close to the surface where he could just pop his head up when he was tired. Even then I knew it is not good to have the thing you want too close to you, not if you want to resist it. No, I knew I would do better in the depths where I would forget what sunlight looked like and forget the taste of the Sunday morning air.

Of course, as you would have guessed it your Uncle Mika could hold out for far longer than me, what with his straw, and though I sat at the bottom, heavy as a stone, smart as a crocodile and laughing in my head at him, I began to feel a burning in my lungs. A little thing at first, but need is need and the need for the Sunday morning air was not likely to diminish. Your Uncle Mika sucked away at it, but me, down there in the darkness with the weeds, I had to live off only what I had taken down with me. So my lungs got to burning, and my lungs got to burning, and all I got see was your Uncle Mika happy near the surface and looking like he might go on forever.

There is only so much a man can take, my bokkie, and I had long past reached it. So finally when I tried to push to the surface, my lungs feeling like they'd take in the water as happily as the air and my vision all gone strangled and dim, well, wouldn't you know it but down there in the muck I had managed to hook myself well and good on the trunk of an old yellowwood, it being, as I have said, a sight murky at the bottom.

It wouldn't have been a difficult thing to get free of. I was a strong boy and a good swimmer, but I was weak from holding in my breathing, and the first thing to set upon me was a panic so strong and so terrible that I flailed like a mad thing.

Your Uncle Mika, he was just about getting tired of playing that old game anyway, and he looks down and he sees me flailing about, and all he can think is the tales the old fishermen used to tell him about the things that lived in the water, the things that none of us quite believed would ever come so far inland. So your Uncle Mika, he hightails it out of there, thinking I'm already dead, thinking that the thing, whatever it is, has already got me. I can't fault him for it, even if he was my own brother, but still to this day I think that is why he sent me off to university even though I was never quite as clever as he was. He always felt the shame of tricking me with that little straw and then leaving me to drown.

So there I am at the bottom of the Breede River, caught up in a tangle with an old yellowwood and not long for the world, I reckon, and soon sure enough the water on the other side of my lips is looking sweeter and sweeter if only so that it'll stop that damn fire in my lungs. That's when I see it: to this day your Uncle Mika doesn't believe me even though he's seen the old lady himself, but I swear that I saw something dark moving through the water, and to be sure, it was exactly the same thing that your Uncle Mika had been afraid of—an old Zambezi bull shark, the grand dame of river sharks, I reckon, her body like a torpedo with a slit-open mouth across the front, head wavering back and forth as she slid oh so delicately through the waters.

They say those sharks are killers, man-eaters, they call them, the slipway greys. Sure as Hell if I had thought drowning would be bad, it had nothing on being taken apart bit by bit by those teeth of hers.

But this one, she just glided past me, a solemn thing, beautiful even though I can't tell you how, until the darkness and the murk closed around her once more.

Who can say if I really saw it? I certainly believed it. It was only a moment later that your Uncle Mika was in the water again, and he was hauling me out by the shoulder, by the hair, by any bit of me he could grab hold of. You see, he'd realized there was no blood, and if there had been a shark, there would've been blood. So after a minute up on the banks, gasping like a son of a bitch, he was in the water again and he was after me and I'm sure that I owe him my life for it.

But that shark, that slipway grey . . . I swear to you, my bokkie, there was nothing more frightening in the world, not even the fear of drowning, than seeing that old thing gliding past. My father, he was a religious man and he spoke to us boys about angels and signs and such, and I swear to you, that day the Angel of Death wore a face and that face was the face of the slipway grey.

I have told you all this for a reason, though, and that is to say that deep water has always had such an effect on me. It is enough to shiver my blood and tighten my balls, if you don't mind me saying. I still cannot shake the feeling that deep water, it was not made for the likes of you and me. It was made for the angels and the demons of this world.

So when Jurie set me to walking down those steps into the cold blackness of those waters, saying that word over and over again, a kind of creeping terror stole over me. All I could imagine was the feel of something against my legs as I crawled through darkness towards the three boxes he told me about, but I did as he told me, and I opened them one by one, and into them I placed the day's lessons. When I woke, cold-soaked and sweating, there it was in my head, and to this day I still know the things I learned. I only have to travel in my mind to the boxes.

As you know, Jurie and I became close friends, and I suspect I owe much of my career to him and his tricks. Indeed, it was the very next semester that I met your Ouma, God rest her soul, and if I thought the first woman had a kind of pull about her, well, there has never been another woman like your Ouma.

The next part of the story happened some time later, once Jurie and I had both taken jobs at the Selebi mine in Botswana. I know you have not been to the mines and so you do not know what it was like there. The job of an engineer is to make a place unfit for man livable, and that is what I did. I was the winding engineer, it was my job to inspect the shafts and make sure there were no obstructions for the man winder, that little elevator the workers used to ride, ninety, a hundred-fifty, up to three-hundred-sixty metres down to the bottom where they loaded the copper and tin into bins.

On this particular day, Jurie and I were riding on the top of the cage of the man winder in order to perform an inspection upon its gears. This was the part that I disliked most about the job, that great fall into the black, just watching that cable unwind slowly as the winding engine driver lowered us down. Jurie, of course, was Jurie and it never bothered him in the slightest, he was the sort of man who could raise a smile on the Devil's lips if he had to. In those days we could not get a radio signal in the mines so we used a system of bells to communicate with the surface: one chime to stop, two chimes to raise slowly, and three chimes to lower. So this time it was three chimes to lower, and down we went, one, two, just like that and the winding engine driver sent the cage a hundred metres, two hundred metres into darkness.

It was at about the two hundred-fifty metre mark where Jurie was fooling around as he did sometimes, knowing that I was a nervous man about such things. Sometimes he would joke about the other men, and sometimes he would sing that old mining song. "Shosholoza," he would sing, "shosholoza, you are running away on these mountains. Eh, boss? Sing it with me." And the sound would echo back up through the mines like Jurie was the tongue kicking around at the bottom of some enormous throat.

Shosholoza, shosholoza, he was singing like a madman, and me chiming three times for the winding engine driver to take us the rest of the way down.

And Jurie's just been singing along—"shosholoza, shosholoza," he's singing like a drunk, "go forward, go forward," he's singing—and suddenly he's hollering up a storm. Underneath us the cage starts to shudder and shake—snick, snick, snick—making a noise. Oh, my bokkie, I don't have to tell you that it is every mine worker's nightmare. That sound. The feeling of the world shifting under your feet and a straight plunge into darkness waiting for you. It sends shivers through me even now, just remembering.

But there it is, the man winder tilting sideways until there's a shower of sparks as it scrapes along the side of the shaft, but not budging too much because now it's jammed solid in the shaft. Then I can see something flashing like a snake in the bright cone of my mining light, something winding through the air, fast now, hooking back and forth. I'm looking around and then I see what it is, one of the stabilizing guy wires snapping free.

It's snapping mad like a hyena put off her dinner for too long, and Jurie's still shrieking, and I can see he's over by the cage's metal guide, and now he's waving his hand around and the air has gone heavy and sour with the smell of blood.

You've seen Jurie smile that goose smile of his, yes, I know it, but you've never seen the way a man smiles in pain, you've never seen the way a man's lips might become something else, might change the very shape of his face when he's staring at the stump of his thumb down there in the mine's darkness, two hundred metres from a sunlight you don't know you'll ever see again.

That snapped guy wire, you see, that wasn't enough to drop us solid—thank God for that—but it was enough to jam us down there. Jurie with just that stub of his thumb bleeding out on the cage. Me with nothing but that bell to tell them what had happened.

"Eh, boss," says Jurie, and I don't even know if he can tell what he's saying, but he's whispering, "go forward, go forward" still as if the song's just kept running through his head, teeth flashing white and glowing in that thin beam of mining light.

I chime the bell once, and the cage, it stops grinding away. At least it's steady for a moment.

I look at Jurie, and Jurie looks at me. He's licking his lips now, I don't know if he can feel the pain, but he's licking his lips just like he's going to settle down to a chicken dinner, like he's so hungry and that scares me all the worse.

"We'll get you, Goose," I say to him, "they'll be coming down here for us, you know that." I'm tearing off something of my shirt, and you can hear that noise, that long rip echoing back up the throat of the mine. Then I'm wrapping it around him, wrapping it around that hand, and I can feel the blood pooling sticky onto my hand, and I can hear him breathing heavy now in my ear. "Eh, boss," he's saying, as he holds his other hand over mine 'til I can feel them almost tacking together with the blood. "Eh, boss. You gotta climb, you gotta climb now."

I know he's right. I know that bell isn't enough, and if we wait, well, Jurie's bones wouldn't be the first to feed the darkness, his blood wouldn't be the first dripping down into the great dark black. But, dammit, if there isn't a worse thing I can imagine at that moment than climbing. But there is need, and I know it, and I know that if I do not climb then Jurie will be dead.

There are vertical ladders—five, six metres each—running up the side of the shaft, so before I think about it, before my brain slams on the brakes, there I am, twenty metres up, Jurie's mine light winking away below me, him slumped over away from the broken guy wire. And then I am climbing. I am climbing and the shaft wall is wet with groundwater leakage, and it is running down the metalwork too, down those ladders I am clinging too. And my hands, my hands are wet with Jurie's blood, but I pull myself up, I pull myself up until after a while I can hear Jurie singing, "go forward, go forward" in that crazy, pain-mad voice of his, or maybe I'm just dreaming it by then.

Because it is just like being underwater. It is just like that, the darkness close around me, and my muscles burning, burning. But I know that if I slack for a moment now, then I will plummet all that way and the dark will take me too.

So I start saying a word.

I started saying that word that Jurie taught me years before, and with every hoist upward I am saying that word now, I am breathing that word out and I am breathing that word in again and I am getting higher and higher and higher away from the blood and the cage and the pool of light beneath me.

And as I climb higher, it is like I am swimming up from deep water now, swimming from the ocean floor up and up and up to sunlight and the Sunday morning air.

But I know I will not make it. I know my strength is failing me.

I am a hundred metres up now. I am a hundred and twenty metres up. If I fall, I will die.

And there is something in the darkness with me.

Something in those dark waters of my mind, something that I sensed was always there with me, has always been with me since I was a child, since the day I was born. And she is sleek, gorgeous and deadly—this thing I know is my own death.

The killer. The man-eater. The slipway grey.

She is coming for me now, drifting along the currents, slick and terminal. Cold and quiet as the lights turning off one by one by one. Her mouth open and tasting. The wide, dark, liquid space of her eyes. The shadow of her, the shape of her. My death come for me at last.

I said, my bokkie, that I have never told this to another person, and that is true. But it was real. It was real to me. I swear it to you and I swore it to your Ouma and, for everything, I know she believed me.

I could feel my hands going slack on the ladder. My back humping out into the open shaft of the mine.

She was beautiful. I wanted her to come for me.

But then. But then, my bokkie, there was something else. Three boxes. I could see them as well as I can see you here, all dressed up fine for Sunday church and maybe a bit impatient—no?—with your Oupa's stories. Three boxes.

So my hands are slipping and in my mind I am opening those three boxes. And do you know what I find? In the first is your Uncle Mika who had taken on the National Service for me. In the second is Jurie, lying in the darkness below me, singing that damn stupid song of his. And in the third is your Ouma who was everything to me. My piece of sunlight. My Sunday morning air. In those three boxes were all the things worth living for.

So I set myself to climbing again and oh, even though it hurt, even though it hurt more than anything, it was still easier than dying. So up I am coming, and I can see that shape of darkness near me. I could touch her. I can see those teeth of hers. But for the second time she passes me by. For the second time she lets me go, and up I come out of the mine. Up I come into the light, and there are the winding engine driver and all the others, waiting for me.

They got Jurie out, not fast, of course, not fast enough to save his thumb but fast enough that even though he was pale and shaking he was still alive. Still singing that damn song of his. "Go forward, go forward," he was singing, "you are running away on those mountains, the train from Zimbabwe."

Now, as I said to you, your Ouma and I, we could never much agree on what it all meant, what it was that I had seen there drifting in the darkness. But let me tell you this one thing, my bokkie, this one thing that I have not told another soul. At the end, after your Ouma and I had come to that decision together and I could see that the lights were going out, one by one, she drew me close to her. Her skin was as pale as old silk, and her touch was as light as a moth's wing, but she pulled me close to her and she whispered into my ear, "I see it. Oh, love, I see it, and I am scared, and I see it, and she is come for me."

Now I know you do not want to listen longer to an old man's ramblings, but as I said, this is a true story. Not a fable. Not a fancy. And I swear to you that it has not grown in the telling. But even now. Even now as I am drawing in breath through these raggle-taggled lungs of mine, these lungs that the doctors tell me will not last much longer, these lungs that feel as if they are breathing in water instead of Sunday air. Even now I know she is coming for me. The grand dame of the river. The slipway grey.

There are three boxes.

Jurie has gone into one, your Ouma has gone into another, and I fear, my bokkie, the last box is mine. But this is how it should be. A man should not live forever.

Because that is what death is. That beast in the darkness where no beast should be. Death is the thing that hooks you and will not let you go. Death is the slow undoing of beautiful things. You should know this, my bokkie, while you are young. Your father will not teach you this.

But here is another secret. The slipway grey has her own kind of beauty, and when you meet her you will know that. There is more to her than the teeth. This is how it is, my bokkie. I want you to know that. When she comes for me the third time, I shall be ready for her. I shall welcome her as an old friend. And when she comes to you, and pray God let that be many years from now, I know that you will do the same.

Acknowledgements

Two years ago, I remember writing the Acknowledgements to my first collection *Hair Side, Flesh Side* in an unnamed sorority house in Seattle—taken over for the summer by the Clarion West Writing Workshop in 2012. If there is a starting place for this book it was in that house, the first room on the left at the top of the stairs: not the room I had been advised to take, the one with the window that opened up to a balcony with a magnificent view of Mount Rainier, but a good room nonetheless, not too hot, with enough room for me, a couple of books, a bottle of Glenmorangie, and a notepad.

On my final night of the workshop I slept in the common room. I had wanted—had *demanded*—that my fellow classmates stay up with me all night so we could have as much time together as possible before I took the redeye back to Toronto. And I tried, but, really, I am like a child and so by two in the morning, I was zonked. So I grabbed a pillow and a blanket and I curled up on the couch. I drifted off to sleep, listening to the voices of my very dear friends—people I hadn't known six weeks before but even now I can't imagine not having in my life. I was sad. The summer was ending. I knew that I would be returning to a breakneck research schedule to finish my PhD dissertation. But I was happy too. Because I was surrounded by friends, and when you are a writer—or an academic—there is a kind of loneliness that comes with the job. One thing you learn in life is that nights spent with friends are rarer than you want them to be.

But when I think about the process of writing this book I don't think about the loneliness. I think about all the people who helped me. I think about people who gave me their time, their support, their love, their knowledge, their companionship. I feel that same sense of happiness. And so of course I want to begin by thanking the Clarion Class of 2012, its instructors and organizers as well, for teaching me so much about the craft of writing. And for reading my stories. All of them.

I want to thank my sister Laura to whom this book is dedicated: you have been my closest confidante, my co-conspirator, and my best friend. You brought home many bottles of champagne so we could always drink to our successes and commiserate our losses. You dragged me through all the dark places on the road, kicking and screaming sometimes, but you did it anyway.

Thanks to my very dear friend Robert Shearman. So many of these stories began with our field trips to haunted pubs or strange museums, wandering around the South Bank and climbing to the top of the CN Tower, with the fateful line: "How about a story where . . . ?" When anyone else would roll their eyes, you always let me get to the end of that sentence. You continue to inspire me. You continue to help me become the very best writer I can be.

And thanks to Sandra Kasturi, Brett Savory and the whole crew of ChiZine Publications. It takes tremendous bravery to run a publishing company. Few see the blood, sweat and tears. I did. I still do. What you have done is nothing short of heroic.

Chris Roberts, thanks to you as well: you make these stories come alive on the page. Your work is gorgeous and subtle, and I'm damned proud to be able to work with you.

Thanks to my family, to Sally Harding and the Cooke Agency, and to all the people who have seen these stories in various drafts and who have kept me breathing during the process of writing them: Nicole Adar, Scott H. Andrews, Nancy Baker, Nathan Ballingrud, Beverly and James Bambury, Brenta Blevins, Peter Buchanan, Michael Callaghan, Bryan Camp, Mike and Linda Carey, Indrapramit Das, Ellen Datlow, David Day, Sarah Dodd, Ron Eckel, M. Huw Evans, Gemma Files, Amanda Foubister, Laura West Friis, Neil Gaiman, Alexandra Gillespie, Sèphera Girón, Neile Graham, Gavin Grant, Paula Guran, Vince Haig, Lisa Hannett, James G. Harper, Mike Harrison, Alyc Helms, James Herndon, Nik Houser, Les Howle, Matthew Johnson, Stephen Graham Jones, Steve Jones, Georgina Kamsika, Michael Kelly, Rachel Letofsky, Henry Lien, Kelly Link, Silvia Moreno-Garcia, George R. R. Martin, Michael Matheson, Sean Moreland, Kelsi Morris, Kim Neville, Kathleen Ogden, Jonathan Oliver, Chuck Palahniuk, Dominik Parisien, Ben Percy, Chris Pugh, Ranylt Richildis, Mary Rosenblum, Michael Rowe, Cory Skerry, Carlie St. George, Simon Strantzas, Ann VanderMeer, Halli Villegas, Kaaron Warren, Greg West, Blythe Woolston, Connie Willis.

And, finally, my deep thanks to the Ontario Arts Council for awarding me a Works-in-Progress Grant and several Writers' Reserve Grants; to the Toronto Arts Council for awarding me a Level Two Writers Grant; and to the Social Sciences and Humanities Research Council of Canada for awarding me a Postdoctoral Fellowship to study at the University of Oxford. Without the generous funding of these organizations, this book would likely not exist.

Previously Published

"Crossroads and Gateways" first appeared in *Beneath Ceaseless Skies*, ed. Scott H. Andrew (July, 2014).

"Death and the Girl from Pi Delta Zeta" first appeared in the inaugural issue of *Lackington's Magazine*, ed. Ranylt Richildis (February, 2014).

"The Hanging Game" first appeared on *Tor.com* (March, 2013).

"I'm the Lady of Good Times, She Said" first appeared in *End of the Road*, ed. Jonathan Oliver (Solaris Books, 2013).

"In the Time of Omens" first appeared in *Fearful Symmetries*, ed. Ellen Datlow (ChiZine Publications, 2014).

"Lessons in the Raising of Household Objects" first appeared in *CVC Anthology Series, Book Three* (Exile Press, 2013). It was shortlisted for the 2013 $15,000 Vanderbilt/Exile Short Fiction Competition.

"The Slipway Grey" first appeared in *Chilling Tales: In Words, Alas, Drown I*, ed. Michael Kelly (Edge Science Fiction & Fantasy Publishing, 2013). It was reprinted in *The Year's Best Dark Fantasy and Horror 5*, ed. Paula Guran (Prime, 2014) and was listed on the preliminary ballot for the Bram Stoker Award.

"The Zhanell Adler Brass Spyglass" was a semifinalist for the 2013 Omnidawn Fabulist Fiction Chapbook Contest. It was shortlisted for the 2014 $15,000 Vanderbilt/Exile Short Fiction Competition.

ABOUT THE AUTHOR

Helen Marshall is an award-winning Canadian author, editor, and doctor of medieval studies. Her poetry and fiction have been published in *The Chiaroscuro*, *Abyss & Apex*, *Lady Churchill's Rosebud Wristlet*, *Tor.com* and have been reprinted in several "Year's Best" anthologies. Her debut collection of short stories, *Hair Side, Flesh Side* (ChiZine Publications, 2012), was named one of the top ten books of 2012 by *January Magazine*. It won the 2013 British Fantasy Award for Best Newcomer and was shortlisted for a 2013 Aurora Award by the Canadian Society of Science Fiction and Fantasy. She lives in Oxford, England.

ABOUT THE ARTIST

Chris Roberts is Dead Clown Art. He is a full-time freelance artist, using mixed media and found objects to create his visual nonsense. Chris has made art for Another Sky Press, Orange Alert Press, Dog Horn Publishing, Black Coffee Press, Kelp Queen Press, PS Publishing and ChiZine Publications; for authors Will Elliott, Andy Duncan, Tobias Seamon, Shimon Adaf, Seb Doubinsky, Ray Bradbury and the wildly talented Helen Marshall. He made the list of recommendations ("long list") for the 2012 British Fantasy Awards, and was nominated for a 2013 World Fantasy Award in the Artist category.

Chris would like to thank Helen for trusting him once again with the oodles of inside artwork he made for the stunning collection you hold in your hands. He's incredibly thrilled and lucky to be the art part of this marvellous pairing, and couldn't dream of a better creative cohort!

Thanks also to his pretty and patient wife, Kelly, and their cute and clever daughter, Amelia; for putting up with his "tortured artist" highs and lows, and for giving him the time needed to make all the things that he makes that were most certainly not here before.

You can watch Chris misbehave at deadclownart.com, or on Twitter @deadclownart.

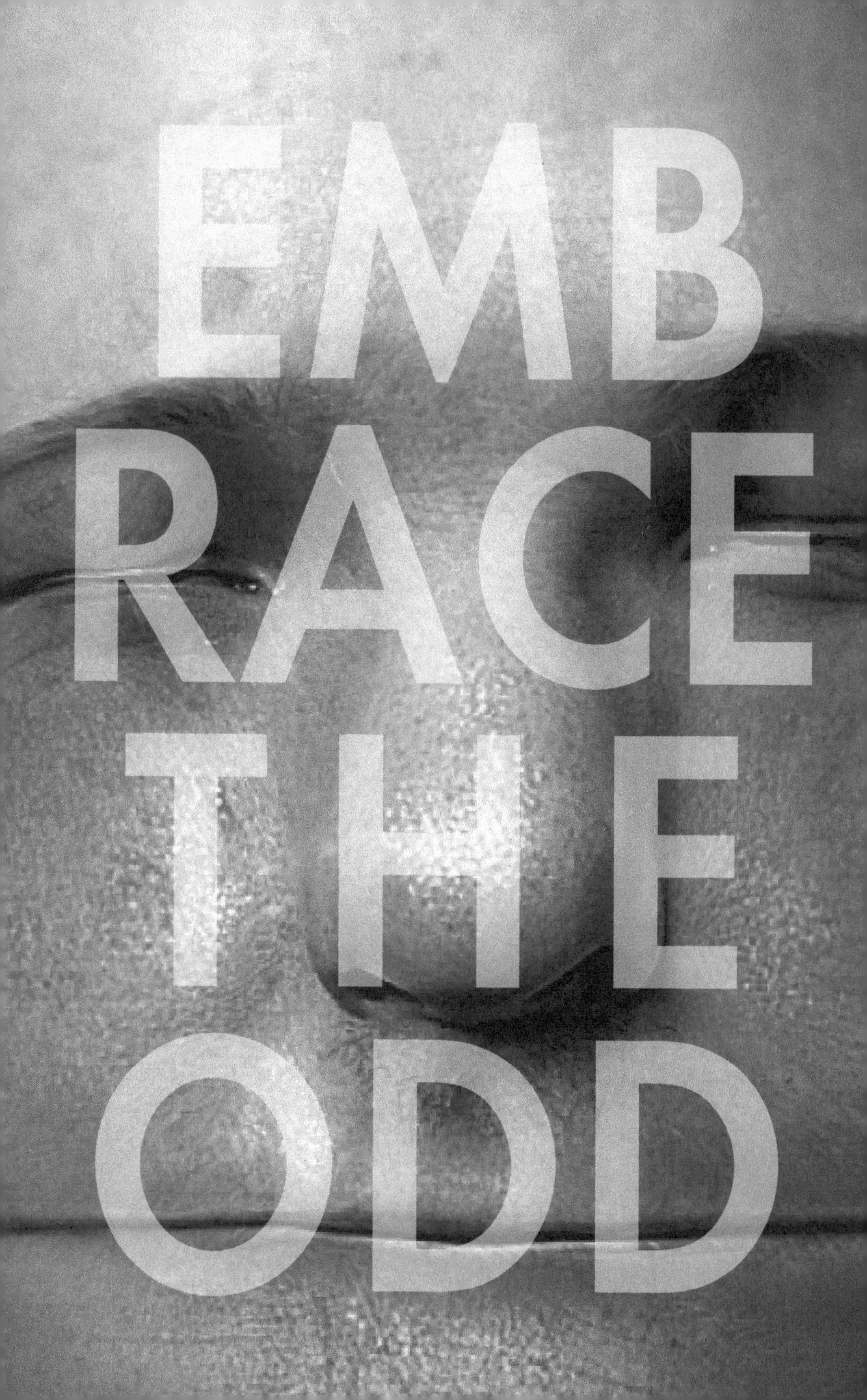
EMB
RACE
THE
ODD

HAIR SIDE, FLESH SIDE
HELEN MARSHALL

Winner of the British Fantasy Award

A child receives the body of Saint Lucia of Syracuse for her seventh birthday. A rebelling angel rewrites the Book of Judgement to protect the woman he loves. A young woman discovers the lost manuscript of Jane Austen written on the inside of her skin. A 747 populated by a dying pantheon makes the extraordinary journey to the beginning of the universe.

Lyrical and tender, quirky and cutting, Helen Marshall's exceptional debut collection weaves the fantastic and the horrific alongside the touchingly human in fifteen modern parables about history, memory, and the cost of creating art.

AVAILABLE NOW
978-1-927469-24-8

ALSO AVAILABLE FROM CHIZINE PUBLICATIONS

THEY DO THE SAME THINGS DIFFERENT THERE
ROBERT SHEARMAN

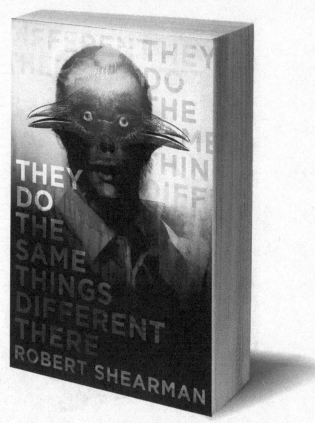

REMEMBER THAT KID WHO WAS IN YOUR CLASS AT SCHOOL? THE ONE THAT SEEMED A BIT STRANGE?

He sat in the corner, right behind the window, and the sunlight never fell on him. He didn't say much. He stared off into the distance. What did he dream of? Worlds just like ours—except countries would disappear overnight, marriage to camels is the norm, and the dead turn into musical instruments. And worlds that are something else entirely—where children carve their own tongues from trees, and magic shows are staged to amuse the troops in the war between demons and angels. They do the same things different there.

You went to school with Robert Shearman, and you never realized. You never bothered to say hello. Time to put that right.

AVAILABLE NOW
978-1-77148-300-1

CHIZINEPUB.COM CZP

WE WILL ALL GO DOWN TOGETHER
GEMMA FILES

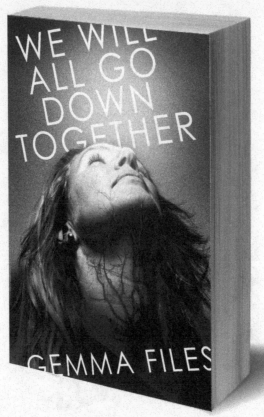

EVERY FAMILY HAS ITS MONSTERS...
AND SOME ARE NOTHING BUT.

In the woods outside Overdeere, Ontario, there are trees that speak, a village that doesn't appear on any map and a hill that opens wide, entrapping unwary travellers. Music drifts up from deep underground, while dreams—and nightmares—take on solid shape, flitting through the darkness. It's a place most people usually know better than to go, at least locally—until tonight, at least, when five bloodlines mired in ancient strife will finally converge once more.

A collection of linked stories by Gemma Files, author of the Hexslinger Series.

AVAILABLE NOW
978-1-77148-201-1

ALSO AVAILABLE FROM CHIZINE PUBLICATIONS